The aluminum was pitted. In many places, time had worn the stonework almost to a matte finish. Earlier crews had taken care of that, and now the limestone gleamed, but the last patches of metal still needed a going-over with steel brushes. That was what Charlie was doing here, up on the scaffolding of what would have been the ninety-fourth floor if there had been any proper floors at this height. . . .

Charlie looked down at that dark patch. . . . this was definitely a splash, and certainly not of oil. You could just see, still, the pattern of droplets that has splattered away from the bigger gout of blood when it had hit the aluminum and the stone, though smaller droplets themselves had long since been worn away by the elements, and only a slight discoloration of the stone betrayed where they had been.

He swallowed again. Not a bird strike. There was too much of it for that—no bird had that much blood in his body. How long had it been here? How long since this level had been cleaned? Had it, in fact, ever been cleaned?

So much blood, to last so long in this spot. Old blood. But from what . . . or who?

Kong Reborn

Russell Blackford

ibooks
new york
www.ibooks.net

DISTRIBUTED BY PUBLISHERS GROUP WEST

A Publication of ibooks, inc.

Distributed by Publishers Group West
1700 Fourth Street, Berkeley, CA 94710
www.pgw.com

ibooks, inc.
24 West 25th Street
New York, NY 10010

The ibooks World Wide Web Site Address is:
www.ibooks.net

ISBN: 1-59687-133-4
First ibooks, inc. printing September 2005
10 9 8 7 6 5 4 3 2 1

Cover design: M. Postawa

Printed in the U.S.A.

In memory of Norman Talbot

Prologue: Skull Island

Far beneath a green forest canopy, six raptors hunted for prey. Over countless millennia, huge reptiles and mammals had cleared broad paths through the jungle's lower tiers of vegetation, and the bipedal raptors trod these nimbly, sniffing the air as they went. They were an efficient end product of evolution–fast, powerful, and intelligent. With their upright, almost human, stance they grew to over ten feet tall. Some weighed more than a thousand pounds. The raptors' weapons were the vicious rows of teeth in their bird-like jaws and their extraordinary recurved claws, the size and shape of a sickle blade–one such claw on each hind foot. Hunting in packs, they feared almost nothing on the island.

The raptors' sensitive nostrils had caught the scent of reptilian quarry. The largest hunter hissed a signal to the rest of the pack. It took the lead as they minced almost daintily, lined up in ones and twos, toward their dinner, stalking their prey like hunting cats. Their rigid tails flicked left and right to discourage the jungle's swarming flies, wasps, and beetles. A dragonfly with wings forty inches across flew over-head, and one raptor snapped at it opportunistically, missing only by inches. The giant insect floated higher and landed safely on a high branch. The raptors returned to their main business, moving stealthily through the primeval forest.

Soon the trees and ferns thinned out and the raptors approached a fast-flowing stream where a small herd of bony-headed hadrosaurs had stopped to drink. These were duckbilled, vegetarian creatures, some of them ten times the bulk of the biggest raptor in the pack. There were two dozen in this herd, from giant bulls to young calves. Not one of them was a match for the raptor pack, and the reptilian hunters had no need to choose the strongest prey. A fat hadrosaur calf had plenty of meat on its bones and would make a fine meal for the whole pack.

As the raptors stepped closer, almost to the edge of the vegetation, the hadrosaurs were still unaware. The pack leader hissed, and the other raptors followed its gaze—their meal had been selected. They took one more careful step, exchanging softly hissed communications. Now the hadrosaurs were aware of them, by hearing and smell—but it was too late. The raptors became a deadly blur of motion. As the hadrosaurs reared up and bellowed, some running in panic, the fast-moving predators reached the calf that their leader had chosen. With powerful leg muscles like coiled springs, the pack leader rushed upon its victim. Sharply pointed teeth and curved front claws sank into the calf near its neck. Then came the killing strokes—quick vertical slices with the sickle-like hind claws ripped the calf open.

All around the pack leader, hissing raptors fended off bellowing hadrosaur bulls. Biting, leaping, and clawing, three of the raptors tackled the largest bull, and it bellowed more loudly in its pain as deep, bleeding wounds opened up on its legs and body.

Blood spilled into the stream. The hadrosaur bulls soon abandoned their futile efforts. Like beaten soldiers, they broke ranks and fled into the forest, leaving behind a trail of blood.

Now the raptors were alone with their kill. The two largest dragged the carcass to a drier spot by the stream and began to sate themselves. The others waited their turn, hissing angrily as scavenger beetles, centipedes, and scorpions scuttled out of the forest to get a share of the pickings. A huge vulture-like bird shrieked overhead but kept a safe distance from the raptors' teeth and claws. Hissing with anticipation, the smaller raptors approached the carcass as the two largest strutted away, satisfied for now with all the meat that they'd gorged down.

But then there was a louder sound—a roar that was really a kind of hissing rasp turned up to the volume of thunder. A huge, jungle-green creature pushed aside the foliage and stepped clear of it. This was a twelve-ton carnivorous monster for which a hadrosaur calf—or, indeed, a raptor—would be just a tasty snack. Like the raptors, it was the product of millions of years of evolution. Its smaller ancestors had stalked reptilian prey in Jurassic times, eons before. Some of them had evolved into the gigantic killing dinosaurs of the Cretaceous period, *Tyrannosaurus rex* and its kin, but this monster was bigger than any of those had been. The evolutionary arms race on Skull Island had produced the most powerful predator ever to walk on dry land: a giant allosaur with sharp, inward-curved teeth eighteen inches long.

It circled the raptor pack, deciding whether the meat they'd slaughtered was worth the effort of fighting over. Even this huge carnosaur would not attack a large enough pack of raptors, but it was more than a match for six of them. Yet those claws on the raptors' hind legs could do it damage and the raptors held their ground, arching their spines, and giving long, loud hisses. The carnosaur roared once again, and lashed its long, muscular tail. Its small brain made a primitive calculation—that this fight was not worth the prize. With a final bad-tempered roar, the giant predator retreated to the jungle to look for better prey.

The raptors held the field.

As always, they ate well.

The allosaur strutted through the jungle on enormously powerful hind legs. It walked hunched over, its tail balancing the weight of an eight-foot-long head that was filled with enormous, flesh-rending teeth. The twelve-ton predator could go for days without food, but now it was getting hungry.

The allosaur was an opportunistic feeder. There were few creatures on the island that it could not kill if driven by desperation. Most sentient creatures fled from it and only the largest sauropods, one-hundred-ton, snake-necked herbivores with powerful tails that could smash down trees, were out of its size range. But a few species formed packs, herds, or colonies that even the allosaur needed to respect. Often, it simply lived on carrion, driving smaller predators away from their kills.

It followed a trail well known to it, leading to a lake that took up much of the island's hinterland. Here, every manner of creature came to drink. The lake was a fine food larder for Skull Island's top predators. As it approached the lake, the massive dinosaur was welcomed with bounty on every side. An armor-plated stegosaur lumbered toward it from the water. Face to face with the allosaur, the tank-like creature stepped away slowly. It turned its back but made no attempt to flee. It twitched its powerful tail, equipped with long spikes of bone. The stegosaur was armed and dangerous; its tail worked like a huge medieval weapon—a spiked flail or mace.

The allosaur roared angrily but made no move to attack. It was not yet desperate enough to tackle such difficult prey.

Down by the water were herds of hadrosaurs, giant gaurs—bull-like Asian creatures—and huge, one-horned rhinos. Birds of all kinds skimmed the lake's surface or waded in the shallows, the largest of them with thirty-foot wingspans. Further out in the water, a small sauropod walked chest-deep searching for soft plants to feed its ever-growing bulk. Such creatures were eating machines, feeding themselves through every waking moment.

The allosaur stepped around the armored stegosaur, keeping clear of the menacing tail spikes. It headed for the lake with its herds of potential prey. Even the largest rhinos and gaur bulls fled in panic as the allosaur suddenly rushed toward them. It didn't depend on stealth but on speed, power, tooth and claw, and the weaknesses of its victims. One or two plant-eaters were always slower than the rest, whether from youth, age, or unhealed wounds. The allosaur was finely skilled at picking them out.

One of the rhinos in the herd ran with a lame hind leg, the legacy of some earlier struggle against the hazards of the island. The allosaur ran in its direction, quickly closing the gap. It leaped at the rhino, which darted to one side, nimble in spite of its bad leg and great size—almost as big as an elephant. Slavering and gnashing its jaws, the allosaur copied the rhino's maneuver. It gave chase to the jungle's edge. Now the rhino was separated from its herd and it had no hope of outrunning the huge bipedal predator, shaped by Darwinian forces to sprint after its prey.

In desperation, the rhino turned to confront its pursuer. It lowered its head, holding the single horn forward. One slash from that sharply pointed, five-foot horn could open up an enemy's stomach, and a less hungry predator than the allosaur might have backed off. The killer reptile and the huge mammal stared each other down, more like mating rivals than predator and prey, neither quite daring to attack first. Frustrated at this impasse, the allosaur hissed thunderously at the sky—and the rhino charged. Its powerful neck muscles weaved the deadly horn from side to side in what could have been a killing motion.

Almost like a matador, the allosaur stepped aside. As the rhino rushed past, the hungry predator swiveled on one cruelly clawed hind foot. It accelerated after its prey and both creatures collided in a fury of muscle, hide, claw, and hoof. Huge jaws and scimitar-like teeth tore a hundred pounds of flesh from the rhino's back and the rhino's stout legs collapsed beneath it. Seeing its opportunity, the allosaur raked at the rhino's side with its strong, curved hind claws, but the rhino whipped around with extraordinary speed for such a ponderous-looking animal. It slashed with its horn, but the allosaur leaped away by reflex. Some of the flesh it had torn off the rhino's back had fallen to the ground near its feet. It swallowed down what remained in its mouth, as the wounded rhino struggled up from where it had fallen. The rhino pawed the ground with one foreleg; it sniffed at the air, readying itself for a final charge.

The taste of rhinoceros meat had whetted the allosaur's appetite. As the rhino rushed past, the allosaur moved quickly. In a moment it was on the rhino's back, almost riding it, and driving it into the ground. Huge jaws clamped on the rhino's neck; rows of razor-sharp teeth cut like shears through layers of hide and muscle. The allosaur bit right through to the rhino's spine. The rhino flexed and twisted in its death throes, trying to shake the killer off its back or bring its horn into play, but the allosaur was too heavy, too powerful, and too agile. When the battle finally ended, the mammal was dead—the giant reptile had triumphed.

Greedily, the allosaur ate its fill. Soon it would find a spot in the forest to sleep and digest its meal. After this repast, it would go for days without food. But whenever it next went hunting, few animals on Skull Island would be safe. Like most dinosaurs, it was not an intelligent creature, but its primitive brain knew that getting food was good. This was what evolution had designed it for.

As it feasted, unchallenged by any other denizen of Skull Island, the allosaur's harsh-sounding cries were those of simple pleasure.

DECEMBER 1999

Among the skyscraper cliffs and the concrete, glass, and steel canyons of Manhattan, the wind could achieve velocities that would otherwise have been impossible. The island's immense structures shaped the wind, channeled and accelerated it. Updrafts, downdrafts, unpredictable vortices, and gusts—all of them could tug and push at you if you worked on the high steel. You learned how to counterbalance, to anticipate the wind and its crazy moods, but it never lost its malice as it howled and shrieked past with the voice of a feral beast. Over the course of an eight-hour day, it could affect your mind…if you let it.

Charlie Old Crow's father was a Mohawk; his mother came from Seminole stock. She had never liked her husband and son working on the high steel, but her people had a reputation for quiet endurance of what could not be changed. In that respect, at least, she'd matched the stereotype.

Native Americans had long been the premier high-steel workers, famous for their "head for heights" and their supposed fearlessness—another stereotype. Outsiders might see it that way, but Charlie knew better. Anyone who was fearless up here was likely to be smeared before long, while the famous *head for heights* was mainly a matter of practice and sticking to the time-honored rules. The primary rule had always been the obvious one: "Don't look down." But there were others: *where* to look; how to take care of your tools and your safety harness; how to watch out for your buddies and know when you could count on them; how not to listen to voices on the wind.

These days the paycheck was less likely to involve true construction work and more likely to be for repair and maintenance at daunting heights. Right now, Charlie had cleaning work to do and he had to shut out the wind—shut it out of his mind no matter how much it screamed.

It was the time of year, of course. No one did high-steel work by choice in December, but when the pay was right you shrugged and wrapped up in layers against the cold—though not enough to affect your nimbleness. When you were suspended up here like a spider from a few narrow steel cables and the wind whipped by you at seventy miles per hour, at a temperature of maybe ten degrees Fahrenheit, you considered carefully what it could do to you, and you made sure all your projecting parts were covered. The effect was like the Antarctic in early spring, an apparent temperature of forty below. Chilblains were certain, no matter what you did. Frostbite happened routinely if you got careless or cocky.

Charlie sighed and looked up at the moon, fat and silvery to the east, now that it had risen above the golden, sodium-lit smog hanging over Brooklyn and Long Island. Up this high you could see five states without trying, even more if the day or night was clear. But tonight was *not* so clear, despite the wind howling up here, more than ninety stories above the city streets. High, ragged clouds streamed overhead, promising bad weather tomorrow—probably snow. But Charlie didn't care. Tonight was his last on this particular job. Soon it would be New Year's Eve and he would be comfortable in his little house in Chappaqua, watching the ball come down in Times Square on TV.

He turned his attention away from the moon. There was work to complete on the edifice, the most respected in New York City, the superb feat of engineering that was the Empire State Building. Charlie was glad of a chance to work on it, if only to clean it up a little. The building damn sure needed it. Decades of pollution had not been kind to the Indiana limestone, while the aluminum and nickel-chrome steel, which were not supposed to oxidize, had managed to do so anyway after all those decades of acid rain and high-ozone smog. The aluminum was pitted. In many places, time had worn the stonework almost to a matte finish. Earlier work crews had taken care of that, and now the limestone gleamed, but the last patches of metal still needed a going-over with steel brushes. That was what Charlie was doing here, up on the scaffolding of what would have been the ninety-fourth floor if there had been any proper floors at this height.

This was what had been intended as the mooring mast for dirigibles until the first couple of attempts had scotched the whole idea. During the second attempt, an airship had almost crashed. Someone had forgotten something important about mooring dirigibles in the middle of a large city: the vicious updrafts.

Charlie unhitched the number-three point of his harness and moved it along to the next-to-last position where he needed to tether himself. He had already cleaned most of the aluminum on this level of the northern face. Accessing the final cornice was going to require a little more time, and he wanted to do it properly before his shift ran out. Here, the metal rose up sheer from the stone in a twenty-foot leap that terminated in a graceful art deco curve. The top was somewhat obscured by the welds and fixing bolts of later additions to the building: the masts that held transmitters for local TV stations as well as microwave repeaters and cellular phone antennas belonging to one company or another. It was an ugly concatenation of girders to Charlie's eye, not part of the original design. The only thing to be said for it was that it nicely caught the ornamental lighting from the building's lower stories.

He sighed and finished repositioning himself, unfastening a cable, fastening it further to the right, checking it…then another, refastening it, checking it. He worked carefully, methodically, taking no risks. Only when everything was checked would he change his footing, shuffling along his plank until he was right near the corner of the building. By its lights and the silvery moonshine, he glimpsed a large dark patch that would be tricky to get at. Finally in position, he unclipped his cordless tool from his belt once more, then started to work with the rotating steel brush on the aluminum surface directly in front of him. It was nice to see the old town getting cleaned up for the New Year, especially this massive aristocrat of the skyline. The grand old building had been one of the wonders of the world in its time, and it still wore an air of dignity and stability, a straightforward, sharp-edged, no-nonsense feeling.

Charlie looked down at that dark patch. It was embedded deep in the ornamental design before the aluminum zigzagged out again to match up with the corner of the building and it spread a little way around the corner, though there was a lot less of it there. He would need to make one more move to get around to it. Carefully, he unhooked his number-three cable, repositioned it, checked it, then did the same with the other two.

As soon as he got close enough to get a good look, he knew that this was not just oxidation. It was black, peeled-looking, a little flaky. He wasn't sure what could have fallen on this surface from above and not been washed away by the rain. *Maybe some kind of splash from that plane that hit the building?* he thought. *Oil or something?* But it seemed unlikely. It would have been there for a long, long time. *When was that, 1945?* It was more than unlikely. *Impossible.* That plane, a U.S. Army B-25 bomber, had come in from the southeast side and had torn into the building more than twenty stories below Charlie's position. Some plane wreckage had gone right through the building, but it would have needed one hell of a splash for anything to get all the way up here.

Of course, it *had* been quite a crash. *All the same...*

Charlie leaned a little closer to the stuff and poked it with one gloved finger. A bit of the blackness flaked away. Leaning back for a moment, he unhooked his MagLite, flicked it on, then peered more closely.

Not black, but a dark, dark brown.

Charlie swallowed. This was definitely a splash, and certainly not of oil. You could just see, still, the pattern of droplets that had splattered away from the bigger gout of blood when it had hit the aluminum and the stone, though those smaller droplets themselves had long since been worn away by the elements, and only a slight discoloration of the stone betrayed where they had been.

He swallowed again. Not a bird strike. There was too much of it for that—no bird had that much blood in its body. How long had it been here? How long had it been since this level had been cleaned? Had it, in fact, *ever* been cleaned? He seemed to remember his foreman, Jimmy, suggesting that the reason this job was so hard now was that they hadn't bothered doing any outside cleaning on the floors between ninety and ninety-eight when they'd put up the TV tower. Either there had been no money or no one had cared.

Still, so much blood to last so long in this spot. *Old blood. But from what...or who?* What might it be evidence of? Certainly not the plane crash in 1945. Maybe something even older...Whatever it was, it needed to be reported. Someone would have to know.

Methodically as ever, Charlie unhooked the number-one cable, repositioned it, hooked it up again. Then he unhooked number two, repositioned it, hooked it up, and went about working his way back to the access ladder on the eighty-sixth floor where he could get inside the building and out of the beast-voiced wind.

ONE

JANUARY 2004

Ever since childhood, Jack Denham had been an early riser, and there was nothing he could do about the habit, even in the winter months when he found himself getting up in the dark.

As he did each day, Jack woke shortly before 6:00 A.M. He staggered to the bathroom and tidied himself up, allowing himself a few minutes in the hot shower to smooth out the aches from a body that was still athletic but not getting any younger. This last summer he had turned forty. *All downhill from here*, he thought.

Jack had risen from a background of family tragedy to become one of the richest men in New York—not yet a billionaire, like Hemming, but with more millions than he could be bothered keeping track of. As a young man, he'd enrolled at Cornell University and had started pre-med. But he'd soon known it was a mistake. Even before his first semester was over, he'd realized that he lacked the right make-up for a medical doctor. He did, though, have what it took to be a first-rate research biologist. He'd graduated Cornell with a *summa cum laude* in biology. Then he'd begun his graduate work, specializing in the particular art that fascinated him: genetic engineering.

Since then he'd never looked back. He'd built his own little empire—not so little, anymore. His career had taken a natural course as the explosive growth of the biotech industry had combined with his native tendency to plan ahead then act fast. In the early days, when he'd started the company with like-minded friends, he'd been a top researcher. These days, though, he missed hands-on lab work. Somehow, he'd left that behind—and with it, the adventure.

He trimmed his short black beard, noticing more gray hairs—another daily occurrence—then dressed in blue jeans, a black sweatshirt, and a pair of high-quality elastic-sided boots. He made his way downstairs to the stainless-steel expanse of the apartment's kitchen, where his housekeeper, Assumpta, had already laid out a minimalist breakfast for him on a silver tray. As always, she'd prepared a tall glass of blood-orange juice, a large pot of Kenyan black coffee, and a rack of buttered toast that was still hot. Somehow she could time the exact minute when Jack would emerge from upstairs, ready for his long day of studying market reports, making phone calls to his network of contacts all over the world, answering dozens of e-mails, and doing what he could to comment on the technical side of his business.

Jack avoided going out. His luxury apartment had everything he needed, from an extensive science library to an extremely rare-for-Manhattan indoor swimming pool and a fully equipped home gym. Once or twice a week he would stroll to his company's complex of offices and laboratories, just a ten-minutes walk away, near the Museum of Natural History. He'd handle any issues that required his physical presence and generally show himself around—demonstrate who was really in charge. Much more frequently, his senior staff made brief visits to the Denham apartment.

"Good morning to you, Mr. Denham," Assumpta said cheerfully, leaning her hip against the breakfast bar. She was a stoutly built Hispanic woman in her early fifties, with hair that fell all the way down her back in a single black-and-gray plait. "It's supposed to snow all day, but that's not going to hurt you."

"No," he said. "I'm staying in."

"How *very* unusual," she said. "I'll leave you alone, then."

Today, more than usually, he needed time to brood, like a bear in its cave. Even at his best, he was bad company for any human being until he'd had at least three cups of coffee. He gulped down some of the orange juice, then took the breakfast tray to his enormous study—originally the living room—where he did most of his work.

The study was a vast area lined on two sides with metal shelving that contained books, magazines, CDs, DVDs, and loose-leaf folders of business documents and scientific reports. A wooden desk, ten feet long, stretched across another wall, most of which was actually a giant floor-to-ceiling window with heavy, royal-blue drapes. Mounted on the desk were a computer, a printer, racks of plastic in/out trays, a reading lamp, spare keyboards, calculators, and several neatly placed boxes of paper and envelopes. In one corner of the room sat two filing cabinets, both covered with piles of paper marked by brightly colored tabs. In the room's center was a large, glass-topped coffee table surrounded by half a dozen low, padded chairs.

Two TV remotes sat on the table's surface, one silver, the other matte black. Nearby—facing the desk and the window—were two commandingly large, state-of-the-art TV screens. By sitting at the coffee table or swiveling the office chair at his desk, Jack could watch two news reports at once—one of the many eccentricities that he'd developed in too many years without a wife or a steady girlfriend to keep him more or less normal. He was well aware of his self-indulgent habits, but what use was it being a millionaire—many times over—if you couldn't do things your own way?

He gently placed the breakfast tray on the coffee table and pulled up one of the chairs. As he used one hand to finish his orange juice, eat toast, and pour coffee, he used the other to fumble with the two remotes, surfing through the news channels on both screens.

This was the most important part of his breakfast ritual. His excuse was the need to see what foreign markets in the Far East had done overnight, but the truth was that he had become a news junkie. He had to know what *everyone* was doing all the time. Jack could access every channel of conceivable interest to someone with his habit, even a Russian TV feed from Moscow that sometimes offered remarkable analysis of events in faraway places like Afghanistan and Iraq.

Jack finished his toast and one cup of coffee, then poured a second, before CNN showed an update of the news story that had seized his attention the previous night and troubled his sleep with nightmares. The anchor overacted her enthusiasm, but Jack was close to trembling. The screen changed to display the image of a creature unlike any he had seen outside of a BBC documentary on prehistoric life or the pages of a book. As it accepted bunches of lush, green grass from its handlers, the creature looked more like an animatronic toy than the real thing. It was a small, brown-furred elephant with short, upward-curling tusks.

"The dwarf mammoth's creators at Bionimals believe that a herd of the beasts could be created before the end of this year," the anchor's voiceover said. "But this could be the start of something much bigger."

Something much bigger. That was the phrase they kept using. It brought an obvious image to mind: gigantic mammoths and mastodons from the last Ice Age, some of which had been preserved in ice, wholly or partly, in the Arctic Circle. Many people would love to see the resurrection of those giants from the past if cloning from tissue samples could bring it about. That was the obvious implication—why not just say it?

Jack knew very well that enough DNA could be extracted from the preserved remains of many extinct creatures to recreate them. A year before, he'd been on CNN with his own extinct pachyderm brought back to life—fully twelve months ahead of Charlton Hemming's company, Bionimals. Now Hemming was striking back, challenging Jack in public. "Anything you can do, I can do in spades," Hemming seemed to be saying to him. The message was almost offensively clear.

One of Jack's favorite projects at Denham Products was to try to resurrect species such as the Tasmanian tiger, the dodo, and the passenger pigeons that had once crowded North American skies. All of them had been destroyed by human hands, by humans' guns. Bringing back those creatures, recent victims of ignorance and greed, made more sense than trying to recreate species such as mammoths and mastodons whose time had long passed, species that no longer had a natural environment. But Denham Products had also been ahead in playing the elephant theme. It had recreated the long-lost pygmy elephant from North Africa, which hadn't been seen since the days of the Roman Empire. Another victim of human arrogance.

Jack had stolen Hemming's thunder, but now the tables were reversed. The dwarf mammoth was getting plenty of coverage and it seemed that Charlton Hemming's star was on the rise, while Jack's was on the way down. Hemming had been doing everything in his power to see to that. Jack's career—his whole mission in life—was on the line. Hemming was trying to destroy him.

No, worse than that—Hemming wanted to swallow him up, to take him over.

Something bigger. To Jack, those words bore a secret meaning, nothing to do with woolly pachyderms from the Arctic ice. Four years before, a worker had discovered a sample of blood on the Empire State Building's uppermost stories, blood that had never been revealed to the authorities, never been mentioned in public. Samples had found their way on the black market to interested parties, including the blood's proper owner—for so Jack considered himself. He'd paid good money for the privilege of buying what was rightfully his. But he knew he didn't have it all.

Something bigger. Something much bigger.
What did Hemming have in mind?
I know what it's got to be, Jack thought.
Kong.

Kong was family business. Jack's grandfather, the moviemaker Carl Denham, had discovered the giant ape on a volcanic island in the Indian Ocean, far to the west of Sumatra, hundreds of miles south of Sri Lanka. The place known in some legends as Skull Island was a mere speck of land in the vastness of the sea, covered in thick green jungle. It was protected by coral reefs and sheer cliffs that rose up from the tropical ocean on almost every side. Its precise location was Jack's other closely guarded secret. The last of the crew from the original expedition had died back in the 1990s, and Jack had the only map, held for him in a secure place.

Skull Island was not marked on any shipping chart, and there was nothing special about it that would show on satellite images. What was so exceptional lay under the cover of its jungle or hidden beneath its waters.

Back in 1933, Jack's granddad had found the island, its people, and the bizarre creatures he'd so often described to Jack when he was a boy. Carl Denham had met the biggest ape the world had seen and had brought it back to civilization. Kong, though, had shown scant regard for civilization's benefits. The giant gorilla had broken loose and terrorized New

York. A squadron of four naval planes had finally taken him out, but Kong had not been an easy target of their mounted Vickers machine guns—he'd destroyed one plane in that last battle and two more humans had died. Bullets had torn through the ape's body, and he'd fallen from his final vantage point at the top of the Empire State Building. He'd smashed against the edges of the building's upper tiers, then plummeted to the street.

Jack had seen old, grainy newsreel footage in black and white, looking slightly undercranked. Kong swatting at the planes, angry, yet puzzled, at this newest, deadliest enemy. One plane falling—crashing against the side of the building. Then Kong himself—reeling, falling…and finally the flashbulb-lit body inert in the street. Beside the fallen giant's immense head was Jack's grandfather, wearing a look of sorrow, yet still talking bravely and calling the shots: Carl Denham—entrepreneur, daredevil, showman, moviemaker, explorer. He was famous everywhere, but he hadn't called the shots for long after that terrible night. He was shortly to be ruined by the lawsuits that inexorably followed.

"All I did," he'd once said to his grandson, "was give the public what it wanted." But when it had backfired, they'd turned on him and pursued him for something else that many people wanted: revenge. Revenge for the terror and destruction that Kong had wreaked on the city.

As for Kong, the planes had gotten him, although Grandfather Carl had quipped that it wasn't the planes—that "Beauty killed the beast." Kong had died for his obsession with a young American woman, an out-of-work actress whom Carl had taken to Skull

Island. *Beauty killed the beast.* Perhaps so. But it had also been human greed and ignorance. Even Carl had realized that later in his long life.

Mankind's rapacity had done the job.

Now what? Jack thought, his mind on Charlton Hemming, the man who wanted to destroy him. *Are you going to do this all over again?*

On one of the TV screens, Hemming sat in a lushly padded leather chair with shelves of books behind him. Jack turned off the other TV; he wanted to concentrate on this.

Even in his sixties, Hemming remained good looking. His hair was silver-white but had scarcely thinned at all. It was combed back in luxuriant waves that just kissed the top of his ears. He wore a dark, beautifully fitted suit, a brilliant white shirt, a red silk tie. Even now, in the dead of winter, he sported a Caribbean tan. His self-satisfied smile displayed capped teeth as white as his shirt.

How can anyone have that many teeth and not be a shark? Jack thought.

Of course, Hemming *was* a shark, an unscrupulous corporate predator. His main company, CenCo, had been stalking Jack for the past two years, doing everything possible to ruin him, if that was what was needed to take over Denham Products. CenCo's subsidiary, Bionimals, was Jack Denham's main rival in the massively accelerating growth industry of animal and plant genetic engineering, which was why CenCo had been so determined to buy out Jack's business. Bionimals had been upping the ante almost every month, announcing dramatic, symbolic projects.

CenCo had relied on its vast resources to help its subsidiary undercut Denham Products on every major tender, though Bionimals must have made no profit, or even run at a loss, on many of its projects. It was a ruthless effort to get rid of the competition. It seemed there was room for only one such company, at least as far as Hemming was concerned, and any opposition had to be eliminated no matter what it took.

Jack spoke to Hemming by telephone almost every day. He'd met him in the flesh several times, both here in New York and at CenCo's Pacific headquarters in California, and knew how physically impressive the man was—at least three inches taller than Jack, who was himself six-foot-two in his boots.

In the past few months, Hemming's plans had started to work. Like a shark, he was adapted to hunt and kill.

"Of course this is a tremendous achievement," the on-screen Hemming said. "But there is more to come. I can promise much bigger things than this."

The camera angle shifted to a young male interviewer dressed in a dark suit, a blue that was almost black. He nodded wisely and said, "What sort of things?"

Hemming was obviously enjoying every minute of it. His mako-shark smile became even broader.

Jack wondered when the interview had been done. Probably overnight, in Hemming's San Francisco office where he did most of his work, though CenCo also owned a massive research and administrative complex in downtown Manhattan, where Bionimals was headquartered. Hemming was probably sound asleep right now, dreaming of world domination, or of torturing flies—or whatever it was that such a man dreamed about.

"We have some other projects," Hemming said on the plasma screen. He folded his hands in front of him, almost rubbing them together in glee. "Some of them will excite the public. Others will do far more than that. This isn't vaudeville, after all. CenCo and Bionimals expect some important products to come from the current research. Products that will help people to live longer and better lives, and make some of their dreams come true."

"You're not talking about cloning human beings, are you?" the journalist said with a nervous laugh.

Hemming dropped his hands in his lap and leaned forward just the tiniest fraction of an inch, staring earnestly down the lens of the camera. "Actually…no." He paused for effect, then sat back with a sort of half-shrug. "That's repugnant to most people in America, so it's off our agenda."

"Then what's *on* the agenda, Mr. Hemming?"

"You'll know that as soon as I can tell you, don't you worry. I think you'll see some developments that will be much more accepted—and maybe even more dramatic—than human cloning." He gave a self-satisfied smile. "As I said, some of it is going to be *big*. *Big* as in symbolic. *Big*…as in important."

Jack finished the last of his pot of coffee just as Assumpta came in to clear away the tray. As always, she knew exactly when to do it. But this was not going to be an "as always" day.

"My, you do look worried," Assumpta said. "Is something on your mind?"

"Yeah," Jack said. "Something big. Something...enormous."

She shrugged tolerantly, and he felt guilty immediately, not meaning to make fun of her, or even to evade her questioning. "Listen, Assumpta, I'm staying home all day—"

"So you told me—"

"Yes, but I'm going to do some things that I've left in the too-hard basket for much too long. I'm going to call Maudie and get her to come over with some of the others." Maude Atchison-Collander was his extremely competent executive advisor.

Assumpta raised one eyebrow. "Is this about Mr. Hemming?"

"You saw him on the TV?"

She shook her head. "I didn't see *him*. But there was something about CenCo on the late news."

"Okay. I need to know what's going on." Had Hemming really been making a coded reference to Kong—something he could recall to people's attention when the time came? In Jack's mind, there was no doubt about it. Hemming doubtless had a sample of Kong's blood and he thought he could clone the giant ape.

That was too much for Jack to stomach. He wouldn't let Hemming win this one.

TWO

When Jack Denham called from home just after 9:00
A.M., Maude Atchison-Collander immediately heard
the tension in his voice. "Come around and see me,"
he said. "Drop whatever else you're doing."

"Right now?" she said, not totally surprised. She
had seen Charlton Hemming on the morning news,
looking as cold-blooded and smug as a lizard that
had gorged itself on flies. For the last half-hour,
everyone in the Denham Products office had been
talking about it. Something was up, something that
went far beyond cloning pygmy mammoths.

"Yes, right now," Jack said. "Is that okay? There's
nothing that can't wait?"

Maudie laughed. "Nothing that can't wait."

Maudie was five-foot-eleven, blonde and statuesque,
with the face of an angel and the gleeful eyes of a
child who has hidden a frog in her parents' bed. She'd
been fired from several corporate jobs because her
previous employers had been smart enough to read
the message in her eyes—that they were *not* smart
enough to equal her and she damn well knew it. She
might not have their family connections and Ivy
League degrees, but she'd devoured every scrap of
information from the perfectly effective courses in
accountancy, IT, and management that she'd taken

at night and she had more rat cunning than any boss whose doorway she'd ever stepped through.

That was how she saw herself and she was pretty certain her current boss saw her the same way. Jack was an excellent research scientist and a smart business operator, but above all he knew how to pick good people. He knew that his best possible protection was someone as smart as him and totally loyal. Maudie had started out as a high-level personal assistant, but had soon become much more. She was Jack's closest confidante. He had recognized what a gem she was and gave her all the backup she needed. She was now really an all-purpose troubleshooter, with authority to handle most of what went on within the building, except for the actual research.

"I take it," she said, "that this is about the Nameless Presence." That was her name for Charlton Hemming.

"You take it correctly."

"All right, do you want me to bring anyone else?"

"I need Mark Illingworth and Graham Riley. If you can find Laurel Otani, so much the better."

"Got it. We'll be there soon." Maudie put down the phone, and yelled out to her own secretary, Alyona. "Get me Mark, Riley, and Laurel. Jack wants to see us right away. I'll meet them in the foyer in a few minutes. Call me on the cell if anything comes up."

"Okay," Alyona said sweetly.

Maudie buttoned on her black, fur-lined overcoat, found her attaché case where she'd left it behind the door to her twelve-by-ten-foot office, and checked that she had everything she might need: her gold-rimmed reading glasses; a thick, yellow legal pad; her favorite monogrammed pen; her cell phone; a folding umbrella; and some vital items of makeup. Everything she needed to go into battle.

"Your guests have arrived, Mr. Denham," Assumpta said, standing in the doorway of the study. Jack had been absorbed in a bound volume of *Science*—his equivalent of light reading.

"Good morning, Jack," Maudie said as he put the volume down on the table's glass surface. She walked all the way into the room, shrugging out of her coat and flinging it casually over one of the chairs. "So, what's it all about?"

Mark Illingworth and the others followed her close behind. Mark was an expert in mammalian genetics—especially, but not solely, that of primates. He was a big, but kind of soft-looking, guy in his late twenties—friendly, sandy-haired, and pale-skinned. He always seemed freshly scrubbed and had a faintly soapy smell. Laurel Otani was a primate zoologist whom Jack had poached from a biotech firm in Tokyo. Like Mark, she was pale, but her skin was as smooth as a doll's and it glowed with health. She was in her late thirties, but looked at least ten years younger.

Graham Riley, known affectionately by his surname, was a year or so younger than Laurel, but he looked much older. Tall and thin, he had a dejected look, partly as a function of his long, narrow face and the way his hair was receding. Back in the mid-'90s, he'd worked for several well-known biotech firms, but he'd ended up at the University of Pittsburgh before Jack had finally offered him more money than he could refuse. Riley was a man with too many

opinions of his own to get along with most bosses,
but he'd become a research superstar at U. Pittsburgh.
He was simply the best scientist anywhere in the
world when it came to animal cloning—especially
cloning primates.

Assumpta stayed at the door awaiting further orders
like a good lieutenant. That was how Jack liked to see
all his people—as volunteers in a cause more than
employees. "Just bring us all some more coffee," Jack
said to her. "I think we're going to need it."

"I'm onto it," she said.

The others sat around the coffee table and Jack said
quietly. "Maudie knows most of what I'm about to
say. I expect it'll be news to the rest of you. First, do
you know the rumors about Kong? All the rumors?"

Laurel spoke first. "Yes," she said in her slightly
pedantic, mildly accented English. "I think that we
probably do."

"Jack," Maudie said, "you're looking flushed. Are
you okay?"

He nodded quickly. "What I eventually want to do
might be...just a little too far upwind of the law, if
you all know what I mean."

Maudie giggled. "Upwind, eh? Is that meant to be
a hunting metaphor?"

"It means we might end up being the hunted."

"I was afraid of that."

"If any of you want to leave now, here's your
chance. Don't say you didn't have fair warning."

Mark and Laurel exchanged glances, while Riley
merely folded his arms. Nobody moved from their
seats.

"Shall I go on?" Jack said. "Here's your last chance
to leave." No one spoke, so he continued. "As you all

know, the pervasive rumor is that a contract cleaning worker found traces of Kong—the big gorilla—over four years ago, up on the Empire State Building—just before the big New Year celebrations for 2000."

"Yeah," Maudie said, "for Y2K—the false millennium celebrations."

Jack laughed. He was just as aware as she was that the third millennium had not really begun until January 1, 2001. "Uh-huh," he said. "They cleaned it up for the false millennium."

"The rumor is not *just* a rumor," Jack said. "What was left of Kong found its way to Hemming. Some of it must still be with him, in a Bionimals laboratory somewhere, and there's nothing we can do about it."

CenCo's interests spread far beyond genetic engineering, into almost every area of finance, property, and commerce. In the late 1990s, it had gained a key interest in the Empire State Building when its real-estate division had purchased a huge share in the Helmsley Corporation, which had owned the building. Anything that happened at the grand old 1930s skyscraper would inevitably come to Charlton Hemming's attention—that included any blood or other tissue from Kong that remained on the building's façade. The Helmsley Corporation had no use for remnants of Kong, but Hemming most likely did. Any strange biological material was grist to Bionimals' mill.

"The thing is," Jack said, "plenty of people who work for Charlton are not especially loyal and some of them don't mind making a large profit on the side, if the chance comes their way. I guess that's why I was offered a sample four years ago…and stepped on a roller coaster."

"Should I be taking notes at this point?" Maudie asked.

"Definitely not, Maudie. Rely on your powerful memory."

She laughed and placed her legal pad on the coffee table.

"Don't write anything down *anywhere*," Jack said. "Not unless I tell you."

Maudie held up both hands like a gunman caught by the town sheriff. "Okay, okay, I get the idea."

"That goes for all of you," Jack said.

Assumpta returned with five steaming mugs of coffee and a plate of homebaked cookies, then left to do her own work.

"Hemming *meant* something when he made that comment on TV," Jack said. "He's softening up the public, getting them ready for the Big announcement."

Riley leant forward, hunching his shoulders. "You believe he was referring to Kong?"

"I'm sure of it. He's going to try to clone the big ape."

"And should I gather that you want to beat him to it?"

"If you gathered that, you'd have the right idea," Jack said. "Let me be quite clear about this: When that offer was made to me four years ago, I accepted it with a clear conscience. Ever since, I've kept my own sample, supposedly of Kong's blood, bought with my own money—not the firm's. I guess you all suspected that."

Riley selected a cookie then sat back in his chair, looking satisfied with what he was hearing. "Let's just say that there's sometimes speculation," he said.

36

Jack shrugged. "You won't find the transaction on any of the company's books. The only thing is, I'd stopped taking it seriously...At least until last night."

He'd had two good reasons for that. The first was that, no matter what tissues had survived, cloning the great apes was supposed to be out of the question scientifically. Until the past few months, Jack would have sworn that you simply couldn't clone an ordinary gorilla, let alone a one-off monster like Kong.

For years, most scientists had doubted the possibility of reliably cloning *any* primates. The published research had found unexplained chromosomal abnormalities when it was tried, quite unlike the successes with domesticated animals like cows, sheep, cats, and pigs. But some labs were starting to get better experimental results. That included the labs at Denham Products. And if anyone could clone Kong, Jack had just the man on his payroll: Graham Riley.

"Maybe Hemming has even started," Riley said. He took a bite of his cookie and chewed it thoughtfully.

"Can it be done?" Jack said.

Riley took his time before he answered. "He has Roxanne Blaine leading his scientific team. She might be able to find a way. If she's told him it can be done, maybe she's right."

Jack nodded at the volume of *Science* that he'd laid down on the coffee table. "I'm sure of one thing: Hemming said what he did for a reason. He wasn't just talking about mammoths."

Laurel spoke up. "It is many years since Kong was killed by the fighter planes."

Riley glanced at her. "That's true."

"What is the possibility that any of his blood might still be usable after all those years?"

"It's been *decades*," Maudie said.

Jack nodded. That was his second reason for not taking the possibility too seriously until now. What use was a DNA sample seven decades old?

Everyone looked in Riley's direction. Riley frowned, as if doing abstruse calculations. He gave half a shrug. "Speaking from first principles?"

"If you like," Jack said. "What's your professional opinion?"

"It depends."

"Well?"

"Speaking hypothetically—"

"Yes," Laurel said. "You are keeping us in too much suspense."

"There's the possibility of a plasma seal. That might get us something usable. Perhaps not perfect—there would be missing DNA, for sure, but we could get around that…"

"You sound very optimistic, for *you*," Jack said with a grin. They all laughed at that.

"I'm not an optimist," Riley said, "but I do like to overcome problems."

Jack looked him squarely in the eye. "I'll be frank with you," he said. "I've made enough money to walk away from this business tomorrow. I swore a long time ago to stop working as soon as it stopped being fun. The trouble is that that's already happened, largely thanks to that bastard Hemming."

"He doesn't try to maximize fun for other people…or so they say."

"I know that, but let's all be clear on one thing. There's no way I'm going to acquiesce in his takeover plans for this company. "What's more, if I can give the bastard a black eye in the process, I will."

Riley nodded. "Don't think I won't applaud."

"Uh-huh. That's understood. But there's another thing. This project goes far beyond my feelings about Hemming. I hope we all have a sense of adventure—if we could remake Kong, it would be the scientific adventure of a lifetime!" Jack felt a flush of embarrassment at blurting it out that way, for it sounded like what his granddad, Carl Denham, would have said.

As Jack spoke, Riley finished his cookie and reached for his mug of coffee. He took a long, unhurried sip, then used both hands to toy with the mug. "Tell me one thing," he said at last. "Where is this precious sample of yours? I'd like to have a look at it."

"It's kept refrigerated in a safe place. We can get it for you this afternoon. I'd appreciate your analysis. I can't even be sure right now that it's what it's supposed to be."

"If I can test it, you'll know soon enough."

The three scientists soon left, but Jack asked Maudie to stay behind. "We'll keep Stanley out of this for now," he told her. "I don't want him compromised when the shit hits the fan." Stanley Levin was a senior partner in Levin Drobnick Mahon, a Wall Street law firm that Jack had retained for the past decade. Apart from Maudie, no one had Jack's ear as much as Stanley. Normally, they checked with him about every move that Denham Products made.

"Gotcha, boss," Maudie said. "Anything else before I head back?"

"Not now. Give Riley and the others what they need. You know where my, er, special samples are kept. We'll take it from there."

"*No problemo*, Jack. I'll just let you know one thing."

"Oh?" Jack said. "More dark secrets?"

"It's not much of a secret. If that bastard beats Denham Products on this, it'll be over my dead body."

"I know, Maudie. Mine, too."

Hemming usually called Jack soon after midday for one of his ever-so-friendly talks; today was no exception. When the phone rang, Jack was at his desk, immersed in reading an online journal with the latest review article about primate cloning. The last thing that he wanted to do was tear himself away and talk to Hemming.

"Jack," Hemming said genially. "How's your day so far?"

"Oh, quiet. I'm just hanging around at home, doing a bit of reading."

"Keeping up with the scientific literature, I suppose?"

"Someone has to do it."

"I appreciate that. That's why I hire the best scientists."

"Really?"

"I'm always looking for talent. For example, you'd go well on my team."

"I'm not much of a hands-on researcher," Jack said. "Not anymore."

"Anyway, that's not what I wanted to ask you about," Hemming said. "Did you catch my little stint on the news last night?"

"I saw the morning reply. Congratulations."

"For the baby mammoth? Thank you. Well, of course, I'm very conscious of your firm's own expertise along similar lines. We'd make a good team if you ever wanted to amalgamate. I know that the market is pretty tough right now. Your share price is still going down, I see—just the way the market shakes out sometimes."

"Sometimes it has a bit of help."

Hemming ignored the remark. "You know, there's some very interesting material you could investigate if you decided to join me in some capacity. I've never suggested that you actually close down Denham Products, you know—some kind of subsidiary arrangement would be good for both of us. There'd be powerful synergies between Denham Products and Bionimals if we changed the corporate structure just a little."

"So you've said before."

"Well, you ought to take it more seriously—think about it harder. It's better than a hostile takeover, and if your stock keeps falling, that's very much in the cards."

"Is there anything *new* you want to tell me, Charlton?" Jack said, losing patience with this never-ending verbal fencing.

"Just one thing."

This is it, Jack thought. *Something more meaningful.* "Yes?"

"That material I was talking about. Part of it went missing soon after it was discovered. These things happen, of course. I imagine that some shady offers might have been made to various individuals."

"Interesting," Jack said. "Were you thinking that someone might have offered *me* this material—whatever it is?"

"Quite possibly. Frankly, some people might have been very tempted by an unusual resource like I have in mind, even if the time wasn't yet scientifically ripe."

"Uh-huh."

41

"Well, the time might be scientifically ripe now. I just thought I'd let you know that I'll be protecting my position vigorously if it ever becomes necessary. I'm giving you the heads-up on that, Jack."

"Well, thanks for your concern, but heaven knows, I'd never want anything to do with handling stolen goods…if that's what you're talking about."

"No, I didn't think you'd want to break the law," Hemming said. "You're a responsible businessman, after all, and you'd never do anything that might impair your firm's effectiveness."

"It's always best to keep downwind of the law," Jack said.

"If that means you like to keep things legal, then we see things the same way."

"Well, sure," Jack said, "but the market's enough of a minefield as it is, even for big companies like yours." *With its rotten record in keeping its best employees, its predatory pricing, and all the rest of it.*

"Don't worry about that," Hemming said. "I don't."

"Still, public opinion can be so fickle. I say, let's all be as effective as we can and stay on the right side of the law. Can I be clearer than that?"

There was a pleased chuckle at the other end. "You always did have a way of seeing straight through to the heart of things."

"So my mother used to say."

"We'll talk soon, Jack. Goodbye for now."

Click.

Very public-spirited of him, Jack thought as he put the phone down. *But what's mine is mine, you old weasel.*

THREE

The Denham Products building covered almost an acre of expensive real estate. Some of its spaces at street level were miniature farms or zoos—big enough to house primates and some domestic animals. Lab 44 was a small, semi-autonomous facility with several rooms where half a dozen apes and monkeys were caged. It included an untidy office for the staff, a central common room where they could go and brainstorm or simply talk over a cup of coffee, and several scientific work areas, including the lab itself. This was a clean environment where Denham Products' primate experts did their most sensitive research using cells and tissues obtained from their collection of primates.

The pride and joy of this collection was a full-grown female gorilla called Matthilde, who was so tame that they let her roam freely through the non-sterile areas.

For the past eight hours Riley had worked patiently in the sterile lab. He and Mark sat side by side on high stools. Everything here was scrubbed and spotless. Beneath the bright overhead lights, Riley found himself sweating; now and then he wiped his brow with a shirt sleeve.

They'd used the lab's microscopes and computer hardware to examine the sequencing of the DNA in the material Maudie had brought to them. It had taken only seconds to establish that they were dealing with blood from some kind of gorilla. Checking that it was a special kind of gorilla, and exactly how much of the DNA was intact, had taken a lot longer. They'd analyzed the sample meticulously, trying to see how much genetic information could be reconstructed, and just how it compared with what they'd expect from a normal gorilla, like Matthilde.

At last, Riley sat back and folded his arms. "This may be do-able," he said without expression.

"It's going to be a bastard to work with this stuff," Mark said. "There's just too much information missing."

"Yes, but it could have been a lot worse."

"So, who's going to give the news to Jack?"

Riley thought for a moment. "You go and call him."

Mark looked at him doubtingly. "You're sure, dude?"

"You'll give it the right upbeat tone. Tell him there's good news and bad news."

It was evening when the phone rang. At the other end of the line, Mark said, "I guess there's good news and there's bad news." He laughed nervously. "That's how Riley told me to put it."

"Tell me the good news first," Jack said.

"The good news is that the sample is genuine."

"It's really Kong?" Jack said, his hopes beginning to mount. Surely there was no other way to interpret what he'd just heard.

"Yes, we're both sure it is."

Jack thought of falling—of the poor beast, wounded to death, that had gone tumbling down for a quarter of a mile from the top of the Empire State Building, crashing into the concrete and asphalt of Fifth Avenue. "All right, what's the bad news?"

"The bad news is that this won't be easy."

"I never expected it to be easy."

Mark was silent for a few seconds. "Sure," he said, "but the material we've been analyzing has really been through the mill."

"How far through the mill?"

"You know what it must have survived, Jack. If it was retrieved at the end of 99, it had been through sixty-six, or sixty-seven, years of wind and rain, sun and snow—and God knows what...It's amazing to see the serum proteins still in place, but a lot of them are."

Jack's heart leapt. "How many?"

"Most."

"*Are you sure?*"

"Don't get too excited," Mark said. "Some of the plasma actually survived, as well as part of the fibrin structure of the clot itself. There must have been a plasma seal."

"Okay, good."

When blood clotted fast enough, its serous component, the "plasma," tended to rise to the top of a given blood mass and seal it. A plasma seal would be spotty, at best, but if any patches of blood remained undisturbed for long enough, if birds and bugs and fungi hadn't gotten at it, there was always a chance that enough red blood cells would be left to get a decent coding.

"But the erythrocytes are pretty much shot," Mark said.

"Crenated?"

"A long time ago, I'd say. It's the sunlight's fault."

That was as Jack had feared. The ultraviolet light that the blood had been exposed to, day after day, for all those years, would have been incredibly denaturing. "All right, tell me the worst."

Mark took a deep breath. "It's not as bad as you might think, given the circumstances. There are some pretty good red blood cells in the sample we have. They must have been trapped right in the middle of the clot. From what we've seen, there was minimal bacterial contamination—there must have been little migration into the heart of the clots."

"Tell me the bottom line, Mark. Put me out of my misery."

"Okay, here goes. It's going to be tough, but maybe do-able.

"That's what Riley thinks?"

"Yeah."

"How much of the genome are we going to be able to recover?"

"I'd say about seventy percent."

"Oh, shit." Jack put his head in his hands.

"I know," Mark said. "I wish I could tell you a better figure. In the circumstances, though, seventy percent is great."

"I know, I know. It's just…well, you always hope for a hundred, or something close to it." Jack smiled ruefully to himself. "You never get it, but you always live in hope."

"We'll have to make do. It's not like this is the first time we've done cloning work with an incomplete genome."

"No, but we'll have problem after problem this time. It's not just the incomplete genome. Damn it, Mark, we don't even know how to *gestate* an animal as big as Kong must have been. We need to make some fast progress with a workable artificial womb, because an ordinary ape isn't going to be able to carry a gorilla like Kong to term."

"I'm sure we can get around it somehow," Mark said. "Meanwhile, Riley and I can work with seventy percent of Kong's genome. There's a good chance that we can reconstruct an animal very much like the original."

"All right, you can go home now. Tomorrow morning, you and me and Riley are going to meet first thing to discuss the technical aspects. I'll call in at the lab about 9:00 A.M., then we can go to my office."

"No problem."

"And make sure Laurel's there. She knows more about gorillas than anybody. I'll get Maudie to come too. Another good brain can't hurt. We'll *make* this work, Mark."

The next morning, Jack found Laurel, Mark, and Matthilde hanging out with two of the technicians in the Lab 44 common room. From here, they could also observe what was going on in the sterile lab using a large round window that they called "the porthole." Right this moment, nothing was happening in there, but if Jack had his way, it would soon be the site of

the most exciting primate experiments the world had
seen.

Mark stood to shake hands with Jack, and exchange
slaps on the shoulder. "It's always good to see you
here in the labs," he said.

"I wish I could be here more often."

"Yeah, life must be tough."

Laurel sat comfortably in a brightly striped beanbag
chair in a corner of the room, "talking" to the three-
hundred-pound Matthilde. She used sign language,
since gorillas could not actually speak; they were
intelligent enough to master a basic form of English
vocabulary, but suffered from a lack of vocal cords.
Some could sign to each other, and to humans, with
astonishing creativity.

"Good morning, *everyone*," Jack said.

The two techs were in their early twenties. One was
a newcomer to the company, a short, fit-looking
woman named Anna-Lena Beck, who'd worked at the
Bronx Zoo before Jack's people had recruited her.
Her closely cropped blonde hair contrasted with
deeply tanned skin. The other was a big man named
Roderick Carwardine. Carwardine pumped iron at
his local gym and he looked almost as heavy as Matthilde. Having someone like that on the team sometimes came in handy when working with apes, for
even a chimpanzee was *much* stronger than a human
being of similar size.

Laurel looked across at Jack with a grin on her face,
and Matthilde's head also turned, though the gorilla
made no move toward the "big boss," whom she'd
been taught to treat with respect. Next to Matthilde,
Laurel seemed tiny, but she had no fear of animals,

no matter how fearsome or strong they were. "Riley called," she said. "He is running late."

"Uh-huh. Maybe we should take Matthilde to the meeting instead. That'd teach him to get here on time." But in truth, Riley's effort the previous day had been sterling. Jack could forgive him this once if he'd slept in or got stuck in traffic. "Well, he can meet us upstairs when he gets here."

Jack poured himself a cup of coffee in a paper cup, then he, Laurel, and Mark left Matthilde in the capable hands of Beck and Carwardine. They took an elevator to Jack's office on the top floor, where Maudie was already waiting in her designer-label jacket and pants, guarding the door like an elegant female dragon. Five minutes later, Riley arrived at the office, looking stressed out and cursing the traffic.

"Let's get to work," Jack said.

Maudie had arranged for a steady stream of coffee, orange juice, sandwiches, fruit, and cookies to satisfy everyone's tastes as they worried away at the problems. Jack was happy to move freely from one issue to another, returning to any particular item as often as necessary to make progress. This was more a brainstorming session than a meeting with a formal agenda. The way he saw it, they'd talk as much as needed, occasionally breaking to refuel—or just to clear their heads.

There were so many *ifs* to ponder. If they could somehow fill the gaps in Kong's genome, and still produce a similar animal…if they could get the engineered chromosomes to replicate properly…if they could find a way to gestate a giant ape and bring it to term…

Another *if* struck him: If they could get away with this legally.

"Okay, Riley," he said, "just what are our chances of pulling this off—purely from a scientific viewpoint?"

"We can only do our best," Riley said. "I'd say we have as good a chance as anyone."

"We've got a *good* chance," Mark said. "Let's be positive."

Jack pondered that. "I'm not so sure," he said. "I wonder if the code that we have intact will even reproduce Kong's giantism." What an anticlimax it would be if they went to a lot of trouble and ended up with something about the same size and shape as an ordinary gorilla.

Riley frowned. "That's hard to say, but we'll sure give it every chance."

"Yes, I know you will." *Seventy percent*, Jack thought. *Seventy percent.*

Denham Products had been able to work with about eighty percent of the DNA of an extinct pygmy elephant when it had cloned that animal. As far as historians knew, the Romans had wiped out the species by trapping every living specimen to fight and die in their gladiatorial arenas. Just one fragment of bone had been found preserved at the bottom of a rubbish jar in Herculaneum.

That had been enough to do the trick, but only because the jar's stone had not been shattered in the volcanic destruction of the city. Well that, and the fact that someone had half-filled the jar with olive oil by mistake and hadn't emptied it before Vesuvius had exploded. Without the oil and the jar to exclude air and any atmospheric moisture, the marrow of that bone would have deteriorated to the point where the

DNA would have been unusable. That sample was far older than the blood of Kong, but it had been preserved almost as well as frozen Ice Age animals. Cloning *them*, as Hemming had done, was actually easier.

Riley fixed Jack with a hard look. "Let's be absolutely clear. You want to clone a whole specimen from this material? A direct heir of the same genetic heritage? Not just splicing bits of his genes into other things—"

Jack smiled gently. He thought of Kong as a "he," not an "it"—as a being that had possessed a personality of its own. Almost human. It seemed that Riley had already fallen into the same way of thinking.

"What's so amusing?" Riley said.

"You're talking the way I keep thinking. *His*."

"I see." Riley glanced at Laurel, then at Mark. He shrugged. "It occurred to me yesterday that you might have it in mind that your grandfather's associate had a raw deal."

"My grandfather's associate? You mean Kong? I suppose he did."

"He was kidnapped from his own kind, thrown into a bizarre culture, maltreated—not necessarily on purpose, don't look at me like that—then plugged full of holes by fighter planes. Sort of like a country kid who came to a bad end on the mean streets of the Big City."

Jack had found, since they'd recruited Riley, that the man's dry humor had a way of sneaking out for a moment, then hiding itself away once more behind his mournful face.

"What are you talking about, Riley?" Maudie said. "Where are you trying to lead us?"

"Well," Riley said, "I'm what-iffing it out. When we're finished, this might be a second chance for the country kid."

"The way I look at it is like this," Jack said. 'When we're finished, Denham Products will have an extraordinary specimen—the only one known to the Western world. Maybe the only one in existence."

"That depends," Laurel said. "Maybe there are more on Skull Island."

That raised Jack's eyebrows. Skull Island was a topic he kept to himself. How much *did* his staff discuss the entire history of this among themselves? He nodded in Riley's direction. "You can be sure that I'll want to treat him kindly. Think of it as making it up to his dad—my granddad's associate, as you put it."

"The most immediate question," Mark said, "is how we patch the holes in the DNA that we have."

"That's your field. I'm sure you can do it. Still, it's open for discussion, if you want."

"Here's what's on my mind, Jack. I could fill in the gaps with DNA from an ordinary gorilla—not Matthilde, but a male."

"A silverback?"

"A male gorilla of whatever age we can find."

"That's not exactly ideal," Jack said, "but I can't see any alternative, can you?" He wished there were not those gaps in Kong's DNA, but he knew he should count his blessings.

"It's a pity that we don't have more DNA samples similar to Kong's," Mark said, "but we can only work with what we've got. It raises another issue, though. Just how aggressive do we want Kong to be? We could try to make him more placid than an ordinary male gorilla. Silverbacks are normally gentle creatures, but they *can* lose their tempers. You don't want an animal as big as we're thinking of deciding to punish one of us, or deciding that we're hostile and have to be driven off."

Laurel was nodding along as he spoke.

"All right," Jack said. "What do you suggest?"

"We don't want to mix in any genetic material that we don't understand. If we want to use anything other than *Gorilla gorilla* genes..." Mark trailed off uncertainly, then added, "The safest thing would be to use the genetic material that we understand best among the apes. The material that's been most thoroughly studied."

"I'm not with you."

"What Mark is trying to say," Riley put in, "is that there's a case—a technical case, at least—for mixing in some human genetic material."

Jack whistled, then sat silent, looking from one face to another, wondering if they were pulling his leg. "That would be dynamite! You're not seriously recommending it?"

"No," Riley said, "I'm definitely not. Quite the opposite. None of us would want to recommend that to you. Even in such small percentages."

"I'd never even consider it," Jack said hastily. Athough, come to think of it, he was not so sure. He wouldn't be the first researcher to introduce human genetic material into a non-human animal. After all, genetic material was merely genetic material...as long as they didn't use so much human DNA that they ended up creating some kind of semi-human monster. Still, whatever the strict ethics of it, the media and the public would have his head if he mixed in any human sequences of DNA in the process of creating a bizarre creature such as a giant ape, a reborn Kong.

"Good, because if you did, I'd tell you to take a hike," Riley said. "I'm committed to all the projects here, but my greater commitment is to science itself. If we started making monsters with human genes, the public would never forgive us."

"Of course not," Jack said. "I was thinking along similar lines."

"I just wanted you to rule it out."

"Then consider it ruled out," Jack said. "Otherwise, do what you have to do. If it helps in some way to add DNA from chimps or pygmy chimps, or other kinds of apes, go ahead with it. Meanwhile, I've had some thoughts of my own about Kong's giantism. Was he a one-off, or could there really be others, like Laurel just implied? Maybe he was a spontaneous, infertile mutation. Maybe not."

Grandfather Carl's expedition had reported no other giant apes on Skull Island, but how much had they understood about the island's ecology in the day or so that they'd been there? They'd had no meaningful discussions with the island's natives, had done no scientific investigations. Carl himself had been a wildlife photographer, not a biologist.

Mark seemed to be trying not to smile.

"Well?" Jack said.

"Riley and I talked about that last night."

"Why doesn't that surprise me? Maybe you should have brought a list of things you *haven't* already talked about. It would be a nice short list."

"I'd say that the 'father' Kong was not a one-off mutation. If he was born with anything like the proportions of a normal baby gorilla—compared to its size as an adult—the mother herself must have been enormous."

"Yes," Jack said slowly. "But maybe Kong was born the size of a normal gorilla baby and just kept growing…and growing. Who knows how old he was when they found him?"

"I tend to think otherwise," Mark said. He glanced at Laurel, who gave a sharp nod of confirmation.

"Yes, and I agree," Jack said. "Well, *that* makes it a high priority getting a viable artificial womb for him. If he's going to be huge, even as a baby, we can't rely on Matthilde or any other gorilla to give birth. We'll need a properly controlled environment for him, as much like a female gorilla's uterus as possible. I can't see us gestating him in an elephant's womb, can you?"

For the next few hours, they worked through the technical problems. Mark would have responsibility for reconstructing Kong's genome, filling in the gaps as best as he could with DNA from a male gorilla and any other non-human animals that were needed. The actual cloning process would be under Riley's control, and Riley would need to be involved with every prior step that might affect its success. Laurel would join the Denham Products team working on artificial womb technology, in addition to her duties in Lab 44. She would also make recommendations on the handling of the cloned ape once it was born.

"I know that's looking ahead," Jack said, "but we have to be optimistic. I don't want to go into this project unless I feel we can pull it off."

Riley looked at Jack thoughtfully. "After we clone him," he said quietly, "just what do we do with him?"

"We'll keep him from climbing tall buildings," Jack said with a touch of sarcasm. Then he added more gently, "At least to start with."

"We will need to build a tailored habitat," Laurel said. "I think several acres in the end."

"Can we make do with less while he's growing up?"

"Oh, yes, but it is better not to wait too long."

"All right," Jack said after a moment's thought, "we'll build a forested space for him, something big enough. As he grows, we'll find him something more. I realize we can't let him roam freely around the labs like Matthilde."

"No, no. He will be much too big!"

"I hope so. That's assuming we can capture the giantism when we finalize his DNA. But to answer Riley's question, he's going to be involved in scientific work, but he's not going to live out his life like some kind of glorified pincushion, with tubes and needles sticking out of him."

"I'm glad to hear it," Mark said.

"We'll create the most humane environment that we can. He'll be our corporate mascot, a living testament to the kind of thing we can now accomplish...and the biggest walking advertisement you ever saw. His existence will make the company grow, and in return we'll see to it that he lives a long, comfortable and honorable life, by way of an apology for humankind for what it did to his 'father.' How does that sound?"

Riley looked unconvinced, but then he gave a quick, resigned shrug. "It's a good intention. Shall we get going on it?"

Maudie waved her right hand. "There's one more issue."

Jack turned to her. "What's that?"

"How do we think we're going to get away with this?"

FOUR

MARCH 2004

The usual daily calls kept coming in from Hemming.
As always, he was full of amiable suggestions about
"coming in under our wing at CenCo." Nothing more
was said about Kong, even obliquely. Though he still
took the calls, Jack got into the habit of terminating
them quickly. This didn't discourage Hemming from
calling the next day, and the next. On the other hand,
Bionimals was going through some business problems
of its own. The market was tough all a round, but the
threat of a hostile takeover of Denham Products
seemed to recede slightly.

Mark and the others worked on the genetic engineering problems, starting to make progress in understanding Kong's genome and how they might best
fill in the missing DNA. Meanwhile, Jack faced a
reality he'd tried to avoid until now. He needed to
talk to his lawyer and at least get an independent
opinion on where he stood.

He picked up the phone and called Stanley Levin,
whom he dealt with every week or two, usually on
minor issues: less important patents, property
arrangements, supply and distribution contracts.

Sometimes Jack had more than that to farm out to Stanley, such as the legal work for a major patent application, or the drafting of a large commercial contract. Apart from Maudie, Stanley was Jack's most trusted adviser.

"Good to hear from you, Jack," Stanley said. "What's up this week?"

"I'm going to need more real estate in town," Jack said. "This will be a big job. I'll need a few acres in Manhattan."

"A few *acres*?" Stanley said skeptically.

"That's right. Do you think you can handle it for me?"

"*In Manhattan?*"

"That's what I had in mind."

"Where? And what do you need that much space for anyway? A wildlife preserve?"

"Something like that."

Of course, it was a good question. The company owned several model farms up and down the East Coast from Massachusetts to Florida. Jack had housed the pygmy elephant down south, and that might make sense for the clone of Kong as well. It was a more suitable climate than New York City, with its long, cold winters, but Jack wanted the cloned ape to be on hand as close as possible, always ready for opportunities to promote the company.

"See what you can do," Jack said. "I won't need it for another year or three."

"Okay. I'll make a note to keep tabs on the New York property market."

"*Please*. I'd be very grateful."

"Anything else you want me to worry about? Some other Mission Impossible for me?"

"Actually, there is one small matter. Can you come to the apartment tomorrow?"

There was a pause at the other end of the line. Stanley must be consulting his electronic diary on the computer screen as he spoke. "Is the afternoon okay?" he said. "How much time do you need?"

"This might take the *whole* afternoon," Jack said. "It's kind of complex."

"That sounds ominous."

"Actually, it might be your lucky day. There's a fair bit of work I'll be needing."

"Okay, okay, I have another client meeting, but I'm sure I can shift it. How about I see you at two o'clock?"

"Fine," Jack said. *If only you knew what you were in for.*

What a pity I can't just kill Denham and make an end of it, Hemming thought.

Bionimals' new chief of science had sent an encrypted report that at least had the virtue of honesty. The problem with employing time-servers and yes-men was that they told you what you wanted to believe—or what they *thought* you wanted to believe—and not the unvarnished truth. This time, he had an analysis that he could trust.

What he liked about this report was not just its honesty. It told the facts almost bluntly, not wrapping them up in soothing jargon. "I CONFIRM THAT WE'VE OVERCOME CERTAIN TECHNICAL PROBLEMS," it began.

Unfortunately, that's not the end of the story.
In all the latest cases, cell division proceeded as

planned, with normal chromosomal replication. Twelve embryos were selected for implantation in female gorillas. Of the twelve, seven were rejected within two weeks. Five developed as planned, but tests showed signs of congenital deformity in all five within four months. At this point, there is still some prospect of producing a viable clone of the giant "Kong" gorilla, but no guarantee can be given as to how long the process might take. Nor can we guarantee that a "viable" clone will not, in fact, be born with undetectable genetic defects, becoming apparent only as development continues to adulthood. This is not uncommon with mammalian cloning, e.g. sheep and cattle, and would not preclude success. However, the risks are increased in this case because of the drastic steps required to fill in missing DNA from the damaged blood samples available. I confirm that we have been able to reconstruct less than seventy percent of Kong's genome. The absence of tissues believed to have been stolen soon after discovery badly compromises the likely success of the project.

You and I will get along fine, Roxanne, Hemming thought. He'd recruited Dr. Roxanne Blaine from the Zöologischegarten in Basel, where she'd worked for the past three years. Prior to that, she'd taught at Stanford, where she'd completed her doctorate in 1996. Roxanne was an expert in animal psychology as well as a gifted geneticist. Obviously she was also courageous and an able administrator. She must have shown a lot of grit to get where she had in the scientific world—not everyone would open doors nicely for a young black woman who wanted to be a top biologist. But she'd made it, regardless of what prejudices she'd faced.

Roxanne also spoke several languages and had represented Stanford in track-and-field events in her younger days. Her résumé showed extensive experience as a biologist in the field, for which she'd hiked in some of the world's most densely vegetated jungles and piloted light aircraft when needed. She had hundreds of hours flying everything from Piper Cubs to Lear jets. This was a woman whom Hemming could respect.

He sent her a brief e-mail response, also encrypted, and routed to be untraceable. He headed it: *Big Man—message understood*. Then, in the body of the e-mail, he wrote simply: *Continue with maximum priority. ANY recommendations for increased resources will be viewed sympathetically*. Then, as an afterthought, he added: *Thanks for your good work*. What she might be feeling didn't really matter, but he'd get her trained to please him.

Unfortunately, even with someone competent in charge, Project Big Man was now well behind schedule. No one on the Bionimals team had the magic hands in solving cloning problems that Graham Riley was reputed to have. Riley was one of those scientists with an uncanny instinct for making experimental apparatus work. But Denham had snapped him up from the University of Pittsburgh even though Hemming had offered more money. Perhaps Riley had sensed that he and Hemming could never work harmoniously together. Brilliant though he was, Riley also had a reputation for drawing boundaries around what he would or would not do.

If Denham Products had obtained its own sample of Kong's DNA, it might be better placed than Bionimals to clone the giant ape. Even Roxanne could not get miracles out of her team. By contrast, Denham had some of the best geneticists in the business working for him, with Riley adding immensely to the potency of the mix. All of which meant that there had to be a Plan B.

But actually, Hemming had *many* plans.

Stanley Levin was a tall man in his mid-fifties, built heavily in the chest and shoulders, but slim around the hips. He was immaculately dressed in a dark blue three-piece suit, yet looked as if he'd be more at home on a squash court, or even playing seniors football in a local league, than giving learned advice to well-heeled Manhattan clients. His face was tanned and leathery, with a ferociously bristling gray mustache. He was almost bald—from too much testosterone, or so he liked to claim.

"Something's on your mind, Jack," he said. "You want to spit it out?"

"Let me give you a hypothetical case," Jack replied.

"Hypothetical it is, then. But you never know when a situation might arise. Am I right?"

Jack took him through it. Kong's death atop the Empire State Building, the loss of blood, the discovery of clotted blood years later, and its getting into CenCo's possession. Then someone stealing parts of it, and selling samples to other interested parties. "And suppose I'm one of those parties," Jack said, "for the sake of argument."

"Consider it supposed," Stanley said. "This is a thorny problem you're giving me."

"All right. Well, I'm heir to any property that my grandfather had in Kong. As far as I'm concerned, that blood sample would belong to me—if anything like this happened, of course."

"Of course."

"So, what do you think?"

"Putting it bluntly, I think you might find yourself up Shit Creek without a paddle."

Jack looked at him, unbelieving. "But, Stan—"

"I can research it, if you like. I know you think that anything to do with Kong belongs to your family, or to you personally. If you really thought that—and you'd stolen the sample yourself or encouraged someone else to—that might be a defense to a charge of theft. It looks to me, though, as if CenCo would have a civil claim to get it back and maybe to get back anything produced with it. If this situation ever came up, I'd advise you to keep out of it." He gave Jack a pointed look that made clear they understood each other. This was not hypothetical.

"I'll keep in mind what you say," Jack said.

"I'm glad to hear that. No one ever went wrong listening to good advice. Not just listening to it—acting on it."

"As I said, I'll keep it in mind...but I do want you to research it further."

"You want a formal memorandum of advice from me?"

"No, not right now." It seemed to Jack that the last thing he needed was formal written advice that he was legally in the wrong. "I just want you to research it. Find some kind of argument in my favor—you know, if this situation came up."

"You're instructing me that it hasn't happened?"

Jack grinned, but didn't feel too happy. "I'm just asking you in hypothetical terms, not giving you instructions about anything that's actually happened, or might be in the cards, or could have happened, or would have, or should have. Okay? Take the facts hypothetically as I've set them out to you, and tell me the strongest arguments I'd have. There's no hurry on this. Don't cut too many corners."

"All right, I'll take it on."

"Bill it to my personal account, not to Denham Products—use your 'general legal advice' file in my name. Just put it down in your records as 'commercial advice and related research,' or something like that. Is that clear?"

"It's very clear, Jack. Whatever is going on, take care. Don't get into anything you might regret."

"Don't worry about me," Jack said, though even this informal opinion from Stanley made him feel kicked in the stomach. He showed the lawyer out, shaking hands with him warmly at the door. "Remember about that property I'm looking for."

"I've got it written down. I'll do my best."

"I know, and I appreciate it."

"Sure, Jack. Take care."

"Give my regards to your family."

When Stanley had gone, Jack headed back to his study, passing Assumpta on the way. "My word, have you seen a ghost?" she said. "All the color's gone out of your face. Is there anything I can do for you?"

He shook his head. "No, Assumpta, not right now." In his study, he rested his elbow on the desk and sat with his head in his hands.

MARCH-APRIL 2004

Mark Illingworth had the vital job of recreating Kong's DNA. He worked long hours every day, weekends included, trying to get all the procedures right. He had to set the stage as well as he could for the DNA transfer and the implantation.

No one could take a single cell and grow a whole organism from it, unless the organism itself was single-celled, or unless that one cell was a fertilized ovum. At some point, the team would need to transfer Kong's reconstructed DNA into ova from Matthilde or other ordinary gorillas, then grow the resulting hybrids into early embryos that could be implanted into a gorilla's uterus. At that stage, Riley would take charge of the project.

Mark shared a bench with Riley and Laurel, though Laurel also had other work to do, especially with the development of Denham Products' artificial womb technology. She, too, put in long hours, but only about five per day here in Lab 44. Riley was here as often as Mark, but most of his research was somewhat different.

The lab was scrupulously sterile, brightly lit, and secured by doors designed to seal tightly and keep out contamination. The instruments that they used had to be free from even the tiniest biological fragments. Many people might have found this environment disorienting, if not actually alien, but Mark loved it. To him, it was home. Like a craftsman's well-oiled tools, everything here had a beauty of its own, a functional elegance that you could love once you understood it.

Mark used precious cells from the Kong blood sample. Using powerful inverted microscopes and a custom-designed computer program, Mark and Laurel taught themselves to augment and reshape the damaged DNA that would be used in the cloning procedure.

Riley acted as their sounding board, but he was mostly absorbed in experiments on chromosomal division in the early stages of primate cloning. His goal was to refine their existing techniques to a state of perfection. They needed to get the conditions exactly right, and to do it routinely. In the past, cloning had seldom succeeded smoothly, even with relatively easy animals like cattle and mice. There had been few successful attempts to clone monkeys, much less the great apes. Occasional claims were made of success even with cloned human embryos, but each of those had been fiercely disputed.

"We won't get too many shots at this," Riley often said as they worked their long hours in the lab. "I want to do it right the first time."

If only that were possible, Mark thought.

Jack seldom visited them in the lab. No doubt he knew better than to interfere with his people's concentration. As a successful research biologist himself, he was the kind of boss who could appreciate how hard everyone worked once absorbed in technical problems—and how little it helped trying to apply pressure. For Mark, at least, the thrill of creation and the fascination of the science itself were enough to keep him immersed in the current set of problems, to sustain his energy in the lab for twelve or sixteen hours a day.

But one evening in late April when Mark, Laurel, and Riley were all back late, there was a firm tapping at the observation window from the common room—the "porthole"—and Mark looked up to see Jack peering at them through the glass. He held up a bottle of French Champagne in one hand, pointing to it eagerly with the other. Then he made a drinking motion.

Mark gave a puzzled if sympathetic smile, but he was at a crucial point right now. He and Laurel were trying to integrate into the Kong DNA some gene sequences from a bonobo, a pygmy chimp.

The replacement DNA that Mark was using to fill the gaps came mainly from a young lowland gorilla named Leonardo—a resident of the Bronx Zoo, where Jack had good contacts. The gorilla DNA would be effective, Mark suspected, but it would not have a positive effect on the psychology of the creature they were designing. Gentle though male gorillas normally were, they could also be fierce. Silverbacked adult males were often violent in controlling and defending their harems of females. Jack himself had first mentioned the idea, right at the start of the project, of including a component of bonobo DNA. Laurel had taken it the most seriously and suggested they try it out. She'd hoped it might have some effect in "tuning down" the clone's psychology from the aggressive level that Kong had shown on Skull Island, and then in New York, all those years ago.

"What do you think Jack wants?" Riley said, looking up from his microscope. "There's no breakthrough for him here today."

Laurel scarcely looked up at all, absorbed in the intricacies of the gene-splicing problem.

Jack beckoned them to join him, but Mark signaled back by extending all the fingers of his left hand. *Give us five minutes.*

Behind the porthole's glass, Jack gave a huge bearded smile, like a rather genteel Greek god.

"Well," Riley said, "*I* can stop work now, even if you two can't. Jack sure seems happy about something."

"Okay," Mark said, trying to concentrate. "Go for it." He continued peering through his high-powered microscope, while tapping twice on his computer keyboard, then twice more. The blood cell he was working on was not one whose nuclear DNA he would actually insert into a gorilla ovum, but he was engaged in a crucial trial of a significant part of the process. If he could just get this right, the rest would probably go okay—at least up to the point when Riley's work would become all important. Mark almost held his breath as he snipped out sequences of genetic code *here* and inserted them *there*.

It actually took more like ten minutes than five, but he was finally happy. He and Laurel looked at each other with grins on their faces, like kids who'd won a Little League game. This was starting to work, and what they'd done today had been recorded by the Chimera computer program that they used for the purpose.

Now they had to switch everything off, discard the genetic material that they couldn't use again, then put the rest away. Those procedures took another ten minutes—nothing done in the lab could be rushed, no matter how keen Jack was to share a drink with them. When they were finished, it must all be as clean as when they'd begun.

By the time they met Jack and Riley in the common room, one bottle of Dom Pérignon already sat empty on the floor. Jack popped open another.

Mark laughed a bit uncomfortably, not used to this level of informality in the workplace, even at Denham Products. "Okay," he said, "what's the big celebration?"

"You three are the only other people working so late tonight," Jack said, slurring his words just slightly. "I knew I could count on you to have a drink with me."

"For what?" Laurel said.

"I've been on the phone most of the evening, talking to government ministers from four countries in central Africa. The bottom line is we've won a major contract—I mean *major*—for New Millet. We beat out Bionimals, even though Hemming tried to undercut us again."

"Someone recognized a superior product?" Mark said.

"Exactly. This makes up for a lot of what's been going wrong since Hemming decided to target us. Our friend Charlton is going to be pissed off like you wouldn't believe."

Mark tried not to follow too much of the company's good and bad fortunes, concentrating instead on the scientific problems that were set for him or those he set for himself. In fact, one of the attractions of the job was the freedom that Jack gave his best scientists to pursue their own ideas. All he asked for, in return, was that they research possibilities which might prove of long-term benefit to the company. Still, Mark had heard enough things to have a sense of the company's woes.

He knew much more about its actual research, for all senior scientists at Denham Products were continually briefed on each other's projects. New Millet was an almost drought-proof genetically modified grain. It had the potential to help farmers in many parts of Africa and Mark knew that Jack was committed to the product for its own sake—or, rather, for the human benefits it could bring—not merely for its potential profitability. If it was going to save the company, all the better. And there was another good reason to feel satisfied. Selling genetically modified agricultural products to suspicious, politically sensitive African nations was always difficult. Doing so against aggressive bidding from Bionimals was a coup—and a smack in the eye for Charlton Hemming.

"I've called all the New Millet team at home," Jack said, pouring a glass of the champagne for Laurel. "But they work proper hours, not like you three."

"It might not be like this for much longer," Mark said.

"In what way?"

"I mean we're making progress day by day on what we need to do to fill in Kong's DNA. If it can be done at all—"

"Yes?" Jack said expectantly.

Mark glanced at Riley, who might have his own ideas, then said, "As far as I'm concerned, we'll be ready to try in another month."

Riley chewed his lip for moment. "I can go along with that."

"Are *you* happy with it, too?" Jack asked Laurel. He handed the glass of Champagne to her, then poured another—this time for Mark.

"For sure," Laurel said. "It is the feeling of the team as a whole."

"I hope Matthilde's agreeable as well," Jack said, "since she's going to be the mama." He raised his glass. "Here's to Matthilde! Hey, we ought to get her in here." He smiled impishly at Laurel. "You want to go and wake her?"

"I don't think so, Jack." As they all knew, it was better not to disturb the research animals' sleeping patterns. Matthilde was probably dreaming happily in her cage. "Not tonight."

"All the same…" Jack said.

"What?"

"To Matthilde!"

"Okay. To Matthilde, then!"

"And to the kid," Mark added. "Don't forget the kid."

Even Riley gave a slight smile at that. He nodded with the others and raised his glass. "To New Millet," he said. "To Matthilde…and to the kid. Perfect may he be and long may he live."

Laurel raised her glass. "To the kid!" she said.

FIVE

MAY 2004

Jack had seen Stanley about five times since they'd first spoken about the legal problems surrounding ownership of the "hypothetical" Kong clone. Stanley had raised the subject a couple of times, but Jack had put him off, not really wanting to think about it more than he had to. Today, he was in a different mood.

The legal offices of Levin Drobnick Mahon were almost as intimidating in their way as the ultra-clean biological labs at Denham Products' headquarters. The décor of the fiftieth-floor reception area was all mahogany surfaces, severe wallpaper, shelves of leather-bound law reports, deep, soft armchairs, and several huge abstract paintings, all—evidently—by the same artist, whose work combined images of darkness with foregrounds of garish orange fire. Behind a crescent-shaped desk sat a startlingly beautiful receptionist with flaming red hair that almost matched the artwork. Seeing Jack, she picked up the phone to call Stanley.

"Dr. Denham is here," she said in a voice that sounded like a songbird's. A minute later, Stanley wandered in from the elevator lobby.

He led Jack to one of the firm's conference rooms, which were slightly more cheerful than the reception area. Here, the décor was pine wood and the paintings tended to be in soft pastels. Evidently the idea was to overwhelm visitors when they first arrived, but keep them soothed while you actually gave them advice on behalf of the firm.

For the first half-hour they worked through some details about the New Millet contract, then Jack raised what was really on his mind. "About that hypothetical question…"

"The one about cloning a large animal?"

Stanley sat up straighter in his chair. "Speaking as your lawyer, I'm glad it's only hypothetical. I wouldn't want to see you in such a mess."

"That bad, huh?"

"It might be, Jack. Pretty bad."

"What about speaking *not* as my lawyer?"

"Speaking that way, I might think it sounded exciting, but that isn't the point. What you need with something like this is someone who speaks *strictly* as your legal adviser."

"Uh-huh."

"Looking at it that way, I'd still advise you to keep well clear of it. Don't touch it with a ten-foot pole."

"What if it was too late to take that advice?"

Stanley pulled his chair closer to the table and laid his pen down as carefully as if lowering a coffin into a grave. "Of course, there are arguments the other way. In that case, I'd do my best to defend you, or try to negotiate you out of trouble. But that doesn't mean I'd want you to do whatever you've done…or whatever you're thinking of doing."

"Goddammit," Jack said, "this sounds like a case of the law being an ass. As far as I'm concerned, anything to do with Kong belonged to my grandfather, including material left behind. If it belonged to him, it was inherited by me. No one has a right to keep it from me."

"I wish it were that simple."

"What's so hard about it?"

"First of all, we'd have to establish that your grandfather ever owned Kong. Mind you, that might not be too difficult; it might not even be contested in the end. But if it came to a crunch, we'd have to discuss all the detail. There are all sorts of problems after that. When your grandfather died, no one took those remnants of blood into their possession. They were just sitting there on the façade of the building where they'd dripped or splashed, or whatever, after the planes shot Kong. Is that the picture I should be getting?"

"I guess so. I'm not sure about the *taking into their possession* part, but you've got the drift."

"Well, maybe they became the property of the building owner, at least after a long enough time. Or maybe not. Maybe they were just like some bank notes that you drop accidentally in a public place, like an airport terminal. You still own them, as long as they lie there. Someone can pick them up and eventually the law will say that they become the true owner, but it takes years. The law calls that process *adverse possession*; if you can hold on to something long enough, you become its owner, even if the true owner turns up. There's an argument that the remnants of Kong never became the property of the building owner, because they were never taken into possession—they always belonged to your grandfather if he wanted to claim them."

"That's what I've been saying all along."

"I know, but then again, the façade of the Empire State Building, ninety floors up, is not a public place in the normal sense. Anyway, it might not even be relevant. Tell me one thing: What happened to the rest of Kong?"

"They burned the carcass," Jack said.

"Your grandfather never tried to keep it?"

"No."

"That's what I suspected. You see, there are lots of problems here. I'm not sure that I 'own' my dog's blood if he gets into a fight when I walk him in the park. No case has ever held that, but maybe the law would go that way if someone wanted to clone my dog."

"Times change."

"Of course they do, Jack. Of course they do. Things become valuable that never were before, and the law has to try to keep up. But in this case, it looks like your grandfather renounced whatever ownership he'd claimed over the flesh and blood that made up Kong. He didn't try to keep the rest of the carcass and he didn't even know about cloning. To him, the blood remnants had no value at all. Perhaps that blood didn't belong to anyone until it was found and someone removed it to a lab somewhere. It was there for the taking."

"In that case, I might have been better off if I'd just gone climbing the building myself and taken it—if I'd known about it."

"I suppose you could have tried. That's a nasty sort of cliff face, though."

"I've climbed worse," Jack said with a light smile. Hiking and mountain climbing had been two of his hobbies for many years. He'd climbed sheer cliffs in the European Alps, in bitter cold, with thousands of feet to fall if he made a single error. "But it's too late now."

"Well, you'd have been in breach of some other laws if you'd gone clambering all over the building, but do I think there'd have been a good argument that you'd become the rightful owner of the blood. But as you say: too late. As for the hypothetical case that you've described to me—someone stealing the blood, then selling it on to you—I'd rather be on the other side, at least from a legal viewpoint. That's my blunt opinion."

"Okay," Jack said, his heart sinking more than a little. "I understand what you're saying. It's nice to discuss these things. I'll have a think about it."

"Please do."

"Let's get back to the New Millet contract tomorrow. I've had enough of the law for one day."

"Any particular time tomorrow?"

"I'll call you and make an appointment."

"That's fine. I'll show you out then."

Fine, Jack thought. *But that's not the end of it.*

He took an elevator to street level and stepped out onto the pavement. The day was bright, clear, and almost hot, so unlike the wintry months when he'd first gotten into this. Time was moving and he was well embarked on a process that he was determined to see through to the bitter end.

Despite Stanley's opinion, he was better equipped to fight than he'd been just weeks before. With the New Millet contract in hand, Denham Products could take some financial risks here and there, endure the expense of litigation if it had to.

Jack walked straight back home. There was no value in disturbing his research teams today. He'd leave them to get on with it.

MAY-OCTOBER 2004

The Chimera software program was named for a mythological monster composed of disparate parts from a variety of animals. It had also come to be the scientific term for a creature engineered from more than one species.

The software allowed Mark to work efficiently with strings of DNA, coiling them tightly, stretching them out, tidying them into the knotted-up little packages that were a genetic engineer's stock in trade. It helped him handle not only planning but actual genetic surgery. It stored a record of every manipulation he'd ever carried out, with a separate field to enter explanatory notes about what he'd done and why. Using micromanipulators, Chimera could undertake a genetic operation. It could be programmed to perform the same operation—say, the removal of a particular gene from a chromosome, and the substitution of another one—again and again, in cell after cell of a sample. More elaborate operations could be constructed by adding elements from earlier successful ones.

But even with this technological assistance, Mark and Laurel had their hands full. Too little was known about the functions of specific DNA sequences in gorillas, or any of the primates, let alone in Kong's unique genome. At the same time, Mark knew all too well that an embryo trying to grow with two or more different genetic and chemical heritages was likely to solve the problem as simply as possible by spontaneously aborting. He dared not modify too much and he had to hope that the DNA he was using to fill in the gaps was similar indeed to the missing DNA in Kong's blood cells.

By comparing different cells, he'd been able to build up some cells to the seventy percent completeness that he'd originally estimated was possible, but that was still too much missing *if* the gorilla genes—or the small component of genes from a pygmy chimpanzee—and the Kong genes were fundamentally incompatible.

Even when the job was almost complete, he could still not be sure that the new "joint" DNA would code for protein structures that would create an animal like the original Kong. If they'd lost too much of the DNA that distinguished Kong from a normal highland or lowland gorilla, they might end up with an ape not that different in appearance from any other gorilla found in captivity...assuming the engineered DNA was viable at all.

There was simply no way to be sure what was going to happen.

By October, the strain was beginning to tell on him. Every morning, in the mirror, Mark saw how much weight he was losing. At the start, he could have afforded losing some of his puppy fat, as he liked to think of it. But now he was starting to compete with Riley for emaciation. As if to distinguish himself, Riley lost even more hair. Only Laurel seemed largely unchanged, but even she was looking tired and care-worn.

Thankfully, Jack stayed out of their way. He saw their weekly reports and must have known he could have done no better.

Finally, almost nine months into his work on the project, Mark was finished "rebuilding" Kong's DNA.

Now came the part that Riley, in his ironic way, liked to call "easy." In fact, it was the part where everything could go wrong: the actual cloning procedure.

NOVEMBER 2004

It's a pity you can't see this, Granddad, Jack thought. *But if this works out, in a year or so, maybe two, everybody's going to remember your name.*

But that was if everything worked out. This was the opportunity for a great scientific triumph, the resurrection of what Carl had once called "The Eighth Wonder of the World," but so much could still go wrong. Since Jack had given the go-ahead, the technical side of the project had come under Riley's control. The rest of the team had waited until he had done his last fine-tuning and was convinced he could get everything exactly right in both the *in vitro* chemical environment and the steps of the procedure itself. Now he was ready.

Jack sat with Mark and Laurel in the back of the lab, keeping as still as he could. They were all masked and suited, but not really needed here. Riley peered through a binocular eyepiece, performing the delicate operation. A thirty-inch video monitor sat beside him on the bench displaying a hugely magnified image of what he was doing. First, it was a matter of removing the nucleus from one of Matthilde's ova, pulling out a more darkly colored mass from the inside of the globular, jelly-like structure that was the ovum. That done, Riley used a microinjector to insert the nucleus of one of Kong's reengineered blood cells into the "enucleated" ovum.

The ovum now contained a complete sequence of DNA: the gaps were filled with genetic material from Leonardo—the lowland gorilla who'd donated his genes—and a pygmy chimpanzee. Biologists called the injection process "somatic cell nuclear transfer."

Everyone held their breaths as Riley completed the process, but of course nothing dramatic took place immediately. The ovum knew its job perfectly well, and so did Riley. He used electricity to stimulate the ovum, trying to get it to fuse with the nuclear DNA that he'd just added. Matthilde's ovum would actually reprogram the DNA from Kong's blood cell, get it to act like embryonic DNA. If the process worked, the ovum would soon begin to replicate and grow exactly as if it had been fertilized by a compatible sperm cell.

With reproduction the natural way, half of the new animal's chromosomes—the gene-carrying structures within the cell—came from the nucleus of the ovum, and half from the sperm cell that had fertilized it. Here, all of the chromosomes were provided by the modified blood cell's nuclear DNA...seventy percent from Kong.

Riley finished the job, looked up, and stood to stretch his legs and back. "That's one finished," he said quietly.

"Well done," Jack said, equally quietly. There was a sense of reverence in here, now that the final process was underway. The atmosphere was as hushed as that of a church.

Maudie tapped at the porthole and waved to them. Riley returned to his apparatus and again they watched his hunched back and shoulders and the images on the video screen. Through the glass, Maudie mouthed the words, "What's happened?"

Jack held up one finger and mouthed, "First transfer." He hoped she'd understand.

Riley began to repeat the process. He would do it five more times, giving them six embryos to choose from. They'd implant at least two or three into Matthilde. After a few weeks, they would see which survived best within her and terminate the others. Eventually, they would undertake a further delicate task, transferring one of the developing embryos into the new artificial womb…if they could perfect the technology in time.

It seemed to take hours, but Riley was finished and cleaned up to his satisfaction. They trooped out to the common room, where Maudie was waiting for them.

Jack shook Riley's hand. "This is a great day," Jack said. "The day we conceived a new lifeform."

"Let's have a drink," Maudie said. "Jack's right. This doesn't happen every day."

"Matthilde should be with us this time," Laurel said.

"Damned right," Jack said. "She's going to be a mommy. She'd better mark the occasion."

Though none of the nuclear DNA would come from Matthilde, she would make a tiny contribution of DNA from her mitochondria—tiny structures that worked like microscopic power plants, found in the outer part of each ovum that she'd contributed. She would also be related to the new kid by providing her ova, and later her uterus, as the initial environments in which his genes could start to express themselves. Cloning research had continually shown how much difference that could make to the way a cloned animal turned out.

It seemed a pity that gorillas—smart as they were—could not be taught all the subtleties of what they were involved in. Jack figured, perhaps sentimentally, that Matthilde would be proud if she could be made to understand.

He went to the refrigerator and took out the champagne that he'd left there earlier. Laurel got Matthilde from her cage and the gorilla romped around excitedly, obviously sensing the good mood that her human friends were in. Jack even offered her a shot glass of champagne, dripping it on her tongue, and she seemed to enjoy the bubbly as much as any of them. Laurel signed to her and Matthilde replied with a complex sequence of finger movements.

"What's she saying?" Jack asked. He had only ever learned the basics of signing, leaving it to others to obtain more fluency in communicating with apes such as Matthilde.

"She says: *Jack good man*," Laurel said. "*Matthilde likes Jack. He should come here more*."

"That's a complicated thought."

"Gorillas are more complicated than you think."

Maudie laughed. "Well, Jack, you've finally found a woman who appreciates you." She swigged down three inches of the Champagne in her glass.

"I guess so," Jack said. It struck him that he hadn't thought of any woman in *that* way for a long time—for far *too* long.

"My, you are all feeling lighthearted," Riley said. "I hope you realize how seldom the nuclear transfer procedure actually works."

"We do remember," Jack said. "We also realize how seldom it's done by someone who knows what he's doing as well as you do. I'm sure it'll be okay. And if it's not, we'll learn something from it and try again." He turned to Laurel once more. "Tell Matthilde that Jack thinks she's a good gorilla and that he wants to talk to her more often. Can you convey that?"

"Not a problem at all," Laurel said, already signing to Matthilde. The two of them, the ape and the human woman, exchanged signs for another minute after that, both of them looking excited, yet serious, whatever it was they were saying.

"What was that all about?" Maudie said, when they finally stopped.

"She wanted to know why we are all so happy."

"What did you tell her?"

"I told her she will soon be a mother," Laurel said, with a shrewd smile, "but I think she did not believe me. She asked me lots of questions about it."

"Well, *I* believe you," Jack said.

"Me, too," Mark said. He raised his glass. "To Matthilde...and to the new kid."

"To the kid," Maudie said. "Don't you think we should give him a name, now we've got this far?"

"Not yet," Riley said. "Don't ever name an animal until it's born."

Jack shook his head at that. "Nonsense. We'll call him *Kong*, of course."

SIX

NOVEMBER 2004–MARCH 2005

The ova that Riley had manipulated got on with their jobs without much fuss. Shortly, there were two daughter cells where there had been just an ovum, and then four, and eight, and sixteen. Only one ovum divided with the common problems in chromosomal replication that so many researchers had found when attempting to clone primates. Soon Riley made a decision about which embryos to implant into Matthilde. He picked the three that he considered healthiest and placed them in the gorilla's uterus where nature could take its course.

From that point, Matthilde was going to be the most pampered pregnant gorilla of all time. Nothing but the best for the mother of the new Kong.

The first few weeks went almost too well. Two of the embryos implanted successfully and Riley soon ordered a selective termination to leave only the more robust of them to grow larger and eventually be born. The new "Kong" now had a definite identity. There was just one creature growing inside Matthilde's womb, growing toward whatever extraordinary fate awaited it.

As the months passed, it became harder and harder to resist Jack's optimism. Riley could almost have joined in, but he knew better. "It's easy to be unborn," he remarked to Jack one morning. "It's easy to die that way, too."

"You know," Jack said, "you're the kind of guy who thinks the glass is half empty when it's half full."

"We're in unknown territory, Jack. No one has done this before."

But it was hard *not* to enjoy what was going on, as ultrasound imaging showed the embryo visibly becoming a fetus. The eyes formed and developed lids; the fingers and toes became defined. Better still, no announcements came from the Bionimals labs. *We must be ahead*, Riley thought. *Wouldn't that be something?* And best of all, Kong kept growing bigger. After five months it was obvious that Matthilde was gestating a creature that was going to be far larger than a normal gorilla baby—larger, indeed, than she could safely bring to term.

Laurel and her team working on Denham Products' artificial womb technology made several attempts to gestate smaller animals, ranging from mice to kittens. Unfortunately, there were many accidents. To Riley's way of thinking, most of them were secondary to carelessness in the birthing process—though he wouldn't have dared put it that way to Laurel. In a few cases, there was some kind of difficulty getting the oxygenated artificial amniotic fluid out of the newborn's lungs. He suspected that the level of oxygenation might have been too high. He and Laurel both made a note to lower the concentration when the time came.

So many things could still go haywire.

MARCH 2005

The process of transferring little Kong to the prototype artificial womb was as dangerous as moving a human infant out of one uterus and into another during the second trimester. Jack and Riley kept out of the way, letting Laurel and her team do the intricate, delicate work. As he watched, Jack's heart pounded, keeping time with the sound of a fetal-heart monitor that gave two beats for his one.

The confidence that they'd all had that they were leading in the race to clone Kong had become near-certainty only a week before, when Bionimals had announced the successful cloning of a full-sized Ice Age mammoth, gestated in the uterus of an African elephant. That certainly counted as "something big," and made Jack feel sure that Hemming had nothing else up his sleeve just yet.

To perform their adaptation of a Cesarean operation, Laurel and her team of veterinary doctors, nurses, and technicians were using a large operating theater on the second floor. They had fashioned the little gorilla fetus a kind of "space helmet" that enclosed its head with a circulating supply of the artificial amniotic fluid. Two of the technicians secured this as tightly as it could be to the "space suit" that enclosed the rest of the developing body; more hands fastened a hammock of soft nylon webbing into place around the precious burden. And then they lifted the whole affair, trailing tubes and monitoring cables, from Matthilde's anesthetized form on the operating table.

Amniotic fluid splashed and dripped everywhere. The scene was a mass of scrub-suited bodies and reaching hands, all straining as they eased the contents of the hammock down into the fluid of the Denham Products prototype "placental tank." And then—

Nothing. On the monitor, the fetal heart beat exactly as it should, uninterrupted, seemingly untroubled. All the monitors came up to speed.

"Piece of cake," Riley said.

At the time of transfer, the fetus weighed five pounds—a good size for a newborn gorilla baby. It had grown that big in half of a gorilla's usual gestation period. Jack had a feeling it would get much bigger still. The giantism gene was working.

For the first time in his life, Jack started coming to work each day, looking through the Lab 44 common-room porthole at the technicians taking care of the support equipment surrounding the placental tank, all in scrub gear with helmets and particulate filters. They'd moved the artificial womb here to place it directly under the control of the Kong team.

The artificial womb itself was not much like any kind of "tank." It looked more like a giant, translucent garbage bag lying on a flat steel base, given shape by an open metal frame, and full of fluid that made it warm to the touch. The bag was penetrated by numerous pipes and nozzles that connected it to carefully maintained six-foot-high storage vats of chemicals. Electronic devices measured the weight of the bag and continually estimated that of the creature growing inside it. To fit all this apparatus, Lab 44 had been stripped almost bare of its benches and usual equipment.

They were taking no chances of some rogue bacterium or virus getting into the fluid. High-infectivity isolation wards in major hospitals had less stringent requirements.

After a few days, Jack decided to stay out, but he still walked to work each morning and went first thing to the Lab 44 common room where he pressed his nose against the glass, watching the small dark shape as it grew. And grew.

SEPTEMBER 2005

As the unborn Kong grew larger, there were more issues about names to sort out. Jack was going to have to name and register this new species as soon as it was a neonate to prevent patent infringements by others and the taxonomy was proving difficult. Laurel was the team's specialist in primates, and—as a side interest—one of their people in the taxonomic end of biology. One morning, Jack took her aside in the Lab 44 common room.

"It is not entirely a new species," she said in answer to his question. "Yet it is not a cross between two previously known species."

As they spoke, Matthilde sat on the floor watching them, her head moving from side to side as if she were a spectator at a tennis match. Laurel's favorite female gorilla had come through her pregnancy with baby Kong unharmed. Six months later, she seemed just as friendly, tame, and intelligent as ever. Meanwhile, her "kid" was still growing. He'd been growing toward birth for far longer than any normal gorilla, since the usual gestation was almost the same as a human being's. He showed no sign of stopping. Fortunately, the placental tank had been designed with that in mind.

Jack sighed. "You and the others talk about everything together…"

"Maybe," Laurel said with a smile.

"Well, you must have a theory about this."

"Not *Gorilla gigans*," she said. "We should keep that for the true giant gorilla. I mean, the first Kong."

"Uh-huh," Jack said. "Maybe so."

"If it is not too immodest for you, one variant might be *Gorilla denhamensis*."

"I think that's appropriate," Jack said thoughtfully. "Not for me: for my grandfather."

Laurel laughed. "Then again, maybe we could be more specific."

"As in *carl-denhamensis*?"

"Oh, yes, we could use that just as easily—"

"But?"

"Mmm, it seems okay…but maybe too long and clumsy?"

Jack considered it, then laughed.

"Mark thinks *Gorilla insulaecranii*," Laurel added. "Maybe that is too obscure."

Jack blanked out at that. "It's almost as long…and it's too obscure for me."

"As in 'Skull Island'…'of the island of the skull.' You see?"

"Oh, okay." There was a tradition of invoking species' points of origin in their scientific names. "Let me think about it for a while."

"Okay then, but not too long—otherwise, he might be born."

"Believe me, I know."

He headed upstairs to his office, feeling a growing sense of anticipation. As Laurel had said, the big day was coming. Not yet, not even soon—if you measured that by hours of days. But it was coming. What kind of future could they give Kong? What would it mean for them all?

Over the next week, Jack thought about all the questions that burned in his brain. There were no immediate answers and he was distracted by the growing dark shape in the placental tank, which seemed to have taken its new "uterus" as a reason to grow even faster. Laurel e-mailed some calculations, showing that baby Kong would not be a fully formed neonate, able to be removed from its artificial womb, for another six months.

The process seemed to be taking forever, but he reminded himself of an elephant's gestation period: the best part of two years. If Kong was going to be a huge animal, he might be developing unusually *quickly*. He now weighed forty pounds, but there was plenty of room in the placental tank. A baby elephant could weigh two or three hundred pounds. That was the size they might expect for an animal whose father had weighed many tons.

"This is a very delicate period," Laurel said, when he called to ask about her calculations. "I hope you are not impatient. His body still needs time."

"Uh-huh, I understand that."

"We must not birth him prematurely."

"Yes, but how's he going? I mean qualitatively. I know he's getting bigger and bigger."

"His lungs are not ready yet."

"So, what do we do now? I feel like we're caught in limbo."

At the other end of the line, Laurel sighed. "I cannot answer that. I think you'll just have to wait."

MARCH 2006

By the following March, Kong was well over two hundred pounds, and starting to challenge the capacity of the placental tank. Laurel was satisfied and it was now a matter of picking a moment. Day by day, Jack held long discussion with her, Riley, and Mark, usually in the common room with Matthilde looking on—the one involved party whom they couldn't consult. In such an unnatural environment, Kong could give no definitive signal that he was ready.

The group of humans who'd created him debated ineffectually among themselves. Now that he was less directly involved, Mark was regaining his remarkable waistline, but Riley's hairline was receding even faster. Finally, Laurel declared that the time had come.

"You want the go-ahead from me?" Jack said.

Riley nodded. "One more time."

Jack didn't even need to think about it. These people were his experts. "All systems go," he said.

"Tomorrow?" Laurel said.

"Yes, and I'll be there with my video camera."

That night, he dreamed that he was pregnant, carrying a huge fetus inside him—which had swollen up bigger than any party balloon. Everyone was there with him, trying to induce labor, getting him to push, but where was his baby supposed to be born from? In the dream, he flailed his arms about wildly to make them give him some space…and woke with a start, confused at first. This was getting very personal, he realized.

In the morning he walked quickly to work, full of anticipation. The actual birth came half an hour earlier than planned. Jack had just gotten into his scrubs and entered the lab when the unborn gorilla, possibly aware of the much-increased activity around him, became excitable and began to kick desperately at the confines of the placental tank. A dozen of baby Kong's surrogate mothers and fathers—Laurel and her team of technicians—converged on the tank, ready for action. There was no use in letting Kong harm the expensive apparatus, or himself.

Time to open the tank.

A minute later, the biggest of the techs—Roderick Carwardine—was able to lean in and he heaved at the burly infant by his ankles. Others rushed to grab the neonate by the waist or the arms, or any other part they could find. Blonde-haired Anna-Lena Beck and a couple of the others began attaching and detaching various tubes and wires. They all moved with a well-rehearsed efficiency—and enough shouting and gesturing to betray their underlying sense of urgency. As Carwardine grimaced with the strain, a loud, nasty coughing noise filled the room: Kong's first attempt to breathe.

Everything happened too fast for Jack to follow in real time, but he caught it all on video. Laurel stepped into the center of the fray, and, rather to Jack's surprise, began to spank the huge upheld form, not on the butt, but on the soles of his feet. Kong responded with a thin, aggrieved bawling. Moments later they'd all managed to lower him safely to the floor, where a big, dark, hefty shape looked at Jack out of two pairs of embracing arms, Laurel's and Mark's. They sat on the floor with the huge infant, looking as pleased as any parents with a healthy son. The gorilla's fur was wet and stuck out all over in spikes like some neo-punk fashion.

"Two hundred and sixty-four pounds and thirteen ounces," Laurel said. Then she looked up and gave Jack a huge smile.

"By the way..." Anna-Lena said.

"Yes?" Jack said.

She laughed. "It's a boy."

Others were hugging each other, even the lugubrious Riley joining in.

"You can name him, now." Riley said, walking over to give Jack a slightly sardonic look. "You have my permission."

"It's a bit too late for that," Jack said. He'd named the new kid so long ago.

"All the same, I'd like to hear it now. Now that he's actually born."

"Kong," Jack said simply, and Riley nodded, satisfied.

Jack knew how odd he looked as he grinned and wept simultaneously. He started to turn away, embarrassed. But then he realized he didn't care. Nothing like that mattered. The tears of joy were welcome.

He let them come.

SEVEN

The day after Kong's second and final birth, Jack stayed home to plan his next moves in peace. For now, he'd used up his reserves of emotional energy. He told Maudie to handle all calls to the office, turned off his cell phone, and unplugged all the phones in the apartment. If Maudie or any of his researchers really needed to speak with him they'd just have to walk over and see him in person.

After his early morning ritual with breakfast and the news channels, he swam twenty laps of twenty-five yards each, enjoying the simple, mindless exercise. The repetitive motions as he plowed back and forward through the water helped him think. He'd need to talk to Stanley as soon as possible now that Kong was actually born. There was legal work to do to protect Denham Products' intellectual property rights. He'd get Stanley to carry out the necessary filings, which might take some days, even with the best briefing Jack could provide.

That, of course, meant coming clean to Stanley about the reality of the "hypothetical" case he had described. *Oh well*, he thought, turning at the swimming pool wall, *it had to happen*. He knew that Stanley had never been fooled, but still…they'd worked on the fictional basis that Jack was asking only about a possible situation.

RUSSELL BLACKFORD

He dried himself and padded back to his study where he'd left his cell phone. On the way, he passed Assumpta, who looked him up and down, surprised to see him prowling about almost naked. "Any requests about lunch?" she asked, deadpan.

"Something light," he said. "Bring it to the study at midday. Maybe a French omelet. Three eggs. No cheese…just something to give it a bit of extra taste. I'm going to call Stanley, then take the rest of the day off."

It struck him that he'd never briefed Assumpta in any detail about the Kong project. No doubt she'd overheard parts of conversations, but then again she expected to hear more-or-less secret discussions between Jack and his senior employees at Denham Products. It came with the job. She didn't ask questions and she didn't leak information. In fairness, he decided to fill her in on the basics. Today could be a day for dealing with loose ends, while otherwise taking it easy. In Assumpta's case, it was better that she find out the story from him than she see it on the six o'clock news.

He called Stanley. "Did you ever have any luck on that property I asked you about?"

"What, the acres you wanted in Manhattan?" Stanley said. "I'd just about rule that out if I were you. I've been watching the market closely, putting out feelers, but there's just been nothing that matches what you want."

Jack needled him just a little. "That's a pity, because the time's coming when I could really use that land."

"Do you mind telling me what you need it for?"

"Well, that's a long story, but it might all be clear in a minute."

"I await illumination then."

"Uh-huh. Well, the light's on the way. The main thing I was calling you about is that I want to meet with you tomorrow—with some of my people. We need to brief you about filing papers, particularly with the Patent Office."

"The genetics division?"

"That's right. This is another patent for a new species."

"What have you got this time?"

Jack thought about that for a few seconds. What he'd told Stanley so far was absolutely routine. The next part was anything but. "It's a mammalian species," he said.

"I see."

"I've been thinking about what to call it. I've decided to run with *Gorilla insulaecranii*…"

"With *what*? How do you even spell that?"

"Skull Island gorilla," Jack said. "You see, my hypothetical case wasn't so hypothetical. Maybe now you can guess why I need that land."

APRIL 2006

When Stanley filed a thick sheaf of papers with the U.S. Patent Office's genetics division, the usual answer came back that they would be dealt with as soon as the USPO had satisfied itself that the species was unique and that there were no other claims to the patented material. When a copy of the USPO's reply arrived in Jack's office, under cover of a brief letter from Stanley, that pushed the process to a brand new stage.

Bionimals would surely have its attorneys keeping abreast of all patent applications that might be relevant to its business, as Stanley did on Jack's behalf. Hemming would soon know for certain that Jack had obtained material from the original Kong and had succeeded in cloning him. Once he responded, it would become an all-out legal war.

It wasn't just Hemming who would know what had happened with Kong. Within a few days, Jack's patent application would be seen by every major player in the biotech industry. Word would get out quickly to the media, who would turn the story into a sensation overnight, whether Jack wanted that or not. He had no choice but to work with the media publicity as far as possible, not against it.

Meanwhile, the Patent Office might end up taking years to deal with his application. He couldn't wait that long—he needed to get on the front foot, to make his own public statements about what he'd done. He thought of toning down the news about Kong, of trying to obscure what it meant, but that would never work. The folks in the news media were not stupid, at least not all of them. This news would soon be grasped and sensationalized no matter what he did or said. He might as well add his own touch of drama.

Using the computer in his study, he found the files for the last few major press releases that he'd drafted with Maudie's help. The announcement they'd made about the New Millet contract was a good model to follow, but what he had to say was vastly more spectacular. He started typing.

DENHAM ANNOUNCES CLONE OF KING KONG.

Jack Denham, president of the international biotech company Denham Products, announced today that his scientists had succeeded in cloning the giant ape known as " King Kong."

Billed in the 1930s as "The Eighth Wonder of the World," Kong was exhibited by his grandfather, Carl Denham, *who brought the animal to* Manhattan in 1933. However, due to a series of unfortunate events, Kong's journey to America came to a tragic end a short time later.

That was a good start. Jack drafted a few more paragraphs working in more references to the events of 1933, but also to the expertise of Denham Products. Of course he'd give Maudie a chance to add her input before he sent it off. But he was struck by the wordiness of the heading. He could do better than that. He retained what he'd written, keeping it as a secondary heading. But on the line above it he typed, in capital letters, the words: "KONG REBORN."

It was late morning in San Francisco when Charlton Hemming first saw the story on his favorite Internet news site, but it would be all over the printed and electronic media as the day wore on. Hemming clicked on the words "KONG REBORN," which took him to some bland, uncritical text that looked more like a Denham Products press release than anything else. This story was so new that the media hadn't yet had a chance to put any distinctive spin on it.

The text was accompanied by a photo of what looked like a baby gorilla, except much larger, playing with a group of Denham's employees, which included an attractive Japanese woman. They were holding the ape's long arms, helping it to walk upright.

Very well, that suited him fine. He would put Bionimals' own Kong project on ice once and for all and use this turn of events to his advantage, as he'd planned from the beginning. He called Roxanne Blaine in New York. "Cancel Project Big Man," he told her.

"Some special reason?" she replied, not mincing any words.

"Yes," he said. "Jack Denham has his gorilla baby. We've lost the race. Now it's up to me and the lawyers to sort it out."

"Consider it canceled," she said without a second's hesitation. "Go and sue the crook's ass."

"I fully intend to. Don't you worry about that."

The storm of public interest began. That night, Jack appeared at short notice on CNN, facing a supercilious young interviewer who started out by trying to make a joke of the whole thing, as if it were just a Denham Products publicity stunt. "How do we know this isn't all monkey business?" he said.

Jack groaned inwardly at the terrible pun but remembered to keep cool. "If anyone doubts our claims, they can look at the photos we've released. Of course, those could probably be faked, but you won't be in doubt for long. When the time comes, I'll let the media meet him." He looked into the camera with the most sincere expression he could manage, and spoke slowly. "I assure you, this is anything but *monkey business*. I'm absolutely serious."

"But what does it all mean? Cloning a monstrous ape that terrorized Manhattan seventy years ago isn't going to feed the world's poor, is it? This seems like a stunt that merely wastes a lot of money."

"No," Jack said, "it won't feed the world's poor, at least not directly. Another of our products, New Millet, will do that." He felt uncomfortable under the bright lights, knowing that every gesture and expression was ruthlessly exposed by the cameras. Hemming always looked more natural than Jack on television, despite the mako-shark smile. The medium favored people who had merely had a knack of *looking* sincere, regardless of their real motives or beliefs.

Still, Jack pressed on.

"The creation of Kong proves a point," he said. "It's given us a chance to demonstrate that our technology is at the cutting edge. We don't believe anyone else could have done it so dramatically. Not that long ago, the best researchers in the field were telling us that cloning apes was impossible."

"Impossible, or just unnecessary and excessive?" the interviewer asked.

"Impossible," Jack repeated. "Check the scientific literature if you want. Well, we've done the impossible here. What's more, it's given us a setting to develop important new technologies, such as our artificial wombs or 'placental tanks.' Those will have unlimited uses in the future. And finally, this is a great adventure." He allowed himself a smile. "You might be surprised how it will capture the public's imagination. It shows that modern genetic technology is real, and what it can do."

"It can make monsters? Is that what you mean?"

"It can create wonders."

"Don't the campaigns against genetically modified foods—what some people call 'Frankenfoods'—show that genetic technology is all *too* real for many?"

"It's all too real for me that some people put their prejudices ahead of human need," Jack snapped back. *Keep calm,* he told himself. It was always a mistake to get angry, even with the most offensive interviewers. They'd just use it against you if you showed any human emotions on air. A favorite trick was to irritate you with stupid, abrasive questions, then use any angry reaction as evidence that you were somehow unfit to wield any power that you possessed. Jack had often seen that done.

He paused for a few seconds, raising his hand to stop the interviewer from asking another question just yet.

"I suppose," he said, very deliberately, "that there's some sort of case for putting 'naturalness' in foodstuffs ahead of providing nutrition for the world's hungry millions that you referred to. I can't see it myself. I imagine that most people are with me on that when they actually think about it."

"But you're hardly in the business of biotechnology for the purpose of feeding the world. Isn't it more about the ego of Jack Denham, grandson of the infamous Carl?"

Jack bridled. "Don't tell me what my motives are." *Wrong approach again.* Once more, he forced himself to slow down. "We now have immensely powerful tools that can be used to cure diseases that were formerly incurable, to feed peoples who suffer from famine and starvation. The only reason to be in biotechnology is to use those tools to improve people's lives. That's what I've devoted my life to; it's what my company is all about."

"But really, Dr. Denham—"

"As I said, recreating Kong won't contribute directly to saving lives, but it will symbolize the power of biotechnology to do good—in this case, perhaps to make amends for the way the original Kong was treated. It's true that Kong terrorized New York, but what about the way *he* was terrorized and finally killed? I intend that our new baby Kong will have a very good life. No one will treat him like a monster. Biotechnology can improve many other lives—human lives, I mean. Everyone should support it."

"Still, doesn't it all seem kind of gross? Why can't you leave well enough alone?"

And why can't you listen to the answers I've already given to your questions? Jack took a quick breath. "You know," he said, choosing his words carefully, "if that way of thinking had prevailed, we would never have invented vaccination or antibiotics. That's also pretty 'gross,' when you come to think about it. What's weirder than deliberately ingesting molds and viruses? And look at the problems antibiotics cause when they're overprescribed! Maybe we should have left well enough alone instead of saving *those* millions of lives."

"Well, there's no comparison with what you're doing here."

"There's no comparison in *your* mind because you grew up with some scientific innovations, so you think they're natural and normal. You're relying on your prejudices, instead of really thinking." As Jack spoke, the interviewer drew back a little. Jack ignored him, and forgot about his own nerves. He stared straight into the camera that was showing the red light, appealing to his mass audience out there—ordinary, good people in their homes watching TV after a day at work, or with the kids.

He had to connect to those people.

He took another breath. "New innovations always seem weird at first, especially now that they proceed from more fundamental science than ever before. But at any point in history, you can find someone who opposed the innovations of the time. Even anesthetiac was opposed. So were contraceptives, but how many people use them now—at least at some point in their lives? Gene technology is no different. Besides, we're only doing more effectively what has always been done, at least since farming and civilization began—pretty big innovations themselves, by the way, looked at from the viewpoint of hunters and gatherers.

"Human beings have been dabbling in genetic material for thousands of years. That's what we've been doing to dogs and cats, to goats and cows and horses…and to fruit and grains and vegetables, and everything we grow or use—since a Sumerian woman stumbled out of her house one morning and said to her neighbor, 'Wow, your beer's a lot stronger than mine, would you give me some of that yeast?' One way or another, it's all been genetic engineering, from then until now. It's touched everything that lives."

He didn't get a chance to say more. "Thank you, Dr. Denham," the interviewer cut in.

Session over.

Jack scored himself about five out of ten for that one. At times, he'd been too sharp tongued—but still, he'd made his points. In one sense, it had been easy. At this stage, the press was fixated on the usual

Frankenscience angle. No one was challenging his right to Kong's genetic material.

So far, so good. So far, no one had called him a thief.

APRIL–JUNE 2006

Next day, Jack arranged for the release of some videotape of baby Kong having his dinner—in this case being fed by Laurel, who had attached a giant nipple to a two-pint plastic bottle. Laurel had dressed in a shaggy mommy-gorilla suit, which helped provide the warmth and tactile stimulation that a baby gorilla needed, even a baby big enough to make Jack look puny. The tapes were horribly cute, and Kong looked harmless and cuddly for a two-hundred-and-something pounder who was growing larger each day.

As the weeks went on, the public was mostly charmed, apart from some radical animal activists who seemed unable to comprehend what a comfortable life Kong was leading. Then there were those who simply disliked biotech for any purpose. Others thought cloning was a sin, no matter what kind of animal was involved.

A dozen protesters parked themselves permanently outside the Denham Products complex. Jack learned to smile whenever he passed them on the way in. They seemed harmless enough. Most looked quite intelligent, though he had to love the middle-aged biker guy with a sunburned face, long, straggly hair, and a large placard that proclaimed in bright orange letters, and with creative spelling: CLONING IS MARONIC.

Not all the flak was so harmless. For the first time in his life, Jack received some truly scary mail, often made up of letters cut out of lines of newspaper print and then pasted to form messages. These ranged from angry reproaches to out-and-out death threats. Jack and Maudie passed them straight on to the police, who were not very hopeful of finding the culprits.

"What kind of person gets a kick out of this?" Maudie asked him one day, wrinkling her face in disgust at the latest death-threat letter—this one pasted together on pink, scented stationery.

They'd met at Jack's apartment for a planning session. Since the New Millet deal, business had fallen off a little. Bionimals was still doing its best to undercut Denham Products at every turn, and it was starting to do further damage.

"I wish I knew," Jack said. "The world is full of people who don't think like you and me. I don't claim to understand them."

"The point isn't to understand them, it's to do something about them," Maudie said, shaking her head vehemently. "Didn't Marx say something like that?"

"Well, whatever," Jack said, "but our friends in the media are still convinced that I'm the weird one around here."

"Thank God you don't look it on TV."

"How do I come across?"

"You're getting better at it all the time. You just seem like a nice, youngish English Lit. professor, or something—"

"Not so youngish anymore." Jack's beard now had less black than gray.

"Boyish, then. Anyway, don't let the bastards grind you down."

"I'll do my best," Jack said. "Sometimes I wish I could put you in the spotlight instead of me. You'd do a better job."

Maudie gave a twisted smile. "No I wouldn't. You're learning to suffer fools gladly. I don't think I ever could."

"I suppose you're right." He laughed. "That's what I like about you—raw, confident intelligence. There should be more of it in the world, not all this pussy-footing around trying to please ignorant people."

"Not that there's any choice," she said. "Right, Jack?"

"No, Maudie, I guess there's not."

"Besides, Jack, you don't *want* to hurt people's feelings. You haven't got it in your heart. You could tear people to strips if you wanted to, but you just don't."

"Maybe, but that's not the best way to be when you're up against someone like Hemming. Him, I'd happily tear to strips."

Strangely though, he'd had less to do with Hemming of late. The daily calls had stopped; it seemed that Hemming was in no hurry to discuss Kong, whether in public or in private. That, at least, was a blessing, but it was surely the calm before a storm. Every day he awaited Hemming's response to Kong. Whatever he was planning, it was going to be ugly.

JULY–AUGUST 2006

They waited for four months after Kong's birth before they introduced more humans to his environment. By now he was becoming more independent and active, but he liked to hang around Laurel for consolation or company.

One ongoing frustration was Jack's search for "green" land in Manhattan to build a large facility for Kong. If the new Kong was going to grow to the same size as his daddy, he'd need room to move. Stanley found some acceptable land in Jersey and on Long Island, but Jack was less than willing to go that far. Jersey had no cachet, and anyway his people weren't wild about the commute in either direction. If it came to that, Jack himself would have liked to keep Kong within walking distance, or at least a short ride on the subway.

Meanwhile, he had the roof level of the Denham Products building transformed into a large, airy, conservatory space—a greenhouse with Plexiglas walls and ceiling to keep out the severe New York winter. Part of the ceiling was covered with collector panels for a passive-solar heating system and there were shades and vents to help fend off the summer heat. The roof of the building—the conservatory's floor—was full of tropical plants, with plenty of plain old dirt and grass growing. The building's stairs came out at one corner, which was cut off from the rest by a twelve-foot-high steel fence, painted jungle green, with a padlocked gate. The rest of the roof, a square with a bite taken out of a corner, was a little one-acre rainforest nestled within the city of New York, expensive but beautiful, with the advantage that security was easy to maintain.

They moved Kong quietly one evening, Laurel having slipped him a sedative in his dinner—the kid was starting to get solids in the form of soft fruits, to supplement his milk—and installed him in a nest very much like his cage in the lab, but considerably larger. It had a metal base, back, sides, and top, and a wire door that wasn't locked. It would swing open easily to let Kong out into the new "forest" any time he wanted. The cage was bolted down and positioned to face the observation area, so it was easy to see how the kid behaved.

The next morning, Jack went to the rooftop with Riley and Mark to see how Kong would take it. The ape's eyes opened, and he looked around curiously. By now, he was four hundred pounds of muscle and bone, teeth, and hide. He was already bigger than Matthilde, as big as a sumo wrestler or as some adult male gorillas. Laurel was waiting in there with him, near his cage, to add a sense of familiarity. Kong looked out through the cage, standing on his pile of brightly colored blankets, then stopped and sniffed the air.

"He's getting the idea," Riley said softly.

Kong looked at Laurel, the nearest thing to his mommy, then at the steel gate that Jack and the others stood behind. He seemed to know that this was where he'd come from. He pushed his cage door open and stepped out into the sudden sea of green. Then, to Jack's delight, his mouth actually fell open.

Jack grinned. It had been expensive, that little jungle. The Plexiglas had cost a fortune to install and he'd had Maudie despoil half the plant nurseries in the state for the small palms and elephant ear and other trees that would suit an environment like this. There were no tropical hardwoods, but there was everything else that a small urban jungle could possibly need. They'd brought in banana trees in fruit, and other tropical fruit trees for Kong to feed from whenever he became so inclined. And there were even rotten logs full of tasty grubs. Maudie's order for the grubs had made a local bait supplier very happy.

Laurel walked back to the other humans as Kong crept through the greenery. He reached out for an elephant ear leaf that hung nearby, felt it in a speculative way, then pulled it close. He tore off a six-inch piece of leaf, chewed at it, made an "ewww" face, and spat it out again. Unfazed by one failed experiment, he hitched himself along a few feet deeper among the trees. He glanced back at his human handlers, then turned again and started to look around.

"He's a real child of the old Denham bloodline," Jack said, thinking of his grandfather. "Quite an explorer."

"Don't flatter yourself," Mark said, laughing. "None of *your* genes went into the mix."

Kong headed over to a palm tree and looked up at it with the same curious expression as the protomen eyeing the black monolith in *2001: A Space Odyssey*. One hand lifted to stroke the trunk of the tree...

Jack watched like any proud parent, losing track of the time. That first day in the conservatory was one of the happiest of his life.

He returned day after day. But then things changed. One morning, as he watched Kong's explorations, the door from the stairs opened behind him and Maudie came into the observation area.

"I had a call from Stanley Levin," she said. "He just got into work. There was already a courtesy call on his answering machine. Someone wants to serve a writ on you. Someone acting for Charlton Hemming."

EIGHT

Dressed in crisp yellow linen, Maudie briefed Jack in his office. "The *someone* concerned is a guy named Tony Jowett, from Nash and Jowett, the law firm that acts for"—she gave a perfunctory smile—"the Nameless Presence. I told Stanley to accept service of the writ on your behalf. There's no use in Jowett sending a law clerk all this way uptown."

"Okay. I guess that's all right."

"Stanley should have it soon. You'll need to talk to him when he's got it. He told me he can read it overnight and find an hour with you tomorrow. Meanwhile, he'll fax us a copy."

Jack's mouth went dry. It wasn't as if he hadn't been expecting this. For the past two and half years, ever since he'd decided to go ahead with Kong, it had been in the back of his mind that Hemming would react, and hit back hard. But you could never be entirely prepared for the shock, not really. "Okay," he said, "we'll wait for it. I wasn't planning on going anywhere."

When the fax arrived under cover of a brief, handwritten note on Levin Drobnick Mahon letterhead, it was easy to recognize what it was. Behind Stanley's note, the front pages of a legal writ were unmistakable. Jack scanned through the formal pleadings, half relieved in a nasty sort of way that Hemming had shown his hand. Now he was alleging theft, illegal entry, theft of intellectual property, destruction of private property, unjust enrichment—everything, it seemed, except jaywalking and littering.

"All right," Jack said at last, "what now?" He imagined the media baying like hounds for his blood. "How are we supposed to fight all this?"

"We'll put that question to Stanley when we meet with him tomorrow," Maudie said. "That's his job, after all."

"Okay," Jack said. "Tomorrow's another day."

"Yup," she said cheerfully. "Things can only get worse."

Next day, Stanley looked every bit as tired as Jack was feeling. In fact, he looked as though he'd been up all night. His entire bald head seemed to be wrinkled with worry. He gestured for Jack and Maudie to take their seats at the pinewood table. "How we fight the case depends on a lot of things," he said.

Maudie gave a force-10 sigh, while Jack merely scowled. "Okay, I'll bite. What does it depend on?" He'd been hoping for a simple answer, not a lot of *ifs* and *ands*.

Stanley sat across the table from them giving Jack an intense, troubled look. "You and I are going to have to go through the documents line by line. Not only that, I'll have to interview everyone else who might be a potential witness. That includes you, Maudie."

She nodded. "Of course."

"Can you two get hold of the guy you bought the sample from?"

"Not easily," Jack said. "I don't think he'll want to be involved." The man had given his name as Kelvin Lee. Jack hadn't seen him for six years.

Stanley scratched his mustache for a moment, then said, "He won't have a choice. Hemming's people will track him down and serve a subpoena to make him testify. It would be good if I could talk to him first, but I'll leave that to one side, just for now. The first stage is to give notice of our appearance in the case and lodge our formal defense with the court. We'll need to answer every allegation in the writ—one by one—even if it's only to say that we don't admit what's alleged."

"Isn't there some kind of statute of limitations on this sort of thing?" Jack said hopefully.

"Sure, Jack. Clients always ask me about that, and I usually have to disappoint them. You get years to sue. How many years you get depends on the kind of lawsuit, whether it's for breach of contract or to get back real property, or whatever it is. With some claims, it's within the court's discretion, and you'd have to prove untoward delay. Remember, Hemming had no proof until now that you had Kong's DNA. The court will let him go ahead."

Jack was having none of it. "They waited until they knew Kong was viable. Now Hemming wants the fruit of all my work. What about the theft of *my* intellectual property? What about the theft of my labor, and the team's?"

"Believe me, we'll countersue for anything we can. I'll make them wish they'd remembered to put in jaywalking, or, better yet, that they'd left you completely alone."

"Yeah, okay. This is your trade, not mine. You don't tell me how to do biology."

"Only when it's for your own good."

"Well, true," Jack admitted.

"I'm thinking, though, if you can afford to counter-sue, you may have legal rights against Hemming that you haven't thought much about."

"For what?"

"For his anti-competitive practices."

That made Jack take notice. They'd discussed Hemming's practices often enough, but never in the context of actually taking legal action.

"I think it's time you did something about it," Stanley said, "if you don't mind escalating the war."

"I'll escalate it, all right. Right now, I'd nuke the bastard if I could."

"What's involved?" Maudie said evenly. Jack had never seen her in such a serious mood. She usually managed a slightly mischievous air even when everyone else was in a state of panic. Today, she was focused and intense.

Stanley leant back with his hands behind his head, and a small fraction of his obvious exhaustion seemed to leave him. "I had a smart young clerk here do a bit of free research for you guys. I wanted to have a better idea of where you stood before bringing this up."

Maudie leant forward eagerly. "And?"

"I think that Denham Products has a case. What's more, everyone knows you're not the only victims. A few words sent to federal officials might not go amiss."

"You'll have to explain all that," Jack said.

"In time, Jack. In time. But there's something else I need to explain at the outset. In fact it's more like a warning."

"Tell me, then. I can take it."

"This litigation is going to get expensive. You've been going on about the company's cash flow problems for as long as I can remember."

"They've been better, but they've been much worse."

"Yes, I know the New Millet contract helped. But you have no idea of what's involved, and I don't just mean my fees. The kind of problems you'll have if this trial really gets going might be phenomenal. If Hemming gets an award of punitive damages, it could bankrupt you. Understood?"

"I've been bankrupt before, in the early days. Or as good as—"

"Sure. And heaven forbid I should interfere in your enjoyment of a previous state of affairs. But what happens to your poor little Kong?"

"I won't let that bastard have him."

"If you lose, believe me, Hemming *will* get him," Stanley said. "Kong is property, a chattel, like a car or a computer. There will be no discussion of custody, Jack, or of Kong's best interests. This is not like a divorce case—Kong isn't human."

"I know, I know."

"Well, let's just be clear about it. Kong is very *special* property. A court might well order that you give up Kong himself, not just pay damages. In that case, Hemming will shut him up in a cage somewhere and milk him for his genes. God only knows what will turn up with your problem child's genes tied into it. Giant cows, giant horses, giant *tomatoes* for all I know."

"Genetics isn't quite that simple, Stan."

"If you say so. But you can bet that Hemming will look at Kong as a moneymaker, not a pet or a personality. They'll clone off pieces of him if they can. Mark my words, he'll spend the rest of his days—how many years for a gorilla? Fifty? Sixty?"

"More like forty," Jack said, "but Kong is not a normal gorilla. I'd guess it might be longer."

"Well, they'll be spent with tubes and needles stuck in him. Then when he dies, they'll stick him in liquid nitrogen and clone from frozen bits of him."

"What do you want us to do?" Maudie asked.

Stanley shrugged. "I faxed you a copy of the writ itself. Before we go any further, I want you both to read the documentation in its entirety."

"I've read it a dozen times," Jack said.

"Then read it another dozen. If you think you understand it, you're probably fooling yourself."

Maudie nodded and glanced in Jack's direction. "Point taken."

"On the other hand," Stanley added, "a lot of this detail in the writ seems wrong, or at least very vague. We'll use that to make life harder for the other side. Now, as for countersuing…"

"Yes?" That prospect gave Jack a small touch of glee.

"Apart from Hemming's business practices, I want to throw in a few other points. I'm not too hopeful, but we just might be able to get CenCo or Bionimals for misappropriation, failure to restore lost property, a few things like that. There's enough in these papers to make it plain that Hemming has, or had, his own tissue samples of the original Kong. Well, how exactly did *he* get them? One thing we'll need to prove is that your grandfather owned Kong."

"Of *course* he owned him. Granddad paid for the ship that went and picked him up. He paid for the advertising and the promotion and the rental on the theater where he was exhibited. Not only that—"

"Okay, okay, I get the picture." Stanley raised both hands in surrender. "But just hope that none of those native people from Skull Island turn up. My guess is that *they* might have an easier time establishing title to Kong's genetic material."

The idea made Jack's mouth fall open. He shut it again and thought about those people—and felt guilty for not having considered them before. The imagined sound of jungle drums and the imagery of wild firelight dances was about the limit of his previous thoughts. It was as if they were not real people, with names and families and relationships. *Not to mention their connection with Kong,* he thought. *Are they even alive, any of them, or their descendants? Who knows?*

As far as Jack knew, no one from Western civilization had stumbled across Skull Island since 1933. Even under all the pressure of law suits and public opprobrium, his grandfather had struggled to keep the exact location secret.

"Here's some good news, though," Stanley continued. If this goes to trial, and you get through it in one piece, you're going to *have* lots of money. You might think I'm naïve about genetics, but I figure that there's a genetic basis for Kong's giantism. If you can solve that, it's probably transferable to other species. I don't care about the details—"

"In a general way, yes," Jack said. "It was never what cloning Kong was about—not in *my* mind. But we'll be doing that research."

"That makes Kong a billion-dollar gorilla."

Jack remembered big, dark brown eyes that had looked up at him the day Kong was born, then of how Kong had first explored his new jungle home. "It's not just that," he said. "There's someone *in* there."

"In where?"

"Behind Kong's eyes. He should be free." Jack glanced at Maudie then back to Stanley as a new thought struck him. "What do you mean, 'if' this goes to trial?"

"There is another option," Stanley said, sounding slightly reluctant.

"There *is*?"

"Possibly a saner approach. Settle."

"Out of court? Settle with Hemming? No. Absolutely not. That son of a bitch is not getting anything out of me, not a cent, and no way is he getting his hands on Kong."

Stanley held up his hands again, motioning Jack to be calm. "It might not come to that. You see, I have a feeling that, when I hold this lawsuit to the light, I'm going to see a secret message."

"Oh? What does it say? 'Jack Denham, You Are Screwed'?"

Stanley gave a smug Cheshire-cat smile. "It probably says, 'You have something I want. Either fight me for it, or meet me halfway.'"

"And what do I have that he wants? Kong? There's no way he's getting that."

"Yes, Kong, of course. But there may be other things that he thinks you could give him. The problem is that we're going to have to serve our own legal documents and start fighting this—maybe even file a countersuit, as I said—just to find out for sure what those things are. Think it over."

"Yeah, that's all wonderful."

"It can't be helped, Jack. That's how the system works. There are probably going to be about fifty meetings between me and my people and Tony Jowett and his people before we get this straightened out and the real issues become clear. Call me if you think of anything, and don't say too much to the media."

"Fine, then. What can I say, Stan? Go and do what you have to do."

"It'll be my pleasure. But just remember that you're playing in deep waters here, and the sharks are circling. Hemming would like to tie you up in years of litigation. You could run into a whole world of grief if you don't act reasonably. And I always thought your general point of view was that life is too short to waste—you have other things to do with it than spend it in law courts."

"I know, I know."

"If we don't resolve this amicably, you won't have anything else to do except litigate your way into bankruptcy. I'm not wimping out on you, Jack. You say the word and I'll fight to the bitter end. But it might not be in your best interests."

Jack was silent for a moment. "You go talk with Jowett," he said. "Find out what Hemming wants."

JUNE 2007

As the months had passed, Jack's desk grew ever more snowed under by paperwork with legalese all over it: requests for better particulars, interrogatories, applications for interlocutory hearings to settle procedural or technical wrangles in one or another suit, or a countersuit. All of it had to be handled. None of it seemed to have any actual effect, but he kept reminding himself that this was real and serious. It might not be resolved today or tomorrow, or next month—maybe not even this year. But it had real ramifications.

Each time he came into the office there was more paperwork from Stanley waiting for him. Today was no exception. When he sat at his desk to work through the in-tray, he found two long faxes with draft clauses from the ongoing negotiations with Hemming's legal team, plus one of Stanley's extended commentaries on how the case was going. As always, he put it to one side to read in detail later. It had to be dealt with, but it all seemed slightly unreal.

Stanley had warned him about this, that litigants often felt as if they were in a phony war while their cases dragged on without result. They could come to believe that it didn't matter, that nothing bad would happen to them—at least nothing worse than the monthly legal bills. "But it does come to an end," he had said.

Eventually the case itself—not some small procedural aspect—would be tried in a courtroom and that could lead to a crushing outcome.

Jack's in-tray had other papers that he could have done without, including an envelope addressed with cut-out letters from newspaper headlines, probably another fruitloop sending him a death threat. Other letters were from media corporations wanting to interview him, but he had no intention of being tried by the media. He sent back some brief letters declining to be interviewed while the matter of Kong was before the law courts. He'd go public on the issue in his own good time.

Since his birth more than a year before, Kong had grown so fast that Jack found himself understanding, a little bizarrely, some parents' laments about how their children grew up too soon. Kong was now six feet tall at the shoulder when he balanced his weight on his foreknuckles, and beginning to fill out with lungs and chest muscles that were huge even for a gorilla. They'd replaced his cage with a much larger freeform structure made of brown hardened plastic. Jack found himself wondering, with some concern, when the giantism was going to finish its work. When would Kong stop growing, and how big would he get?

There were many exaggerated stories about the first Kong. Some old newspaper articles from the 1930s talked about a gorilla that stood over fifty feet tall, reared up on its hind legs. From talking to his grandfather and studying actual newsreel footage, Jack knew better than that: Kong had been about half that height—though that was big enough.

Before her death, Ann Darrow had once told Jack how Kong had treated her like a truly huge man who saw her as a lover. As she'd described it, the experience had been frightening, but not like riding around like a flea on some whale-sized monster. All the same, was "baby" Kong going to end up the same size? Why, in fact, wouldn't he, if he had the original Kong's giantism ? An ape that big would weigh more than any bull elephant. It would be one of the largest, strongest mammals ever to walk the earth.

What would it mean to own a creature like that?

NINE

It came as a surprise when Jack got a phone call just after six one morning. He switched off the two TV sets in his study, grabbed the phone, and gulped down the toast he'd been eating.

"Boss," Mark said, sounding very urgent. "You'd better get down here now." There was a loud sound of objects crashing and breaking in the background.

"Why? What's happened?"

"We've got trouble with Kong."

When Jack reached the top floor *of* Denham Products, he found Kong's "jungle" was in chaos, as if a tornado had done a crazy dance through it. There was a shambles of uprooted bushes and trees, with dirt, planting medium, and gorilla feces flung everywhere. Kong's favorite toys and his small "jungle gym" of ropes and tires lay smashed, some of the toys half-buried under greenery and tree trunks. Out in what remained of the greenery, Kong was moving around angrily, making a noise that could only be described as roaring. At two years old, he was a huge animal.

Mark and Laurel were there with half a dozen other Denham Products staff. One animal keeper, a tall, lean young woman named Christine Archer, held a rifle designed to fire tranquilizer darts. She had this trained on Kong—obviously, just in case. Archer was popular with the team as someone who spoke her mind and was always quick with a joke. She was a New Jersey girl who seemed to think and talk at a million miles an hour. Right now, she looked very serious as Kong rushed this way and that, seemingly frustrated. His movements were sudden, explosive, using all four of his powerful limbs. As he ran, his front knuckles bore the weight of his immense upper body. Jack had never seen him like this, an awesomely powerful destructive force. He recalled all the humans whom the first Kong had killed, both on Skull Island and here in New York.

Kong was still growing, but he was far bigger than any normal gorilla that had been bred in a zoo or found in Africa. He was growing faster than an African gorilla, as if his body wanted to take full advantage of the giantism as soon as possible. He towered over human beings, and was correspondingly massive. Laurel, who knew the dimensions of gorillas better than anybody, had estimated that he now weighed over a ton.

Jack went up to her and Mark. "What happened?"

"We have no idea," Mark said. "He got up as usual, went and found himself a mango, ate it...went to get another one, couldn't get at it—it was just out of reach. Then he seemed to blow a fuse. He pulled the next branch right off the tree. Maybe he liked the feel of that, 'cause next thing he was stampeding around the place. He just went on a rampage."

As they spoke, Kong seemed to calm down a little, but he still had the look of an angry giant who was totally pissed off and looking for one more thing to take it out on before calling it a day. As long as he didn't take it out on anything *human*, Jack thought. Kong was far from being an adult and his fur still had the reddish tinge of a juvenile's, but the power in his deep chest and huge arms could tear even the strongest of men apart if they ever came to grips.

"But why?" Jack said. "Why is he so upset?"

Mark shook his head again, then sighed. "The symptoms would normally be those of stress."

"Stress? Here?"

"This is not his natural habitat," Laurel said.

"You mean he doesn't like it here?"

"We are doing our best, but nothing we do can be perfect."

"Besides," Mark said, "we have little information on how similar to normal gorillas he is psychologically. There were strange stories about how his father acted." They always referred to the first Kong as the ape's father. It was simpler that way.

"I have a fair idea about that," Jack said.

"There have always been questions in my mind about his fine brain structure and how the giantism might affect it," Mark said. "That's one reason why I tried to make him more placid when I filled out his genome. But who knows?"

Laurel nodded seriously. "For him, this is an unnatural existence."

"Okay," Jack said. He knew they'd done their best under almost impossible circumstances. There was no way that Kong was ever going to turn out as gentle as a social worker. His big daddy had fought dinosaurs, derailed trains, crushed humans who didn't get out of his way. No matter how well the new Kong was socialized, he was always going to have his turbulent side.

Jack looked out at the wrecked conservatory. Kong met his gaze from among the plucked-up, thrown-down greenery, looking quieter now, tired out but still discontented. Abruptly he sat down and the expression on his face made Jack gulp. It was dangerous to anthropomorphize primate expressions and maybe Jack was projecting his guilt—but maybe not. The giant ape's round, human-like eyes seemed to say so clearly, *What's the matter with my world? Why aren't things right?* Perhaps even, *What did I do wrong?*

"Poor boy," Laurel said.

Mark scowled in response. "You call that a *boy*?"

"What will he do now?" Jack said.

"He'll go to sleep," Mark said off-handedly.

"What?"

"Mark is right," Laurel said. "He does sometimes—"

"—After he's moody," Mark added.

Jack looked at them both. "You mean he's been like this *before*?"

Mark shook his head quickly. "No, no, no, I didn't mean to give you that impression. This is the first time he's acted so violently. But sometimes he just seems morose. He sits rocking, absorbed in himself. Other times, he gets a bit aggressive, though nothing like this. He's never hurt anyone. Sometimes he chucks things around, like we all did when we were kids. Then he has a nap and he seems to feel happier."

"Yeah, okay. I get the picture, but this kind of *chucking* things won't be a regular part of his life, I hope."

Laurel gave a worried frown. "It might get worse before it gets better. There is the problem of oncoming puberty."

"Isn't it a little early for that?"

"Actually, yes," Mark said. "You'd be right if this was a normal gorilla. If he had a full-time mother, he might hang around with her for as long as three years. He might even nest with her at night after that. That's normal gorilla growing-up time."

"But?"

"He's two already and he's growing *very* quickly. Just as well in a way—humans can't give him the same kind of care as a mother gorilla, no matter how intensively we work with him—"

"We have given him all the interaction that we can—" Laurel said.

Jack cut her off. "Wait a minute. When is puberty coming?"

"We cannot be certain."

"Think of him as like a ten-year-old boy," Mark said. "Ten years old, going on fifteen."

"All right, I'm getting the idea. You're talking about hormonal changes, though?"

"For sure," Laurel said.

As they watched, Kong began morosely pulling some broken branches together. "And in primates," Jack said, thinking it through with increasing concern, "like us for example, puberty can mean increased aggression—right?"

"Often," Laurel said as Kong started to drag the branches over to his plastic cave to use as a nest. He looked right now as though he'd never hurt a fly—a huge, but tame beast.

Of course, Jack had always known what a risky undertaking this might be, that he was leading the project to create a potentially dangerous animal. Ann Darrow had seen the first Kong fight and kill a huge carnivorous reptile, some sort of carnosaur similar to *Tyrannosaurus rex*. Even when military planes had attacked him, he'd destroyed one of them before the others had shot him down.

For a few moments, no one said anything. "When he dozes off," Jack said at last, "can you give him a sedative? We'll be wanting to get people in here to tidy up and do some replanting."

"No problem," Mark said. "I wouldn't recommend keeping him out more than eight hours, though."

"That should be plenty of time."

As they watched, Kong lay down in his nest. His eyes closed.

"What happens when he does this again?" Jack said. "Maybe when he's even bigger?"

Mark shook his head, then said, "We'll handle it."

Jack looked at him for a moment. "So you say."

As he took the stairs back to his office, he felt as tense as Kong must have been when he'd thrown his tantrum. The whole weight of the world seemed to be on his shoulders. He sat back in his chair and closed his eyes, just to rest them for a minute or two... Something must have made a noise, for Jack twitched awake to see Maudie sitting opposite him, across the desk. She twiddled her thumbs meaningfully, while looking at the ceiling.

"Was I asleep long?" Jack asked, embarrassed. This was the first time he'd ever drifted off at work. The sheer interest of his main projects normally sustained him even through the toughest days.

"I don't know," Maudie said, resuming a more orthodox posture for talking to her boss. "I just came in. Sorry I disturbed you."

"No, that's all right." He stretched. "Has the clean-up team arrived? I mean for Kong."

"They're on the roof."

"Good."

"That's not our main problem, though," Maudie said quietly. "Riley just came and had a word with me. He's not entirely happy about Kong's hissy fit."

"Oh?"

"You should talk to him yourself. You know he has strong views about things."

"But he sounded you out first?"

"That's right." Maudie looked him steadily in the eye. "I'm your buffer against these sorts of problems. You fry the big fish, boss; I try to fry the smaller ones."

"Okay, but what's Riley saying?"

"He says the city is just not a good place for a gorilla, especially one the size that Kong is going to be."

Jack nodded reluctantly. "He's right about that, but it's not his business. We brought him into the firm as an expert on cloning, not as an animal psychologist."

"I know, but I think it gave him a shock when he heard what happened this morning."

As they spoke, Jack remembered that desperate look in Kong's eyes, a look that said the world shouldn't be this way. It was all the more painful because Jack couldn't explain it to anyone else without sounding sentimental and pathetic. *I've done Kong an injustice*, he thought. *The same injustice that Granddad did to his father. Neither of them belongs here.* "Do you want to talk to him?"

"To Riley? Yeah, go and get him now. It's time to sort this out."

Maudie left and soon returned with Riley. She sat and stretched her legs, but Riley merely leaned against the doorway in his crumpled suit, looking stubborn and not the least embarrassed. Jack realized that his cloning expert would not have hesitated to confront him with his concerns. He'd simply done the tactful thing, talking first to Maudie.

"Okay," Jack said to him, "so what's your plan for Kong?"

Riley's eyes widened in surprise. "You agree with me?"

"Yes, but what can we do about it?"

"He needs something much bigger and better than this. I don't think we can fool ourselves about keeping him within commuting distance."

"No, I don't either. Stanley has found some properties, but none I want."

"Right, well you need to find a home for him that's really a home. Some place for an animal that's growing fast and will soon be much bigger still."

"I accept that, but you haven't answered my question. What do you want me to do? We'll spend whatever it takes."

For the first time, Riley looked almost afraid.

Jack laughed good-naturedly at his discomfort. "Out with it, then."

"If he had a home, I'd say rehome him. But he doesn't...or, rather, this is it. We need to build him something better, and not in the city."

"I think Jack's agreeing with that," Maudie said.

Jack nodded her way, then gazed at Riley candidly. "I've been thinking, too." He opened and closed his mouth as an idea that had been forming finally crystalized in his mind. His nap, just now, seemed to have helped it along. He'd been so tired lately with the stress of the litigation. Now it all seemed easy. "Kong does have a home. A genetic home."

"Skull Island," Riley said. "But I thought the place was lost. Can anyone find it again?"

"Jack, you had *plans* for Kong," Maudie said. "Remember? You don't need to throw them all away just because there's been one glitch."

"It's not just one glitch with Kong," he said. "It's everything that's happened since he was born." Jack held up his hand to ask for her silence as he focused on the main question. "Don't worry," he told Riley. "I can find the island."

"I won't ask you how," Riley said. "I guess what 1930s technology could find, twenty-first century technology can find again. We've got satellite imaging, all of that—"

"It's nothing so complicated."

What Jack and Maudie knew was that a downtown bank held all of Carl Denham's maps and notes from the 1933 expedition. His final bequest had been to the young man who, according to a letter Jack had found in his papers, was "in some ways, more my son than my son was." Jack had been through the papers many times, in the privacy of the bank's box room. Maudie had seen them, and had authority to retrieve them in an emergency, but only Jack had ever had the chance to study them closely. He could pinpoint exactly where the island was, within a few miles.

"Conditions might be different now," Riley said. "Who owns Skull Island?"

This time, it was Jack's turn to blink.

"I mean," Riley said, "you can't just turn up on someone's private property and turn a giant gorilla loose on it."

"Maybe you can, if there are others already there," Jack said slowly.

"Oh, come on! You think this is going to be like setting your pet goldfish free in Central Park Lake? Show up in the middle of the night, dump him, run away again? I don't *think* so."

"No, I don't think so, either." Getting to the island seemed possible, but what about when they got there? That island was full of creatures that could be dangerous not only to visiting humans, but also to baby Kong. Big as he was getting, he had not been taught to face gigantic carnosaurs and God knew what else: all the creatures that Carl Denham, Ann Darrow, and the others had seen more than seven decades before.

Jack recalled one of his childhood talks with Ann in which she'd acted out her encounters with terrifying creatures that had included some kind of pterosaur big enough to lift her from the ground. Another creature had been an amphibious monstrosity that sounded like a cross between a giant water snake and an elasmosaur. It had given the original Kong the fight of his life. Even if she'd exaggerated, those creatures must be formidable.

He'd spent many, many hours as a child, and in his adult life, studying the animal life of the Mesozoic

Era, inspired by the tales he'd heard from Ann and Carl. He had some idea of what Skull Island must be like. How would Kong adapt? This was not going to be easy, especially while also fighting large-scale litigation in the New York courts.

But the more he thought about it, the more it seemed that it had to be done. It was the only logical way.

"It's going to be a huge investment," Maudie said worriedly.

"So be it."

"All right," Riley said. "Well, you're going to have to find out who owns the place these days. If anybody. What about the people who live there? Are they independent, or have they been swallowed up into some entity like the Federated States of Micronesia? Over six thousand islands, and no one's ever counted them accurately—"

"Not Micronesia," Jack said gently. "Wrong part of the world."

"Well, wherever, and *who*ever. I don't know where this island of yours is located, but you'll have to take it up with somebody—the French, the Indonesians, whoever it is."

Actually, Jack doubted that it belonged to anyone. "New times, new problems," he said. "But I don't believe that anyone knows about Skull Island. If there's a government somewhere that has information about it, I'd bet it's hidden away deep in a top-secret archive. And I can guarantee that the information has never been published. If it had been, I'd know."

"All right, then," Riley said. "I'm in a crazy mood today." His long, mournful face seemed to militate against any such possibility, but even stranger things had happened. "Let's postulate the best case. Suppose we get Kong there and the island is uninhabited by human beings."

"Right."

"If, as we've all theorized, 'father' Kong was not a one-off mutation…we don't know how many others might be there."

"Uh-huh," Jack said, "not to mention other monstrosities." The giant reptiles that Carl and the others had seen were more dangerous than any ape, elephant, or other living animal could be. It was for that reason, Jack supposed, that the natives of the island—or perhaps their ancestors—had built the huge stone wall that divided their village on the edge of the sea from the rest of the land. It must surely have been to keep out the island's monstrous creatures. Only those that could swim or fly would have been able to reach them—perhaps an occasional pterosaur or amphibious reptile. "The natives seemed to have a fairly long-standing relationship with Kong, though its nature might seem a little weird to us—they practiced a form of human sacrifice."

"Nice people," Maudie said.

"Perhaps not, but put yourself in their position, living in a place full of monsters. You'd want to find a way to propitiate them. It seems that Kong was their point of contact." Jack laughed and shook his head to show he was not wholly serious. "It's just one of my theories. All we can say for sure is that they captured Ann Darrow and tied her on a kind of altar for Kong to have his will with her. I don't know what Kong did with those 'brides' he was offered by the natives, whether he ate them or what. Anyway, there's no telling what relationship the islanders might have had with a whole family of giant gorillas."

Maudie looked thoughtful. "And all those other creatures."

"Yes, true." Jack considered the ramifications of what he was saying. "If we go through with this, it's going to take money—*tons* of money."

"That's what I just told you, boss."

"Finding money is your specialty," Riley said.

"Not with all this litigation over my head."

"Well, I'll leave that to you. Here's another point. If there aren't any other gorillas on the island, what are you going to do, just maroon Kong with no one of his kind and no humans to fuss over him? Gorillas are intelligent, sensitive creatures…and essentially social."

"Okay, okay," Jack said. "I get your point."

"Hear me out. This one has grown up with lots of company, plenty of people to be with and play with. If you just dump him there, he's going to become desperately lonely. You can't leave Laurel behind to play mommy to him."

"Yeah, well, what can we possibly—"

"If it turns out they are all gone," Riley said, "we'll just have to clone another Kong…but next time the ovum is going to stay a girl."

"You can do that?"

"In principle."

Jack could see how it could be done, with some tweaking of DNA from a normal gorilla. The giantism was not sex-linked for the same reason that the first Kong had not been a one-off mutation: his mother, back on Skull Island must also have been a huge beast to have given birth to him. It could be done—of course, it could be—but it would cause too many new problems to bear thinking about.

What was certain was that the company's finances needed to be turned around. Despite all his talents, and those of his team, Jack could not deal with every problem at once. Right now, the world was throwing too much shit at him.

TEN

Kong did not trash the place a second time, but his growth was spurting like a teenage boy's. He could stretch up to fifteen feet or more and possibly weighed three tons. His appetite had become insatiable. Jack felt wary whenever he observed the big ape and all the staff were careful around him. Though he was allowed to wander freely in his rooftop jungle, he was watched at all times by keepers with tranquilizer-dart rifles—just in case. He continued to have "moody" patches, but more often he just seemed morose.

On the legal side, things had gone no better. Each day, in front of the mirror, before going downstairs for his toast and coffee, Jack reminded himself of Stanley's advice, that a month, or two, or three—even a year or three—was not a long time in major litigation. Not until you reached the actual trial. "That's when you have to watch yourself," Stanley had told him. "A beautiful case can crash in flames just because of some admission made by a witness. You can build your case for months, then it falls apart in seconds."

That was all very well. Jack just wished the case would get *somewhere*. This waiting, negotiating, hoping to resolve the whole thing before trial was like slow torture. Even worse, he was having no luck with his plan to "repatriate" Kong. He'd considered financing it out of his private fortune rather than making it a project for Denham Products, but harsh reality had soon dispelled that idea. Financing something like this was beyond even his considerable means. As for raising a loan to cover the costs, his own bank seemed unwilling to discuss anything containing the word "Kong." Fair enough, he supposed; he would be cautious, too. It was not as if he were proposing a money-making venture. Other banks had sent him away with honeyed words...and no funds. Some private investors seemed enthusiastic, as long as there was something in it for them—which there clearly wasn't.

It was *very* annoying, but he kept plugging away at the problem. One difficulty was his refusal to give the location of Skull Island to anyone. Even Maudie didn't know the precise details and giving them to investors was out of the question. The information would inevitably leak and that would defeat his whole purpose.

One afternoon, he returned to the cramped little room at the bank to go through Carl's papers, just to steady his thoughts and emotions. He read one more time through the letter that had been left for him by his granddad with all the maps and other papers:

I hope that some day you or one of my other descendants may return to Skull Island to help put right whatever damage I may inadvertently have caused. My time was one in which people thought less deeply about their impact on foreign cultures and often assumed that their own social environment was inherently superior to those they found—that whatever they found was theirs to use as property, to loot or exploit as circumstances allowed. We were an arrogant generation.

It would certainly do no harm for my descendants to look in on Skull Island—discreetly—and see whether its inhabitants are prospering. Not merely the human inhabitants. And if they are not, please try to help them, however you can, in atonement for the damage caused so many years ago.

There was a challenge that Jack could not refuse.

When he returned to the apartment, Assumpta helped him out of his tweed jacket. "Stanley Levin called," she said. "He asked if you'd call back."

"Did he say what it was about?"

"Charlton Hemming."

Jack called Stanley from the phone in his study.

"Remember that 'secret message' I once told you about?" Stanley said. "The one I said we'd find in the lawsuit if we held it up to the light?"

"Yeah. And does it say, 'You have things I want'? Like Kong?"

"Here's what you can give Hemming," Stanley said. "First, you can help him avoid looking like big business bullying a talented entrepreneur. Better still, you can make Bionimals, and CenCo itself, look like caring companies—"

Jack laughed out loud, "I'm a millionaire but I'm not the Good Witch of the South—and *that's* who you'd need for that job."

"Yeah, I know—someone who could make Genghis Khan look like a Boy Scout leader." Stanley paused. "The thing is you've got the job whether you want it or not. Meanwhile, I know your business has problems, but so does Hemming's. CenCo has taken a lot of hits recently, and it's not just *us* taking restraint-of-trade actions against all of its associated companies. That's on Jowett's mind, believe me, and Hemming's, too—that and a lot of other things."

"You're saying that my bargaining power has increased?"

"It's not looking too bad at all. It would be good for Hemming if he could show some signs that he's not such a bad guy."

Jack grunted skeptically.

"Don't be like that," Stanley said. "I'm totally serious. And there's one other thing. It has to have occurred to you by now that financing for your repatriation project is going to be hard to come by. Has it occurred to you that Hemming has something to do with that?"

"It's occurred to me, all right, but it's hardly a commercial prospect for a bank, anyway. And we don't have any proof that CenCo even knows about it—"

"Word gets out," Stanley said, "and it's marvelous how banks pick up on what would please or displease the head of a major corporate conglomerate."

"Stan, this is all interesting, but what's the bottom line?"

"Hemming wants something more."

"Of course he does—he always wants something more. That's the nature of the beast."

"Jack, listen to me. What he wants is nothing that will harm you financially, but it may be something you won't like."

"And what's *that*?"

"It's simple, Jack," Stanley said. "Just give him the keys to Skull Island."

Jack froze. "This whole exercise was meant to put right an old wrong," he said. "If we wind up doing another wrong, bigger than the first one—"

"What do you want to do, Jack? You're going to have to resolve this, one way or the other. Still want to go to court?"

"Can you come over here now? Assumpta can cook dinner for us. Let's thrash this out once and for all."

"Anything for Assumpta's fine cooking. I'll get a cab right away."

While Assumpta prepared dinner, Jack led Stanley into the study to consider options over a glass of beer. "All right, Stan," he said. "Go ahead and see what you can negotiate, but if we're getting close, you'll need to get back to me on every important point."

"Of course, Jack. But I think you can get out of this in good financial shape, as long as Hemming sees it as a 'win-win.' He's motivated by greed, not revenge."

Jack gave him a long, meaningful look. "That's where you're wrong," he said. "Greed might be what motivates Charlton's *lawyers*—"

"Ouch."

"I mean, on his behalf. They might just want the best deal they can get for him. But I know Charlton

Hemming better than you do. He might settle gener-
ously if it's in his financial interests, but he'll get even
with us later on—one way or other."

"We'll close off any opportunities," Stanley said.

"You can try." Both men were silent for a time,
thinking, then Jack added, "Maybe it's time that
someone visited Skull Island—it can't be kept isolated
forever."

"Agreeing to that would make all the difference—"

"I know, but I don't want Hemming trashing the
place. Imagine what a barbarian like that could do
there, given half a chance!"

"I don't think he wants to trash it so much as
exploit it for himself. If he knows that it's full of new
species, his eyes must be seeing dollar signs every
time he thinks about it." Stanley shrugged. "Any new
plant or animal might have commercial potential. Tell
me if I'm wrong."

"That occurred to me even when I was young," Jack
said. He finished his beer and gazed down into the
empty glass, trying to sort out his feelings. "But I
always wanted to leave the island pristine."

"Do you really think that's possible in this day and
age? Someone else will find it sooner or later."

"I've kept the secret so far."

"Could you keep it *forever*, Jack?"

"No, probably not. If someone with Hemming's
resources threw everything he had at the problem, he
could probably locate the island."

"Which brings me to another point."

"What's that?"

"Any documents you have that are related to the
location of Skull Island might be relevant to the out-

come of the trial, inasmuch as they could help prove that Carl Denham really owned Kong."

"You're kidding me."

"Jack, believe me, I'm not kidding you. I haven't pressed you about whether such documents exist, but I'm telling you now. Tony Jowett brought it up again in our last meeting. He says we made incomplete discovery of relevant documents. In other words, we're holding out on him. He says there are papers that he has a right to see."

"If any such papers exist," Jack said.

"Of course. But if they do exist, we'll have to make them available to the other side. Not only that, if you ever *had* such documents, but they've been lost or destroyed, we'll still have to say what happened to them."

"I'll take it under advisement."

"Please do."

"Do you think this whole trial is just a ploy to find out the location of Skull Island?" Jack asked. "Was Hemming thinking that far ahead when he served the writ on us?"

"Maybe even before that."

It had never occurred to Jack, until now, that the actual location of Skull Island, or those old papers he had received from his grandfather, had any relevance to the case. It was fortunate that the map of the island, with its latitude and longitude, had not become public years earlier in the lawsuits that had been filed against Carl. But no one had disputed his ownership back then. How times changed! Anyway, those cases had never gotten very far—Carl had settled each one, eventually using up all the money that he'd had.

What do I do now? Jack thought. He knew better than to lie about the papers that he had from Granddad. If he tried to lie, it would probably come out in the end, when Hemming searched his bank records, or if Maudie admitted it at the trial. He couldn't get her to perjure herself. As Stanley had advised him, it only took a small admission and your whole case might collapse, especially if you'd tried to build it on lies or evasions.

All the same, he wasn't going to hand over the map of the island just like that.

"Let me think about it, Stan," he said. "There might be some old documents."

"*Might* there?" Stanley said heartily. "Only *might*?"

Jack changed the subject quickly. "If we settle this, I've got to keep 'creative control' with Kong, no matter what Hemming wants. If he asks too much, we're going to slug it out in court. I don't care how bad our chances look, some things are non-negotiable." He tried to sound stern and unworried—a tough client keeping the steel in his attorney's spine—but he wished he felt more confident.

"All right, but it has to be said that the odds are not as good as I'd like."

"You've been clear about that from day one."

"I'll drive a good deal for you, Jack, but I strongly advise you to accept it when I do, especially if you care about Kong."

"I hear what you're saying."

Jack thought ahead to when this would finally be over. Kong was still not fully grown, but it was going to be hard transporting him. Skull Island was a long way off, and it wasn't the sort of place where you could just charter a 747 and land at the nearest airport. That might be the first leg, but Kong would be hell to keep sedated on a long flight. There would have to be ocean transport, support staff, logistical support for the support staff, food supply, fuel, weaponry, internal security, external security, communications.

If he was going to do it, the sooner it was done the better, and in the best financial environment possible.

For the next hour, Jack and Stanley hammered out the possible elements of a settlement: what Hemming wanted; what Jack was prepared to give him; what Jack demanded for himself. They only called it quits when Assumpta entered the study to say that the roast chicken was ready.

"Okay," Jack said to her, "we're almost finished." She returned to the kitchen and Jack started to check some calculations—then he gave it up for the evening. "Stan?" he said.

"Hmmm?"

"Am I doing right?"

Stanley looked at him with a surprisingly compassionate expression. "That calls for a value judgment."

"Yes, but you know what I mean. This whole thing, from the cloning to what we're planning now—assuming we pull it off."

"Since when do you not pull off anything you're set on?"

"That's not the answer to my question." Jack had always gotten through his problems, and he knew he would again. Deep inside, he still believed that…but was he doing the *right* thing?

"You don't suppose people become lawyers to answer questions, do you?" Stanley said, and smiled just slightly. "You become a lawyer to ask them, Jack."

DECEMBER 2008

The final meetings took little time—so little that Jack became annoyed with himself thinking he could have resolved it earlier. But Stanley shook his head at that idea. "That's not how it works. These things settle when the time is ripe."

All the same, Jack wondered if he'd been too stubborn, given himself unneeded heartache. *But that's a family trait,* he thought, *and one that's paid off in the past.* The process wasn't pleasant, but it was one that he'd had to go through. He'd done right to grit his teeth and deal with it.

But then he found himself in the back of a stretch limo with Maudie and Stanley, riding downtown to Bionimals' New York headquarters to sign an agreement that was close to completion. The legal teams had drawn it up, and only a few last points needed to be settled to everyone's satisfaction. Jack and Hemming would both attend this last meeting personally to see if the deal could be done there and then. Stanley looked exhausted, but pleased enough. Maudie was quiet, unreadable. Now they were so close to the end, Jack was almost having cold feet.

"I really dislike the idea of going down there, hat in hand," he said as they passed the corner of Fifty-Ninth and Fifth.

"You don't even *wear* a hat," Stanley said. "Anyway, you've got to be there. It's symbolic."

"It symbolizes that Hemming has won."

"Consider it an olive branch, Jack. A generous gesture. We'll expect some generosity in return."

"It's not the gesture that I had in mind."

"Me, neither," Maudie said, surprising Jack by how bitter she sounded.

Seeing Stanley's chastened look, Jack couldn't help but laugh sympathetically. "Never mind, Stan. I know how hard you've worked on this. And you're right. It's a just cheap gesture."

The limo pulled up in front of the CenCo conglomerate's New York building, which included the headquarters for Bionimals. It was all glittering black stone and shining black glass, a monolith with—to Jack's eyes—no information to impart. Nothing but the message *We take what we want.* Their hired chauffeur opened the car's rear door and Maudie got out first, gracefully unfolding her gazelle-like legs, followed by the two men. They climbed the steps to the front door of Hemming's castle.

A dark-suited corporate flunky met them in the lobby—a man in his twenties with no sign of personality. They rode up thirty floors without a word, then the flunky ushered them into a vast, beige-carpeted acreage, a floor occupied by a central reception area with glass-walled offices and conference rooms around the edges.

Hemming stood there waiting. They shook hands—Jack rather unwillingly, but he didn't propose to be boorish—then Hemming led them to a large corner space, completely surrounded by glass.

His legal-team leader, Tony Jowett, was sitting at a large wooden table. He was a thick-set, red-faced man in his fifties, with thin gray hair. On his left sat a younger man who also looked like a lawyer. Papers were strewn in front of them both. On Jowett's right was a black woman who looked about thirty-five. She was slender, severely dressed, with thick, beautifully coifed hair—an extremely attractive woman, despite her harsh demeanor. The table was empty in front of her, and she appeared aloof from the proceedings, absorbed in her own thoughts. Jack had never met her before, but she was a scientific colleague, and he'd often seen her photo. Dr. Roxanne Blaine, Bionimals' chief scientist.

Stanley greeted Jowett, ignoring the others, and they all sat. Hemming chose one end of the table with Dr. Blaine on his left. He reached forward to pick up a remote from the center of the table, then pushed a button on it. The internal glass walls went frosty.

"Jack," Hemming began, "I appreciate your finally being able to come and settle with us on these matters. I just wanted to go over a few details so we're not in doubt about them later." He sat back in his padded chair. "Here's the deal, then. First, Bionimals and CenCo are dropping all legal actions against Denham Products and any associated firms or individuals. We'll give you a formal release from liability and withdraw the actions. That can be done today. I've specifically named Dr. Riley, Dr. Illingworth, and Dr. Otani in the release from liability, and I'll add anyone else you want to name, including your source of the blood sample from Kong. You only have to say so and he's also on the list."

"Put him in," Jack said. "We gave you a name about ten exchanges of documents ago."

"Mr. Lee," Roxanne Blaine said with distaste, as if naming some species of vermin.

"Fine," Jack said. "Include that name if you want."

"And," Hemming added, "there'll be no counter-suits, no more litigation. Each side will release the other from any possible liability for everything that's happened."

"That's all agreed," Jack said.

"Both sides will bear their own legal costs incurred to date."

"Of course. I'll sign a release, or whatever you call it."

"All the wording for that has been settled," Jowett said to him, "provided you're happy with it. Have you seen the proposed clauses?"

Jack had already gone through the papers, guided by Stanley, with Maudie reading over his shoulder. They'd both advised him it was okay and he could see nothing wrong with the wording himself. "It's all fine."

"All right," Stanley said, "that brings us to the core terms of the settlement."

"Denham Products is proposing to return your clone of Kong to Skull Island," Hemming said.

Jack nodded.

"As you've seen from the draft papers, we won't try to stop you. In fact, we're going to help you." Earlier in negotiations, Hemming's people had made offers to assist in finding bank finance, but Stanley had driven an even harder bargain. "We are agreeing that CenCo and/or Bionimals will fund this operation completely," Hemming said jovially, "up to an amount of thirty percent over a reasonable projection of transport, research, and logistical costs."

"Very generous," Jack said grudgingly. But there was a catch, which they'd get to soon enough.

"There are always overruns," Hemming said. "It's stupid to assume otherwise. Now, in return for this funding, Bionimals acquires title to half of all living or dead animal species, known or unknown, and any otherwise interesting genetic samples that are judged as suitable for research purposes by the team we are sending on the expedition and brought back to the U.S. afterwards. Which half of the samples we acquire will be decided during the assessment period by a team of both Bionimals and Denham Products staff. The main concern will be to achieve a rough equality of advantage."

"Agreed," Jack said.

"With recourse to arbitration if needed," Maudie added.

Hemming nodded agreeably and smiled his toothy smile. "Certainly, my dear."

There was more detail at the margins of the agreement, including a provision for giving Bionimals access to Denham Products' artificial womb technology for use in projects over the next three years. Beyond that date, the same technology would be leased to Bionimals on fair commercial terms.

But the guts of it all was the Skull Island expedition. Hemming would actually finance it, but he wanted what amounted to an equal share in the proceeds. More fundamentally, he was forcing Jack to turn the expedition into a commercial venture.

"One more thing," Jack said.

"Yes?" Hemming offered what was evidently intended as an especially benevolent smile.

"The ecology of the island has to be preserved. That overrides everything else."

"I agree absolutely," Hemming said. "We're not going there to mine it, or log it. Think of it as a renewable resource." He glanced at Jowett. "We'll insert a sentence about that."

"There's already something there," Jowett said.

"Good. Put in something more."

"If you say so."

"We're as one then, Charlton," Jack said. "At least so far."

"Additionally," Hemming said, with his mako-shark smile on full display, "Bionimals has the right to film the entire operation, and will possess the only title to that film, and to later feature film rights, book rights, and licensing of materials having to do with the expedition."

Jack nodded at that as well. Stanley's face didn't move a muscle, though this was one of the areas where he and Jack had disagreed most violently. Stanley had been unwilling to give up the licensing rights and had gone on about it for several days until Jack had made it plain that he had other concerns. "I don't care about the profits on T-shirt sales," he'd said. "Let's give Charlton that one and dig in somewhere else." Stanley had not been convinced, but he'd let it go. When push came to shove, a client's instructions were sacred.

"And finally," Hemming said, "our chief scientist goes along on the expedition. In all matters concerning the acquisition of biological samples on the island, Dr. Blaine will have equal authority with you. That authority includes the actual samples chosen and the methods used to acquire them."

Blaine nodded slowly, but her face gave nothing away.

"Of course," Hemming added, in a sweetly reasonable tone of voice, "we'll all have access to any advice and assistance that we want, but someone has to have the authority. It will be shared equally."

"Go on," Stanley said.

Hemming obliged. "From the time the agreement is signed and the litigation is withdrawn, our chief scientist will also have equal authority with you in the handling of Kong…since Kong's correct handling and safe release on Skull Island are absolutely essential to the entire operation."

Jack looked at him for a long while, and then quietly said, "Yes." He felt defeated as he uttered the word. Once again, Stanley was not letting his face move, but this was the spot on which he and Jack had disagreed even more violently than about the licensing issue. Jack did not take kindly to sharing authority over Kong with anyone. Only when it had become plain that this was a deal-breaker, and that the repatriation would not happen without it, had Jack finally agreed. He eyed the woman Hemming had chosen as his chief scientist, trying to guess what motivated her. She appeared slick and cool, totally confident in herself.

Well, Jack thought, *whatever Hemming has told you about me, you're going to find out that you're not dealing with a pushover.*

"And all these terms are agreeable to you?" Hemming said.

"None of them are agreeable," Jack said.

Hemming raised an eyebrow. "No?"

Jack eventually offered a thin smile. "But I agree to them."

Hemming smiled back, satisfied. Even Blaine let out a small sigh of relief. That was something. She wasn't made of ice after all.

"Excellent," Hemming said. "Now there's only one last matter. Once we clear this up, we can sign off on the paperwork."

But Jack was already shaking his head. He knew what was coming.

"The location of Skull Island," Hemming added, not taking his eyes off Jack.

"Sorry," Jack said. "I won't divulge that information at present."

Both Stanley, and on Hemming's side of the table, Tony Jowett, looked shocked. "Jack!" Stanley said, and bent his head close to whisper.

But Jack held firm. "The answer is definitely no. I realize that's where you got to in the agreement, and I said I'd go along, but I've been having second thoughts."

"We have a problem, then," Hemming said, unruffled. "My people can hardly plan logistics and funding for an expedition when we don't even know where it's going."

"That information will be released to you," Jack said, "after the team is assembled, briefed, and worked-in, and not until all possible logistical matters which *don't* require the location have been settled."

"Oh, come on, Jack, be reasonable!"

"I have been," Jack said. "A lot more reasonable than circumstances require. I could have fought this every inch."

"Don't get into that—you really don't want to litigate this. I know where I stand, what my rights are."

"You're missing the point, Charlton. Your thought is probably that I'll do anything I can to make life hard for you, get a little last-minute payback?"

"You mean it isn't?"

"No, and I'll tell you why. All that might be understandable, but I have other concerns." He warmed to his theme quickly. "Even if I could trust *you*, I don't want anyone *else* getting hold of this information and doing something that might interfere. There are too many possible ways for the information to be leaked…too many places for it to go. The location stays with me until the last possible time, when we've got all the logistics handled."

"You've missed *my* point," Hemming said. "How can we handle that if we don't even know where we're transporting the expedition to? It could be in any of the oceans of the world, for all I know."

Jack doubted that Hemming was so deeply in the dark. Surely *some* information had leaked from the first expedition, enough to give him a few general clues. Still, it was a fair point to make. "I'll define a circle six hundred miles in diameter," Jack said, smiling. "You can be sure that the island is somewhere in that circle—perhaps not in the middle, but *somewhere*. Initial logistics can be planned for somewhere within that ballpark."

"A pretty big ballpark, Jack."

"I just hope it's big enough. It needs to be big enough to keep anyone from forestalling us if the information leaks." *As you know damn well it will.*

Hemming sat staring at the table for a moment. Then he exchanged glances with Roxanne, who looked put upon, but nodded slightly. Finally, he spoke to Jowett. "Alter the papers to that effect. Let's get it over with."

Jowett and Stanley looked across the table at each other, their faces betraying just a touch of exasperation. Stanley flipped to a fresh page in his legal pad, jotted some words on it, finally tore the page off, and handed it to Jack. Jack read it carefully, wanting to be sure. When he was satisfied, he nodded and handed it back. "Okay."

Stanley pushed it over to Jowett, who read it and looked thoughtful. He stretched past Roxanne to show the paper to Hemming. Hemming scarcely glanced at it before he nodded.

"We have an agreement, then," Jack said.

Jowett typed swiftly on his laptop, then nodded to his assistant, Palmer, who stepped out of the room and returned with a one-page printout. This was passed around until everyone was confident about the new wording.

"All right, then," Jowett said, "I'll print some copies of the full agreement. It can be signed now."

"Is that fine with you?" Hemming said to Jack. "There's nothing else?"

"Nothing else," Jack said. "That should about do it."

Hemming's tanned face looked back at him, wearing a suppressed, not especially triumphant smile—but all Jack could see was a phantom image of shark teeth.

I should be furious, Jack thought. *He's beaten me.* But at the same time, he was aware of being filled with a sudden, fierce delight. *No one's beaten who feels like this.* The thing was, it was going to happen: Kong could go home at last. *This* was what he had been waiting for. Completely without warning, the joy in his life was back—the thrill of adventure—and he was going to find a way, despite everything, to turn it all to his advantage.

He grinned at Maudie, then laughed out loud in Hemming's face. "We've got a million things to do," he said. "Let's get on with it."

ELEVEN

Kong was still nowhere near as big as his "father" had been, but the kid was obviously working on catching up. No wonder some reports had exaggerated the old Kong's size, back in the 1930s. When you saw a beast like that, it looked like a walking, furry mountain.

Even the keepers with their rifles seemed jittery as their eyes followed Kong's movements, although they'd watched him as he'd grown, and he'd never shown aggression toward them. These days, only Laurel went into Kong's territory without fear. For those who cleaned out the area each day, it was a careful, potentially dangerous procedure. Jack had increased their pay by fifty percent to make it more worthwhile, but he couldn't expect them to go in there forever, exposing themselves to the mercy of such a powerful animal.

Yet, Kong was magnificent! Jack had no regrets about anything he'd done.

"A penny for your thoughts," said a familiar voice.

Jack turned to see Maudie, bundled up against the cold in her long, black overcoat and a pair of fur-lined Italian boots. "Any problems?" he said.

"Not even one," she replied. "I had a word with Stanley, who assures me that all the papers are in order. The lawsuits on both sides have been formally withdrawn. Your relationship with the Nameless

Presence is now controlled by the agreement you both signed."

"As long as he honors it."

"Exactly, Jack. He'll try to break you when he sees an opening. He may be your new business partner, but I know what men like him are like. He's not just after profit—a man with an ego like that will want to destroy you."

"I'll be careful."

"I know you will be." She stepped a foot closer to the fence, watching Kong, who was now very still. He kept his distance, but regarded them through the bars. "Now that's all done," Maudie said, "Bionimals will want access to Kong."

"They can have it when they request it," Jack said. The agreement included provision for Roxanne Blaine to meet and assess Kong before any attempt to move him back to Skull Island, and to have an equal say in his handling. Jack knew he had no choice about that, but he'd taken an instant dislike to the woman. In fact, he'd met few people who seemed so thoroughly willing to be disliked.

"I'm sure that their Dr. Blaine will get someone to call us and make an appointment."

"Yeah…well, I'll cooperate as long as she does, but I won't be doing anything to make her life easy."

Kong wandered over, as if to greet them. The keepers stepped back a few feet, training their dart rifles carefully, but he sat down without any show of aggression and merely peered at Jack through the gate with a very serious expression on his face. Even on his haunches he seemed to stretch into the sky, looming over the little group like the huge statue of some noble warrior or athlete. Jack noticed that his fur was getting thick and growing darker, losing the hint of red. No silver had appeared in it yet, but that would probably come as he grew older and the African gorilla component of his genome showed through.

"I wonder what's he thinking," Maudie said.

"I wish I knew," Jack said. "He can't know that he's going home."

"He seems so gentle. When he's sitting like that, it's hard to believe the destruction his dad caused."

"Well, you saw how he tore up this place, even before he got this big."

"I know."

"Still, you're right. I don't quite see him wrecking trains and battling dinosaurs."

"Not yet, at least."

As they spoke about him, he hardly moved, but merely looked down from his much greater height, turning from one to the other as if attempting to follow their conversation. After a time, he stood and stretched…and his head seemed to reach to the clouds. Finally, the fur-covered Titan shifted to all fours and walked back into his miniature jungle.

"Maudie," Jack said, "when I'm away you'll have to run this place without me. I'll be in touch, but you'll be boss for the day-to-day decisions."

"Can do," she said brightly. "You have a good time hunting dinosaurs."

"I guess that's part of what I'll be doing—but not exactly *hunting* them. Come on, let's leave Kong alone. We can make some contingency plans in my office."

As they left Kong and his keepers and descended the stairs into the building, Jack wondered about those animals on Skull Island. The way Carl had told him the story, many of the seamen hired for the original expedition on the *SS Venture* had been killed in the short time they'd spent on the island—not to mention dozens of islanders when Kong had gone crazy and burst through the huge wooden gate in the wall that separated them from the hinterland. More seamen had died when their raft had been attacked by an enraged reptilian creature that had dwelt in a lake they'd tried to cross. The others had been killed by Kong himself when they'd attempted traversing a deep ravine—the giant ape had thrown them from the massive log they'd been using as a bridge.

On the expedition that Jack had planned, they would avoid the water as much as they could and generally be careful. They'd also go heavily armed. He hated the thought of killing any of the island's rare creatures, but they might have little choice.

The descriptions he'd had from his granddad sounded like dinosaurs and related beasts from the Mesozoic Era, but there were anomalies. Besides, Jack could not see how prehistoric reptiles could have survived for millions of years on a remote island. The island's geological history would be well worth investigating. Even if the creatures that Carl had seen *were* dinosaurs, they could not possibly have survived totally unchanged since the Jurassic or Cretaceous Period.

Well, they'd soon find out.

"You seem deep in thought," Maudie said when they reached his office.

"I was just thinking about the creatures on the island. You know, I grew up like a lot of boys, reading everything I could find about dinosaurs and everything else related. I guess I knew I might go to Skull Island one day. It's a bit of a shock realizing that the time has come."

"I'm sure it must be. I'm even a little bit frightened on your behalf."

Jack sat behind his desk, steepling his fingers as he spoke. "I used to beg Granddad for stories about the island—the natives, the roaring dinosaurs, the midnight drums when they tried to sacrifice Ann. We used to have sessions out in the garage when he visited—to get away from my mom and dad."

"Well now you're going to see for yourself," Maudie said. "I wish I could go, too."

Jack considered that for a moment, slightly surprised. "In a way, I'd like to take you," he said. "You're the best employee I've got...maybe the best friend I've got, if the truth be told. But I need you back here."

She gave a satisfied smile, though the color that showed on her cheeks might have been a blush of embarrassment. "That's very true."

He realized he was grinning at her, but not at anything to do with what she'd said. Instead, he was wondering what a dead man—if his soul survived—would think about this new adventure. *Granddad*, he thought. *If you're there, watch what happens now.*

By the end of the day no calls had come from Hemming or Blaine, but a draft media release arrived from CenCo, sent by e-mail from Hemming's secretary. Obviously, with the agreement finalized and the litigation withdrawn, it was time to make some kind of public statement. The covering e-mail message suggested that a press conference be held at Bionimals' headquarters next morning, with Roxanne to fill in for Hemming. There was even an additional attachment setting out what line she would take with the press.

It rankled, of course, to hold the press conference on Bionimals' territory—it symbolized which company was the senior partner, who had the upper hand. Then again, that building might well have facilities and it would seem petty to complain. Interestingly, Hemming did not plan to be there himself. It looked as if he wanted to promote Bionimals in its own right, rather than as a subsidiary of CenCo.

Jack strolled to Maudie's office down the corridor and sketched out the scenario quickly to see what she thought.

"What do you want to do about it?" she said.

"I'm not sure. I don't like being upstaged, but at least Hemming won't be there."

"You've got a big advantage, Jack. Kong is on your territory."

"Yes," he said with a grin. "That's so true."

"Then press your advantage, General Denham!"

"You're right, as usual." He saw what he had to do.

The next day, all was quiet outside Bionimals' HQ except for a single camera crew set up at the top of the steps on the way in. Jack passed by with a happy winner's smile. He was greeted by the same faceless underling who'd met him as last time he'd been here. They took an elevator to the seventh floor, where more reporters and photographers were milling around. He entered the large room that had been chosen for the press conference, past TV cameras and still more photographers. Someone shoved a microphone in his face: "Any comment for us, Dr. Denham?"

"Lots of comments," he said. "I hardly know where to start."

"Tell us if you're happy about the agreement."

"Happier than you can imagine. I'll have plenty more to say in a minute."

Roxanne Blaine was waiting for him at the podium in the front of the room and she greeted him with a token smile. Without meeting his eyes, she extended her hand for him to shake. He took it as briefly as possible, forcing an insincere smile of his own as cameras clicked. That photo opportunity over, he stepped aside to let her start the proceedings.

"I'm pleased to announce the beginning of a great venture, which might benefit all humanity," Roxanne said, standing at a wooden lectern but not consulting any notes. She nodded at Jack, then looked into the eye of the TV cameras. "Dr. Jack Denham and his team have performed a miraculous feat of science in cloning the giant ape known as 'Kong,' which terrorized Manhattan in 1933. I can't even begin to explain the technical difficulty of their project, reconstructing Kong from severely damaged DNA that had been exposed to the elements for nearly seven decades. The scope and precision of the undertaking compares with NASA's Apollo launchings, which put men on the moon in 1969, or, much more recently, to the Human Genome Project."

Jack had to admit that she spoke superbly; she blended earnestness, smiling benevolence, and absolute confidence. He suddenly saw her in a new light.

"You know," she continued, "everybody in the biotech industry respects and admires Jack Denham's work." She looked like she was sucking a lemon as she said that bit, but she soon recovered her benevolent expression. "That did not stop Bionimals or other relevant companies in the CenCo Group from taking legal action to protect our legal rights as we saw them. We believed that the DNA which Dr. Denham's team had used was rightfully ours."

"Well, was it or wasn't it?" someone called out.

Roxanne gave a dry laugh, which drew a few nervous chuckles from the audience. "The fact is, however he did it, Jack got there first, and what he and his team did was awesome. I know that Jack believes strongly that he had a moral right to Kong's DNA." She shrugged. "Maybe he believes he had a legal right as well, and he certainly was prepared to fight the issue tooth and nail."

She paused for effect, looked slowly around the room, making eye contact with many of the individual reporters. Then she turned to Jack and nodded to him again, this time in a very formal way. More cameras clicked and a few people actually clapped.

Roxanne went on. "Charlton Hemming—the Chairman of the CenCo conglomerate, as you all know—asked me to convey just one thought to Jack, in front of everyone assembled here. He said to tell Jack, and to tell you all, that he always respects a fighter.

"At times like this, it's best to settle differences, and see if there's some mutual advantage to be gained. We've negotiated this issue hard, and I think that Charlton's hair has grown whiter, but we've settled and all the litigation has been withdrawn. What I want to announce today, side by side with Jack Denham, is that we have an outcome that will be in *everyone's* interests. We're going to work together to give Kong what he really needs—I mean the new

Kong, created from the first Kong's DNA. We'll give him his freedom, transporting him back to his ancestral home, a place called Skull Island." She stopped at that point, and smiled for the cameras. "Don't blame me, folks—I didn't make up the name."

That got a loud round of sympathetic laughter.

Roxanne held up one hand to still her audience. "Skull Island's precise location will be made available to you at an appropriate time, which is certainly not today. The island is a land that time forgot, if you'll excuse me that hackneyed phrase. It's a lost world, if I may use another—a place of the most extraordinary fauna and flora, some of it resembling forms hundreds of millions of years old.

"Which leads me to the rest of this announcement. We'll be exploring Skull Island in a systematic way for the first time. This will bring some profit to Bionimals—I don't deny it—and not just to Bionimals, since Jack expects his cut as well. He may be an idealist, but he's a *hard-headed* idealist." Again she looked around the room slowly. "You know, we like that at Bionimals!" That got her another good laugh, but once again she silenced the room with a single imperious gesture. "What matters even more is the profit this could bring to science and scientific understanding…and to humanity in general. I guarantee that no one will be disappointed—no one with a heart, no one with an interest in health and life. No one at all with a human spirit. This will be a profitable adventure for mankind."

Jack applauded spontaneously. However this woman had behaved to him so far, she was *good*. She was like a queen ruling her court.

Those last words, about an adventure for mankind, provided Jack's cue to step forward, which he did. Roxanne's effort had inspired him, shown him what was possible. Something inside him said that he could match her performance.

After all he'd been through, he was in a wholly new mental zone. He felt tranquil in a way that he'd never experienced before when stuck in front of microphones and cameras. There was such a feeling of rightness about the fundamentals of what he was doing—the return to Skull Island and repatriation of Kong—that the rest had lost its importance. For now, he no longer cared about questions of scientific superiority or the legal rights.

He nodded appreciatively at his audience and the TV cameras. "You know," he said, "there's a reason why I'm grinning like a loon. It's because what we will be doing is the *right* thing."

He knew he was radiating a happiness that could not be faked. The happiness of a real winner.

"We're preparing an expedition to Kong's true home, Skull Island," he said, "just as Dr. Blaine described. That gives us a great opportunity to explore a place unlike any other known on Earth, with fauna like nothing else Western scientists have seen. From all accounts—those of my grandfather, Carl Denham, and others—it is an almost prehistoric land. Whatever freak events in geological history enabled it to survive into modern times, its scientific implications are staggering. Not least are the potential consequences for human health and welfare that might come from finding entirely unknown species, worthy of biomedical as well as traditional biological study.

"Ladies and gentleman, imagine it for yourselves. We'll be bringing the most ancient corner of our planet into contact with twenty-first-century science and technology."

Roxanne joined him, shoulder to shoulder to take questions. She pointed at an enthusiastic-looking young reporter in the front row

"Which one of you stole the DNA?"

"We're not getting into questions of legal liability," Roxanne said frostily.

"Dr. Blaine is absolutely right," Jack said. "We have no more claims against each other's companies. That's all in the past."

"How can you reassure the public?" another journalist asked.

"I have no idea," Roxanne replied with a disarmingly gentle smile. "Reassure them about what?"

"Genetic technology for a start. The original Kong wrecked half of New York City—"

"That's an exaggeration."

"Exaggeration or not, haven't you now tampered with nature?"

"Oh, puh-lease," she said theatrically. "Give me a break."

"Really, Dr. Blaine, you've made a monster. Not you, I suppose. Dr. Denham has. Don't you think people will see it that way? Some people might think this symbolizes everything that's wrong with genetic science—"

"I don't think so." Jack cut him off impatiently. "Most people understand the benefits and they won't see Kong as a monster—not when we show him this afternoon at the Denham Products building where he's housed. You're all coming along, right?"

"Genetic engineering is thousands of years old," Roxanne said quickly. "Humankind has been *tampering* with the genes of dogs for twelve thousand years or more—almost as long as that for goats, sheep, cattle, and pigs." She shrugged. "Maybe just three or four thousand for birds."

"In fact," Jack added, "those are all conservative estimates. The point is that genetic engineering is older than civilization itself. The only difference is that we can now do it faster, much faster than the most intensive breeding programs. That's a reason to be careful, but not a reason to talk about 'creating monsters' and 'tampering with nature.' People have been tinkering around with genes for so long that you might say it's one of the things we do, as a species. It's part of our repertoire for survival." How much more should he say? He decided to plunge on for just another minute. "I'm always frustrated by the suspicion of genetic engineering. I wish I could make you see it the way *I* do—the endless possibilities for improving people's lives, curing what has always been incurable, *treating* illnesses and disabilities that we've previously just *endured*."

"Another question?" Roxanne said.

After half an hour, the questioning finally ran down, and Jack was glad to get out of there.

Back at the Denham Products building, Kong put on a good show for the press just by being himself. An animal so impressive didn't need to do much to overwhelm the senses. There were astonished gasps as he walked slowly on his hind feet and forek-nuckles, toward the group of humans. Kong stopped at the twelve-foot metal fence, his round, curious eyes almost level with the top of it. With all these people gathered, it seemed like a very flimsy barrier. As he looked down at the humans gathered to see him, the giant ape gave what sounded like a contemptuous snort. He looked like a slightly puzzled giant inspecting a nest of annoying bugs.

"Oh, my God!" a young reporter said. "He's *huge*!"

Cameras clicked, video cameras rolled...and Kong merely yawned.

All the original team members were there: Maudie, Riley, Laurel, Mark, and several of the keepers and technicians who'd looked after Kong since the early days. Roxanne Blaine watched Kong intently, evidently fascinated by the extraordinary sight. Anyone seeing him for the first time had to be amazed, not only by his enormous size and strength, but also by his obvious appearance of intelligence.

Kong soon moved back from the fence and took up a position twenty feet away. He lay on his side, watching his new visitors dispassionately, and occasionally scratching his face.

"Isn't he going to do something more?" one of the reporters drawled in a jaded, world-weary voice. It was the iguana-like man from the day before.

"What do you *want* him to do," Jack asked, "start eating New Yorkers while whistling the theme music from *Jaws*?"

That provoked some nervous laughs.

The demonstration was brief, but it made a point—Kong was not monstrous in any way except for his great, ever-increasing size. He was visually overwhelming, far bigger than any ape or the biggest bear on Earth, but not deformed in any way. He did not act violently or otherwise like an unhealthy animal. He was simply magnificent. Maudie shepher-

ded the press representatives downstairs, leaving Jack
with his scientific and technical team, plus Roxanne,
to watch over Kong.

"Kong seems quite happy," Roxanne said with a
trace of surprise. "Is he usually like this? I thought he
might be depressed stuck up here by himself with just
a few handlers for company."

"He liked the visitors," Laurel said. "But you are
right, he is usually not as happy."

"I see." Roxanne turned to Jack. "I have to go now,
but I want to spend some time observing Kong and
interacting with him. Can that be arranged?"

"Of course it can," he said.

"Give me a couple of hours, then. I'll be back."

TWELVE

When she returned to the rooftop, Roxanne had changed out of the sleek corporate attire that Jack had always seen her in previously. She looked much more like a working scientist. Under a midlength leather coat, she wore low-slung gray jeans that emphasized her slim, athletic body, matching boots, and a rather elegant black cashmere pullover. It was not exactly what she'd need for the jungle of Skull Island, but fairly practical and casual. Her demeanor, however, was as icy as usual.

"Back for more, huh?" Jack asked pleasantly.

"Yes, Dr. Denham."

"You might as well call me by my first name."

"If you like. I appreciate your cooperation, Jack."

It was obvious that the feeling of dislike between them was mutual. Everything about Roxanne's tone, expression, and body language suggested that it actually pained her to deal with him. That seemed strange. Jack had made his share of enemies over the years, but few people had ever reacted to him like that. He didn't have the same gift for smarminess as Hemming and some others, but he was an intelligent, articulate, reasonably good-looking man. Not to mention rich. Most people—especially most women—found him charming enough when they met him in person. Roxanne Blaine was clearly not charmed at all.

"So, what now?" As Jack spoke, Kong ran over to them with his surprisingly quick four-limbed gait. Jack hoped that he'd put on a show of aggression, but that was unlikely.

The two keepers guarding Kong had both been with the giant ape from the beginning. One was a tall, lean, weather-beaten man named Gibson, who was in his forties. The other was Joey Díaz, who was somewhat younger, darker-skinned, and nearly bald.

Roxanne turned to Jack. "Who goes in there with him?"

"Mainly Laurel," Jack said. "She's kind of his surrogate mother. We try to keep others out of there as much as we can, except to clean up after him. He's usually gentle, and he's never actually hurt anyone—or even threatened someone—but he has his nasty moments."

Kong put his face closer to the bars, as if trying to smell the newcomers, especially Roxanne. She held her ground, even when he bent and sniffed at her. After a minute, he shambled off to his nest.

"I'm not sure you should get too close to him," Jack said.

"I'll be careful," Roxanne said, "but I need to go in there."

"What?" Jack said. "You've got to be joking."

"Why? From now on, I'm half responsible for this animal's welfare. I want to understand him as well as I can. To do that, I need to interact with him."

"You're talking about *interacting* with an animal that could pull your head off the way you'd pull a cork out of a bottle."

"From what you're all telling me, he hasn't uncorked anyone so far."

"He might start with you, though, because he's known everyone else who goes in there from when he was an infant. Laurel and I, his keepers, and all the people who work here are the closest thing he's got to a family."

Kong watched them all closely from the comfort of his nest. No one who saw him would take him to be a killer, but who could be sure how he'd react to strangers in his rainforest?

"Sooner or later, you're going to have to introduce me to him properly," Roxanne said. "It might as well be now. It's my job to work with him, and I can't do that unless he and I form some kind of bond."

"All right, you can go in there with Laurel," Jack said, slowly feeling as if he were conceding defeat. "She knows him better than either of us—better than anybody. I always defer to her judgment and I advise you to do the same, assuming you ever take advice."

Gibson and Díaz opened the gate to let the two women inside. Laurel stepped up boldly to Kong, where he sat quietly in his nest, almost catatonic. She reached on tiptoe to pat him on the arm and he looked down at her sadly. She gestured and spoke to him, though Jack couldn't make out the words. Roxanne stood only a step behind her, hands on her hips, observing closely.

"Introduce me to him," Roxanne said.

"Sure," Laurel said. "You can talk to him if you want." She took the Bionimals scientist by both shoulders, turning her as if to "offer" her to Kong. "This is Roxanne," she said. "Roxanne. Friend."

Gibson and Díaz raised their dart rifles to their shoulders, ready to fire if needed. "*Roxanne* is a *friend*," Laurel said, conforming her speech to the gorilla's fairly simple concepts. She turned to Roxanne.

"Roxanne," she said, then turned back to the giant ape, "this is Kong."

Roxanne stepped closer to him. "I'm pleased to meet you, Kong."

Kong lowered his head to sniff at her, while she held her ground. He reached out a huge, leathery hand, and Roxanne slapped his palm as if giving high-fives to a buddy. Kong gave her another quick sniff, then turned and bounded away. She stayed in position fearlessly as he spun around again, eyeing her from a distance with a quizzical expression.

"What do you think?" Jack said to Gibson, speaking quietly so that Laurel and Roxanne wouldn't hear him.

"She seems to know what she's doing," Díaz said, lowering his rifle.

Kong sat in the middle of a group of palms and fruit trees. He scratched his chest idly, no longer seeming to care about the humans. Jack frowned. He was not bonded with Kong to anything near the same extent as Laurel was, but it did bother him that Roxanne, another zoological specialist, could waltz in here as she had and form a bond with the ape. Kong actually seemed to like her. Why should this cold, interfering woman from Bionimals be able to treat Kong as though he was *hers*?

He felt an irrational urge to open the gate, go in there, and try to take part in the show—compete for

Kong's attention. It was childish, but there it was. *You're a jealous fool, Jack Denham*, he thought.

Laurel walked back to the gate with Roxanne close behind and Gibson let them out.

The trouble with Roxanne over the next few days was her aura of resentment toward Jack, as if she'd been forced to work with a lunatic who happened to have achieved the task of cloning Kong. Jack supposed the distrust was about even on both sides. While she was obviously competent, she was a loyal employee of Charlton Hemming, which was sufficient proof that she was not all good.

Jack came into the office each day, sometimes letting Roxanne work alone with Laurel, sometimes overseeing what they were doing, sometimes even entering the enclosure with them and Kong. They'd agreed to conduct a battery of physical and psychological tests designed to assess the ape's capacity for thought, his response to various stimuli, his current stress level, and even his sense of self.

One test involved waiting for Kong to sleep and positioning the biggest mirror that they could man-handle up the stairs and into his rainforest. They placed the nine-foot mirror twenty feet from Kong's nest. While Kong slept, Laurel used a hypodermic needle to extract a sample of his blood to be analyzed. Within a day or two, they would have a lot more data about his current state. Jack wished that he had a doctor as painless as Laurel must have been in inserting the needle. Though Kong stirred slightly, his eyes never opened. "This should tell us lots,"

Laurel said to Jack, as she headed past him to take the blood sample downstairs.

By the time Kong awoke, she had returned. As they watched from the observation area, Kong stepped rather warily from his nest. He looked around as if to see what had changed, then noticed the mirror.

"Here's where things get interesting," Roxanne said.

"Yes," Laurel said. "For sure."

Kong immediately saw his own image, which he must have interpreted initially as another young male gorilla. He tried snarling at it, even rearing up on his hind legs and slapping his chest loudly with both of his giant hands. For several minutes, he went through a variety of postures and displays, attempting, so it seemed, to establish dominance over his reflection.

But then he seemed to be puzzled. He walked up close to the mirror, huddling right down to look at the reflection, then backed away from it, not exactly looking dominated by a new rival so much as cautious, as if he expected a trick. He looked over at Jack and the other humans behind the conservatory's gate, then back at the mirror. For a least a full minute, he made a series of less dramatic motions, twisting his head from side to side, while watching the mirror carefully. Once again, he moved close to the mirror, watching the image as he pulled different faces— snarling, flaring his nostrils, giving a gorilla's equivalent of a smile. Then he sniffed the shiny glass surface. Seemingly dissatisfied, he sat back on his haunches, scratching himself and watching how his actions were reflected. Eventually, he seemed to lose interest; he simply returned to his nest and went back to sleep.

Whatever concept Kong had of himself, he'd clearly worked out that something odd was going on. He'd quickly abandoned the belief that his reflection was a rival male gorilla. He was neither frightened by it nor concerned to establish his dominance.

"We'll take this a step further next time we visit him," Roxanne said.

The plan was for them to visit Kong again late at night. While he was sleepy, Laurel would insert hidden, minimally invasive electrodes beneath his skin, integrated with tiny radio transmitters. Those could provide some detailed data, moment by moment, on many of his vital signs, including his blood temperature and heart rate. To continue the experiment with Kong's sense of self, they would use a bright red dye to mark a couple of dots on his facial fur—then they'd see how he reacted at the mirror when he saw himself in the morning.

Jack made a mental note to come into work before sunrise.

The morning was bitterly cold with light snow on the ground, and Jack walked to work—early even by his standards—dressed in his Burberry overcoat, plus gloves, a light-brown cashmere scarf, and a woolen cap. Without removing any of those items, he went straight to the roof of the building and waited for the sun to rise over the city. There was some faint light through the clouds already and more lights glowed dimly on the roof to allow Kong's keepers to see what he was doing. The two keepers on shift were Christine Archer and a blond, tanned guy named Mitchell.

"Kong's been sleeping like a baby," Mitchell said.

"A big baby, but still a baby," Archer added in her rapid-fire voice.

As the sun began to rise, reddening the clouds in the west, Laurel and Roxanne came up to join Jack and the keepers in the observation area. Jack exchanged nods with Laurel, and somewhat more remotely with Roxanne. No one spoke a word as they waited for Kong to uncurl from his sleeping position and start to move about. He was especially slow about it this morning, perhaps tired or stressed from the previous day's events and the demands they'd made on him. Eventually he shuffled out of his nest, giving the humans behind the gate what Jack would have interpreted as a dismissive glance if it had come from another human being.

He peered over his shoulder at the mirror, seemed to hesitate, then walked over to look at his reflection—examining it from different angles as if he were trying to scrutinize his skin for acne. As he watched his reflection, Kong lifted his fingers to the dots of red dye that Laurel had put on his fur. He tugged irritably at the dyed hairs, plucking some out, then shuffled away back to his nest, where he sat quietly, staring back at the humans as if to say, *What now? What else do you want from me today?*

Mitchell opened the gate for them and Jack, Laurel, and Roxanne stepped into the enclosure, Laurel going first. Kong walked over to join them. For the next hour, Jack watched as Laurel and Roxanne talked to Kong reassuringly, played ball with him using a giant beach ball, rewarded him with kind words when he responded. The enclosure was well stocked with piles of the fruits that made up the majority of a gorilla's diet, but Laurel offered him individual melons and bananas when she was especially pleased with him.

As the session continued, Roxanne petted Kong's massive tree-trunk arms to reward him more physically. At one point Kong stepped toward her and she stepped back, looking him in the eye but not encouraging him to touch her. He could easily have reached out, and nothing could have stopped him, but instead he sat back and eyed her with what Jack could have sworn was a hurt look—more like a jilted admirer than a gigantic, muscular beast.

He did finally stretch out and poke her with one battering-ram finger, causing Roxanne to stagger, even though his touch had been quite gentle. Before anyone could act on either side of the gate, he jumped away, as if he'd had an electric shock. Roxanne regained her balance and turned quickly to the keepers. "It's all right," she said quickly. "He didn't hurt me. He wasn't trying to do anything bad."

She stepped closer to Kong, looking up at him and speaking to him softly in reassuring phrases. "Good gorilla. You didn't hurt me. Good Kong." Kong stooped to touched her again, so gently this time that she didn't even move.

Eventually they the conservatory, leaving Kong alone, and took the stairs back to Jack's office.

"It's clear that you and your team have done a good job under the circumstances," Roxanne said. "But you have an underlying problem that isn't your fault. It's simply that gorillas are intensely social animals. Obviously, Kong is far too big to socialize with ordinary apes, and it's not good enough using humans as a replacement."

"Don't you think we might have thought of that, already?" Jack asked. "Actually, we've had long discussions about it."

"That's good, then. I want you to know that I totally support the idea that Kong needs a natural habitat to roam in. It's not healthy for him living alone, with no others of his kind. We all have to make sure that life is as good to him as it possibly can be, now that he's been created. Are we agreed about that much?"

"Of course we are," Jack said, "but I wouldn't have expected it to come from *you*."

"No? Then there's a lot that you don't know about me."

"Probably. What else did you want to say?"

"What else? Well, my opinion on that first point doesn't matter so much, since you and Charlton have already reached an agreement to repatriate Kong. Charlton has his own reasons, but it was the only logical thing to do. What I'd like to know is just how disturbed Kong is by what he's been put through so far."

Unusually for her, Laurel bridled at Roxanne's words. "That is not a disturbed animal."

"No?"

"You saw him. He is tame, intelligent, and quite good-natured."

"Of course he is, Laurel. But he's also bored and lonely."

Laurel nodded reluctantly.

"Meanwhile," Jack said, turning on Roxanne, "that was a stupid thing to do, letting him touch you like that." He glared at her furiously. "What good would it have done if you'd gotten yourself killed?"

"No good at all, but I didn't, did I?"

"Luckily."

"It had nothing to do with luck. I was totally in control."

"Whatever you say."

"All right, since you don't like my company, how about I get out of your way and go and check on the data that we have? The blood analysis will be interesting."

"We'll have it this afternoon," Jack said.

"Then I'll come back later. I want to talk to Charlton first."

"If you're talking to him, tell him that the less delay there is with the expedition the happier I'll be. Or should I call him myself?"

"He understands that already, but organizing something like this is not like running a Sunday school picnic."

That point was fair enough. Of course the logistics were difficult, as Jack had found when he'd done some preliminary calculations with Maudie. "All right," he said. "I'll leave it to you and Hemming. Just impress him upon that I want to leave on the earliest practical day. I'd leave tomorrow if I could."

"It won't be tomorrow, but it will be the earliest day that's reasonably possible. I'm looking forward to it."

Sure enough, the blood tests showed signs of an animal under stress. For the next week, they went through a routine of spending one hour with Kong every morning. Kong seemed to relish his time with Jack, Roxanne, and Laura, but the reports that came back from his keepers were not encouraging. He was more withdrawn than ever, spending most of the day sitting in his nest, rocking back and forth, showing little sign of life except when he wanted something to eat. Even that was getting rarer. He'd also started a habit of looking out over the edge of the roof, through the wall of Plexiglas, whenever Jack and the others left him.

At the end of the week Jack held a lunchtime meeting with Laurel and Roxanne at his apartment. "He's surprisingly sane," Roxanne said. "He might have been a lot worse than this. He's also extremely intelligent—the pygmy chimpanzee component of his DNA may have added to that."

Jack sipped on the vodka martini that Assumpta had made, absorbing the implications of Roxanne's opinion. "And you say he's *surprisingly* sane?"

Roxanne nodded. "You could have ended up with a skewed and neurotic gorilla. I wouldn't describe him that way—the human company that he's had has done him some good. But he's not really happy, either. All the data we've gathered show an animal who is suffering stress. His heart rate is much higher than it should be when he's outwardly calm. He's not having a happy life, no matter how hard you've tried to give him one."

"I accept that," Jack said. It seemed pretty obvious.

"Not only that, his blood has traces of ACTH at a level that suggests an animal whose physiology is in the early stages of a chronic emergency reaction."

She was referring to adrenocorticotrophic hormone, a chemical secreted by the anterior pituitary gland. Their data told the story of an animal that was spending too much of its time aroused as if ready to flee or fight...despite Kong's usual appearance of placidity, the safety of his living quarters and the fact that he had no real challenges from day to day. There were no predators to chase off, no other males to face down. Something invisible, and intangible, was stressing him out.

"What do you want to do now?" Jack said.

"There is another thing first," Laurel said.

"Yes?"

"He has grown enough to look for a mate."

Roxanne nodded. "Laurel's right about that. Ideally, we do need to find him a mate. He should at least be somewhere where he can roam around and look."

"All the more reason to take him back to Skull Island," Jack said.

"You make it sound like we *disagree*."

"No, I didn't say that."

"The important thing is that he's not too stressed to be transported. My fear was that the data might have looked a lot worse...especially the data on the condition of his heart. I thought we might have reached the point where we didn't dare move him—where any new stress might bring on a heart attack."

Jack kept a poker face, but he knew that she was talking good sense. The more he dealt with Roxanne, the more he realized that he'd need to be sure of his ground in any dispute, because it was obvious that *she* would be. Much as he still disliked her, he liked the idea of having her as a grudging ally if tough decisions had to be made about Kong's welfare, rather than as someone working against his plans.

"Right now he has nowhere to go," Laurel said, "and we are his only friends."

"And we need to try harder," Roxanne said. "The least we can do is give him more human company."

With that agreed, they finished up quickly and headed back to the Denham Products building.

Though cold, the day was clear and bright, the sun high overhead in the wintry sky. Crossing the street to the building, Jack looked up…to see Kong standing on two legs and staring straight at them through the Plexiglas wall.

It seemed that he'd figured out where people entered and left the building because he was looking just where Jack always walked on his way from home. Kong was actually looking for them. That thought sent a shiver up Jack's spine; it brought home once more how smart the giant gorilla was.

Even so, Jack did not anticipate what happened next.

THIRTEEN

Kong pounded his huge fists against the thick Plexiglas, roaring his displeasure. He wanted *out*. Gibson raised his rifle, loaded with a dose of tranquilizer sufficient to drop a six-thousand-pound rhinoceros, but hesitated to fire—that was an absolute last resort. But then cracks appeared in the Plexiglas as Kong desperately flailed at it; his great body shuddered with the motion and his roaring filled the air like thunder. He turned from the glass, leaping into the air, and landed with the force of an earthquake. His teeth were bared in a rictus of anger and he roared deafeningly. He was going berserk. A second later, he hurled himself at the Plexiglas wall and a huge vertical crack appeared. Kong bounced off the glass, angrier than ever from the pain and frustration. In a few more seconds he'd be free.

There was no other choice—they'd have to stop him.

Kong was running frantically, rushing this way and that in every possible direction—not an easy target. It was important to make the cleanest possible hit so that the dart penetrated properly into his body. A glancing impact was as good as useless.

Gibson squeezed back the trigger and fired. The dart missed, but then Mitchell fired and took Kong in the back, below his shoulder blades. It was a well-aimed shot, but not a clean hit, for Kong was in rapid motion and the dart didn't penetrate—it went spinning crazily through the air.

They'd just made Kong *really* mad.

Jack didn't wait for the others. As Kong's roars echoed over the city, he ran across the road, dodging traffic. Cars slammed their brakes, tires squealed, horns honked. There was a harsh metallic thud as a small sedan crashed into the back of a large van. Car alarms were going off. As Jack reached the opposite curb, a motorcycle swerved around him at thirty miles per hour. He raced up the building's steps and through the doors, heading for the elevators.

He went straight to the top floor, cursing the elevator all the way, wishing the damn thing would go faster. As soon as the doors opened he was out of there like a sprinter off the blocks. He pushed through a small throng of his staff, including Maudie and her secretary, to reach the stairs, then took them three at a time as he ran to the roof.

It was a scene of total chaos.

Kong had smashed through the walls of his conservatory and was now descending the side of the building. A dozen people milled around the observation area, none of them sure what to do. Trees had been smashed, some of them uprooted. Dirt, fruit, and feces had been thrown everywhere. Gibson and Mitchell, the keepers on duty, were covered with foul-smelling muck.

"What happened?" Jack asked.

Mitchell was wiping dirt and gorilla shit from his face with a towel that someone had handed him. He looked at the soiled towel with disgust. "Kong suddenly decided he wanted out. We fired. I hit him, but not cleanly, and it just made him go even crazier. He seemed to work out that the shots had come from us. Next minute, he was running around, wrecking the place, throwing things." Mitchell shook his head in awe. "You have no idea what he can do. Next thing, he's broken out and we didn't dare fire again. He could be a squashed monkey if he landed in the street from up here."

As they spoke, there was another squeal of braking tires from the street below and the slam of metal on metal. More horns honked. More alarms went off.

Jack hesitated for a moment. "Give me that," he said, grabbing Gibson's loaded dart rifle in both hands. He ran down the stairs without saying a word, then took the elevator to street level where the traffic was now snarled by several damaged cars parked at the curb—and one with two of its wheels on the sidewalk. Drivers were arguing heatedly near their cars. Broken glass was scattered everywhere but no one seemed to be hurt. A crowd had gathered on the other side of the street, gawking up at Kong as he climbed down the building, using its windows as hand- and footholds.

No, not again, Jack thought. This was like 1933 all over. Imaginary scenes of Daddy Kong's Manhattan rampage flashed through his mind, given more texture and realism from the old newsreels that he'd watched as a child. Jack vividly recalled the images of Kong climbing the city's skyscrapers, then falling like Lucifer from the top of the Empire State Building. He couldn't let it happen again like that.

Directly beneath Kong was another scene of chaos, where pieces of the Plexiglas conservatory wall had fallen. Miraculously, it seemed that no one had been killed, but two parked cars had been smashed. One car alarm was going off but it was just one among many. Near this wreckage, Laurel stood with Roxanne, who was shouting frantically into her cell phone, covering her free ear against the noise of the alarms.

Jack raised the dart rifle to his shoulder but he didn't dare shoot. Depending on where Kong fell, people might be killed.

And then the giant ape suddenly let go, dropping the last twenty feet to the ground. He hit hard, landing on all fours, but seemed to absorb the impact okay, for he suddenly reared up on his hind legs. The giant gorilla pounded his chest and roared in what seemed like triumph.

From somewhere behind Jack, and to his left, a woman screamed. All around, frightened men were yelling. People were fleeing. Horns were honking. All those alarms sounding. Kong still roaring. All furious but unintelligible. It was sheer panic in the street, total pandemonium.

On his hind soles and his foreknuckles, Kong made a dash for the road—just as a police cruiser appeared from the nearest corner, its lights flashing and siren blaring.

Kong began to cross the street, stepping over stationary cars, whose thin metal roofs collapsed under his weight. Panicked drivers dove out of their vehicles just inches ahead of him. As Jack watched, as horrified as everyone else, Kong picked up a compact car that was in his way and effortlessly tossed it to one side. It landed on top of an abandoned SUV with a shriek of heavily impacted metal. Kong seemed to like the noise of it. He overturned another car, then pounded on it with both huge fists, smashing it into shapeless junk.

Another police car arrived, from a different direction, and then an ambulance and a fire truck. Two cops left the first car. They drew their guns and ran toward Kong, zigzagging through the piled-up traffic.

Burdened by the weight of his own rifle, Jack ran to meet them as fast as his legs would go. "Don't shoot!" If he could just get one really clean shot with a tranquilizer dart. But, damn it, he had to make it count; he cursed himself that he hadn't thought to get extra darts.

Kong was stalled, for now, in the middle of the street, looking all round as if calculating the best way to trash the city. He looked up and down the avenue, then at the buildings rising overhead, like a jungle of metal, glass, and concrete, whichever way he turned. He sniffed the air—and chose his direction. Smashing cars aside as he went, he headed for Central Park.

As if to ruin Jack's day as much as possible, a brightly painted news helicopter approached from above, its rotors thrumming noisily. Kong lifted his head and roared at it. More helicopters followed as Kong smashed past cars. A couple of shots rang out from the police guns, but there were too many fleeing humans—the cops hesitated to fire. By now there were six or seven helicopters approaching: mostly from the news services, but a couple of police choppers as well. The maddening noise of car alarms filled the air in Kong's wake. All the noise was starting to drive Jack crazy. What must it be doing to Kong?

As he followed the giant ape, dodging his way through the glass and metal wreckage, Jack realized one thing *very* clearly. If they ever did get this situation under control—and if Kong somehow survived it—the giant ape could not stay in New York another day. Much less could they keep him in a city when he was fully grown. No enclosure could hold him and a full-grown Kong on the loose would be calamitous.

Kong disappeared around a corner, still homing in on Central Park—he must have been able to smell it through the polluted city air. People ran, cars revved and honked, trying to escape. Jack caught sight of the giant ape again as he lifted a full-sized Chevvy into the air—it was about as long as he was tall—and contemptuously chucked it aside. For just that moment, Jack had a clear shot. He brought the rifle to his shoulder and squeezed the trigger. The dart rifle fired with a loud pop and a whoosh, and the dart struck cleanly, stabbing into Kong's back on the left side, a couple of feet above his waist. Kong wheeled to face Jack, snarling angrily.

Even more police rushed to the scene. A loudspeaker blared out from one of the NYPD choppers overhead, but Jack couldn't make out the words clearly above all the other noise. Two mounted police on horseback appeared from the direction of the park and Kong's roaring drove one horse to panic. It reared up, whinnying, dropped back on its front hooves, then kicked and bucked like a rodeo bronco. Kong waded through the wreckage on his hind legs, heading in Jack's direction; with each step, he swung his huge, hairy fists and pounded the already-broken lumps of glass and steel that lay in his path. His blows smashed vehicles beyond recognition, flattening them or twisting them into pretzel shapes.

But then he seemed to sag…and a second later he fell, face down, flattening yet another empty car under his three-or-more-ton bulk. For a few seconds he lay there, then slowly pushed himself upward with his outspread hands. The tranquilizer was affecting him, but would it be enough? It seemed he was not drugged heavily enough to pass out—but perhaps enough to slow right down. Jack walked up close to him, taking his place in front of a group of cops. He held out his hands, as if the cops' 9 mm. guns were trained on him, not on Kong.

"Please, everyone," Jack said, "just stay as calm as you can. He's not going to hurt you. Don't panic…*please*. Don't fire any guns." As he spoke, he caught a glimpse of Mitchell heading his way, brandishing the other dart rifle. Frantically, Jack signaled to him to hold his fire. Roxanne and Laurel followed close behind. Suddenly, Laurel broke into a run, dodging this way and that through the wreckage and getting past Jack himself. She raced the last few feet over to Kong, fearlessly embracing him—which was like trying to embrace a shaggy, panting mountain.

Jack could not be sure that no one had been killed or seriously hurt, but he was hopeful. As far as he'd seen, the passengers had fled in time from all of the cars that Kong had pounded or crushed. Kong now looked peaceable, tired out from his efforts and the tranquilizer, yet somehow content with his escape— like anyone who'd done a good day's work and wanted a well-earned rest. Mitchell stepped up close to him, the dart rifle trained on Kong's chest, a very easy target now that the gorilla was not moving about.

"No need to shoot," Jack shouted frantically. "He's asleep for now."

Roxanne stepped up close to Jack, shouting over the din. "I've called Bionimals."

"What?"

"I've called Bionimals. We've got a cage big enough to hold him, built for transporting mammoths. We'll just have to coax him into it."

Jack grunted. "You better put in a call to Hemming, then, as well."

"And what do you want me to tell him?"

Jack glanced at Kong, who was starting to doze off. "Tell him we need to move up the timetable. Tell him the expedition needs to leave *tomorrow*."

FOURTEEN

The Californian sky was overcast with continual drizzling rain as the huge Lockheed C-5A Galaxy transport plane touched down in San Francisco. A sizable group gathered on the tarmac, waiting as the plane taxied to a hanger at the far end of the airport.

There were police, airport officials, workmen, CenCo security staff, and a few security-cleared CenCo executives, including Hemming himself. A truck was parked here, to transport Kong at this end. Nearby were half a dozen smaller vehicles. Any reporters, well-wishers, or protesters who had turned up at the airport had been kept well away.

Jack shook hands with Hemming, somewhat reluctantly. "Welcome to sunny California," Hemming said with a wink.

"Yeah, thanks." He turned and introduced the Denham Products staff members who accompanied him: Laurel, of course, and Mark; Kong's "keepers," Gibson, Archer, Diaz, and Mitchell; and a select group of technicians and scientists with extensive backgrounds in animal and plant bilogy. Fifteen people in all.

Hemming nodded dismissively. "Let's get on with it, then," he said to Jack.

Jack stayed close to the operation as Kong's cage was winched down the ramp then raised onto the truck. Each time they moved his cage it was a major effort, one that put Kong under more stress.

Stay calm, kid, Jack thought. *Try to stay calm.* If anyone were killed or hurt in this operation, there'd be irresistible pressure to have Kong slaughtered. *Just be patient, big guy. It's all going to get better...*

Once the cage was safely chained down, Jack joined Hemming, Roxanne, and Laurel in a chauffeured car and they headed out of the airport, saying little to each other. More cars followed behind and then the truck with Kong, escorted by police motorcycles and other safety vehicles. They took local streets to avoid clogging the freeway. There was soon a thrum of rotors overhead, alerting Jack that news helicopters were following them. Craning his head to look through the rear window, he spotted three brightly colored choppers, standing out vividly against the gray sky.

If the San Francisco news agencies were prepared to go to so much trouble just to photograph their path from the airport to the wharf, Jack hated to think what the situation would be like when they actually arrived at their point of departure. You had to give the press some access, but it could turn out like a circus. Then again, how could it have been any other way? You couldn't keep something like this hidden so you might as well do it with a blaze of fanfare. As long as it was quick, you could grin and bear it.

They approached the wharf where the *Tropical Explorer* was moored. This was a large research vessel that Hemming had hired and fitted out—a three-hundred-foot ship with its own biological labs. They drove slowly toward the wharf, past a crowd of people with the usual placards protesting cloning, biotech in general, and research that involved animals. It was raining more heavily now and some protesters huddled in dull green raincoats.

Jack's car passed through the first security checkpoint into an area that been kept clear of protesters, but it was thronged with other people, some in uniforms, some in suits, some in more casual clothing. Among them were reporters and photographers, as well as officials and CenCo staffers. The police waved the car through a second checkpoint and into a high-security zone. The driver parked almost in the shadow of the ship.

A few seconds later, the other cars pulled up. A young police officer directed Jack and the others to a low wooden building with a wide verandah that faced the berthed ship. Jack struggled over to it in the rain, lugging his heavy suitcase and dodging puddles. He went through the embarkation routine with the port and immigration officials. Right now there was no hurry—it would be quite some minutes before the truck with Kong would arrive since they'd left it well behind in the traffic from the airport. Jack sorted out his paperwork while the rain grew heavier still, beating down hard on the building's roof.

As he signed the last of many government forms, a uniformed man age about sixty stepped forward to shake his hand. "Jack Denham?" the man asked. "I'm Brian McLeod, the ship's captain." McLeod was almost as tall as Jack, with an erect, military posture. His hand was callused and strong.

"Is everything in order?" Jack said.

"We'll be ready to sail once your cargo truck arrives. Leave your luggage here and I'll get it stowed in your cabin. Then come to my cabin for a drink once we're underway."

The captain left Jack and approached Hemming. Finished with his forms at last, Jack headed to the verandah at the front of the building, where he waited for the arrival of the truck that was transporting Kong. Laurel, Mark, Roxanne, and some of the others joined him while Hemming spoke to Captain McLeod.

Just then, someone cheered as the truck with Kong reached the outer police cordon. The cheer was answered by a few shouted curses. A minute later, as the truck approached the ship, a collective sigh went up from everyone present. The truck drove slowly along the side of the wharf in low gear, then parked near a pair of large cranes. Ignoring the rain, Jack walked over to see Kong. Laurel followed a moment later, tugging at Jack's arm to show that she'd borrowed an umbrella from someone. He took it from her and held it over them both.

Gibson and Archer followed to check that everything was okay.

The main thing was to ensure that Kong wasn't too agitated. Once he was safely on the ship, he'd have to adapt to the roll of the waves, but at least they could give him more room. Roxanne joined them, obviously finished with whatever instructions Hemming had been giving her. She hadn't bothered with an umbrella and her thick, jet-black hair was soaking. For a few minutes, she and Laurel talked to Kong, trying to reassure him.

Kong looked at them with an intense but unreadable expression, then turned away and gazed resignedly around the wharf. If a human being had acted in that way, Jack would have called it sulking. You couldn't be sure what an animal was thinking or feeling, but it was hard *not* to attribute emotions to anything as human-seeming as a gorilla.

Hemming had headed for the medium-security zone allocated to the press, flanked by a couple of policemen. At least the security arrangements kept the press from getting near Kong himself. Jack left Roxanne and Laurel and headed over to shadow Hemming. Once he left the high-security zone, the TV cameras circled him like buzzards and a skinny Asian man thrust a microphone at him. "Dr. Denham, what are your feelings at this moment?"

Jack gave a rueful smile. "I'd like to say I'm exhilarated, but it wouldn't be true. All this attention isn't good for Kong."

"Talk a bit about what you do feel, Dr. Denham."

"As of this moment, I have a stressed giant gorilla on my hands. I want him safely on board the ship and then we can calm him down and look after him. He'll have every comfort on the voyage, but he can't possibly understand what's going on right now. I wouldn't want to be in his place."

"So, you're mainly worried about Kong?"

"Yeah, his welfare's on my mind. I'm feeling a little stressed myself."

"How long will it take you to reach the island, Dr. Denham?"

Jack gave a knowing smile. "Good try, but I'm not answering that. I don't want a camera crew waiting for me when I get there." That was another fear right now: landing on the beach at Skull Island in a few weeks, only to find a score of reporters and cameramen waiting for them. *Welcome to this tropical paradise!*

"No more questions, please," Jack said, holding out his hands imploringly. "We've got work to do."

He approached Hemming and they shook hands formally for the cameras. "Have a good voyage," Hemming said with his broad his mako-shark grin.

"Yeah, Charlton. Thanks."

Back at the ship, workers were rigging up Kong's cage, ready for a crane to lift it to the ship. It was time to board and Jack saw that some of his people were already standing on the deck looking back over the ship's railing.

Thankfully, the rain was easing off a little. Jack ran his fingers through his soaking hair, trying to mold it into some kind of civilized shape. He waved to all the TV cameras in the near distance and gave a smile that he hoped would convey both his pleasure at what he was doing and something more than that—a certain rueful acceptance of its necessity and the problems that had to be overcome.

He gave a final thumbs-up sign, then boarded the ship. A short time later, the *Tropical Explorer* pulled away from the dock.

The journey to Skull Island was at last underway.

FIFTEEN

JANUARY 2009

Captain McLeod carefully steered the *Tropical Explorer* through a gap in the coral reefs on the island's south side. Up in the bow of the ship, Jack leaned against the safety rail and watched through a pair of binoculars. They'd sailed all morning under heavy low-lying clouds but these had now cleared and the early afternoon was sunny and bright. Only a plume of volcanic smoke rising from the highest part of the island marred the brilliant blue of the sky.

For Jack, the view of the island was breathtaking, not merely for the beauty that it shared with many other islands in the tropics, but because of what it symbolized to him: the culmination of all his efforts and the reality behind all of his grandfather's stories. His heart beat faster as he thought of the secrets that lay hidden within its jungles and behind its cliffs.

As they'd drawn closer to Skull Island, a small crowd of passengers and crew had gathered to watch from the bow of the ship. It included all of the scientists and technicians on the voyage, plus most of the seamen who were rostered off duty or able to take time away from their tasks. Penelope Ross's film crew captured every moment of their approach.

The ship dropped anchor half a mile out to sea, avoiding the shallows and rocks and outlying spurs of coral. Like Jack, Roxanne had brought along binoculars and through them she'd watched obsessively during the ship's approach, occasionally passing them to Laurel, with whom she seemed to have become friends during all the weeks they'd now worked together.

Not long before, Jack would have opposed any friendship shown to Roxanne by his own people, but he'd given up on that. She could be cold and controlling, but he couldn't fault her professionalism. Perhaps it was her misfortune to have chosen Charlton Hemming to work for.

There was a decidedly festive atmosphere on the ship's deck. Bottles of beer and champagne flowed freely, and many of the passengers had stripped down to cut-off shorts, sarongs, or swimsuits. Jack wore the khaki shorts, white T-shirt, and deck shoes that had become his regular outfit on the voyage. Just for once, Roxanne showed a touch of frivolity. She wore a brief, hot-pink bikini, a turquoise anklet, and a pair of sunglasses with bright red plastic frames, the better to enjoy the sunshine while they still had a chance before starting their serious, and possibly dangerous, work on the island.

She kept her distance from Jack, talking mainly to Laurel, who looked more demure in a floppy yellow hat and a brilliant white one-piece swimsuit. Jack had seldom paid attention to how attractive the two women were. He looked upon Laurel purely as an employee, or really a colleague, while he still thought of Roxanne as a rival, though not exactly as his enemy—not anymore. But they were both very intelligent and desirable young women, once you looked at them that way. Not all *that* young in Laurel's case, but some of the worry lines had fallen out of her face over the past few weeks. She actually looked younger than when they'd left New York.

Jack was reminded, rather unpleasantly, of how long it had been since he'd allowed himself the time to have a proper girlfriend, much less contemplate a permanent relationship. Work had always come first in his life and perhaps he'd grown dependent on it, or even neurotically attached.

"I didn't think that Skull Island would be so beautiful," Mark said. He wore baggy orange board shorts, a bright red T-shirt, leather sandals, and a straw hat. On the geneticist's plump frame, the effect was startling.

"The island is fabulous," Penelope said breathlessly.

Jack had to agree. He now faced a crescent-shaped bay whose waters lapped against high cliffs, except at the western end, where a finger of white sand, two miles long, extended into the sea. This was cut off from the rest of the island by a structure that, seen through binoculars, was clearly the ruin of a colossal stone wall. Jack had heard stories about that wall from his grandfather, and from Ann Darrow: about how Ann had been taken by the islanders to the wall's other side and tied to a stone altar, where she'd been offered up as a "bride of Kong."

Here Jack was, at last, returning to the scene of those incredible events. The thought that the stories were all true, that all of it had really happened, sent a shiver up his spine. He'd never disbelieved it, but now here it actually *was*, right before his eyes: the beach, the steep cliffs, the huge stone wall and its broken gate.

Looming over all this was a volcanic mountain, rocky and bare at the top. It was from there that the plume of smoke rose into the sky. From this angle, once you looked beyond the shoreline, the landscape appeared almost vertical, though this was an illusion. As Jack knew from Carl's stories, there was a whole hidden ecosystem between the mountain and the sea. All the same, the impression of a vertical landscape often came to mind when you saw a volcanic island from offshore. It was much the same, on a far larger scale, with the big island of Hawaii, where Jack had been scuba diving. That island was dominated by the brooding peaks of Mauna Kea and Mauna Loa, whose slopes appeared to go almost straight up if you watched them from a boat out near the island's reefs.

If he had not been told of the mountain's supposed resemblance to a human skull, he supposed he might not have noticed. But that skull shape was just what he was looking for to confirm that they'd really found the right island. Seen from this angle, the caves, indentations, and rocky prominences at the top of the mountain created enough of an illusion to justify the name Skull Mountain—and Skull Island for the island itself. Undoubtedly, they'd come to the right place. What more evidence could they need?

Even with the binoculars, he could see little detail at this distance. In the island's hinterland there must dwell numerous creatures such as no one from the Western world had ever captured, and few had ever seen. But there was no sign of them from the ship, or, indeed, of anything sentient. The only life he could see right now was the lush, green vegetation beyond the sand or above the cliffs. Nothing moved on the beach or in the air. Nothing made a sound.

Roxanne stepped over to him. "We're here at last."

Jack turned to her, lowering his binoculars. While he'd been watching through them, she'd covered up slightly, wrapping a pink-and-orange floral sarong around her hips. Perhaps she'd felt embarrassed being quite so scantily dressed next to a man whom she disliked. Then again, who knew what her thought processes were? During the time in New York, and then the weeks they'd worked together on the ship, they'd developed some professional respect for each other—at least, he *hoped* the respect was mutual—but she was still cool and standoffish.

"Jack, look down there," she said. "In the water just below us."

The water was bright and clear, showing pink, orange, luminous green, and purple coral far beneath the surface. Dense schools of small, colorful fish swam past the ship's bow, followed by a dozen much larger fish of a kind that Jack had never seen before.

"Oh, my God," Laurel said. "What are they?"

Soon everyone was looking down into the water.

The big fish were silvery—though darker on their backs, almost black—and somewhat rounded, with blunt jaws that made them look like marine bulldogs. The biggest of them must have been seven feet long and bulkier than a human being. They showed no fear of the ship, or even any curiosity. Oblivious to anything else, they swam after the smaller fish, chasing them from different angles as if trying to herd them.

"They're something like giant trevally," Jack said.

"But they're huge," Roxanne said. "*Huge.*"

"I know."

"I've never seen anything like them before."

"I've seen reef trevally that look something that, but those suckers are twice as long."

He glanced across at her and saw how her dark eyes had gone wide with wonder. "I think we've found our first new species," she said.

Jack turned back to the intricate movements in the water. "Yes," he said as he watched. "And we've only been here a few minutes. I wonder what else is in store."

"What do you want to call them?" Roxanne asked. "Or do you think we need to land a specimen first?"

"To classify them properly...yes."

Roxanne and Laurel glanced at each other, grinning, and they both grinned at Jack just as openly. The wonderment of the island seemed to have melted any remaining animosity, and for the first time Jack had a surge of feeling toward Roxanne almost akin to friendship. It might not last, but it was something.

Roxanne said, "We'll capture one, then. But I guess they're basically monster trevally. That'll do for now—it's as accurate as anything else we could call them."

"Okay," Jack said, "that's just what they are."

"Yes, monster trevally," Laurel said with a laugh. "But I will need to think of a Latin name."

"Okay, I'll leave that to you."

Penelope and her film crew began taking footage of the swirling patterns of the fish, hunters and hunted, as well as of Jack, Roxanne, Laurel, and Mark, all in the highest spirits they'd shown on the entire voyage. Penelope was a bleached-blonde, tanned, immaculately groomed woman from London, who spoke with one of those perfect accents that would work well in a BBC nature documentary. Though she was almost Jack's age—somewhere in her early forties—she was bouncy and athletic in the lean kind of way that cameras loved.

She thrust a microphone in Jack's face as one of her cameramen—a young Indian guy named Jagat Lal—did the filming. "So tell us, Jack," Penelope said, "what's your first reaction to seeing the island? Not to mention those incredible fish, the first new life form the expedition has found."

"It's stranger and more beautiful than we knew," Jack said. "I'm itching to see what other creatures live on the island. We'll start exploring as soon as possible."

"And you, Dr. Blaine?" Penelope said, pushing the microphone in Roxanne's direction.

Roxanne stepped away from the camera focused on her. She quickly struck a pose like a professional TV journalist, one foot forward, her body turned slightly to one side. She somehow combined relaxation and a dynamic quality. "I think we're all struck by the beauty and strangeness of what confronts us," she said as if it had been rehearsed. "Of course, we all want to start exploring. This may be the greatest adventure in any of our lives."

"Anything more you want to say right now?" Penelope asked her.

"I can't convey the thrill of being here at last, or the anticipation we all feel." Roxanne laughed. "Let the games begin!"

It was too late in the afternoon to begin major exploration of the island, but there was certainly time for a first look at the peninsula where the island's natives had lived when Carl Denham's party had visited over seventy years before. Seen from here, there was no sign of any human activity. *Were any of the islanders still there*, Jack wondered, *or had they vanished completely? What signs had they left behind?*

The party at the ship's bow broke up as they went to their cabins to change into more practical clothing, or just to freshen up. Jack exchanged his deck shoes for a stout pair of hiking boots. When he returned to the deck, Roxanne was already there, wearing the stylish but sensible clothes that she'd favored on the ship: khaki shorts that came almost to her knees; a matching, smartly pressed, short-sleeved shirt; and a pair of plain white tennis shoes. She seemed to have a limitless supply of these, for they always looked spotlessly clean.

At their joint request, the crew prepared one of the *Tropical Explorer*'s two twenty-foot amphibious launches. A dozen people crowded onto the launch: Jack; Laurel; Roxanne; Mark; Sanderson; Penelope Ross, and Lal; Hashemi, the first mate; two hulking Canadian seamen—Kowalski and O'Connor—who were part of the ship's regular crew; plus two of the techs, Roderick Carwardine and Anna-Lena Beck, from Denham Products.

It might not be the party that Jack would take when he began some long hikes in the jungle—for a start, he was sure that Mark was not physically fit enough to last the distance—but it would give some feel of the island to a good cross-section of the team. Between them, they had a valuable range of experience, even if they were not all batting for the same side.

One thing that Jack had learned in the last few weeks was that everyone on the ship seemed capable of working with the others, regardless of who actually employed them. It would be interesting to see whether this continued when the chips were down and new animal species were discovered for exploitation. Underlying any good feelings, there was still a ferocious rivalry between CenCo and Denham Products. At some point, loyalties would be tested. Roxanne, Sanderson, and Penelope's team were working for Charlton Hemming—not for Jack. So, in a sense, were the ship's crew, who'd been hired with Hemming's money. But for the moment, they were all functioning smoothly enough as a unit.

They took supplies of water, dart rifles and more conventional weapons, plus all the movie gear that Penelope and Lal needed.

As Hashemi piloted the launch toward the shore, the place seemed almost too quiet. Other than the tropical fish that they'd seen, there were still no signs of animal life. They landed on the beach and encountered a cloud of insects—a species of fly that Jack did not recognize, somewhat larger than a housefly, with a shimmering purple body. The launch lowered its caterpillar tracks and began to crawl up the sand until it was totally clear of the water.

A dozen large birds flew overhead from the cliffs on their right. These were nothing monstrous, but they were still a species Jack didn't recognize, some kind of black-feathered eagle. As he watched, most of them soared up over the colossal stone wall, flying inland toward Skull Mountain. Two broke from the others and headed out over the sea, flapping their wings occasionally as they climbed the air in lazy, intertwined spirals…almost like a genetic double helix.

Jack and Roxanne stepped out of the launch together, as if claiming the island for Denham Products and CenCo. Both of them carried loaded dart rifles, just in case. Those monster trevally had been the first sign that some of the creatures here were on a different scale from anything that Jack had experienced in his earlier travels around the world. Several of the others on the launch, including Hashemi, Kowalski, and O'Connor, carried large-bore Winchester hunting rifles in case lethal force was needed.

"God Almighty, look at that!" one of the seamen called out.

Jack looked up, and saw a truly gigantic bird, white this time, its wings scarcely flapping. It was much like a gull, or perhaps an albatross, but bigger than any albatross known to science, whether from modern times or from fossil records. Its wings must have been twenty feet or more from tip to tip. It circled them three times, gliding not more than fifty feet over their heads, then evidently decided they were not prey. Flying low over the water, it headed in the direction of the ship. Then, perhaps a hundred yards from the shore, it plunged downward, almost vertically.

It stabbed into the water and picked up one of the monster trevally in its beak. Judged against the size of the gull itself, that fish must have been over five feet long. The gull headed toward the cliffs at the eastern end of the bay, then vanished among the rocks and trees.

Jack swallowed. His heart seemed to be in his throat, trying to get out. "Another new species?"

"It's not in any book I've ever read," Roxanne replied flippantly. "I'd be tempted to call that a monster gull, but I don't think words like 'monster' and 'monstrous' are going to do justice to all the things that we're seeing. We're going to have to get more creative when we name them."

"I know," Jack said, waving away the annoying purple flies from his face. "Otherwise, it's going to get repetitive."

"We'd better pool our imaginations, Jack. Something tells me that this place is going to test our limits in more ways than one. Maybe in every way."

The two of them led the exploration party toward the stone wall. When Jack's grandfather had been here, the upper end of this sandy peninsula, just this side of the wall, had been the site of a village. The natives' thatched huts had nestled among tropical trees. The trees were still there—some of them a hundred feet tall—but the village itself was gone. A few ruins remained, shattered wooden frameworks bleached by the sun, but it looked as if no one had lived here for decades, perhaps since the time of Carl's expedition.

By contrast, the wall looked as though it would last forever. It was seventy feet high, forming a mighty barrier between the top of the peninsula and the rest of the island. Both ends of it merged into the cliffs, and the barrier would have been impenetrable except for one thing. Just as Jack had been told, the fifty-foot-tall double gate where the original Kong had burst through, snapping the huge wooden bolt that had once held the structure shut was open.

The wall and the gates were covered in moss and creepers. No one, it seemed, had tended them for many, many years. Perhaps that last night of Carl's expedition, when the enraged Kong had burst through and attacked them, had spelled the end for the islanders' civilization. As Jack had heard the story, Kong had killed many of them and flattened the whole village in his rampage before he'd been subdued by the gas bombs that Carl had brought for protection. Whether or not the islanders had survived the breach in their protective wall and the loss of their god when Kong was taken back to America, it was clear that they had all died out long ago. Either that, or the last of them had left for somewhere more hospitable.

"I want to go through, there," Roxanne said, pointing through the gate. "Do you agree?"

"Absolutely," Jack said. "I wouldn't miss this for the world."

"No, I wouldn't either, but it could wait for tomorrow, if you'd prefer."

Mark shook his head at that. "No way are we going to wait."

Jack laughed good-naturedly at this display of enthusiasm. "You heard the man."

They formed up in a long line, with Jack going first, together with Frank Hashemi. The tall first mate carried his hunting rifle and Jack his tranquilizer dart rifle. After them, in single file, came Roxanne, Laurel, Sanderson, and the two Denham Products technicians—Anna-Lena and Carwardine—then Penelope and Lal. Kowalski and O'Connor formed a tough, well-armed rear guard.

Jack stepped forward warily. He climbed the smooth stone steps that led up to the gate wondering what lay beyond. No land animals had yet appeared, but there must be some not too far away.

At the top of the steps, he and Hashemi approached the gate slowly, then walked through the gap quickly, both of them half crouched, ready to fire their weapons if needed. From the distance came a shrill scream from something wild, but there was nothing out there that Jack could see, no sign of sentient life bigger than the bothersome insects. He called the others forward, then continued leading the way.

The area on the other side of the gate was over-grown with grasses, low bush, creepers, and vines, but he could see the outline of what must surely be the altar where Ann Darrow had been offered as a sacrifice. In the distance stood more vegetation, including a few truly huge trees. Behind all that he could still see the slopes and cliffs that led up to the sinister peak of Skull Mountain.

They had at least a couple of hours before sun-set—not enough time to get far and still return to the ship before dark. Besides, they were not equipped for truly serious hiking. But surely they could use some of the remaining daylight to get a quick idea of the terrain. With Jack and Hashemi still in the lead, they pushed forward into the jungle, which was not all that thick at ground level, though the path was crossed by branches, fronds, and vines. Several more species of insect landed on them, some trying to bite as they brushed them away. A creature like a centipede, but thirty inches long, suddenly scuttled out from a rotten log just ahead, running as if they'd terrified it.

A few minutes later they came to a dense spider web that stretched across their path for ten feet from one low palm tree to another, visible only because of the insects and broken pieces of bark caught in it. Jack held up his hand to halt the line behind him. At first he could see no sign of a spider, but then he realized he'd been looking in the wrong place. It was up in the top left corner of the web, partly hidden by a drooping frond. The spider was a spectral creature, almost white, with surprisingly thick legs. It looked to be two feet across.

Jack shivered involuntarily. He was not especially afraid of spiders or anything else that crawled, whether snakes, centipedes, or large insects, but this particular creature brought back childish fears. He imagined what it would have been like walking into the web with its thick, sticky strands, then having a thing that size race toward him. The thought was somehow more frightening than being eaten alive by one of the huge carnosaurs that Ann Darrow had told him about. He'd pledged to preserve the ecology of the island, but this horror was almost too much. If he'd had a more suitable weapon than the dart gun, he might have been tempted to use it. But that was irrational. The spider was not threatening them.

There were more screeches in the distance, then a louder, deeper sound, like a lion's or a tiger's roar.

"I think this is a good place to stop exploring for today," Roxanne said. She didn't look as shaken as Jack felt, but she added, "We've seen a lot, and it's time to go back and think about it."

Jack opened his mouth to argue. They'd only come a few hundred yards and it wouldn't be all that difficult to find another path, avoiding the frightening spider and its lair. But Roxanne was probably right. They'd had a sample of experience that bore thinking about before they pressed on any further. That was all he'd set out to achieve for one afternoon. The evening would be a time for serious discussion of what they'd seen and what it meant to them. Everyone could spend the night getting used to the idea of where they were and how strange this place was. Tomorrow they could start exploring it in earnest.

"Shall we get back to the beach, then?" Penelope said. "I'd like to get some more reactions there, from Jack and Roxanne."

"That's fine," Jack said. "We've still got a bit of time."

As they retraced their steps, Roxanne broke off some leaves and small portions of fern fronds. "Botany's not exactly my field," she said, "but a lot of these plants don't look familiar."

"Yes," Jack said. "I was thinking that, too. They're modern plants, most of them, but not the usual forms."

As they approached a clearing not far from the stone altar, Hashemi suddenly said, "Don't move!"

At the other end of the clearing was another animal from no species that was known to science. Gazing straight at them was what Jack saw as a giant-sized version of a bull gaur, a buffalo-like animal from Asia. The gaurs of India and southeast Asia were massive animals, weighing up to a ton, but nothing like this. Black-skinned and almost hairless, the giant gaur stood nine feet at the shoulder, with sharp-pointed horns that spread sideways, then up, extending three feet on either side of its oversized head. Its body was deep-chested and muscular, planted on powerful legs. It must have weighed three tons or more. No one would have a chance against such a creature if it charged at them.

They backed away from it slowly, raising their weapons, as it simply sniffed the air and stared in their direction. "Take it easy," Jack whispered to Hashemi. "We can go around him."

Suddenly, the gaur turned to its left—*across* their path, not toward them—and ran in what looked like terror. From behind it came a bloodcurdling noise that combined the worst of hissing and rasping, turned up in volume almost to the level of thunder. The lower trees shook and fallen branches cracked under the tread of giant feet. Jack signaled a retreat, as what could only be a living breathing, raging dinosaur burst into the clearing from the tree cover, racing on two legs. It ignored the humans, following instead on the heels of the gaur.

The creature's scaly hide was jungle green. It ran with a hunched gait, its long body flattened out, and its immense tail held off the ground to balance its eight-foot-long head. Its huge jaws were filled with long, inward-curving teeth shaped like scimitars. If it had reared up into a fully vertical position, it might have been twenty-five feet, perhaps thirty feet, tall. As it was, the monster seemed to take forever going past them, like a long freight train. There was little here to measure things by in any exact way, but it seemed to be over sixty feet long, maybe much more—bigger than any Tyrannosaurus or any other carnosaur that Jack had ever read about.

Following the giant gaur, it plunged out of sight like a mile-long train disappearing into a tunnel. It shook the trees and snapped off branches in its headlong rush. Soon there was the sound of a beast bellowing in its death throes.

SIXTEEN

"We'd better get out of here," Mark said in a low, urgent voice.

They ran for the broken gate, rushed through it quickly, then down the stone steps. Lal stumbled under the weight of his camera, sprawled on the steps, but somehow managed not to fall any further. Kowalski, one of the big Canadian crewmen, helped him to his feet. Soon they were all back on the sand. Lal seemed okay. As fast they could with their equipment, they ran to where they'd left the amphibious launch. Jack half expected something to have happened to the launch, but it was still there, unharmed and untouched.

"Did we get any footage of those monsters?" he asked, breathing raggedly.

"I got some of the big bull," Lal said. "Just a few seconds of the T. rex."

"It was not a T. rex," Laurel said. "Similar, but not the same."

"She's right," Jack said. "I noticed it, too. It was something bigger and nastier. Did you see its forearms and the claws on its hands?"

"What do you think it was?" Roxanne said. "Some kind of allosaur?"

"Maybe," Laurel said, "but much bigger than Allosaurus itself."

"Yeah," Jack said, "maybe so. It was sure bigger than any allosaur I've heard of. It's something that's evolved along the same lines as a tyrannosaur, but even bigger and nastier. I don't know what to call something like that, and I hope I never come any closer to one than we did just now."

"Well, we can't be too sure of that," said the Bionimals guy, Sanderson. He stroked his full beard as he spoke. "For all we know, the island's full of those things."

"Probably not *full* of," Laurel said.

Roxanne nodded and said, "A carnivore that size probably roams a pretty big territory. I'd hope there aren't too many around."

Sanderson seemed to think it over. "Good point, but we have to assume that there are more of those monstro-rexes where that one came from. There's enough of them to have been breeding all these years. That suggests a viable population."

"Either that, or *our* monstro-rex could be the last of his kind," Roxanne said. "I think we'd all consider that unlikely."

"Unless you believe in wild coincidences," Sanderson said. "If we've run into one on the first day we're here, I'm betting there are plenty more on the island. What's more, if we're going to explore this place seriously, we're likely to run into them. We'd better all be ready, wouldn't you say?"

"Of course," Jack said.

That "monstro-rex," he'd already realized, was probably of the same species as the carnosaur that had attacked Ann Darrow when she'd been on the island in 1933. The first Kong had fought and killed that creature, which showed what a powerful beast

216

Kong must have been. But Kong Mark II was not fully grown, and Jack had to wonder how he'd fare if abandoned here to cope as best he could with reptilian monsters like that. For the first time in months, Jack wondered whether he was doing the right thing.

"All right," Hashemi said. "Let's all get back to the ship. Any objections?"

"Soon," Penelope said. "We seem to be safe here for the moment. I still want some comments for the camera and it's going to look so much more impressive if we take the footage here rather than on the ship."

"There'll be plenty of time for that another day," Jack said.

"Well," she said, "if you *insist*."

It occurred to him that they'd never be safer on the island than they were right now. Nothing could attack them from beyond the wall without following them through the gate and down the stairs. That might be difficult terrain for a giant carnosaur and they'd see it well in advance. Nothing smaller posed a threat to them, armed as well as they were.

"No, I'm not *insisting*," he said with a laugh to break the tension. "Let's do what you say—but get it over with quickly."

Whether they were safe or not, his heart was still pounding from its close encounter with the dinosaur. He'd flirted with death before, climbing unforgiving mountains where survival had depended on nerve and skill, but that had not been as terrifying. Then, there'd always been something he could do; he'd understood the challenges and he'd had the skills to survive them. Facing that huge reptile, he'd encountered something totally outside his experience.

He didn't know what he could have done if it had attacked them.

Lal set up the shot so that Jack was framed by the colossal stone wall behind him. "This was your first day on Skull Island," Penelope said, walking casually into the frame. "What were your impressions, Dr. Denham?"

Jack took a deep breath. *Mustn't seem too panicky.*

"We've had a quick look round," he said, sounding as calm as he could, "nothing more than that." *Try to sound professional.* "It's clear already that this place is a cornucopia of new species, both animals and plants. Some of the creatures we've seen resemble living animals from other parts of the world, but not the huge carnosaur that literally crossed our path this afternoon. It was a creature like nothing that has walked anywhere else on Earth since the end of the Mesozoic Era, sixty-five million years ago. Nor does it quite match any known dinosaur species. Evolution has continued here and we've not so much gone back in time as seen the ancient times of the dinosaurs brought up to date and mingled with creatures we already know."

Penelope signaled for Lal to stop the camera for a moment, and she beckoned Roxanne into the frame to take Jack's place. "Please share your thoughts about your first steps on Skull Island, Dr. Blaine."

As always, Roxanne spoke with a slickness and professionalism that Jack could only admire. The woman was just made to be filmed. If she hadn't been a scientist, she could have starred on TV. She'd probably provide the star power for Penelope's documentary when it was finally finished and in the can.

"There's an eerie feeling about this place," she said. "In many ways, it's anomalous. An ancient civilization has been here and doubtless made its mark on the fauna of the island, but now it's vanished almost without a trace. As we stand here on the beach, there's hardly a sound to disturb us, but something strange and dangerous could appear at any time, as we've seen already, with aquatic, terrestrial, and flying creatures like nothing in the biology books that we studied in college. It's driven home to me even more that Kong belongs *here*, in this place so unlike the modern city where we tried to bring him up. However dangerous it is here, this is where he belongs—and where I hope to find more of his kind."

Jack shook his head silently. Impressive, intelligent, and even beautiful as Roxanne was, he and she were such different people. Their reactions to the island couldn't have been more contrasting. While he now had misgivings about repatriating Kong, her thoughts had gone the opposite way. Their experience with the jungle, the spider, and the carnosaur had actually confirmed her resolve.

It was always a surprise to him when someone whose intellect he respected reacted differently from him to the very same experience. It was not that he thought he was always right. *Surely*, he thought, *I'm not that arrogant*. It was just that it showed how all people were alien to each other. *At some level, we're strangers. We're not the same under the skin, not as individuals. We're all so totally different.*

Quietly, with their weapons at the ready, they reboarded the launch and headed back to the *Tropical Explorer*. No new creatures appeared on the shore or in the sea. No more giant birds flew past. For now, Skull Island looked like any other unspoiled paradise in the tropics. Within a few minutes they reached the ship, and the crew winched them aboard.

After all the excitement and the brief moments of terror, he was psyched up, ready for more exploration. He'd have to contain himself until the morning, but he couldn't have been more eager. The island was everything that his grandfather had said it was and more. It was a whole new world, waiting to be explored.

One high priority before going to bed would be to call Hemming on the satellite phone. Jack and Hemming had seldom spoken during the voyage, though Roxanne had given her corporate boss weekly briefings on their progress and location. From the most recent update, Hemming would know that they'd reached the vicinity of the island. Much as Jack begrudged it, Hemming was entitled to be told that they were here and to make whatever statements he wanted to the press.

Even Roxanne seemed to know little about what was on her boss's mind these days. Much as he tried not to think about matters back in the U.S., Jack had begun to wonder whether Roxanne had done something to lose Hemming's trust. That evil old corporate shark never *had* known how to treat his best staff. But maybe it was wishful thinking. Roxanne never said anything disloyal about the man.

Before anything else, Jack called a meeting in the common room to discuss the day's events and the next phase of the expedition. The ship was designed to carry more people than its actual crew since it had been built to ferry scientific teams around the world's oceans. Thus there was plenty of space in public areas, such as the galley and the common room. Jack requested the presence of all the scientific and technical staff and invited everyone else who wanted to attend. He specifically asked each person who'd been in the initial landing on the island.

Hashemi and some of the crew reorganized the common room to make it more like a classroom, turning its sofas and lounge chairs so they all faced in the same direction. Jack and Roxanne settled themselves at the front, sitting at a pair of ordinary dining chairs that Kowalski had brought in from the galley. A few people sat on the padded arms of the lounges. Sanderson, Hashemi, and Captain McLeod stood against the rear wall.

All of the scientists and technicians showed up, as well as the others who'd been on the island, the rest of Penelope's camera crew, most of the ship's crew who were not actually rostered on essential duties, and two of Kong's keepers—Díaz and Archer. Gibson and Mitchell were watching over Kong's pen and would need to be briefed separately.

"Let's get the ball rolling," Jack said. He turned to Roxanne. "Do you mind if I start?"

"It's okay with me," she said.

"All right," he began, "let me sum up the afternoon the way I saw it." As he spoke, the cameras rolled. Penelope would have footage of this meeting from three different angles. Jack smiled bleakly into the camera at the back of the room. "I'd say that we had a successful, if slightly scary, first visit to the island," he said. That gained a few brave laughs from those who'd been there. Buoyed up, he continued, "The main thing is that no one was hurt, despite the nature of the creatures that we saw. I'm sure that those of you who *weren't* there have already heard the stories. Am I right on that?"

"I reckon you're right," Archer said, speaking very quickly as always. She perched lightly on one arm of the faded red lounge chair that embraced Carwardine's considerable bulk.

"Okay. Well, I'm here to tell you not to believe what you heard. Ladies and gentleman, believe me, *whatever* you've heard…it was worse than that. Want to take over for a while, Roxanne?"

"I'll assume you all know what Jack is referring to," Roxanne said, without directly answering him. "We now know—if there was ever any doubt—that we'll need to take special care at all times. The creatures that live here have no fear of us, and some of them are very, very dangerous."

"I'll second that," Mark said quietly from his position near the back.

"Right," Jack said. "Tomorrow we'll begin a major exploration of the island. I'll be up early in the morning, talking with Roxanne and the captain about who, exactly, we need in the exploring parties. You'll be glad to know we can't take all of you."

"Oh, *please*?" Mark said.

"Right, that's all I have to say for now. I'll hand the floor back to Roxanne for any more observations that she wants to share."

"Thank you, Jack," she said, handling the transition smoothly. "As you all know, the primary purpose of this expedition was, and still *is*, to repatriate Kong to Skull Island. We intend to start that process tomorrow. We'll be taking Kong with us when we leave the ship and we hope to find other apes like him. Given my own duties under the agreement between Charlton Hemming's group of companies and Denham Products, I'm treating that as my highest priority and I'm personally committed to it—more than ever after today."

After what Jack had seen on the island, that last comment didn't thrill him at all, but he could hardly argue against it when Kong's repatriation had been his idea in the first place.

Roxanne went on. "Many of us here are scientifically trained. Those of you in that category will have been wondering, like me, how this island and its ecology came about. There's a wealth of knowledge to be gained here by studying the island's life forms and its geological history. We might also find out much from archeological investigation beneath the ruined village site on the sandy peninsula that you've all either been to or at least seen from the ship. At some stage, I hope that all of that can be done. I'll certainly recommend to Mr. Hemming that he give it his full support.

"It's apparent that some of the island's animals are further mutated and evolved versions of creatures dating from far back in Earth's history. The gigantic carnosaur that we encountered today, which you all either saw or heard about, was not a *Tyrannosaurus rex*—strange as that might seem to some of you. T. rex died out at the end of the Cretaceous Period, roughly sixty to seventy million years ago. That creature looked like a pumped-up version of an even older creature, perhaps an allosaur from the Jurassic

Period, over one hundred million years earlier. I think we all agree on that."

"I agree," Jack said. "It's not my specialty, but I do know my dinosaurs." He winked in the direction of Laurel, seated in the front row. "I always knew it would come in handy one day."

"On the other hand," Roxanne said, "the mammalian forms on the island are much more recent arrivals. Some came from this part of the world—southeast Asia or the Indian subcontinent. Some may have been brought here by human beings—perhaps in ancient times—and they've since evolved further in isolation from others of their kind.

"What we know for certain is that Skull Island contains a wealth of genetic structures, both animals and plants, all previously unknown and untapped by science." She gave a smile that seemed to say that she was in charge, in control, and that no one needed to worry too much because she was a step ahead in thinking about their problems and issues. "Now, would anyone else like to share their observations about what we saw, or to make any other comments? If so, you may have the floor." Then she added, as an afterthought, "You okay with that, Jack?"

At least she was *trying*, he thought. "Sure," he said, "that's okay. Anybody want to say something?"

"Yes," said Sanderson, who was still standing up the back of the room, looking relaxed in shorts, sandals, and a bright Hawaiian shirt. "I have a few points."

Roxanne nodded. "Go ahead."

Sanderson paused for a moment, stroking his beard. "It's not such a big deal for this first expedition," he said, starting slowly, "but there's even more scientific knowledge to be gained here than you might be implying."

"Go on," Jack said. "Tell us what we've missed."

"Well, maybe you haven't exactly *missed* it, but let me just spell it out. We have here what looks like a fairly young volcanic island—only a few million years old, I'd guess by the look of the landscape. But it must have been connected once upon a time to much older land that's disappeared from view. Are you with me so far?"

"Right."

"It's *got* to be right because of what we've all been saying. We've seen the descendant of a creature something like two hundred million years old. The land mass where the big carnosaur—whatever we decide to name it—evolved must have been isolated from the rest of the world all those years ago."

"I understand your point," Jack said. "This part of the world must have had a complex geological history."

Sanderson gave an approving nod. "Complex...yes...and maybe violent. If we're going to go back two hundred million years, everything around here—and north up to India if it comes to that—was part of Africa. The rocks that make up the island and the ocean floor beneath us were down near Madagascar somewhere. This all moved—the Indian tectonic plate broke away from Africa all those millions of years ago and started moving north and east, though we're missing a lot of detail about how the process happened."

"Yes," Roxanne said thoughtfully, "there must have been huge upheavals."

"Damned right there must have been. Studies of the island and the ocean floor around here could solve a lot of puzzles about exactly how it happened. This place would be like a banquet for a research geologist. Science has a lot to learn here, a helluva lot, not just about the development of life on Earth, but the history of Earth itself."

Jack folded his arms and said, "I've been thinking along similar lines."

"I thought you might have been," Sanderson said, giving a respectful nod.

"And I'm happy with what you said," Jack added. "We'll let researchers from all disciplines come here. Whatever causes and influences have led to this place being like it is, it's now unique on the face of the planet. There's an enormous research potential."

In his dour way, Sanderson looked pleased enough. "All right, then, that's all I needed to say."

Somewhere deep in time there must have been incredibly violent geological episodes as continents sheared away from each other and land rose or sank into the sea. Combined with more recent events, this had all created an extraordinary ecology. Jack's mind for scientific research was excited by that, but the fragility of the island would have to be kept in view at all times. "By all means let's study it," he said, "and try to work out how it happened, but we have to preserve this place. We've found one of the world's natural treasures. No matter what, we mustn't harm it."

"You'll get no debate about that," Sanderson said. "Not from me."

"Or me," Roxanne said.

"Yes," Jack said. "I realize that. You're both right. There'll need to be more studies. One thing I'd personally like to know is how gorillas got here from Africa and how they evolved to such on enormous size. As Roxanne pointed out, they can't have been alive when this part of the world was isolated. One of the things we'd all agree on is that there were no gorillas in the world two hundred million years ago. It looks clear that they were introduced by the ancestors of the natives who lived here, though we can't even guess why."

"Maybe some ritual significance," Laurel said.

Jack considered it for a moment. "Okay, maybe we *can* at least guess. And that's as good a guess as any."

"An educated guess, Jack," Laurel said. "It makes sense. We know the islanders worshipped Kong. Maybe there was always a gorilla cult. Why bring them here otherwise?"

"You mean Kong is descended from ordinary gorillas?" Archer said. "Like, from *Africa*?"

"For sure, he must have been," Laurel said. "We know that the DNA is very similar."

As Grandfather Carl had described the islanders, they'd spoken a language similar to those in some of the islands of Indonesia. On the other hand, they'd been black-skinned, which suggested that they'd originally come from Melanesia to the east, or from Africa far to the southwest. It seemed that they must have had at least some connections with Africa. There was no other way that African mammals could have reached here, across thousands of miles of ocean.

"I suppose you and Mark have already discussed this theory?" Jack said with a grin. "You know, like everything else."

"A few discussions, Jack," Laurel said. "On a voyage like this, there is not much else to talk about."

Mark laughed. "She's got a good point there, Jack."

"Well," Roxanne said, "we're not going to solve all these puzzles today. Let's not even start on the *botany* of the island. What I saw was a mix of familiar modern forms, plus a few ancient forms that I studied in text books, plus mutated versions of both—plants not known to science. The riches here are even greater than I'd imagined and we'll have to bring in more specialists to sort it out."

"That's one thing we all agree on," Jack said, making clear he'd brook no opposition.

"Yes, but on this expedition, we can only make a start in cataloguing species and identifying some that we'll take back for detailed study and maybe commercial use. In other cases, we'll just take tissue samples."

"Agreed. Absolutely right."

"We'll discover as many species as we can," Roxanne said, "and start naming them, at least informally. But we have years of investigation ahead of us. I hope that Bionimals and Denham Products can work out a basis to do that together. As I'll be telling Charlton Hemming, there's obviously scope for a much more open-ended agreement."

"I haven't even thought about that," Jack said. "Dealing with Charlton is not—" He decided not to say any more about what he thought of Hemming, not on camera. "Well, we'll have to work out something. We're getting ahead of ourselves."

"Meanwhile," said Captain McLeod from the back near Sanderson, "if you're going to explore any further, you'll have to go better armed than ever. These creatures you've described could be dangerous enough, but you don't know what else is waiting out there."

"That's true, too," Jack said. "No offense to anyone else...but it's probably the best advice I've had all day."

Even as a boy, Jack had imagined himself on the island confronted by its dangerous creatures. As a matter of fact, he'd not had peaceful thoughts about Skull Island. At least in Jack's experience, boys were pretty damn atavistic creatures—they thought more about fighting and killing monsters than conserving them for posterity. That streak of violence in their imaginations was all part of growing up—except that some mature men acted like they'd never grown out of it.

Now that they were finally here, they had to assume the worst. The captain was right—there might well be even more dangerous creatures out there on the island than the carnosaur they'd seen, or than anything Carl, Ann Darrow, and Jack Driscoll, the first mate of the *SS Venture*, had encountered. The stories from the *Venture* expedition could give them some idea, but Carl and the rest had been here for just one day and night.

Carl had told Jack all the gory details about how so many people died during that short time. He'd often acted out his vivid account of a huge stegosaur that had charged him and his party, but had not actually harmed anyone. They'd stopped *that* monster with gas bombs and bullets. Most of the deaths had been caused by the first Kong, when they'd pursued him trying to rescue Ann Darrow from his clutches.

Several others had been killed by a huge sauropod that must have been something like an Apatosaurus, going on Carl's description. It had capsized their raft and crushed half a dozen seamen in its jaws.

The Apatosaurus, or whatever it was, had clearly been bad-tempered and territorial—perhaps, in that regard, more like a hippo than a flesh-eating animal. The long-necked Mesozoic sauropods, Apatosaurus and its kind, had been plant eaters, and it was hard to imagine them evolving to become carnivores; the basic engineering of their bodies just wasn't right. But that had made no difference to all the men whom the brute had killed back in 1933. Once you were dead, you were dead, whether or not what killed you had also wanted to eat your flesh. Carnivores would not be the only danger when they stepped again onto the island.

They would need to be careful of everything that moved, anything that might bite, sting, charge, crush, claw, or otherwise pose a danger. The island's lakes and rivers would be especially perilous, since their dangers could be concealed beneath the surface. Jack had always thought it best to keep out of them. In Africa, hippos caused far more human deaths than lions. It was better to confront Skull Island's equivalent of a lion than its local version of a hippo or a crocodile.

"Apart from what we've seen today," Jack said to the group, "we have the experience of my grandfather's expedition. I realize that there are many rumors about what happened on the island and I'm sure you've all heard things."

"We have," Mark said with a wink. "But I think we're more receptive now. You know what I mean?"

"Uh-huh. Well, I got the story straight from Granddad's mouth. I'm going to brief you all on what I've heard, while I have you here together. When you know what I know, my decisions might make more sense."

"Fire away," Roxanne said. "You have a captive audience."

After the meeting they ate a late-night dinner in the galley. Jack was lost in his own thoughts and the others were equally self-absorbed. The celebratory mood when they'd arrived, not so many hours ago, had been sobered by the realization that this place was not merely exotic and beautiful. It could easily be the death of them.

Jack finally pushed away his half-eaten plate of rice dessert. "Time to make some phone calls," he said to Roxanne. "Apart from anything else, I want to find out what your boss has in mind."

"All right, I'll go with you," she said, still toying with her own dessert. She put it aside unfinished, drank down a half glass of orange juice from a plastic tumbler, then stood to walk to the communications room. Jack followed a step behind.

Before they called Hemming, Jack made a quick call to Maudie's office in New York, just to be sure that nothing had happened that he needed to deal with. "Anything new?" he said when she answered the phone.

"Nothing to bother you about," Maudie said. "The papers have been running stories about Skull Island, but no one has actually followed you there as far as I can tell."

"Well, we sure haven't seen any journalistic life forms here, not unless the prehistoric monster we came across today was carrying a tape recorder."

"You're actually at the island?"

"As predicted, yes—and we've started exploration."

"You will be careful, won't you, Jack?"

"As careful as I can be." Jack said. It seemed to him that Maudie hadn't taken his remark about a prehistoric monster very seriously. He decided not to worry her by explaining. "Anything else before I go, Maudie?"

"We keep getting threatening messages," she said, "but I don't want you to bother about those. Everything is being recorded and security's tight. You can let me handle it."

"I'll have to, Maudie. You're the one on the spot."

"I do seem to be, don't I? Listen, Jack, do you want to make any announcement—now that you're there?"

"The less said the better. I'll keep my mouth shut about it as long as Charlton does."

"Right you are. Go get 'em, tiger!"

"Okay, I'll sign off now. We have to call Charlton."

"Fun and games with the Nameless Presence, Jack? Good luck."

Jack handed the phone to Roxanne to call Hemming at his home in California, where it was still early morning. She keyed in the number, frowned, tried again, then shook her head, looking puzzled. "I'm getting an answering machine message," she said. "I'll try his office, but he should be home right now." For the next few minutes she tried calling several numbers, all without success. Hemming wasn't at home or work, and his private cell phone was switched off. She left a trail of messages, then shrugged. "This isn't like Charlton. He's never out of contact."

"No?" Jack said. "Well, maybe this is a good precedent."

Her eyes narrowed warningly. "No comment, Jack."

"I know it's not your fault if your boss is a jerk. He's lucky to have such a good representative here."

"Thank you for the compliment," she said as carefully as if walking on eggshells. "It's not something I'd have expected from you."

"Oh, I never doubted your *ability*."

"No? Meaning you doubted something else?"

"The feeling would have been mutual, then, wouldn't it."

She merely looked at him as if itching to say something.

Jack left the room to clear his thoughts and walked down to the main deck. Across the dark water sat Skull Island, almost invisible in the night—just a slightly darker shape against the general darkness.

SEVENTEEN

As Charlton Hemming stepped from the Lear jet that he'd chartered in Singapore, the heat, humidity, and sweet scent of Colombo, Sri Lanka, combined to bathe him. Even late at night, he could still tell he was near the equator. These southern Asian countries were *so* different from the San Francisco winter. He breathed in the tropical air like perfume.

As a Very Important Person, he cleared the immigration line quickly. He passed through customs without mishap—and there, sure enough, was Armando Falconie waiting for him. Everything was going as planned.

Falconie was a tough-looking, dark-haired man. He was much shorter than Hemming, only about five foot nine, but he seemed almost as wide as he was tall. He wore blue jeans, army boots, and a white T-shirt within tight sleeves not displayed biceps like cannon balls. Beneath the shirt, his pectoral muscles stood out almost as prominently, while his stomach was obviously as flat as a washboard. Falconie was possibly in his forties, with his closely cropped hair going gray at the temples. His face was thickly stubbled. His tanned, muscular forearms and thick wrists were covered with coarse hairs long enough to curl.

Within his own dubious profession, he used the codename *Falcon*. Hemming's contacts had recommended him as a man with a reputation for ruthless competence combined with absolute discretion. Those were just the right qualities for what he'd have to do in the next few days. Before this Skull Island frolic was over, some accidents would have to be arranged, some bones would need to be broken. In fact, a lot worse than that would have to be done before it all came out right. Falconie—or Falcon—was just the man to do it.

He didn't come cheap, of course, but that didn't matter to Hemming. *You pay peanuts, you get monkeys.* Falconie was a highly trained ex-commando, extremely professional, a smooth operator. He was someone you could trust to do a job for you—then walk away with no loose ends or other complications. His reputation and livelihood depended on all of that. One successful job could lead to referrals for others.

Falconie took Hemming's suitcase and they walked briskly to the airport's parking garage.

"Any problems here?" Hemming said.

Falconie stared directly ahead. "None at all. How about you?"

"No problems, but it's been a tiring trip." Hemming had spent almost two days traveling in various aircraft and now he felt sleep deprived. Still, he'd bounce back just fine when he woke in the morning. That kind of stamina had served him well through a long career in business. A bit of lost sleep here and there would not be a problem.

"You'll be okay," Falconie said, as if reading his mind.

"I'm sure I will be, Falcon. I have a lot to look forward to."

"Good." That was another fine thing about Falconie: he didn't make small talk or try to be clever. Hemming appreciated that in his hired help.

They climbed into Falconie's rented Toyota and were soon on the main road to the city center, whisking along in the dark at sixty-five miles per hour. It occurred to Hemming that Denham must now be at Skull Island. *I wonder what dear Jack has found for me so far. What sort of creatures?* It was hard to believe that the island was only three hours away—at least the way Falconie would be traveling there, in a V-22X Super-Osprey that CenCo had bought especially for this project. Modified for maximum range, rather than military strike capacity, the Super-Osprey could easily get Falconie and his team to the island and back.

Over the past few weeks Hemming had briefed them all thoroughly. Falconie and the others would be taking over on the island—contractual arrangements with Denham or no contractual arrangements. They'd arrange some kind of accident for Denham, which shouldn't be too difficult on a dangerous tropical island. If Roxanne or anyone else had to be expended in the process, so be it. Indeed, no one who'd sailed on the *Tropical Explorer* need return to civilization. If push came to shove, anyone was expendable, as Hemming had told Falconie in the clearest terms. Roxanne had been a good employee in her way, but her use-by date was up. If she survived, fine. If not, Hemming could buy other scientists. He'd begun to do just that.

The Super-Osprey would be equipped to bring specimens back here to Sri Lanka. It had taken some time to sort out, but Hemming had bought the land he required and gained all the permits that he needed in return for an agreement to hire local workers. Everything was falling into place but the work they'd do here in Sri Lanka seemed almost like a side issue, at least for now. Hemming's highest priority was to take care of Denham once and for all. No amount of luck would save his rival's thieving hide.

Falconie pulled up at the brightly lit glass tower of the Parkway-Voyager Hotel, one of the most opulent places to stay in Colombo.

Sweet revenge coming right up, Hemming thought. Everything was falling out just as he'd seen it would five years before when he'd laid down a coded challenge to Denham Products—almost dared Jack Denham to attempt cloning Kong. If only Denham understood how he'd been outsmarted and manipulated at every turn. It was *almost* a pity that he wouldn't live long enough to find out.

SKULL ISLAND

Kong had calmed down since the first days of the voyage, when he'd been "moodier" than anyone had ever seen, throwing about any objects that were placed in his pen and spending much of the day and night roaring his displeasure. Then he'd settled back into the dulled state that he'd shown in the later months of his time in the New York City conservatory. He'd even seemed *happy* whenever Roxanne or Laurel climbed into his den to talk to him and play ball.

Right now, he sounded angry. Very angry. Loud growling sounds, mingled with occasional thumps, came from the direction of his pen.

In the ship's dim lights and the dull moonshine, Jack crossed the main deck to visit his huge problem child. "Hey, kid," he said, "what's wrong?" Most likely, Kong could pick out distinctive odors that he'd never smelled before coming from the direction of Skull Island. Whether they signified freedom to him, or simply something strange, they were new and doubtless unsettling.

Gibson and Mitchell were stationed on one side of the pen's metal roof, playing cards within a circle of light only slightly brighter than the rest of the deck. Occasionally they cast nervous glances down into the pen itself. Kong was certainly agitated, thumping around down there. Thankfully, they wouldn't need to confine him for long.

At least he hadn't tried to escape, as if he knew the problems it would cause. For better or worse, he was still growing and Jack was sure the pen wouldn't hold him if he really tried to get out. No one had measured Kong lately, but he was now at least twelve feet tall at the shoulder, maybe even more—and half that height again if he stretched up on his hind legs. They couldn't weigh him aboard the ship but Laurel had guessed he was at least four tons. That was still not as big as his city-terrorizing daddy had been, but Kong was definitely working on it.

Jack greeted the keepers in a quiet voice, not wanting to disturb the ape even more, though Kong was surely aware of him. "You guys will be glad when this is over."

Gibson looked over Jack's shoulder, nodding to acknowledge someone else on the ship's deck. "It's a problem for you two in the end."

Us two? What?

"Not for long now," Roxanne said, as Jack turned to face her. She must have followed him onto the deck and then down here to the pen. He'd been too absorbed to notice.

"I didn't know you were there," he said. "You must walk like a cat."

"I'm sorry. Want to talk?"

Jack followed her to the rail at the side of the ship.

"What are you thinking about?" she said.

"Lots of things," he said, facing her. "About Kong...about Hemming. What happened today. How we're going to handle things tomorrow." He still felt shaken from his first excursion to the island, yet also exhilarated—and he hardly knew where to start in identifying new species and choosing the first for detailed study.

Roxanne nodded. "I've been thinking, too."

"About the expedition?"

"Mainly about Kong."

As if cued by hearing his name, Kong gave a powerful roar.

"What about him?" Jack said when the roaring stopped.

"I'm going to miss him, you know," Roxanne said. "Does that sound stupid?"

"No, of course it doesn't. I'm going to miss him, too."

"But I'll be glad when we finally set him free. Maybe we can do it tomorrow...or in a day or two."

"With any luck."

"You don't sound too certain."

Jack thought before he replied. "I'm worried about letting him go on the island. After what we saw today—"

"What we saw today should make no difference," she said with a touch of impatience. But then she added, more gently, "This is the environment that he's adapted to. I think he has a right to live here in peace, without humans bothering him. Don't you?"

"After today, I'm not so sure. He hasn't grown up with dinosaurian monsters like that allosaur, or whatever it was. I'm not sure whether or not he could survive here."

"It's not up to us how he fares in the future. What he really needs is his freedom."

"But be realistic," Jack said. "Freedom can have its downside."

"That's what dictators say."

"Not only dictators."

She seemed to scrutinize him in the dim light. "What's got into you, Jack?" she said. "All through your negotiations with Charlton what you really wanted was for Kong to be returned to the island. Now we're here, you start to question it."

"It's not exactly *returned*, though, is it? He was cloned in New York City, thousands of miles from here. He grew up with human beings as company, not prehistoric reptiles, not even others of his kind…if there are any. You can't just equate him with the animal that he was cloned from. For a start, nearly a third of his DNA comes from other sources. But more importantly, he's had no chance to learn the dangers of the island. I don't know how long he'd survive if we let him go."

"That's not your responsibility."

"Yes it is. I brought about his existence. I'm his *creator*." He smiled at that, despite himself. "Sorry to start sounding like a mad scientist."

Roxanne laughed conspiratorially. "Between you and me, you do a good impression of one."

"But if Kong has a short miserable life, I'm the one who'll be to blame. I'm starting to think that this was all a mistake. I should have left well enough alone...not even created him."

"And maybe *I* would have been the one to create a clone of Kong," she said with a shrug. "Then it would be my responsibility, right? Or Charlton's?"

"You might never have succeeded."

"Well, *that's* true, anyway. You probably had a better blood sample, and *we* didn't have Graham Riley on our team."

Jack looked out over the dark sea.

She stood closer to him at the rail. "Jack?"

"What?"

"In the end, we'll have to release Kong. We don't have any other choice."

"I know that," he said.

"We can't take him back to New York. For better *or* for worse, this is the only place for him."

"I know, I know. I'm not saying we should take him home with us."

"Then I really don't understand your thought processes."

This was the most meaningful discussion he'd yet had with her. He was struck by the recognition that she was not an evil person, self-contained though she was. "I guess you don't have a very high opinion of me," he said.

"Your opinion of *me* isn't all that high either."

"That's not true."

"No?"

"Well, it's a lot higher than it used to be. I know you're good at what you do, I respect the way you work with Kong. I just don't understand—"

"Why I work for Charlton Hemming?"

"Actually, yes."

"Maybe because he's treated me honestly."

"Are you sure of that? Charlton is a law unto himself. He respects no one—or if he does it's never for long. You shouldn't trust him one inch, Roxanne. Take care when you deal with him. Damn it, why am I even telling you this? It's not my responsibility."

Roxanne looked confused. "Whatever you think he's like," she said at last, "or whatever he's done to you or anyone else, he's given me good work. He's paid me fairly. Most of the time, he's listened to my advice. I can't ask for much more than that from an employer. Believe me, it's better than I've experienced from plenty of others."

"All right, I don't expect you to bad-mouth him. If I told you more about him, you probably wouldn't believe me and you'd think even less of me than you do now."

"You're not the only one who's told me that Charlton can be ruthless, so don't worry about me calling you a liar. But I'm not involved in that side of things—whatever exactly *that side of things* might be." She laughed again. "I'm employed by Bionimals as its chief scientist. I do good work to the best of my ability. End of story."

"All right. He's your boss. I'll keep my peace about him."

She shook her head and made a wry face. "I didn't mean you have to censor yourself."

"No?"

"Actually, no."

"Uh-huh." He decided to change the subject anyway. "The thing is, we can't just drop Kong in some random spot on the island and hope for the best."

"No," she said thoughtfully, "but he'll get used to the island. And if we *don't* set him free, I'm worried about the consequences for his health. Believe me, it's kinder to release him here than if we kept him locked up somewhere. At least the challenges here are those he's evolved for."

"That hasn't escaped me," he said, "but we could have a dead gorilla on our hands if he meets one of those carnosaurs that we saw today."

"Look at me, Jack."

"What? What do you mean?"

"Read my lips. I Only Want The Best For Kong—got it?"

"Yes, I know you do."

"That might not be uppermost in Charlton's mind, whatever is in his mind…but it's what he's paying me for. As far as the Kong *side of things* goes—right?—Charlton just wants a nice movie that shows a successful return to Skull Island. He's got no reason to want to screw that up, and I *certainly* don't want to. Just assume that everything I suggest to you is in good faith, whether you like me or not."

"It's not a matter of liking you or not liking you. I'm past that now."

"*Really*, Jack?" she said incredulously.

"Yeah, really." All the same, he still felt uncomfortable. She seemed just too assured of her own ability, her righteousness—and, he admitted to himself, her beauty. From any angle she looked good enough to be almost an affront to ordinary people, and she used all that power without effort. Jack waved his hands in the air feeling downright confused—by how he felt about Roxanne. By everything. *"Whatever!* I don't know."

"Are we deadlocked about Kong, or what?"

"Of course we're not deadlocked. We'll do everything as planned. Just because I have misgivings doesn't mean I'm going to give up at the last minute."

She touched his arm lightly. "Thank you. I'll go to bed now. Today wasn't easy for either of us."

After she'd gone he could still feel her touch. At that moment she'd been almost affectionate, not at all her cold, focused, superior self. It occurred to him that she might even find him attractive. If so, *that* feeling was certainly mutual. He tried to dismiss the thought, but it wasn't all that easy. He found himself getting sexually aroused by the image of her in his mind, especially as she'd appeared earlier in the day, in her pink bikini, acting more carefree than usual. And now the memory of her light touch on his arm.

Well, she probably hadn't meant anything by it. It was just another of her patronizing tricks.

At this rate, he realized, he would have a sleepless night—worrying about the island, Kong, Hemming, and now whatever it was he found himself feeling for Roxanne.

Disgusted by all this mental confusion, he headed for his cabin.

Tomorrow was another day. Things would probably get worse.

EIGHTEEN

As always, Jack woke early. He'd tossed around on his bunk for much of the night, getting increasingly frustrated at his inability to sleep. But it hadn't over-ridden his inbuilt programming. He was up at 6:00 A.M. He showered quickly, pulled on his T-shirt, khaki shorts, and deck shoes, then headed to Kong's pen to check how things were going. Kong was still prowling around the floor of his pen like a angry prisoner who'd been denied parole, but at least he'd made no actual escape bids.

Satisfied on that score, Jack called in at the ship's galley to scrounge some toast and coffee. Captain McLeod and some of the ship's crew were already breakfasting in the galley, together with Penelope Ross and a couple of the techs. The captain eyed Jack up and down. "You look like you've been in a fight," he said in the slightly bantering way that he'd shown throughout the voyage, once they'd all grown used to each other.

"What makes you say that?" Jack said.

"It's just that you look worse than usual."

"Give me my three cups of coffee, and I'll turn human. You know how it is."

Penelope smiled knowingly. "What I think the captain's trying to say…"

"What?"

"Is that you look even less human than you *usually* do in the morning."

"Fair comment," Jack said. "You've pretty much described how I feel."

He went to a sideboard nearby and returned with his first cup of coffee. "Is something wrong?" Penelope asked.

As if in answer, Kong delivered one of his best roars of frustration. It echoed through the galley like the sound of an earthquake. Jack gave a rueful smile as if to say, *Does that answer your question?* "It's nothing that you can help with," he said. "But Kong knows something has changed. He can feel that the ship has stopped moving and I'm sure he can sense the island. We'll have to take him there before it drives him nuts."

He drank his coffee quickly and felt slightly better for it, then excused himself to collect another cup—plus a large plate piled up with buttered toast. He'd just demolished the coffee and all but one slice of toast when Roxanne arrived. "Your foster child is throwing quite a tantrum," she said.

"Tell me about it."

"I think he can smell freedom."

After breakfast they both went to Jack's cabin to make some plans for exploration of the island. Today they would do some reconnaissance. Tomorrow they'd send out two exploration teams, each with the task of identifying new species but one with the additional responsibility of returning Kong to his natural environment. A third team would maintain a base camp on the beach, leaving just a skeleton crew on the ship.

Jack had prepared large maps of the island, based on the original from his grandfather, but overlaid with an eight-by-eight grid to help with locations. Each square on the grid represented four square miles. If the landforms marked on the original map were roughly to scale, they could orient their way around the island fairly effectively—though much of Grand-dad's old map showed little detail since the island had never been fully explored. Their first step would be to check it out from the air and at least get some idea of how well the maps corresponded to the reality.

Roxanne was in a cooperative mood and they made good progress. After a couple of hours they agreed to stop and freshen up, then meet back on deck to start the day's big task. It was time to set Kong free.

Once again there was low, heavy cloud cover over the island and as far beyond as the eye could see. There was even some mist hanging over Skull Mountain. But by mid-morning, a gentle breeze from the west had started to clear the sky.

Jack took his position with Captain McLeod at one end of Kong's pen, but keeping a safe distance from the operation. Penelope and her cameramen operated from higher vantage points on the ship. Watching like hawks, their dart rifles trained—just in case—Kong's regular keepers were stationed at the four corners of the pen's steel-grid roof. Gibson and Díaz wore sensible khaki outfits, but Mitchell was barechested. His bright, electric-blue shorts clashed impressively with his rugged work boots and black socks. Christine Archer wore faded blue jeans and a white T-shirt. She was barefoot but still as tall as Mitchell and Diaz. Only Gibson had a few inches advantage over her. Archer puffed on a cigarette nervously waiting for something to happen.

Half a dozen of the ship's crew, led by Frank Hashemi, stood back from the pen armed with large-bore hunting rifles—they were ready to back up the keepers in a real emergency. Another two seamen sat on the pen's roof—on its four-inch-thick bars—working to unlock the bars manually. Once that was done, the two halves of the roof could be winched up by small cranes at either end. The roof could then open out like a drawbridge.

Roxanne had always wanted Kong to be free to move around on the ship under human supervision. The captain had expressed no objection to Kong's being allowed to wander with the explorers on the island, so long as he was under Laurel's control or Roxanne's—but not on his precious ship where Kong could do damage and there was nowhere for his crew to run. In his current mood, Kong would cause panic if he got out of his pen onto the main deck. *Just be patient, big boy,* Jack thought. *We're almost there.*

"Finished!" exclaimed one of the seamen perched out on the grid of metal bars. He and his buddy crawled back to the deck, while others started the motors of the cranes. Roxanne and Laurel stepped away from the pen as its roof peeled away. Soon the enclosure was an open metal pit. Jack stepped closer to observe Kong, who looked upward at the humans gathered around the edge of his pen. The gorilla slapped his enormous chest and roared defiantly.

Seconds later Kong's explosive roar was answered by a distant roar from the island. Something huge had made that sound, though Jack could not tell what kind of animal. It had sounded nothing like the carnosaur they'd encountered on the island, but heard at this distance, half a mile from the shore, it might have been anything else—from a big cat to another giant gorilla. Kong roared again, as if in response, and another roar from the island answered him. He roared yet again, but this time there was no answer. Kong merely growled and then he was silent, as if sulking.

Quiet or not, he could flare up angrily at any moment. They would have to sedate him before setting him free on the island, but Jack was fearful of sending even Roxanne or Laurel down there while Kong was so cranky. Most likely they'd be okay. The giant ape would never harm either of them deliberately, but there was always the off-chance that he'd forget his own strength. Did he understand how flimsy human flesh and bone was compared to a brute his size? It was so damn hard to guess what he must be feeling or, in some way, "thinking." In the past, he'd yielded patiently when given a sedative injection, but there had to be a first time for any act of rebellion.

Jack caught Roxanne's eye and gestured for her to join him. Amidst the noise of Kong's roaring, Jack explained quickly what was on his mind, conveying it as much by emphatic gestures as by sounds. How could they best sedate the gorilla so he could be moved to the island? "As far as I can see we have no choice," he said. "Either we wait until he settles down, which could take hours—"

Roxanne arched an eyebrow. "Or?"

"Or we'll have to use a dart rifle. No matter how fond he is of you and Laurel, you're not going down *there* while he's acting like this."

To Jack's slight surprise, she didn't argue the point. "I don't want to wait," she said, "and I basically agree with you. I might be stupid enough to go into his pen myself, but I wouldn't send anyone *else*." She gave a sly smile. "And that proves your point, doesn't it?"

"Huh?"

"If I wouldn't send anyone *else*, I must know it's dangerous."

"That sounds logical, I suppose."

"Of course it's logical. I'm not getting anywhere near him in a confined space when he's like *this*."

"We'll tell Laurel."

"Kong won't like it, though. He's going to feel betrayed. He's already worked up about dart rifles. The more often we do this, the more he'll lose trust in us."

"That's rather anthropomorphic," Jack said.

"Kong *is* anthropomorphic—in many ways, he's almost human. Don't you feel that?"

"Of course I do." Jack had known that for a long time—that sense of somebody at home, and not just a mindless brute, behind Kong's round eyes. "Look, I'll get Gibson to do it. The poor guy can be the villain again."

Roxanne nodded quickly. "You talk to Gibson. I'll have a word with Laurel."

A few minutes later, they'd prepared the heaviest dose of tranquilizer that they could risk. Uncomplainingly, Gibson did the dirty work. He leaned carefully over the edge of the pen, trying to get a clean shot at Kong as the ape rampaged up and down. Finally, he squeezed the trigger on the dart rifle, taking Kong in the shoulder. Kong slapped the wound as if he'd been stung by an insect. He stopped in his tracks, looked up at them angrily—and roared his displeasure.

Great, Jack thought. *Just great.* Never mind Kong's loss of trust in humans, how was he going to get the ship's crew to trust *Kong* after all this?

As expected, Kong struggled for some seconds to stay alert, but he finally seemed to give up. He sank to the floor, rolling over onto his side. Archer tugged on a pair of battered-looking shoes while they all waited for Kong to start snoring. After another minute, when it was plain that he was safely in dream land, the Kong Squad—Laurel, Roxanne, Kong's four keepers, and a group of seamen—descended the ladder into his pen. Their next task was to attach an apparatus of huge leather straps and strong steel chains that they needed to lift Kong's four-ton bulk into position.

This was another tricky job. Kong was far too heavy for human hands to move. It was a matter of getting as much of the harness as possible around his huge arms, while Hashemi and Kowalski started up the Jayhawk helicopter and flew it overhead. The rotors thrummed and dust blew everywhere as the chopper came down and hovered near the pen. Once the harness was safely clipped to a bracket on the chopper, Hashemi was able to lift Kong into a better position. That helped the Kong Squad to readjust the harness. After a long, gradual process of adjustments and improvements, they finally got Kong ready. Mission accomplished, the Kong Squad climbed the ladder to the main deck.

While this was going on, Captain McLeod oversaw the final packing and readying of the two launches to go to the island.

At last the Jayhawk lifted Kong up out of his pen. Jack gave Hashemi and Kowalski a thumbs-up sign, and the chopper made its way slowly across the half-mile gap to the shore.

Laurel walked over to Jack. "Very well done," she said.

"I didn't want to shoot him," Jack said.

"No, it was best. Now we should get to the island."

"Yeah, before he wakes up."

This time more than thirty of them crowded onto the launches, together with tents, blankets, canteens of fresh water, food and medical supplies, biological equipment, gallons of insect repellent, extra clothing, matches and firelighters, radios and radio tracking equipment, cameras and microphones, several sizes of guns, and everything else that they'd need to establish an onshore base and start full exploration of the island. By the time they landed, the clouds had mainly cleared. Hashemi had set down the chopper in a position well away from the sea—not far from the base of the colossal wall where the islanders' village had been. Like a house-sized furry toy, Kong lay where his harness had been lowered onto the sand.

Engaging their caterpillar tracks, the two amphibious launches crawled up the beach.

Mark was first out, using his straw hat to brush away the swarming flies. Laurel was close behind. Kicking up dry sand as she ran, she raced over to Kong to check that he was okay. Jack followed, giving a thumbs-up sign to Hashemi and Kowalski where they now stood beside the Jayhawk. "Well done!" he called out.

"I think the big monkey should be okay," Hashemi said when Jack had gotten close enough to talk to them. "He slept like a baby the whole time."

There was a loud squawking in the sky. Jack looked up to see four creatures flying overhead—not birds this time, but giant airborne reptiles.

"My God," Hashemi said, "Look at the size of those things. What the hell are they?"

The flying reptiles swept low enough to give an impression of just how big they were. It was obvious that they had no fear of humans. "I don't know," Jack said, "but I sure would like to find out."

"Some sort of pterodactyl?" Kowalski said. "Are those the things you were talking about last night?"

He was referring to Jack's account of the *Venture* expedition and the huge pterosaur that had attacked Ann Darrow. "Those creatures are not quite what I imagined," Jack said, watching them in awe, "but I guess they might be what tried to carry off Ann. I always thought she was exaggerating." The pterosaurs circled once, but didn't attack or come any closer. They flew off out to sea, perhaps hunting for fish, like the albatross that Jack had seen the previous day.

"You don't have a name for them?" Hashemi asked.

"No. They don't match anything in the fossil record. They're bigger than anything we've ever found fossilized."

"That's what I figured."

The biggest known prehistoric pterosaurs were Quetzalcoatlus and *Pteranodon longiceps*. Some very large fossils had been discovered of Quetzalcoatlus in particular. It had been blessed with a wingspan of thirty-five feet or more, as big as a light plane's, but the wings of these creatures flying above the island had seemed to go on forever. Their span might easily have been twice that of Quetzalcoatlus.

Let's see, Jack thought...If *Quetzalcoatlus had weighed up to five hundred pounds—an estimate made by some paleontologists—a pterosaur twice that big in each dimension would weigh eight times as much. Something like two tons each!* What he'd just seen, he figured, were flying reptiles that had been evolving for many millions of years since the original days of the dinosaurs, gradually changing and growing bigger. *Imagine something like that swooping in on you.*

Back in 1933, Ann had almost been carried off by a flying creature that she'd later identified as a Pteranodon when she'd been shown some artists' recreations of prehistoric life. That had always bothered Jack, for no Pteranodon in the fossil record had been anywhere near large enough to do what she'd described. But those creatures he'd just seen had looked quite similar to *Pteranodon longiceps,* though on a vastly greater scale. It was not so hard to believe that one of them had tried to make a meal of Ann.

Clearly, this island had its own definition of size.

There was another squawk and Jack gasped. Another of those airborne monsters flew straight toward them from the direction of Skull Mountain—roughly north of their position. It stayed above them, circling, and made no move to attack. Hashemi raised his rifle and fired a warning shot in its direction. The pterosaur climbed higher into the air, lazily, almost contemptuously, then flew back over the jungle.

They all took a few minutes to get their breath back, then started to set up a camp among the trees near the old stone wall. Jack went over his map of the island with Roxanne and a few of the others. Though it showed little detail of the island's landforms, the most prominent were clear enough: this sandy peninsula; the rocky peak of Skull Mountain; a river that flowed in this direction from the north; and the vaguely sketched boundaries of a lake or series of marshes. For the moment, that would have to do.

As they worked, Kong slowly awoke. First, his limbs moved slightly. Then his eyes opened and he sat up, looking as groggy as a drunk with a bad hangover. Most who didn't know him well kept their distance, but his keepers stood guard and Laurel talked to him with the kind of solicitude you'd show an accident victim waking up in hospital. When he was ready, she offered him fruit from their supplies and a hollow gourd full of fresh water. It looked like a thimble in his huge hands. He drank it in a gulp and she gave him more—another thimbleful. He'd have to find his own water once they started exploring.

Jack walked over to join Laurel as Kong suddenly shook his whole body like a wet dog. He rose onto all fours and looked down at them from a vantage point more than twice Jack's height.

Jack waved the keepers away, wondering what mood Kong would be in, but the giant ape merely stood still, appearing uncertain. Laurel stepped back toward the shore, calling out to him as she went, and Kong eventually deigned to follow her. He sniffed curiously at the air and swatted away some buzzing insects. Once he had the idea that he was free to roam around on the sand, he made a sudden rush toward the sea, then ran back toward the camp, stopping when he reached Jack and Laurel.

Roxanne joined them, grinning all over. "You're a good gorilla," she said. "You like being let out, don't you?"

Kong made another dash right through the center of the camp and up the steps at the base of the ruined wall. For a moment, Jack feared that he was going to settle any discussion about what to do with him by fleeing through the gateway into the jungle—and claiming his freedom once and for all. But then he returned, moving faster than Jack had ever seen him move. It was obvious that the ape's entire mood had changed. This was the happiest he'd seemed since he'd been a mighty infant, just learning his way.

Turning to face the great stone wall and the jungle behind it, Kong reared up on his hind legs, thumped his chest, and let out a powerful roar.

"Go, Kong!" Roxanne said.

From the jungle came the answering screeches of birds, then a frightening shriek from some unknown animal. Kong roared again as if he'd been challenged by the jungle sounds—and roars came back at him from the far distance. They could have been the sounds of lions or of some kind of animal Jack had never seen. For several minutes, the competition went on—Kong roared and the jungle answered, then Kong roared again. Eventually, the noise from the jungle became still more distant, and finally it ceased.

But there was one more roar in Kong—his most powerful yet. As he let loose with all his lung power, it seemed like the giant ape's cry of rebirth.

The sound of liberation.

NINETEEN

By early afternoon, Jack and Roxanne had established
their base of operations with a small cluster of orange
Mylar tents among the trees near the stone wall.
Clomping around in his heavy hiking boots, Jack was
getting sweaty and tired, but nothing had happened
to cause any fear. From the near distance came a
steady droning of what sounded like cicadas, mingled
with the varied songs, shrieks, and raspings of birds,
but nothing nasty had emerged from the jungle. No
creatures had disturbed them, save for insects of all
sizes, and the giant birds and flying reptiles that
occasionally flew overhead.

As his human friends worked and planned, Kong
settled down among the trees at the perimeter of the
tents, occasionally getting up to look around, sniffing
at the vegetation but never straying far from the camp.
Now that he was free, he seemed perfectly content.
Even this beach was giving him a world to explore,
though he had yet to learn how much more awaited
him on the island.

Penelope and her crew took endless footage for
later editing. Kong's keepers still kept careful watch
over him, but the rest soon ignored him as they went
about their work. Jack was pleased to see how quickly
any misgivings had dissolved away. All right, so there

was a giant gorilla romping about among them, taller than some of the trees. But as his curious, all-too-human eyes looked down on the dwarfed men and women, everyone could see that he had no malice in him. *But that might not be a good thing*, Jack thought. Maybe Kong needed a meaner streak to survive in a place like this. How would he adapt to his new life among giant flying creatures, mutated dinosaurs, and whatever beasts had roared at him from the jungle?

Jack and Roxanne chose a half-buried log closer to the sea as a good place to sort out some final details of allocations to groups. They took hunting rifles just in case of attack from the air, but the giant birds and pterosaurs still kept a distance—seeming not so much respectful of the humans as aloof and indifferent.

All the names were scribbled on a small notepad that Jack had brought along. Some names had double question marks beside them. Some marks had been scribbled out, then replaced. It was all a mess on the page, but there weren't too many sensible possibilities. In the end, it wasn't too hard finalizing arrangements with Roxanne. One more time, they discussed each individual, taking particular abilities into account. Each of the groups responsible for exploration needed strong scientific and technical expertise and all three groups needed obvious leaders.

With some reluctance, they settled on Laurel to lead the group at the base, supported by Hashemi and Mark. It was a pity that she couldn't go with Kong, but Jack and Roxanne both needed to be in that team, since they had equal authority for Kong's handling. Jack wanted Laurel back here. She and Mark had scientific expertise that would be valuable in the exploring teams, but Jack needed people with scientific knowledge and seniority to stay at camp and make decisions. Mark's skills would become more and more valuable as the venture continued, but he was clearly not in shape enough for a long hike in steaming jungle with a heavy backpack—not everyone had the right fitness and experience for that.

Jack made sure that Mark and Laurel would have backup from other Denham Products staff whom they could trust, including Gibson, Mitchell, and Díaz. With Roxanne's agreement, he assigned O'Connor, one of the two big Canadians, to the base group, plus one cameraman to cover any events of note.

The rest of it then fell into place. Jack and Roxanne would go with Kong. They added Christine Archer to their group, which gave them even more experience with handling Kong. Penelope also had to be included to direct the most dramatic footage from the expedition: any last farewell to Kong would be a highlight of the movie she was making. They chose one of her cameramen who had not gone with them the previous day, using Jagat Lal to strengthen the experience of the second exploring team.

The other team would have no responsibility for Kong and could concentrate entirely on scientific observations and cataloguing. Jack and Roxanne assigned that team most of their scientists and technicians, with Sanderson nominally in charge.

It was then a matter of ensuring that both exploring teams were adequately supported by seamen with guns, muscle power, and practical experience from previous scientific expeditions. Roxanne made perfectly sensible suggestions about the balance of the teams, and Jack found that he couldn't fault her judgment and efficiency in a task like this. He was coming to wonder why he'd disliked her so much when they first met, but then he reminded himself of the simple reason: She had treated him like scum.

It seemed that they'd both moved a long way since, and not just geographically.

"This isn't so hard, is it?" he asked, looking up from his notes.

She looked at him intently and said in a cold voice, "What do you mean?"

Slightly flummoxed by her tone, he said, "We've been working well together." Or maybe, he thought, he'd only imagined that. He'd expected a more sympathetic reply.

There was a long, strained silence. "I must admit you've surprised me," Roxanne said at last.

"I've surprised *you*?"

"Jack," she said patiently, "I know you have your own way of seeing things, but look at it from my point of view. Everything I knew about you before we met told me that you were a cowboy...not much better than a thief."

"Well, no one's called me *that* to my face. Not even Charlton."

"I'm not *calling* you anything; I'm only telling you what I thought back then. You have to accept the fact that the blood sample you used to clone Kong was *stolen* from Charlton. I don't care how you got it or what justification you thought you had. Bottom line, Jack, you created Kong using stolen goods—and then you used some pretty sharp legal tactics when you were challenged."

"Well, that's not exactly how it seemed to me."

"Just look at things from someone else's point of view for a change," she said a bit more heatedly. "You had no right to Kong's DNA, but you got it on the black market—and then you managed to bluster through the problems that you'd caused. What was I supposed to think, that *you* were the good guy?"

Jack was speechless. Whoever the *good guy* was, if you wanted to look at the world in those simplistic terms, it damn sure wasn't Charlton Hemming.

"Was I supposed to kiss you when we met," she said, "and tell you that you're my hero?"

"I guess not," he said, getting angry. "I guess I just expected you to act professionally."

"No you didn't. What you expect from women isn't professionalism. You expect us to baby you...and fawn over you. Maybe even *flirt* with you, like your pal Maudie does. Hasn't it ever struck you, Jack, that you're a charming bastard who avoids serious relationships—but women spoil you to death? *I* wasn't in any mood to act like that when we met, but I defy you to tell me when I was ever unprofessional."

"All right," he said, truly angry now, "so that's how you feel."

"No!" She looked upset at the idea. "This is coming out all wrong—that's *not* what I'm trying to say. I'm not meaning to rub it in or to punish you. Look, maybe you're a nice guy for all that—in your own way. I've started to think you actually are, all right? And maybe Charlton is a jerk, or even worse." She stopped as if she'd wanted to say more about that, but then thought better of it. "Whatever. Maybe this, maybe that. The fact is...*your* professional ethics back then left a lot to be desired."

"I see." He placed the scribbled pad on the log beside him and folded his arms.

"How else could anyone objective see it? And it's not just Charlton who was hurt by what you did. What about *my* work, Jack?"

"Well, you and Charlton, and lots of the others, might be better off in the end."

"Because you gave us the location of this island?"

"That's what I meant, yes."

"Jack..." Roxanne gave a long, frustrated sigh. "Maybe we *are*, maybe we aren't, but making us better off wasn't exactly what you had in mind when you used material that you'd stolen—or purchased from someone who'd stolen it, or from someone they'd sold it on to, or whatever exactly you did." She shook her head. "As if it makes any difference."

"You should blame Charlton for alienating his employees. I bought what was there to buy, and I probably wasn't the only one."

"Well, from where I sit, I think you're lucky that you had something else to give Charlton in your negotiations." The heat had gone out of her voice, replaced now by a colder form of anger. "If you'd had less to bargain with, you'd now be in a helluva mess—and you'd *deserve* it." She took a long breath, then said more gently, "Anyway, that's all in the past."

"You've really been bottling this up, haven't you?"

"It was waiting to come out," she said with the hint of a smile. "I've wanted to tell you what I thought of you, to put you in your place, ever since I met you. And I've kept wanting to do it, even when I started to see more in you than that. In fact, that made it even more important." The smile became slightly more than a hint. "You've surprised me since we've been working together. I've been amazed at how professional you can actually be."

Jack's anger had already passed, but he felt deflated by the conversation. At first, he'd written off Roxanne as a hard-nosed, interfering bitch who didn't deserve the time of day, just another heartless scientific mercenary whom Hemming had stretched out an arm for and hired with the aid of his fat checkbook. But now her good opinion meant a great deal to him. Perhaps it was the isolation from the rest of the world, but this particular heartless mercenary suddenly struck Jack as one of the most wonderful people he'd ever met.

"I don't think I could explain my motives to you," he said. "If you'd lived my whole life from childhood until now, it would all make sense. But you'd have to had to grow up as a little kid with my granddad and all his stories about Kong…and about this island. Maybe if you'd gone through all that, we could talk about it on the same wavelength. Otherwise, I don't even know where to start."

She placed a hand on his knee, her dark skin contrasting with the khaki of his hiking shorts and his own much lighter skin tone. "I've been through a few bad experiences myself, Jack. Surely you don't think I've had life easy? But you can't let any personal experience override your sense of ethics."

"You still don't understand," he explained. "There's no question here of *overriding*. Every ethical bone in my body says that Kong was meant for me."

"So you say, and I've gone along with that in public—"

"Well, true."

"Yes, but I could never do what you did. It wouldn't matter what it meant to me personally—"

"It's not the same thing," he said, almost pleading with her. "I wish I could make you understand. There's so much experience that we don't share—"

She laughed kindly. "Please listen to me, Jack. You're missing the point."

"Which is?"

"The point is, I know that you're not a bad person...even if you *have* been spoiled in every way, and even if you made one bad call. At some level, I guess I always hoped that, but I couldn't believe it."

"Of course I'm not a bad person," he said, disgusted at the very thought.

"There's no *of course* about it. Where would science be if we all went around saying 'of course'? Anyway, it's forgiven and forgotten. We can disagree about that one thing. The point is, I've seen in all the time I've worked with you that you're still a good man and a good scientist. Is that enough? Can we get along on that basis?"

"I'm not a cowboy, after all?"

"Oh, you're still a cowboy. I thought I made that clear."

"What?"

She grinned at him frankly. "Look, are we going to be friends or not?"

Her hand was still on his knee and he put his own hand over it, feeling her warmth. "Come on," he said, grinning back at her, "we'd better tell the others their fates."

TWENTY

In Sri Lanka, Hemming slept the sleep of the just and innocent, and didn't wake until mid-morning. After a light room-service brunch, he sent some e-mails to his office in San Francisco, then called Falconie's room. "Falcon? Meet me downstairs."

In the heat and glare of the early afternoon they drove to Bionimals' new facility thirty miles outside the city. They passed jigsaw countryside—old farms with pigs and chickens alternating with square, colored-glass buildings flanked by manicured lawns.

Long before he'd settled his dispute with Denham, Hemming had seen how events would play out. CenCo had created a new company, Island Properties, to work with Bionimals on Skull Island–related issues. The new company was under Hemming's direct control. Once he'd had some idea of Skull Island's location, he'd moved quickly and acquired most of a foreign university's technology park here in Sri Lanka. It was good property that he'd snapped up at a bargain rate.

This was the first time Hemming had visited it in person. At its driveway entrance was an unobtrusive metal sign: ISLAND PROPERTIES PARK. Beyond was a cluster of low-rise buildings in a mix of local and Western architecture. Stark walls of ice-blue glass were relieved by murals depicting traditional images—

Hindu gods, stylized Indian elephants—and splashed by green palm fronds.

Falconie parked next to the first building in a space marked "CEO," then led Hemming to the door. They took an elevator to the second floor. Through a set of glass doors they came to a low-ceilinged waiting room, where a tiny Asian receptionist dressed in a white, short-sleeved uniform sat behind the desk. Huge ferns dominated the room, spraying out from high-glaze ceramic planters. "This is Mr. Hemming," Falconie said to the receptionist.

"I am very glad to meet you, sir," she said. "Please go straight through."

An opaque glass door slid open and they walked along a short hallway, past some closed wooden doors, to a bright office where Dr. Ramon Valdez was waiting for them. Through its floor-to-ceiling tinted windows, the office looked out over the facility's spacious grounds. Here they had animal enclosures, laboratory buildings, living quarters for the local staff, and even an aircraft hangar.

"Mr. Hemming!" Valdez said enthusiastically, offering his hand. "I'm glad you've arrived."

"Please," Hemming said, taking his hand with practiced bonhomie, "call me *Charlton*."

"Okay," Valdez said with a slightly nervous laugh. "I'll soon get used to it."

"You settling in then, Ramon? I hope that everything's just as you were hoping."

Valdez was a short, wiry man with a mop of dark hair. He'd made his name at Harvard, then working for In-Dreams Biotech in San Diego. Hemming had paid him well to move to CenCo as his personal science advisor and his local administrator for the Skull

Island project. From now on he'd be working between Skull Island, Sri Lanka, and San Francisco, reporting to Hemming directly. He smiled, eager to please. "I've been here for five days now," he said. "I couldn't be happier with all the facilities or the local staff we've hired."

"If there's anything else you need, just let me know. Anything at all. Don't worry about bothering me or about the expense. Whatever it takes to make the project work, tell me and you've got it."

"Please, Charlton, sit down," Valdez said, pointing to a set of low chairs. "You too, Mr. Falconie. Really, we have everything I could ever need. I'm going to like working with you."

Do this right, Hemming thought, *and I can make you very rich. Do it wrong, and you'll wish you'd never heard of me.* Making himself comfortable, he said, "When can you fly out to Skull Island?"

"We're almost ready...Charlton. I need another day, maybe two at the most."

Hemming exchanged glances with Falconie. "You happy with that, Falcon? All the equipment's what you wanted?"

"It's just what I ordered," Falconie said, "and we checked the Super-Osprey yesterday before I met you at the airport. It's ready to go. Give me two days to make sure everything else is working right."

"Take the time you need," Hemming said. "But do it right." He looked Falconie in the eye. "Understood?"

"Understood."

"My old friend Jack is going to get a big surprise when you two call in on Skull Island. You and your team."

"We'll ruin his party," Valdez said. "Poor old Jack!"

More than you know, Hemming thought. Coming to work for CenCo on short notice, Valdez clearly had an eye for the main chance—but he was a scientist, not a killer. Dealing out death was very much in Falconie's domain. He was a professional who'd done more than his share of crimes but never been charged with anything. Once they were on the island, he'd make sure that good old Jack Denham had a very *permanent* accident. *Soon, my dearest Jack, you're going to wake up dead.*

The first thing to do was to break the news to Laurel that they wanted to leave her out of the exploring teams and assign her to take command at the base. At first she protested, but Jack placated her as best he could. "You and Mark have an important job here and there'll be plenty more time for you to explore the island. Besides, there's another reason."

"Yes?"

"Roxanne and I both have to go with Kong. Only one other person knows him as well as Roxanne—and that's you. If anything happens to Roxanne and there are still decisions to make about Kong...well, you're the only one who can really advise me. If it comes to that, you can take over if something happens to *me.*"

"Which means," Roxanne added gently, "that you'll soon have to say goodbye to Kong."

Laurel nodded slowly and there were tears in her eyes. She'd doubtless worked all that out already. "I know," she said. "Please take care of him."

That done, Jack and Roxanne organized the teams to leave next day, assigning each person on the island to their own team, Sanderson's, or Laurel's. They

spent the afternoon making short reconnaissance
flights in the Jayhawk, checking their maps for accur-
acy. From the air Jack could see little of the island's
wildlife beneath the jungle canopy—but Carl Denham's old map was accurate enough. There was the
volcanic mountain and *there* the lake where the
explorers had been ambushed by a fiercely territorial
apatosaur, back in '33.

The lake gave Jack his first glimpse of the richness
of the island's ecology. As the chopper went lower to
observe, several kinds of huge, long-billed birds flew
in lazy circles over the water. Far out from the shore
in the deeper part of the lake, near-submerged reptiles
swam, some of them extruding long, snaky necks,
while others displayed little more than nostrils, like
crocodiles cruising patiently for prey. In the shallows
at the water's edge waded an entire herd of giant
reptiles, munching on soft marsh plants. They
resembled Mesozoic hadrosaurs—duckbilled herbivorous dinosaurs that might well have been prey for
allosaurs or T. rex back in the Jurassic and Cretaceous
periods. Seen from the chopper, the true size of these
evolved, mutated hadrosaurs was not fully apparent—there were not enough clear points of comparison—but the largest of them might have been fifty
feet from bill to tail.

As he returned to camp Jack knew that he'd see far
more in the morning.

In the last hours of daylight, he joined up with
Sanderson to lead the newbies to the island on a brief
tour behind the stone wall and its wooden gate. This
was almost an anti-climax. The largest creatures they
saw at first were the giant insects and centipedes, then
some kind of greenish creature crossed their path—a

reptile or amphibian four feet long. Its head and body had a froglike look, but it moved on four splayed legs like a lizard. Whatever it was, Jack never got a good look for it dashed across their path into tall grass and bushes—and just kept going. Nothing here showed fear of them, but nor did the creatures show great interest—all of which was fine with Jack. He liked the idea that nothing on the island had evolved to consider humans its natural prey.

When they returned to the camp that was enough for one day. After dusk they compared notes and stories, with much faltering and shaking of heads as they tried to describe what they'd seen and felt. Jack retired early, exhausted from the day's work and his poor night's sleep the previous night. He fell asleep quickly in his tent, but not for long. At about midnight he woke up, suddenly alert, from a bad dream about the creatures of the island. In his dream, Hemming had come here and started to take things over.

Jack rolled onto his side and tried to forget the dream, but now his mind was racing with plans, contingencies, worries, issues, and doubts. Everything troubled him at once. Kong. Hemming. The expedition. Roxanne. For another hour, he lay awake in the pitch dark, listening to occasional noises from the jungle, wishing that he could shut down again and just go back to sleep. There was so much to do in the morning—but try telling his poor, over-stressed brain that! Worse, every minor ache from the day's work decided to become a painful cramp.

Finally giving up on sleep, he fumbled for his hiking boots, pulled them on without lacing them, and went out into the starless night to the night to check on

Kong. A gentle, surprisingly cool breeze blew from the sea.

Kong had made himself a nest of palm fronds, down near the shoreline. He lay there peacefully while Laurel sat cross-legged on the sand nearby, dressed in a pair of loose shorts and a long T-shirt. She watched silently over Kong's huge, sleeping form. She had a Winchester rifle braced against her thigh, just in case; she held it steady with one of her small hands. A few of the seamen stood around with rifles and lamps, taking their turn at watch. There was little that Jack could say to any of them. The grandeur of what they were going through exceeded any words he might find—though he was sure that Roxanne would have thought of something memorable.

He nodded to Laurel as he stepped over to her to give her shoulder a reassuring squeeze. "Thanks for everything you've done," he said. "Don't stay up all night."

She looked up sadly at him. "I know, Jack. I will get some sleep."

"Just make sure you *do* sleep. You've still got an important job."

"It's okay."

He knelt beside her and watched over Kong for another hour, or maybe two—he soon lost track of time. Eventually he began to yawn and returned to his tent. Even then, he tossed and turned—but at some point he must have drifted off, for when he next checked his watch it was his usual waking time: just shy of 6:00 A.M.

God, he needed some coffee.

Come on, Jack, he told himself. *Time to face another day.*

One of the biggest of his life.

TWENTY-ONE

Sanderson's team left first, with instructions to head north and east until they reached the farthest tip of the island, then head roughly west, eventually tracking around the whole perimeter. That would require two nights away from their base, maybe even three. Jack's team would start out on a similar route, but then head back across the middle of the island toward Skull Mountain, which was somewhat off-center, near the northwest corner. Again, they planned on taking two, possibly three, nights for the round trip. And both teams would avoid waterways, with their hidden dangers.

Laurel was in tears as she said farewell to Kong, and the gorilla seemed confused as Roxanne coaxed him up the steps to the stone wall and its high wooden gates. As he stood at the top of the steps, Jack wondered again what culture had built this. Surely this wall must have been thousands of years old. If the builders had been an African people, that fit with the unavoidable conclusion that gorillas had been imported here by human beings. Laurel had suggested that it was for a ritual purpose, and that was the best theory they had, but so much was unexplained about that lost civilization.

The natives of the island—descended, perhaps, from those who'd built the wall—had vanished. There was no one else to communicate with about it. Archaeological digs might find evidence, but that would have to wait until long in the future.

"Kong!" Roxanne shouted, as if calling her family's dog. "Come on! We're taking you home." She stepped through the gap between the wooden gates.

The ape sniffed around curiously, almost as if he could detect signs of the bloody battle that had taken place here three quarters of a century ago between the donor of his genes and the humans who'd caused the first Kong such frustration. Whatever he could smell, he followed it through the gates, where Roxanne and some of the others had gone on ahead.

This party was slightly larger than the one that had begun exploration the previous day. Its final makeup was Jack, Roxanne, Archer, Penelope, and one of her cameramen, Swain plus nine seamen from the *Tropical Explorer*, including Kowalski, who'd co-piloted the Jayhawk to land Kong here on the island. It added up to fourteen humans and one giant gorilla.

Jack and Roxanne carried dart guns and tranquilizer doses big enough to take down creatures weighing several tons. Except for Penelope and Swain, the rest carried hunting rifles—from Winchester Magnums that could stop a charging elephant to lighter weapons for shooting small birds and mammals. Their packs were heavy with supplies: clean water from the ship, compasses, calculators, flashlights, and binoculars; a mobile radio; plenty of preserved food; tents and ground sheets; biological, medical, and first-aid basics; insect repellent; and enough ammunition to support a small-scale revolution.

Once Kong was through the gate, Jack caught up with the rest of the group. As they stepped out into the unknown on the other side of the wall, rifles at the ready, he felt as if he were leading a military unit, not a scientific expedition. But much as he hated the thought of harming the island's ecology, he had no intention of being eaten alive by any of its creatures.

Jack took the lead, his dart rifle at the ready, while Roxanne followed immediately behind him, then Christine Archer, carrying a lightweight rifle. With a strong squad of crewmen from the ship as their rear guard, they followed the same path that Jack had taken the day before. Kong now bounded ahead, bending trees out of the way with his massive body. Now and then he doubled back to rejoin them, almost like part of the team. Every few hundred yards or so, he froze in his tracks for half a minute—looking about with apparent wonder or sniffing at the ground and the foliage.

Soon they passed the point where Jack's original group had stopped the first time they'd explored beyond the ancient stone wall. They found a narrower path that avoided the huge spider web. Jack took slow, deliberate steps in the sticky equatorial heat. Too much effort and he'd soon be exhausted. He kept his eyes sharply focused on the path ahead.

By now, they were getting deep into heavily shadowed rainforest. No large animals appeared, but there were the constant sounds of birds singing, chirping, and squawking. Behind the bird songs, the droning of insects made a uniform wall of sound. Occasionally a parrot or a macaw flew across the explorers' path with a sudden flash of bright color. Despite all the insect repellent that Jack and his team had brought, several kinds of flies swarmed around—and sometimes much larger insects. More giant centipedes scuttled on the jungle floor, some even larger than the ones they'd previously seen. At one point, a huge dragonfly floated around their heads, its shimmering three-foot wings like translucent sails. It left them after five minutes when it didn't find whatever it was after.

Camouflaged insects—green and brown—sat on the trunks and branches of trees, almost invisible until you approached them. Some of these were more the size of house cats or animated monkey wrenches than of regular beetles, bugs, and mantids. Now and then, Jack heard roars or shrieks up ahead, or behind them, and he tensed at those louder noises, spinning round quickly with his dart rifle at the ready. Kong had gotten used to the jungle sounds. He seldom answered with more than a low, threatening growl. So far, nothing caused them any serious problems.

Kong discovered a species of fruit something like a mango but bigger than the biggest watermelon. It grew on a kind of tree that Jack had never seen before. These trees were twenty or thirty feet high, but Kong easily stretched out to pick the ripest "mangos." In the ape's giant hand, the huge, juicy fruits looked no bigger than cucumbers, and he devoured them with the hunger of a starving man. Jack thought of stopping him until they could check a fruit sample for toxins, but of course that was just what they could *not* do forever. They wouldn't be able to nursemaid the Kong once they'd left him on the island. For better or worse, he would have to adapt.

For the first hour or two, the walk seemed quite easy, despite the heat, the humidity, the insects, and the weight of their packs. Perhaps they'd just been unlucky the previous day in encountering that giant carnosaur, but Jack was conscious that the very same specimen could not be far away: surely the island's various predators must range within definable territories. And then there were the shrieks and roars that they'd often heard in the distance, sounds that suggested the force of powerful lungs. If those cries had come from carnivores, they must be huge and dangerous.

The foliage thinned out and they came in sight of the lake. Yesterday, Jack had seen his first herd of the island's megafauna—but that had been from the safety of a helicopter. Seeing *en masse*, and at ground level, the lake provided an awesome experience. A huge herd of giant gaurs—cows, calves, and a scattering of massive bulls—had gathered near the water's edge, some of them drinking, some frolicking in the shallows, some keeping lookout, gazing uneasily back into the jungle or across the water, sniffing at the air. There must have been hundreds of the ponderous beasts—perhaps a thousand tons of meat on the hoof. Kong stopped in his tracks to watch them closely but not getting too near.

Jack waved back the human members of his team. Disturbing a herd of huge animals like this could well be a bad move. If they got the bulls angry, it might be the last thing they ever did. Not only that, it was best to keep away in case so many tons of prime beef attracted predators. Jack had no intention of getting in any arguments with one those giant, mutated allosaurs, not if he could avoid it.

But this was at least a time to stop, put down their packs for a few minutes, and take some documentary footage. Birds flew over the water, ignoring the gaur herd, occasionally squawking. They ranged in color from creamy white to a gray that was almost like charcoal. Some were no bigger than swans or herons, but others were more the size of a Piper Cub. Now and then, one dove for fish, breaking the surface of the lake water and coming up with something silver and wriggling. The large hadrosaur herd that Jack had seen from the chopper had either dispersed or moved on to other feeding grounds, but a much smaller group of the duckbilled dinosaurs waded near the shore—just half a dozen of them, paying no attention to the gaurs. Their scaly hide was the same muddy green as a crocodile's, though these creatures were strict vegetarians.

Then, as Jack gaped at the sight, a stegosaur the size of a steam locomotive shuffled out of the jungle no more than a hundred yards ahead. It made its way slowly down to the water as the herd of gaurs parted to let it through, then closed ranks behind it. Some of its bony plates, in two rows along its spine and down its tail, must have been ten feet long. The end of its tail was equipped with murderous curved spikes, like long spears of bone.

"Oh my God," Roxanne said at Jack's side. "Who would have believed that it could be like this?"

"I did," Jack whispered, as the huge dinosaur took its position at the water's edge. It lowered its head to drink unhurriedly, master of its domain—at least until one of those gigantic carnosaurs might turn up.

Jack tried to imagine a fight between two such beasts, if the carnosaur decided that the stegosaur was food. Come to think of it, that actually seemed unlikely with all this mammalian meat to choose from. Except out of desperation, why would any carnivore bother picking on a creature so large and well-equipped for battle? If there were more herds of hadrosaurs and gaurs, the whole island must be like a huge, easy food larder for its top predators.

"You know, Roxanne," Jack said, "I always believed Granddad and the others. I knew that they wouldn't lie about what they'd seen here. But all the same..."

"What?"

He shook his head, not exactly surprised—but still *amazed*. "I believed it was all here, but I guess I never understood what it really meant, that it could be like *this*."

Kong sat back on his haunches, apparently just as fascinated as the humans. He was almost still, just waving away the flying insects that came to investigate him.

"Can we have some reactions from you both?" Penelope said to Jack and Roxanne. "Tell us what you're thinking as you see this incredible sight."

"What can I say?" Jack said, glancing at her over his shoulder. "*Incredible* it is."

"Could you face the camera please, Jack?"

"Oh, sure." He followed Penelope's instructions, while trying to think of something suitably uplifting to say for posterity. Swain angled the movie camera in his direction. "It's seventy-five-odd years," Jack said, "since outsiders last visited this island and saw anything like what we're now seeing. Speaking for myself, I feel very privileged."

"Dr. Blaine?"

Roxanne turned from the water, letting it provide her with a sensational backdrop, and fell into her practiced posture for the camera. "Speaking personally, this is one of the supreme moments of my life."

Swain stepped toward her as she spoke. "Right now," Roxanne continued, "I can only watch in awe at nature's marvels." She made a sweeping movement with one arm. "We came here with a scientific mission, but this moment feels as if it even transcends the aims of science. We're seeing a side of nature that defies the mind and the senses. This place is a window into the depths of time." That said, she returned to watching the stegosaur, which had evidently drunk its fill. It slowly walked back to the jungle, the herd of gaurs once again parting without a fuss as if this sequence had been rehearsed a thousand times.

"Thank you both, dears," Penelope said. "That will be just fabulous."

According to the map, this lake was their cue to skirt directly east, or as close to it as they could manage. Water stretched in that direction as far as the eye could see, though the shoreline was obscured by trees and outcroppings of rock. They'd want to keep away from the lake as much as possible to avoid confrontations with its megafauna, but it was a handy landmark if they ever needed it, as well as an inexhaustible source of wonders. Jack struggled once more into the straps of his heavy pack. "That's enough rest for now, folks," he said. "We'd better move on."

As they worked eastward by the compass, they headed at an angle that took them gradually away from the water and back into the tropical forest. The emerald vegetation soon became thicker than ever, but whatever large animals had criss-crossed the jungle in their travels—whether the gaur herds, the mutated Jurassic dinosaurs, or something Jack couldn't even imagine—had trodden paths that were sufficiently wide for humans to proceed with no great trouble.

The paths were wide enough even for Kong's four-ton bulk.

All the lower tiers of vegetation—palms, tree ferns, and the many plants that Jack could not quite recognize—grew around the lords of this forest. These were massive hardwoods with buttressed trunks ten or twenty feet across. Their upper branches merged to form a green canopy nearly two hundred feet overhead. The very tallest trees, the giant emergents, rose through the canopy, their trunks like bare wooden towers. Whatever branches they had began somewhere out of sight, up above the canopy. Deep in the forest, away from the sea and the lake, the canopy and lower vegetation filtered out most of the sun.

Down here, so far below the forest canopy, Jack felt like a pygmy—dwarfed by the trees, by Kong's immensity, and even by the breadth of the path that had obviously been cleared by the movements of giant creatures. Branches and vines sometimes tangled in front of him—but there was plenty of room to duck under these or shove them aside. Now and then as he ran on ahead, Kong broke through overhanging branches or tore away dangling vines.

Then, as they descended a slope that led to a ditch of shallow muddy water, Kong brushed against a tangle of lime-green vines with two-inch-long thorns that formed a wall along the left side of the well-trampled path. The vines unraveled with astonishing speed, sending out separate tendrils that snaked into the gorilla's fur like the tentacles of an octopus. Kong roared with pain and anger. He jerked back, yanking at the vines as more of them stretched out to encircle him. Some tendrils snapped as the four-ton gorilla pulled away. Others came loose from him, but ripped off fur and pieces of flesh. Soon Kong was free, but he ran on ahead for fifty yards as if in a panic, like a dog with a burning tail.

He stopped suddenly and spun around to face Jack and the others, roaring and roaring in distress. It was like an accusation.

"Come back, Kong," Roxanne said, gesturing to him. "Come back. Everything's good."

Kong roared again. Who could blame him? That sentient killer vine was like nothing Jack had ever seen or heard of. Even Granddad hadn't encountered anything like that in his brief time on the island—or he hadn't thought to mention it. The place evidently had even more dangers than they could have guessed. Kong had just discovered one of them.

Roxanne kept soothing the giant ape and he finally calmed down, but didn't return to them past the killer vine. The group of humans passed through there carefully, keeping close to the right hand side of the path, well away from the vine. Jack glanced nervously all about, hoping there was nothing just as dangerous on the side they'd chosen—that this was not like passing through the gap between Scylla and Charybdis, those monsters of ancient mythology. Nothing else bothered them, but Jack gulped as he saw the collection of old bones, giant insect husks, and half-rotted reptilian creatures entangled in the lower parts of the killer vine.

That could easily have been some of us.

After four hours of walking, with several short stops to rest and recover, they encountered more large animals. At a small stream, narrow and shallow enough to step across on logs and stones, a group of hadrosaurs gazed up at them from the other side.

These looked harmless enough, but you could never be sure. They were a smaller species than Jack and his team had seen back at the lake—though the largest was as big as an Indian elephant. These saurians were a brighter green and they had elaborate bony crests, almost like spiral shells. There were three of them, one adult and two smaller reptiles. *A mother and her kids?* Jack wondered.

He leveled his dart rifle in case of attack, but after a moment's curious staring the hadrosaurs ignored them. They drank some water from the stream then wandered off with a four-legged gait into the depths of the jungle, their long, muscular tails held straight back behind them. The encounter was eerie, as if they'd just met life forms from another planet.

Kong bounded across the stream, stopping on the other side for a long drink. Jack crossed with greater difficulty, balancing on slippery stones while still carrying all his heavy gear. When they'd all reached the other side they needed a well-earned break. Their watches showed it was already well past noon, though you could never have been sure otherwise in this steamy jungle, whose foliage blocked the sky. Time to stop for lunch. This terrain was exhausting even for experienced hikers; if they pushed themselves too hard, they'd stiffen up too much to function in the morning.

For their lunch break, they chose a wide, safe-looking section of the path where a couple of old logs provided easy seating. They took their time to eat a meal of canned meat, dried fruits, energy bars, and oatmeal cookies. As well as water canteens, they'd brought powdered electrolyte drinks and small plastic tumblers to drink from. They'd all been eating well on the ship, which they'd restocked when they had stopped for four nights in Indonesia. No one was likely to starve from a few days on this diet.

When they started walking again, as refreshed as possible considering the circumstances, Kong ran on ahead as had become his habit. After they'd gone another mile or so, he suddenly stopped at the edge of a clearing. As the humans caught up, the gorilla looked back over his shoulder as if needing reassurance. He sniffed the air all round, then took two steps forward. Jack signaled the others to stop. He switched the safety of his dart rifle to the "off" position as he checked the jungle all around, watching for any movement in the trees, listening for any threat. As if in answer, a harsh sound, almost like tearing metal, came from just ahead of Kong through the thinned-out foliage.

Jack took one deliberate step. Then another. And another. He moved as stealthily as he could in his heavy boots. The rest of the group followed just as cautiously—until they'd caught up with Kong and could see what had troubled him.

"Oh my God!" he heard Archer say. "Would you look at that!"

Lying in the clearing was the broken, half-eaten carcass of a huge crocodilian animal, perhaps fifty feet in length. Something had torn its limbs away and peeled long strips of meat from its bones. Two evil-looking birds, creatures as shiny-black as crows or ravens, and similarly shaped, but bigger than ostriches now fed upon it. One of them seemed to defy Jack, staring him straight in the eye. Its beak opened wide, and it made that harsh, metallic sound again—it was actually a deep-throated, arrogant cawing.

Well, Jack thought, he was not going to be daunted by these scavengers. He stepped past Kong, moving crabwise around the clearing to avoid the birds. He targeted his dart rifle at the one on his right. With so many guns aimed at them, the birds were surely not a threat. Jack glanced behind to see that everyone was following in good order, that no one had taken fright. Swain busied himself shooting movie footage, making sure-footed catlike movements, even while concentrating on what he was filming. Most of the others had their fingers on the triggers of their rifles as they picked their way carefully past the giant scavenger birds. The birds themselves held their positions. They watched without fear, but made no move to attack. After a minute or two, they resumed their scavenging as if the puny humans were beneath their notice and even Kong was not a threat to them.

Kong suddenly rushed ahead through the center of the clearing, apparently having decided that the giant scavenger ravens were harmless. They looked up as his tons of muscle and fur blurred past, but made no other movement.

"Wait," Roxanne said. They had reached the end of the fifty-foot reptile's tail, well away from the closest of the carrion-eaters. Roxanne stepped over to the tail, and crouched down. "Cover me with your rifles."

Jack saw what she was doing. She lowered her own dart rifle carefully, shrugged off her backpack, and took out a small metal box containing biological apparatus. She had cutting instruments, hypodermic needles, and thin glass test tubes. She was going to take a tissue sample. As she worked with deft, efficient movements, Jack wondered whether she really hoped to clone a monster like this when they returned to New York City. Though they'd considered cloning some specimens from small samples of tissue, a monster on this scale was never what Jack had in mind. But then again, just studying its DNA was bound to be scientifically important.

At some point, he realized, they should start sampling everything they saw.

In a few minutes Roxanne was finished and they began walking again. None of the birds had attacked. They left the clearing behind and the jungle became thicker and darker. After another hour, a compass check and some calculations showed that it was time to turn more sharply north, then west, hoping to catch a glimpse of Skull Mountain. By this time, they should be east of the lake, and they could track its shoreline as they moved north. They could get no real view of the mountain from here, but Jack was sure he was right about their location and the ground was sloping upward in a roughly northward direction. They'd done enough for one day.

Gorillas were newcomers to the island, their lineage dating back mere thousands of years—no more than an eyeblink in geological time. But in that eyeblink, they had mutated and evolved to compete with the great reptilian beasts from the Jurassic Period that dominated the island. Over generations they had grown. And grown.

Nothing dared invade their colonies. When banded together, the giant gorillas had no natural enemies—they were invulnerable to predators. They encountered trouble only when they roamed alone, or in groups of two or three, searching for fruit to feed their huge stomachs. Even then they were seldom attacked. The largest males were a match for the island's thundering carnosaurs, themselves the product of evolution over millions of years since the Age of Reptiles. Even the vicious packs of raptors that terrorized Skull Island's other creatures seldom took gorilla prey. The giant apes had grown too strong for that to happen.

Over the centuries they'd established their own spaces: huge nesting places where dozens of gorillas might sleep in a single colony; wide paths where they traveled and foraged; many kinds of places that were special to individuals; healthy fruit trees that made larders for the colonies. Each nesting space was an area on the forest floor that had been shaped by a gorilla colony over countless years. Here where the gorillas made their homes, giant trees still rose and the green canopy of branches arched over all. But the busy apes had thinned out the lowest layers of jungle, leaving only grasses and a few much-prized fruit trees. In these vast shared spaces, gorilla dynasties formed and gorilla politics played out as the adult males competed for dominance. Males and females mated, young were born and grew to maturity—and the cycle renewed itself.

Beneath the muted sunshine of one such nesting area, two giant males confronted each other. Females, youngsters, and smaller adult males watched tensely, for the outcome of such battles affected them all. The two giants reared up in display; they were well over twenty feet tall on their hind legs. They roared and snarled, showing off their powerful lungs and huge, strong teeth. Neither male backed away. They slapped with open palms at their massively muscled chests, each asserting dominance over the other—with neither willing to yield. Like wary human combatants, they circled each other, moving now on hind feet and foreknuckles, each looking for signs of weakness. As yet, neither would submit. Where dominance was concerned, too much was at stake to give it up lightly.

The two giant apes became more angry and desperate. They circled more rapidly, still not coming to grips. Such battles were largely ceremonial—usually one gorilla would back down after merely symbolic violence. But these two were quite evenly matched and neither would concede to the other without a test of strength. They snarled again, then both reared up once more to display their full size. The thick fur on their backs bristled as each tried to outstare and intimidate the other. One roared and slapped its chest, then the other followed suit. Both dropped back to all fours, still angry, their rivalry unresolved.

They charged, hitting together with a thunderous impact. Like sumo wrestlers, they gripped, shook, pushed each other; they tried to get closer to inflict bites. They had now gone far beyond ceremony and intimidation. Until one showed submission, they would treat this battle as a fight to the death. Now and then, a giant gorilla did die in the never-ending struggles for dominance within the colony. Though they were not carnivorous, their powerful jaws and teeth could inflict fatal wounds.

The two apes shook each other, seeking advantage, and at last one proved more powerful, slowly pushing its opponent back inch by inch. In another second, the stronger gorilla exerted itself to the full and threw its rival to the ground. Eight and half tons of bone and muscle slammed against the earth. The fallen giant quickly regained its feet, reared up, and slapped its chest to show it was far from beaten—and the two huge animals came to grips once more.

For one whole minute they seemed equally matched, but the stronger gorilla slowly gained the upper hand. It forced its rival to the ground and tried to bite its throat. Knowing it was beaten, the weaker ape went limp. Every muscle relaxed as it ceased to struggle. Warily, the victor backed away. The fur on its back was still erect and it never stopped staring and snarling.

The beaten ape did nothing special to submit. It simply ignored its conqueror and showed sudden interest in a ripe fruit tree near by. On feet and foreknuckles, it romped over to the tree and reached out to pick one of the melon-sized fruit. Face was saved, but the outcome was clear to every gorilla in the colony. One giant male had prevailed and the other had been beaten. The winner of the battle reared up one more time; it roared at the canopy overhead and slapped its chest. Its point made, it loped over to the fruit tree to eat alongside its beaten rival. For now, the conflict was forgotten.

Order was restored and all was peaceful in the colony.

TWENTY-TWO

Even here, in the middle of a lost jungle hundreds of miles from nowhere, Jack's body clock seemed determined to get him up at dawn. He'd finally had a decent night's sleep, despite the trying circumstances, so he patted his hair back as much as he could, running a palmful of water through it. He reached for his dart rifle, strapped it around his body, and left the small tent that he shared with Kowalski.

Time to look around.

Further up the slope where they'd camped, Penelope and her cameraman, Swain, were doing a short early-morning watch—everyone had to take a turn in case of any dangers. Both of them carried hunting rifles now instead of their film equipment and looked every inch the experienced hikers that Jack knew them to be. The trouble was that no one was experienced with this ecosystem. It might harbor dangers that they still couldn't think of, even after the past two days. The killer vine was a case in point, something Jack had never considered. Before they'd stopped the previous day they'd passed another two tangles of that stuff—so it was prevalent enough on the island to be a real danger. Who knew what else might grow here, in an ecology that had followed its own bizarre evolutionary path?

To find a spot to camp, they'd avoided clearings that were covered with animal tracks. It would have been all too easy to be run over in the dark by gigantic creatures that might be totally herbivorous, but quite capable of crushing them as they pounded by. Eventually, they'd found a sparsely vegetated area of the jungle where the ground rose sharply. No sooner had they chosen this as their place to stop than a new factor had entered their calculations. Jack had looked up as some water fell on his face from the darkening sky. Even as he'd put his hand to his cheek to make sure what he'd felt, the rain had come harder. And harder still. Soon it had been a torrent, almost deafening in their tents. Any harder and Jack would have feared being swept away. As things were, it was just as well they'd chosen high ground.

He'd radioed Laurel to let her know they were all okay, then gone to sleep, leaving Archer and Kowalski to take the first watch in case of any dangers.

Hours later, in the early morning, the rain had ceased but the sky was still gloomy and the sloping ground outside the tents had turned to mud. Jack let the others sleep. Several of them had taken watches during the night and they all needed to be well-rested for today's long hike. Not that many yards away, farther down the slope, Kong lay on his side, snoring. Almost touchingly, he'd made no attempt to desert the security of the humans he'd grown used to. Perhaps he was still more comfortable with human company than with the strange lifeforms of the island.

"I bet you wonder where Laurel is," Jack said quietly, approaching him. "Things won't be the same for you, very soon."

"Talking to yourself now?" asked a familiar voice. Roxanne stepped out from behind a group of palm trees on the other side of Kong. She carried her dart rifle in one hand, pointing its barrel at the ground.

"You couldn't sleep?" Jack said.

"I slept the sleep of the just," she said. "But only for a few hours. I woke up some time ago, and it was like: *zing!* You know what I mean?"

"I know the feeling all too well!"

"It's too exciting to sleep. This is like a whole new world to explore. I think the excitement is going to kill me."

"That might not be a good choice of words."

She gave a half-suppressed laugh. "No, maybe not. Partly, I can't believe my luck. Not only am I here, I'm still alive to enjoy being here. After some of what we've seen, that's a bonus."

Jack picked his way over the muddy ground, edging his way past Kong to get closer to her. She held out her free hand to help as he contemplated jumping a deep, slippery-looking ditch. With his right hand, he braced the dart rifle against his chest. With his left, he took her hand—and kept holding it tightly when he'd made it over the ditch. "I didn't think we'd end up being friends," he said, choosing his words with special care. "Life works out strangely, doesn't it?"

"Doesn't it, Jack?"

She leaned closer to him and then they were suddenly kissing, the sweetest kiss he'd tasted in a *long* time. When their lips finally parted, he offered a thin, rueful smile. "I wish we'd worked this out a bit earlier."

Roxanne put her hand to his beard, scratching it gently, like someone petting a cat. She stroked the side of his neck with her fingertips—then his shoulders and chest. "You feel good," she said.

"I'm not a cowboy anymore?" he asked, still resenting that accusation.

"Didn't I tell you? I *like* cowboys. I just think they're bad news." She stepped back and looked at him quizzically. "I hope you're not bad news, Jack. Or *are* you?"

"If you can't work that out by now, you never will."

"That's true." With exaggerated movements, she checked him out—looked him up and down, peered at one side of his face then the other. "Well," she said at last, "the news looks good from here. Let's just say I've seen worse."

They kissed again but drew apart quickly. Nearby, Kong had snorted and twitched in his sleep. Jack looked around to see what was bothering him, but the only sign of animal life was a large, brightly colored bird flying overhead. That and a few tiny insects, like baby mosquitoes or gnats. Maybe the gorilla was simply having nightmares.

Whatever had disturbed him, Kong suddenly pushed himself up with his huge arms and it was like part of the hillside was moving—a mountain come alive. Even on all fours, he seemed to tower into the clouds. Once again, Jack felt pygmy-like. Kong roared, but relatively softly—it was almost like a monstrous yawn. He made no move to come any closer, but walked up the slope, sniffing around the little group of tents.

"That settles that," Jack said ruefully. "No one will sleep now."

"I was going to roll Christine out of my tent and take you to bed," Roxanne said with a smile. She made a hangdog expression. "I guess that'll have to wait."

"Don't worry, I'll be here waiting."

"Promise?"

"Yeah," he said. "I promise. I'll promise you anything you like."

"Anything at all?"

"As long as it's not about business."

"This isn't about business, Jack. It's about us. Tell me that you love me."

"Of course I do."

"*Promise me, Jack.*"

He put his hand on his heart. "Solemnly and sincerely."

Penelope and Swain filmed a few minutes of their breakfast, capturing some rueful comments about the mud, the rain, and the food. The latter could actually have been much worse, but it gave them all something to complain about.

Straight after breakfast, Jack radioed the base to find out if anything had happened. Laurel answered. "Lots of news," she said. "I heard from Sanderson's group after you called last night. They were also okay."

"All right," Jack said. "That's a relief."

"And they called again just now. Still okay, Jack. Taking lots of biological samples."

"That's great. Have we heard at all from Maudie…or from Hemming? I left a message for him the other night."

"Yes, Jack. Hemming called Captain McLeod, but did not want to talk."

"Didn't want to talk?"

"That's what the captain said. That is all, Jack. The only other thing is…it is very *wet* here. Rain, rain…"

"Here, too. Did it cause you any problems?"

"For sure it did, but nothing we could not handle."

"Uh-huh. All right, we'll be in touch now and then throughout the day."

He gave Laurel their estimated coordinates on the Skull Island maps that they used. There was no substitute for reporting positions frequently. The maps were valuable to the exploration parties as they navigated their way around the island, but also to the personnel at the base and back on the ship if a rescue operation was ever needed. The expedition had tracking equipment that could be used to home on a radio signal, but such devices were always fallible.

"Good luck, Jack," Laurel said. "You take care."

"Will do. Out for now."

Burdened by their packs, they hiked slowly in the direction of Skull Mountain, letting Kong sniff around or stop to eat, whenever he wanted. They took short breaks whenever anyone was tired. The packs were still heavy, even with some of the food eaten. With the tropical heat and with hordes of insects beleaguering them, there was no point in knocking themselves out.

After an hour they came to a huge fallen log from a tree that must have been almost twenty feet in diameter at the base. Its fall had made a clearing somewhat smaller than the one with the scavenger ravens they'd passed the previous day. Jack headed for one of the tree's thick branches, where it lay across the ground at an angle to the rotting trunk. He was glad to remove his pack and rest his tired feet.

Roxanne followed and sat beside him, taking off her pack but keeping her dart rifle handy. Kong sniffed around excitedly, like a dog that had found an emptied garbage can.

"You know where we are on the map?" Roxanne asked.

"I've got a good idea," Jack replied. "Do you want to work it out more accurately?"

"We really should…in a minute."

Jack opened his water canteen and took a swig, letting some of the water splash down his chest. "How are you, anyway?" he asked. There relationship had changed so much in the past two days. Now he felt solicitous about her where once he'd have liked to take her down a few pegs. "Are you okay?"

"I've walked in my share of jungles," she said with a grin. "This isn't much worse."

"I'm sure that's true," he said, returning her grin with one of his own.

Roxanne gulped down some water from her own canteen.

The rest of the group stood about or sat on other branches. Archer joked with the seamen, among whom she seemed to have found admirers. Penelope and Swain took film of the jungle all around, then some of Jack and Roxanne consulting together. "Look serious," Penelope said. "We don't want the movie-going public thinking that this was a picnic."

As Jack checked the map, a flock of small, bright birds erupted from the trees—straight in front of him. There was a sound that he had heard just once before, a rasping, sibilant noise as loud as a steam train. A huge, tooth-filled head appeared from the foliage then snaked forward. It was the same kind of carnosaur that they'd seen on the first day. Whether it was the same specimen, or another of the species, it rushed at them on its long, springy legs.

Jack stuffed the map away as shots went off all round. The monster staggered, turned ninety degrees, and lashed out with its tail. Archer cursed loudly. As the tail swung over his head like a huge club, Jack leaned forward to seize Roxanne and drag her down to safety. Kong must have been lashed by the muscular tail, for he answered the carnosaur with a roar of pain and anger.

Jack and Roxanne rolled on the ground. She'd had the presence of mind to keep hold of her dart rifle and she tried to get into position to fire. Someone else was quicker, firing off a heavy round from a hunting rifle. The round hit the carnosaur in between its arms, staggering it. But other people lay hurt—it had struck them with the first powerful tail sweep. Still others were rushing about looking for cover but it was surely too late for that. The monster lunged forward, roaring with pain and anger from the bullets its huge body had absorbed. It caught one man with a downward blow of its savagely clawed foot. A second later, it had snatched up Swain in its jaws. In another second, it had mauled him beyond recognition, dropping the lower part of him on the ground and swallowing the rest.

Kong ran back and forth as if in state of panic, neither fleeing into the jungle nor approaching the carnosaur. With the suddenness of a rattlesnake, the reptilian monster struck at him—but it had miscalculated the explosiveness of Kong's own movements. Kong reared up as tall as the giant reptile, though it might have been three times his mass. The gorilla moved in a flurry of fur and muscle, slapping and punching at the carnosaur's throat. Somehow, Kong got in under the carnosaur, forcing its head up, and tore at its throat with his teeth. The two gigantic creatures fought savagely, shaking each other almost faster than the eye could follow. The dinosaur snapped at Kong's body with its jaws and raked him with its clawed forelimbs, but Kong held on like a bull terrier.

Suddenly the carnosaur shook itself free and butted Kong.

Kong was hurt, whimpering in pain as he writhed on the ground. He tried to roll away from the monster as it came after him. For a moment, it seemed like the end for Kong—but the carnosaur was also hurt. It hesitated, shaking its head as it shrieked and hissed. Jack could now see how badly its throat was torn and bleeding from Kong's attack.

Roxanne had time to aim carefully. She squeezed the trigger of her dart rifle. As the recoil slammed her shoulder back, the dart plunged straight into the carnosaur's stomach. "That won't be enough," Roxanne said, trying to find another dart.

The monster uttered its terrifying hissing rasp and came toward them but Kong rushed into its path. He roared back at the mutated dinosaur as if challenging it to another round of battle. *Kong,* Jack thought, *you're going to get yourself killed.* Big Daddy Kong had once defeated something like this, but he'd been fully grown. It might be curtains for his "son." But then Kowalski fired a round from his Winchester Magnum, which took the carnosaur right behind its beady eye, caving in its skull. Others now fired shots from high-powered rifles and the huge reptile dropped forward suddenly, at Kong's feet. Jack found his pack and his own dart rifle, while Kowalski pumped one more round into the monster's skull, just to make sure.

Kong stood over his fallen enemy, slapping his chest in triumph. Christine Swain rushed over to him, craning her neck to try to see his injuries. Roxanne was just a second behind.

"How is he?" Jack called out.

"There are some claw wounds on his chest and shoulders," Swain said.

"Deep?"

"It's hard to tell," Roxanne said. "Maybe he'll be okay."

Both women backed away from Kong as he did a kind of victory dance. He jumped up and down and beat his hands against the earth.

Jack tried to take stock. At first sight, Kong wasn't that badly wounded. They all regrouped—or all who'd survived the attack. Of the living, Penelope seemed worst hurt—the carnosaur's tail had hit her hard on her right shoulder and upper back. "It's like someone slugged me there with a brick," she said. "I don't think I'll move that arm for days." Jack checked it out quickly—nothing seemed to be broken, and it wouldn't stop her walking, but she'd surely develop some dreadful purple bruises. Several others had been hit by the carnosaur's tail, but they'd all be okay.

Two men were dead, both from the first seconds of the carnosaur's attack. Swain had been half eaten. The other man's body was a sickening mess where the carnosaur's foot-long talons had opened him up. If not for Kong, that monster might have torn *most* of them apart before they could have taken it down.

All the sudden, Jack realized being on Skull Island was no fun anymore. The creatures here were dangerous beyond understanding. Nothing that big should have been able to move so fast—the human brain couldn't comprehend it. No modern terrestrial creature combined such enormous power with that kind of speed and ferocity.

This was no place for human beings to have come with nothing more than hand-held weapons. They should have brought armored vehicles—some kind of mini-tank, perhaps, small enough to follow the jungle paths. Right now, they didn't belong here. *Not like this.*

The dead seaman's name was Tighe. Jack had hardly known him, beyond knowing his name. They'd probably exchanged a dozen words on the whole journey since leaving San Francisco. Now, suddenly, Tighe was gone—his life was forfeit. Somewhere back in the civilized world there must be folks who'd lost a son, a husband, a father. Every death mattered. Likewise with Swain. To *someone*, his life had been all-important.

"Damn you!" Jack said out loud—directing it at himself. He'd been over-confident. Things had been going almost too well. One minute, they'd all been fine—trekking in the jungle had been tiring, but it hadn't seemed too dangerous. Everything had been under control, or so it had seemed. Now he felt vulnerable and foolish. Surely he'd heard enough about this place from his grandfather. Men had died that time, too. He should never have taken the island so lightly.

Insects were already swarming on the carcass of the dead carnosaur—and the remains of Swain and

Tighe. Dull-plumaged vulture-like birds started to arrive. They were not as big as the twenty-foot gull that they'd seen fishing for monster trevally or some of the water birds that had circled the lake for fishy prey. They were not as big as the huge scavenger ravens that Jack's party had come across in the jungle the day before—but they were big *enough* for all that. Back home, they would have matched up well against any eagle or condor.

"We'll have to bury these men," Roxanne said. "We can't carry them around in this climate." What she left implicit was that the bodies would soon start to rot. Then there were the gory logistics of trying to carry them. They really needed body bags to place the bloody pieces in, maybe get them back to the base camp, but they'd brought nothing like that. Besides, what good would it do? One way or the other these men would have to be buried here on the island.

Roxanne looked thoughtfully at the carcass of the carnosaur, as if she wanted to take a tissue sample. If so, she gave up on the idea and turned away.

Some of the insect and avian carrion-eaters were already trying to get to the remains of Tighe and the cameraman, and Jack realized that something must be done to lend some dignity to the deaths. With Kowalski's help, Jack beat a path through the scavengers. He winced at the dreadful sight and smell as they gathered Tighe's body and what was left of Swain's.

"We'll carry the remains to a better clearing," Jack said. "We can't bury them here with those goddamn vultures all around."

There was no choice but to abandon the camera equipment as the least necessary gear they had.

Penelope looked ashen but she didn't argue. Swain was gone and she would have enough trouble trying to drag her own gear. Everyone else was loaded with equipment that was necessary for survival.

Kowalski and one of the other crewmen carried Tighe's body, while Jack and Roxanne struggled with Swain's gruesome remnants. With nervous glances in all directions they found their way out of the clearing. Kong ran on ahead of the humans, sometimes looking back or stopping to let them catch up. Jack and the rest walked in silence, looking for somewhere to bury their fallen colleagues and wondering what else awaited them in the jungle.

For now at least, no new danger emerged, and the group found a smaller clearing where the earth was deep enough to dig shallow graves with branches and stones. After they'd covered the bodies, Penelope said a blessing over them. As she sat to rest her bruises, the others worked together to drag some heavier branches, then a large slab of stone, to place on the mounded earth. Two or three hours had passed since the attack when Jack finally had a chance to rinse some of the blood and dirt from his hands, using as little of their precious water as possible. As they'd seen, there was plenty of fresh water on the island but no one knew what diseases it might harbor, so it was best to stick with what they'd brought from the ship.

It was time to radio Laurel and report the bad news. "We had an encounter with one of those carnosaurs," he told her. "We've lost two men."

"No!" she said. "Who was killed?"

"Swain, and one of the guys from the ship—name of Tighe. Do you remember him?"

"I do, Jack. But I did not know him. We hardly ever talked. This is terrible."

"Please relay it to the captain. I don't see much choice but to press on for now. Going back might be as dangerous as moving forward. But we'll be extremely careful."

"Yes, please do."

"I'd never have believed one of those things could move so fast, not even after all the books I've read. It's one thing to read about estimated speeds. It's another thing to see it."

"Don't blame yourself, Jack."

"I'll call again later. Have you heard from Sanderson?"

"Not since breakfast time."

"I'm worried about the other team. Radio them and make sure they're okay."

"I will."

"Tell them to take every possible care. If we hadn't had Kong with us, more of us might have died this morning. The big guy deserves some kind of medal. Sanderson and the rest don't have a giant gorilla to help them out." *And neither will we on the way back,* Jack thought. *Not if we stick to the plan.* There was one other possibility, he realized, which was to get Hashemi to fly the Jayhawk and airlift them back to the beach. Once they'd seen off Kong, one way or another, that just might be the most attractive possibility. The chopper could home in on a radio signal so all they had to do was find a good place for it to land.

"I will call Sanderson's team," Laurel said. "I will pass your warning to them."

"Uh-huh…that's good."

"And if anything has happened, Jack, I will call *you*."

"Yeah, Laurel. That's great, I guess. I'd better go now."

That done, Jack led the group back in the direction of Skull Mountain, wondering whether they'd ever find signs of other giant gorillas on the island. Some of those distant roars could have been like Kong's—it was too hard to tell. They walked as if navigating a minefield, looking out at every step for killer vines, spiderwebs, and all the other hazards. Twice they saw killer vine tangles in narrow sections of their path and they detoured to avoid the danger. Insects buzzed at them, sweat poured down their bodies, and they never knew what might be behind the next bush or tree. Jack felt disgusting, with a residue of dirt and blood still on his hands and clothes. More than once, he wondered if the time had come to give up on the whole expedition. This island was aptly named. It was a place of death.

After an hour, Laurel radioed him. "I cannot reach Sanderson's party," she said.

"Oh, shit," Jack said. "You're kidding—" A thousand thoughts flashed like sheet lightning across his mind.

"No, I cannot get through. I keep trying, but the radio isn't working."

"Not working?"

"Dead, Jack. The channel is dead. Maybe just an electrical fault—I don't know. Also, we have lost the homing signal. We cannot track their location."

Their radio units were designed to send a continuous, unique signal that could be tracked from the base, the ship, or the Sikorsky helicopter. If that signal was interrupted, it indicated damage or a malfunction.

"All right, let me think for a minute," Jack said. His first panicky thoughts had been of carnosaurs or worse—but those had had been premature. *Okay*, he thought, *something must be wrong with their equipment.* He still disliked the idea of Sanderson's team being out here in the jungle and out of contact. If they could not be reached, that didn't prove the explorers had come to harm—but it damn sure didn't mean they were still alive. That remained to be seen.

Beside him, Roxanne said, "We can try to find them."

"Okay," he mouthed back at her.

Maybe Sanderson and the others were fine but Jack could only wonder. "Do you have their estimated location?" he asked Laurel. "Their last location, I mean?"

"Yes, Jack, but they might have moved on. Mr. Hashemi is flying over there now, in the Jayhawk, but I cannot be optimistic. The jungle must be so thick—"

"That's true, unless they can find a clearing." *Assuming they're okay. Please, let them be okay.* "We're going to detour and see if we can find them. After what we've seen here, human lives have to take priority. Finding specimens can wait."

"Understood."

"Give me that location."

Laurel gave him a grid coordinate on the map, which was toward the cliffs on the island's eastern side. Sanderson's team were supposed to have hugged the perimeter of the island—to keep near the sea, once they reached it. By now they might have gotten as far as the island's easternmost edge. If they had, they may or may not have hiked several miles north. It depended on a host of imponderables: how fast they could walk; what stops they had taken; what obstacles or problems they had encountered. With a few calculations, Jack would be able to narrow the probable location to about three squares of the grid. But that was the best he could do. In this jungle, you could get within a few hundred yards of other humans— even less than that—and never know it. Finding Sanderson's party might be like finding the proverbial needle in a haystack.

But something had to be done.

"If you hear from Sanderson," he said, "or manage to get through to him, tell him to go right to the tip of the island—the northeast tip. Got it? Tell him to stop there. That's where we'll head, too. There are so many paths through the jungle we could walk right by each other." At a rough guess, the tip of the island was at least six miles away, but there seemed to be no good alternative.

"Will do, Jack," Laurel said. "Is there anything else you want?"

"If Hashemi finds them, we'll need to take stock. Call me if it happens."

"Of course."

"Signing out for now."

They turned north and east, a direction far out of their way, but they'd already allowed for a possible third night in the jungle. As for repatriating Kong, it mattered little what direction they took right now. If there *were* other giant apes on Skull Island they might be located anywhere. That issue aside, nowhere in the jungle had seemed better than anywhere else to become a gorilla's new home; they might as well leave Kong in one spot as another.

For the first mile they met nothing more dangerous than a mating pair of gigantic hadrosaurs, the male bellowing like colossal bull. They gave the hadrosaurs a wide berth and continued for another ten minutes without mishap...inured by now to the sweat, the insects, the blood, and the dirt on their skin. Suddenly, there were hissing noises all round—not so loud as they'd heard from the carnosaur, but clearly the voices of more than one creature.

A pair of reptiles appeared ahead on the path. These were much smaller than the gigantic carnosaur had been, but almost as dangerous looking. They stood about ten feet tall on two legs, peering around intelligently. One glance told Jack what he was up against. They had long, sinuous necks and long rigid tails held stiffly behind them, and were patterned in several shades of green, yellow, and brown. Their skulls were shaped almost like those of eagles, but with sharp, shark-like teeth.

Hissing, arching their necks, snapping their jaws, they stepped forward with a cautious, prancing gait. Jack raised his loaded dart rifle. These creatures were small enough to be taken down.

He fired. At the same time, Kong roared.

A third reptile appeared almost behind them. Then there was a fourth, leaping from the bushes. Each of its hind legs had a huge, recurved toe-claw—something like the shape of a sickle. *Raptors. Good God—those creatures look like raptors!* A fifth appeared through the foliage. It opened its jaws and attacked.

TWENTY-THREE

The island's green jungle and its single beach of white-gold sand shone like jewelry on a blue velvet background...and it was going to make Falconie a tidy pile of loot. He slowed the Super-Osprey to approach the beach. As he drew closer and switched the plane's giant turboprops to VTOL mode, he could make out the bright orange tents of the Bionimals-Denham Products camp. Their research ship was anchored half a mile from the shore.

In its VTOL mode, the Super-Osprey became, in effect, a giant helicopter with twin, wing-mounted rotors. Falconie glanced across at his co-pilot, a 290-pound black man named Lucius Coffey.

"Ready, Donut?" Falconie said.

"Ready if you are, man."

Falconie had no real idea why Lucius was known as "Donut" to anyone who'd been with him in the military. He'd never seen Lucius eat a single donut in his life—or any other kind of cake or sweets, if it came to that. His bulk came from consuming vast quantities of beer and beef, assisted by years of fanatical weight training. Much of him was hard, thick slabs of muscle, but he was softer round the middle than would ever have been allowed in his days as a military commando. If you met him for the first time, you might think the nickname referred to that "spare tire" of flab, but Falconie knew that it had been with him for much longer than the spare tire. Maybe it was a dumb joke about the his surname—pronounced like "coffee."

Whatever.

Falconie took them down.

They'd brought enough personnel, food, equipment, and firepower to take over the whole expedition. Seated back there in the rear compartment was Hemming's new science boffin, Valdez, plus four of Falconie's oldest buddies—all with combat experience in the U.S. forces. Their cargo included large and smaller specimen cages, dissection kits, and liquid nitrogen containers for organic samples.

From his first meeting with Hemming, back in the U.S., Falconie had realized that you couldn't take half measures with a job like this. If the animals of the island were as dangerous as Hemming had thought they'd be, you had to treat them like you were in a war. That was why he'd brought assault rifles, high-explosive impact grenades, and plenty of ammunition. It was no use trying to pussyfoot about saving the goddamn dinosaurs they'd be facing. Too many men had died on that first expedition, the one in 1933. Falconie had checked whatever was publicly known about the events on the island, who had died and how—and who had come back alive. The moral was, you had to be ready for anything—and then have the guts to *use* your firepower and fight your way through it.

From what Hemming had told him, no one else had properly grasped the situation. You could go hunting *elephants* with elephant guns, but these goddamn monsters weren't going to be anything like elephants. "Goddammit," he'd said to Hemming that first time, "doesn't anyone take this *seriously*?" Hemming had been smart enough to get the point. The man was not a fool.

As they landed the aircraft on the island's broad beach, the powerful rotors threw up a cloud of sand. Once he was sure the Super-Osprey was stable, Falconie cut the power to its rotors, then prepared to disembark. Three figures approached from the tent site, and he nudged Coffey on the arm. "Some company," he said. "Let's see what we can find out."

"Brother, let's rock," Coffey said.

Kong threw himself at the first dinosaur in the pack, lifting it off the ground over his head. He slammed it straight down, where it writhed and then quickly found its feet. It rushed Kong, agile and swift as a cat, all fangs and claws.

Jack reloaded and fired at one of the other hissing monsters. All around him, others fired their rifles. One reptile went down from a clean head shot, but another seized Penelope with its teeth and front claws. Almost faster than the eye could follow, it raised a hind leg, ripping Penelope open with a vertical slice from its huge, sickle-shaped claw. Red carnage was everywhere. A long-clawed foot tore into one of the seamen.

Jack no longer tried to think—he just hoped to survive the next few minutes. And hoped the same for everyone else, especially Roxanne. He couldn't lose her now.

More of the reptiles appeared. They were not exactly like any dinosaur that Jack recognized, but why should they be? All of these reptilian creatures had been mutating for millions of years.

Kong was far bigger than "his" raptor, which might have massed one thousand pounds, but probably no more. Kong held it off the ground as it snapped at him and thrashed with all its limbs and its tail. Twisting it savagely, he broke its back. After what seemed like several minutes—but must have been far less—one of the creatures was dead from gunshot wounds, another wobbled on its feet from a clean hit with a tranquilizer dart. Kong had killed "his," then another, and he ran after the others in a fury of fur and teeth. The whole pack of them fled into the jungle. Kong slammed his chest in triumph—the raptors had met their match.

Jack looked around in a state of incomprehension. If not for Kong they would all be dead, so quickly had the creatures attacked. As it was, they'd started out with fourteen in their party. As he took in the gruesome tableau, it seemed they were down to nine. The carnosaur had killed two. Four others had died in the ferocious rush from the pack of smaller reptiles, torn apart by those terrible slashing hind claws. Penelope was dead, as were Christine Archer and two of the crewmen from the ship.

Archer was the only one whom Jack had known well—a happy, friendly young woman with a vivid personality and a great work ethic at the company. Everyone there had liked her, and she'd worked her heart out looking after Kong. Now she was dead—*just like that!* The flame of a human life could be snuffed out so quickly. What was left of her lay crumpled, bleeding from her terrible wounds. The raptors' claws had opened her up more swiftly than a maniac could have done with a sharpened ax.

But Kong had fought like a four-ton demon. That had saved the survivors.

Just what had those creatures been? To Jack's eye, they'd resembled dromeosaurs, like Deinonychus or Velociraptor, but that was probably an illusion, just as the giant carnosaur had not been a real *Tyrannosaurus rex*. When Skull Island had become isolated, back in Jurassic time, dromeosaurs had surely not yet evolved—no fossil records of them dated back so far. But they had always been a logical design for one evolutionary niche in the dinosaur world: relatively small, incredibly fast predators with vicious teeth and claws. The Mesozoic dromeosaurs might have been the most efficient killing machines of their time. What had surely made them more terrifying was their highly evolved intelligence.

These local raptors must have evolved in parallel with Deinonychus and the rest, as ichthyosaurs and sharks and killer whales had all developed similar bodies and the same modus operandi. From what Jack had just seen, the basic dromeosaur design certainly worked. Skull Island's homegrown raptors had been deadly and hunting in a pack had made them more so.

All of that passed through his mind in seconds—he knew his dinosaurs, though he'd only just begun to learn what dealing with them could mean in real life. But it brought to mind another thought. *What about Sanderson's party?* Jack was already uncomfortably aware that *they* had not set out with a giant gorilla to help against Skull Island's deadly predators. What had happened to them? More than ever, he needed to find the missing party, then get the hell back to the relative safety of the beach. Kong might just have to fend for himself. From what he'd shown today, he would be up to the task.

But what were they all *doing* here? Perhaps the beach was safe...but perhaps not. As for the explorers, would any of them be alive by tonight?

Seconds later there was a harsh cawing and one of the jungle's ostrich-sized black ravens flew into the clearing to feast on the fallen humans and reptiles.

Jack was at his wit's end. "Well," he said to Roxanne. "Now what?"

"Try this now," Jagat Lal said.

He passed the microphone to Sanderson, who looked at it skeptically for a moment. "Thanks," Sanderson said, wondering if they would ever get through to Laurel Otani and the others back at the beach. With his free hand he brushed away an unwelcome fly the size of a Goliath beetle, which kept wanting to hover near his face. The marshes were full of insects like that. Pesky brutes. These Goliath flies were not the biggest insects that they'd seen on the island, but they were all too friendly. Insect repellent didn't seem to discourage their attentions.

"Thank me if it *works*!" Lal said.

"No, no. Thanks anyway, whether it works or not." There was one good thing about being in a group of scientists and techs and a nature photographer: Get them focused and they could dismember or cobble together most kinds of electrical or electronic equipment. Lal had cannibalized his sound gear to rebuild their radio unit and try to get it working. Sanderson had a feeling that their day's luck might be about to change. "Base?" Sanderson said, operating the mike. "Laurel? Is anyone there? Can anybody hear me?"

There was a sound of static from the reconstructed radio unit, but no answer.

"Goddammit!" Sanderson said.

Somewhere out there in the mud, water, and fog, a huge sauropod, maybe a hundred tons, was lying in wait to attack them one more time. *God only knows what else is there in the marshes.* There were many places where he'd have preferred to be.

Ramon Valdez stepped from the Super-Osprey, dressed in loose khaki clothing and light canvas boots. He looked around at the beach and the sea as three people approached from the cluster of tents near the huge stone wall. So this was Skull Island!

His job was to take over here, whatever Jack Denham or anyone else might think about it. Like many biological scientists, he'd crossed Denham's path before, and knew the man had a strong personality—he wouldn't be easy to face down. Valdez glanced at Falconie for reassurance. Falconie gave an amused, almost contemptuous wink. Hopefully, Denham and the others would see reason, Valdez thought. At least Roxanne Blaine should be on his side—like him, she was Hemming's employee. She should know where her loyalties lay.

"Who's in charge here?" Valdez asked, hoping he sounded less nervous than he felt.

One of the three who'd come to greet them was an Asian woman whom he'd never met, but instantly recognized as Laurel Otani. He'd seen her image in scientific reports and on the news. The fat young man with her was less familiar, but Valdez had seen his image, too: Mark Illingworth, sometimes written up as Kong's real creator, the man who'd done the work to fill the gaps in the gorilla's genome. The third in the group was a tall, forty-something man whom Valdez didn't recognize.

"I am in charge of the base camp," Otani said.

"I see. Then where could I find Jack Denham?"

She gestured toward the jungle behind a monumental wall of stone at the top of the sandy peninsula. "He is in one of the exploring parties."

A few pounds seemed to lift from Valdez's shoulders. "You're Laurel Otani, then?"

She gave him a *do-I-know-you-from-somewhere?* look.

"You might know me by reputation," he added quickly. "I'm Ramon Valdez, at your service. You may have read some of my work in evolutionary biology."

"I do know some of your work, Dr. Valdez, but—"

"But what am I doing here? Is that what you'd like to know?"

"Not to put fine a point on it—yes," Illingworth said. "Exploration of this island isn't meant to be a free-for-all."

Valdez gave the man a nod, "And I know who *you* are, too, Dr. Illingworth. Congratulations on the fine work that you did with Kong. You're a top genetic engineer, if I may say so."

Illingworth nodded back, more curtly. He introduced the other man, whose name was Gibson.

"Is Captain McLeod well?" Valdez said.

"He's back on the ship," Illingworth said. "Anyway, he's fine."

Valdez was starting to warm up. With Falconie, Coffey, and the others flanking him, this might be surprisingly easy. "I'd like to confer with him as soon as there's a chance," he said.

"What, exactly, is this all about?" the tall man—Gibson—asked slowly.

"That's what *I'd* like to know," Illingworth said, trying too hard to sound tough. Falconie's team had an intimidating presence.

"Let me make the position clear," Valdez said. "I've been employed by Charlton Hemming to look after his interests on this island—"

"You're with Hemming? What the—"

"Please, young man! Please let me finish. "I'd like to introduce my colleagues, who'll be helping us from now on." Valdez quickly went around, naming them all. "Armando Falconie, Lucius Coffey, Johnny Jones, Kurt Ettinghausen…" He went through the whole group, knowing that Otani and Illingworth—and the non-entity with them—would not remember all their names from this first meeting. But they'd have to get used to the newcomers quickly because they were here to stay. From now on, this well-trained, disciplined group of people would be at the heart of all the efforts on the island.

Otani and the others raised their eyebrows at the appearance of Falconie and his team. They were dressed in matching olive drab outfits, with body armor under their uniforms, and M-16 assault rifles strapped across their bodies with grenade launchers attached. They carried army helmets and wore webbing crammed with magazines and grenades.

Otani and Illingworth exchanged uncertain glances. "I am very glad to meet you, Doctor Valdez," Otani said.

Illingworth nodded. "Likewise."

"The pleasure is mine," Valdez said, offering Otani his hand. "Now, my dear lady, you'll need to brief me. Shall we go to your tents?"

"All right," Illingworth said. "If you're with Hemming, we'll have to run you through what's happened."

"That's what I had in mind."

"Come to the tents, please," Otani said, looking nervously at all the military hardware. "I will explain about the expedition. Jack and Roxanne are both in the jungle—probably back tomorrow."

"Tomorrow?"

"Yes, or maybe the next day."

"That's fine." Valdez took the deepest breath he could without it showing. At least he hoped it didn't show. "There's one thing you need to be clear about."

"And what's that," said Illingworth.

"Now that I'm here, I'm in charge of this expedition."

"Jointly with Jack, perhaps," Illingworth said. "I'll leave it to you and Roxanne to sort out who deputizes for Hemming."

Valdez laughed and shook his head. "But I'm here now, and they aren't. Understood?"

"Anyway," Mark said, faltering slightly, "come and meet everybody."

"I'd be delighted to, of course."

As they approached the tents, there was a harsh, squawking sound overhead. As Valdez looked up, Falconie exclaimed, "What in the name of God?"

A huge jet-black bird landed twenty feet away. It was much like a raven, but bigger than any man. The bird made no move to flee them or attack. It merely watched with bright, beady eyes.

Valdez stared back at it, terrified. But then he remembered who he had with him and what they were capable of. With a touch of bravado, he said, "Someone teach Mr. Nevermore a lesson. I don't like his attitude."

Beside him, Falconie selected "automatic" on his M-16. Four three-round bursts of fire blasted the oversized scavenger off its clawed feet. In a few seconds, it was a shattered corpse on the sand. Otani appeared shocked, but that was not a problem for Valdez.

"Thank you, Armando," he said with a pleased smile.

"Come on," Illingworth said. "We *really* need to talk."

"Of course, Mark," Valdez said with a smile. He realized that he could come to like working this way. "Tell me all about it. Then we'll see what needs to be done." *Yes*, he thought as he followed a pace behind Illingworth, his team of ex-commandos ready at hand to do his bidding. *Being Charlton Hemming must feel a bit like this. All the power that money can buy, and people just waiting to act at your behest whenever you snap your fingers.* Valdez felt a little drunk with his new-found power. He could come to like that a lot.

TWENTY-FOUR

"Let's finish that thing off," Kowalski said, pointing at the carnivorous dinosaur that Jack had taken down with his dart rifle. He carefully aimed his large-bore Winchester and fired a round into the head of the tranquilized creature.

Roxanne crouched down to take a sample from one of the dead raptors. As the vultures and other predators gathered, Jack and the others shifted the four human bodies. There'd be no time for any but the shallowest graves.

"This whole idea was crazy," Jack said when Roxanne had finished her work.

"You mean the expedition?" she said.

"Yes," he said firmly. "I should have left well enough alone."

"I'm sorry you feel that way."

"Well, we'll talk about it later. After the funeral."

"I need to know everything that's been happening," Valdez said. "Take me through it step by step."

Otani's look showed him how unwelcome that was.

"Something wrong?" he added.

"Come this way," Otani said. She pointed out a shady spot near the tents at the base of the colossal stone wall. "This is where we meet while the sun is out."

They had a folding card table here, plus a few canvas-backed chairs. Valdez took a seat deciding that it would have to do in the circumstances. This was hardly a place for civilized comforts. *That* was not what he'd come here for.

A whole group gathered round to see and hear what was going on, but that didn't bother Valdez. He had all the backing he needed if anyone wanted to issue some kind of challenge to his authority. Illingworth sat opposite him, resting his clenched hands on the surface of the table as he leaned forward. "Before we go any further," he said, "this island's ecology must be extremely fragile. You're a good enough scientist to understand that."

"Of course I do," Valdez said.

Illingworth sat back, his pudgy face flushed. "Then I have to protest about the way Mr. Falconie shot that bird. For all we know, it could be rare. Correction—*any* creature on this island is probably rare."

"Come now, Mark," Valdez said, "don't exaggerate. We're all here for one purpose and that's to exploit the island for our employers. To do that we'll have to take as many specimens as we can."

"That does not require killing," Otani said. She'd quietly taken a seat beside Illingworth. "For that reason, we brought dart rifles, cages, and DNA sampling equipment. Killing is a last resort on this expedition. Mr. Hemming knows that just as much as we do. I assume you have been told about that."

"It's all in the legal agreement," Illingworth said, "if you care to have a look at the detail. No one is supposed to trash the island. That was an important point that Jack and Hemming agreed upon."

"We'll preserve it as well as we can," Valdez said, losing interest in what these two had to say about it. "Preserving ourselves comes first. Now, I suggest you forget about that issue. If there's any contractual problem, you can take it up with Charlton later on. I don't think it's worth arguing about right now." He turned to Falconie, who was still standing, keeping a distance behind him. "What do you think, Armando?"

"With respect, his opinion on scientific matters is hardly relevant," Illingworth said.

Falconie shrugged. "It's not an issue at all."

Illingworth looked like his face would explode. "This is not the sort of attitude I'd have expected from CenCo's people."

Valdez raised his eyebrows theatrically to show his impatience with this stupid scolding. "You're not in much of a position to argue the point, I'd say. Still, I'm not here to destroy your precious island. Charlton is as concerned to preserve it as anyone."

"That's not the vibe you're giving off."

"Oh, Mark, *please*. I'm not working for some nine-teenth-century capitalist who thinks that you can lay waste the same resources that you're exploiting. Charlton Hemming is a sophisticated man, and so am I. All the same, you don't want to treat the island with too much respect. Make sure it respects you."

"Are you sure you haven't been drinking on the way here?" Illingworth said.

Valdez shot him a warning glance. "That's not very nice, Mark. Anyway, forget about all that and tell me what's been happening. Charlton will want me to report."

Illingworth sat there with a disgusted look on his face. Or *was* it just disgust? Could something have gone wrong?

"Come on then," Valdez said, "it can't be that bad. Or if it is, maybe we can help out." *Which is probably the last thing you'd want from us.*

"We've had problems. We've lost people in the jungle."

"Deaths?"

"Yes, deaths."

"See what I mean?" Valdez said cheerfully. "This is a dangerous place. Don't you think you'd better brief me about it?"

Otani described the basics of how they'd worked since coming here. Two parties had begun initial exploration. Denham and Roxanne led one, while Sanderson led the other. "We have heard from both exploring parties since they left," she said. "On our latest information, two were dead in the Denham-Blaine party. We have been unable to contact the Sanderson party since early this morning. Their radio set is not working—and we have no tracking signal from the unit."

"What have you done about it?" Falconie put in.

"We are searching for them now, by helicopter."

"We know where they were at breakfast time," Illingworth said, "and we know the way they were headed—"

"But you don't know where they are now?" Valdez finished for him.

"There's just a small area of the island where they could have gotten to by now. If they've stuck to the plan, it's only about ten square miles to search."

"I see. *Only* ten square miles of thick, tropical jungle?"

"And Jack's group has also diverted to that same area," Otani said. "We will find them, one way or another."

"All right." Valdez took a minute to think about it. She seemed like a brave little thing—he had to give her that. "It sounds to me like your leaders have made a mess of this expedition," he said.

"That's hardly fair," Illingworth said.

"No? You seem to have mislaid a lot of people."

"We're only just learning about the island. This won't be typical."

"From where I look at it, it's just as well I arrived when I did."

Otani sat up straighter, and folded her arms across her chest. "No, I do not think so."

Falconie took half a step forward, but Valdez held up his hand in a soothing gesture. He was really enjoying this. He should have joined Charlton Hemming's employment years before. He leaned forward toward Otani and said in a confidential voice, "Then whatever you think isn't relevant. You'll need my help to sort this out."

"Try now," Lal said, making a last adjustment to the exposed circuitry of the battered radio unit.

"Base?" Sanderson said into the mike. "Can you hear me?"

Then an answer at last. "This is Laurel Otani."

"Sanderson here."

"Oh my God! We were so worried."

"I'm sorry we've been out of contact."

"We thought you could be dead."

Sanderson took a deep breath before breaking the news. "Most of us are, Laurel. We're in a slightly drier patch of mud in a swampy area, maybe two miles east of where I radioed from this morning. We'd been heading toward the coast as planned, but there's no simple way to get there on this side without cutting through the marshes."

"Due east of your old coordinates?" Laurel asked, businesslike.

"Slightly north as well. I can give you our coordinate location, the way we've calculated it." He told her the reference. "We were attacked," he said, "trying to get through."

"Attacked?"

"Yes, by a pair of sauropods...something like apatosaurs. Huge, long-necked sons of bitches. Our radio got damaged in the process."

"How many of you were killed?"

"There's only five of us left." He told her their names: himself and Lal; Roderick Carwardine; Anna-Lena Beck; and a man named Whitlock, one of the crewmen from the ship. The rest had been crushed by the gigantic sauropods, which had refused to go down, even under heavy fire from the large-bore rifles that some of the party had carried. Finally, they'd taken out the smaller of the two monsters, which now lay only fifty yards distant, stretched out in death among the mangroves, mud, palm trees, and tree ferns. A group of giant scavenger birds had been feeding on it ever since.

The other apatosaur—which might have weighed a hundred tons—had lumbered off deeper into the marshes at surprising speed, presumably to lick its wounds. It was still out there somewhere. Carwardine and the other two were patrolling with their guns in case the huge dinosaur came back. Sanderson didn't want to face it again.

At the other end of the radio link, Laurel was conferring in tense, urgent tones with several more people. Sanderson could make out words, but not the whole sense of their debate. Then she spoke into her radio mike: "Sorry, some other people have arrived on the island."

"What?" Sanderson said. *Who else could have arrived?*

"That does not matter so much. The main thing is, we can find you. Frank has been searching for you in the Jayhawk. If your equipment is working, he can track your radio signal. Please find a clearing. It would help if you could light a fire. Do you think that is possible?"

"It'll have to be," Sanderson said. He saw something in his peripheral vision and started with surprise. But it was only one of the island's giant dragonflies, which seemed to be totally harmless. It flew by about ten feet away.

"Give me your coordinates, then find a clear area big enough to land the chopper," Laurel said. "If you can do that, Frank will get you out."

Only a few days before it had all seemed completely logical, the *only* solution to what to do with Kong...and with Denham Products' litigation problems. Now it had all gone bad, with six people killed that Jack knew of. Then there was Sanderson's party. What had happened to them?

Kowalski retrieved the precious water canteens but they couldn't manage all the other gear. Silently, they did their best to make graves in the damp earth not far from the area where the raptor pack had ambushed them. Half of the team worked at burial duty, while Jack and the rest stood in a circle, facing outward into the surrounding jungle. They kept their fingers on their triggers, ready to fire at a second's warning.

Jack scanned the foliage around him for any sign of life larger than the ubiquitous insects, spiders, and centipedes. If more raptors appeared, it might just spell the end. He just hoped the reptiles were intelligent enough to have learned a lesson—that armed human beings and a giant gorilla were too dangerous a target to be worth attacking.

He couldn't fool himself about all the graves they'd been making. Burying the dead gave the living a sense of dignity and closure, but those shallow graves would not last long—not with the rains and the jungle's animals. They probably wouldn't last a day. Everyone who'd been killed would surely end up as meals for the endless lines of scavengers that seemed to prosper here on Skull Island. And he didn't fool himself, either, that he'd still be alive if not for Kong. Some of them might have survived the attack from the giant carnosaur, but the raptors had meant business. In the midst of the battle, as more had kept appearing, he'd lost count of their numbers. At least eight or nine, he figured.

After the makeshift burial, he took Roxanne aside. "I'm supposed to lead this expedition in conjunction with you," he said.

"You don't need to tell me that," she said warily. "What's on your mind?"

Part of him was angry with her, as if what had happened were somehow her fault. Another part tried to calm the first part. Despite the dangers of the island, she'd stayed enthusiastic about repatriating Kong, but what else could they do? She was to blame for nothing that had happened. *Take it easy, Jack. You've only just found out that you love each other. Try not to fight with her.* "Rox," he said, "I want to go back—as quickly as we can. If we find Sanderson's group, or their remains, that's it for me. We head straight back to the beach. There's no point letting more people die."

"Those creatures might not attack again," she said thoughtfully. "Whatever they were, they seemed intelligent—"

"Far too intelligent for my taste."

"Yes, I know, but they might have learned a lesson."

"I was thinking the same thing. But what if they *haven't* learned their lesson? Or what if they figure out how to be smarter next time?"

She seemed to consider it. "I've never seen a predator attack something that's already beaten it off. They'll go after easier prey."

"You've never seen a predator like *that*," Jack said, getting frustrated. Neither had he, if it came to that. No one had ever seen creatures quite like this, not even in the books.

Roxanne looked him up and down. "You're not exactly *consulting* me—are you, Jack?"

"I'm trying to—"

"No, you're *telling* me. *You* want to get back and *I'm* just supposed to accept it. "

"It's not meant that way."

"Yes it is—and do we just give up on finding other apes like Kong? That was our whole purpose."

"We don't have to give up," he said, knowing he was under stress and trying to work out what he really thought. "I don't know, Roxanne. Let's look for Sanderson's team, then at least regroup." It came out sounding almost wheedling, which made him despise himself. "If we stay on the island, we can work out what to do about Kong."

"Oh…*if we stay on the island*, is it?" she sneered. "So now you want to abandon the whole expedition?" She'd started raising her voice and angry tears came to her eyes. "Listen to me, oh mighty Dr. Denham. We knew it was going to be dangerous when we came here. It was clear to me—even if it wasn't to you—that the dangers would be worst in the first few days until we learned about them. Right? Don't think I'm glad to see people killed, because I'm not. But I'd braced myself for something like this to happen…and I'd thought long and hard about how I'd react." She was trembling, now. "*Are you telling me you hadn't?*"

"Rox—"

"It's bad enough dealing with the island and its lifeforms—"

"*Please!* You're not thinking straight."

"Aren't I?" she said. "Aren't I just? Has it ever occurred to you that you might not actually be the straightest-thinking person in the world, after all? That just now and then someone else *might* be thinking at least as straight as you are, or maybe just a tiny bit straighter?"

Feeling even more frustrated, he said, "Look, we have to find the other team."

"Then let's do it. We can argue when we've found them."

Jack squeezed her arm, trying to show affection, but she pulled away. "All right," he said. "If that's the way you want to be..." Her goddamn emotions weren't his responsibility.

The sky above the chopper was blue and clear. The marshes below were partly obscured by mist but Sanderson's radio unit was sending a clear signal for Frank Hashemi to home in on. As he followed the signal, Hashemi looked out for any smoke rising up from the ground. *Please,* he thought, *where exactly are you?*

Close to the horizon, a flock of pterosaurs—perhaps a dozen—slowly approached the chopper. Occasionally, one of the huge flying reptiles flapped its wings lazily as it glided above the green canopy of the forest. Nearer to the chopper a pair of black eagles cavorted above the marshes. They ignored the noise of the churning, thrumming rotors.

Where are you, goddammit? Hashemi thought. All he'd need to pick up the Sanderson team was a reasonably clear space to take the chopper down. Somewhere in those marshes—just an area big enough for the Jayhawk. According to the electronic tracer, Sanderson was right down...*there.* And then Hashemi saw a single line of wood smoke climbing vertically into the still sky. He went lower. Sure enough there was the big tech from Denham Products, Roderick Carwardine, waving his khaki shirt for attention.

Hashemi took the chopper down. *Boy, will you guys be pleased to see me!*

There was a whole group of them down there. He recognized Sanderson, Lal, and the others—just five of them. According to the report from Laurel Otani, most of the team had been killed, and not even by carnivores. Hashemi kept the chopper hovering a couple of feet off the muddy ground and the survivors ran toward it, hunching against the wind from the rotors. *Come on, then!* The sooner they could all get out of here, the happier Hashemi would be. It would take just few seconds for them to scramble aboard, then they could be up, away, and in the clear.

That was when things went crazy.

The creature that charged out of the vegetation was the size of a blue whale, though nothing like it in shape. You'd have to take the whale's body, paint it a muddy yellow, then stretch out its tail and neck. Mount it on thick, powerful legs like huge cylindrical pillars. That was what it was like—a one-hundred-ton, bad-tempered behemoth rushing at them with the force of an out-of-control locomotive. It bellowed with territorial rage. "Get in now!" Hashemi screamed from the cockpit, as if *that* could somehow transform Sanderson and his team—turn them into Olympic sprinters. He knew it didn't help but he had to let out the tension. "Come *on!*" But the huge dinosaur began to overtake them; it crushed Sanderson beneath one of its enormous, pillar-like legs, then trampled Carwardine and Lal.

The remaining man, Randy Whitlock, reached the chopper first and managed to crawl aboard. Anna-Lena Beck, the little blonde lab technician from Denham Products, was hard on his heels. Screaming in fear, Anna-Lena threw herself at the chopper—just seconds ahead of the enraged dinosaur.

"Good girl!" Hashemi called out.

But they still had to take off!

As the Jayhawk started to rise, the gigantic sauropod reared up on its hind legs, its head arching God-only-knew how many feet into the sky at the end of its long neck. The dinosaur still had forward momentum as it suddenly dropped back to all fours, its forelimbs striking the Jayhawk from above. The rotors must have cut into it, for it bellowed more loudly and shrilly than ever, as if in pain, and a cloud of blood exploded in the air—thousands of droplets splashed the glass cockpit.

"Climb, baby, climb!" Hashemi said as the chopper rocked. The rotors were clearly damaged—they must have crumpled like foil as they'd cut like a circular saw into the sauropod's bulk. There was no choice but to descend before he lost control completely. Urgently, he radioed the base camp. "We're damaged!" he shouted. "We can't fly. We're going down!"

As if it hadn't learned its lesson, the enraged sauropod charged again at the chopper. This time, its long, serpent-like neck struck the damaged but still spinning, rotors, which nearly decapitated it—the primeval creature's head stayed attached, but held by what seemed like a mere thread of butchered meat. Like a headless chicken, the sauropod was too stupid to know when to stop. It just went crazy—bucking and leaping, plowing its whole body into the chopper, which went over on its side, the rotors biting into mud, roots, and dirt, and deforming further under the strain. Surely the goddamn monster was dead now, but no one was telling it that, or else it wasn't listening. Whatever bizarre neurophysiology it had, it just wanted to keep going.

It bucked for another minute, even as its severed neck jerked about spurting blood. Finally, the monster collapsed and its hundred-ton bulk fell toward the crippled chopper like a giant's hammer dropping from the sky. In his last seconds Hashemi saw through the cockpit glass that pterosaurs were swooping his way. Like vultures, they had an interest in death. For one last moment the sauropod seemed to hang in the air—as if time had frozen. Then it hit the chopper's cabin with a crushing impact that nothing human could have survived.

TWENTY-FIVE

Jack ground his teeth as his group of explorers silently worked their way north and east. But then things changed—a radio call came through from Laurel, back at the base camp.

"Jack," Laurel said, "are you okay?"

"Negative," Jack said, taking the microphone. "We've now lost six people. We've had no time to call you."

"*What?*"

"No time to explain. We're headed for Sanderson's last position. The rest of us are okay right this moment." That was the most he was confident of saying. Things looked bleak after the attack from the raptors.

"Jack, a lot has happened here as well. We have company."

His mind just went blank at that. *Company?* "What kind of company?" he asked.

"I have no time to explain. People sent by Charlton Hemming. One of his scientists…and a support team."

Scientist? Support team? "What scientist?"

"Ramon Valdez. Do you know his work, Jack?"

Listening at Jack's side, Roxanne said, "Valdez? I don't believe this—"

"What's Hemming playing at?" Jack asked.

"*Jack!*" Laurel spoke so sharply that he almost jumped. "I am sorry," she said, "but there is no time for this. We must consult urgently."

"Okay. Tell me—"

"We heard from Giles Sanderson—"

"Good—"

"No, not so good, Jack. Most of his team are dead. We sent Frank to pick up the survivors."

"Hashemi? In the Jayhawk?"

"Yes."

"Did he find them?"

"He made contact, Jack, but that is the last we heard. He radioed us that the chopper was going down. We can still get a homing signal, but nothing else. No one answers radio calls. Maybe they are all dead. We have no way of knowing."

"All right." Jack tried to think it through. *What the hell could take down a Jayhawk helicopter?* "We're heading in that direction. We'll search for survivors. From what you've told me it doesn't sound good." But he figured he had a duty to *try*. No one deserved to be left behind. He could imagine all too vividly what it might be like to be injured here on the island and left by your friends to die.

But how were they all going to get back? A dozen inconsistent plans leapt into his head—none of which seemed workable. Maybe if they kept Kong with them they could shoot their way to the base camp, fighting through any more attacks from the island's creatures. If the Jayhawk had been damaged—*again, by what?*—then that ruined the idea of getting out by helicopter. Even with Kong there was every chance that they'd be killed off one by one, or three by three, if they remained on foot. This island seemed determined to take all their lives.

But if they did keep Kong with them, released him back near the beach, then just got the hell out of here and back to civilization... In that scenario, maybe *some* of them would survive. Maybe he was deluding himself about that, but the mind went on hoping, no matter what, long after things seemed hopeless.

"Listen," he said. "We'll do our best to find Sanderson's party. If any are left alive, we'll get them back somehow. We'll probably need to camp one more night."

"No, Jack," Laurel said. "There is another way."

As Laurel told it, the new team that Hemming had sent with Valdez were armed with military weapons. They'd arrived in some sort of VTOL craft, which she referred to as a Super-Osprey—that meant nothing to Jack, but Roxanne nodded as if it made perfect sense to her. They had equipment to track signals from Jack's radio or Sanderson's. If Jack could get his people close to Sanderson's coordinates, the newcomers could find them, search for survivors from the other party, and airlift all of them back to the beach in one or two trips.

Jack had no choice but to agree. *Beggars can't be choosers.*

"All right, Jack," Laurel said, "they will reach you shortly. The team leader's name is Falconie. Head for Sanderson's position and they will soon be there for the pick-up."

"Roger that," Jack said, but the idea of being rescued by Valdez or his people gave him a sour taste. He signed off and they continued in Sanderson's direction.

Any gift that came from Hemming was tainted—and what was that old shark doing sending in a secret team anyway? Nothing in the contract allowed for that and it looked like a bid to gazump the whole expedition. As for Ramon Valdez, Jack had nothing personal against him—he scarcely knew the man. Valdez was respected enough for his science, and there was no doubt about his credentials, but he'd always seemed like a little sycophant who'd sell his soul to the highest bidder. If he'd taken a job with Hemming, that just added to the impression.

All the same, Jack had to admit the facts. Valdez's group might be their last best chance.

As they hiked in silence through the steamy jungle Jack tried to count his blessings but they seemed to be thin on the ground. At least some of his party were still alive. Kong continued to bound ahead, brushing aside any obstacles, then stopping to let the humans catch up. Maybe they could get through this. It seemed that the island had defeated them but maybe they wouldn't all be destroyed.

Except, Jack suddenly realized, something was terribly wrong.

Kong stopped, sniffing the trees then the air. As the humans gained on him, he stood up on his hind legs, looking slowly from right to left and back again, like a field commander scoping out the site for a battle. Jack raised his dart rifle and checked each bush and tree, one by one. Kong's ears pricked and his fur began to bristle. In another second it stood up all over his back. The giant gorilla must know something that his human friends didn't. Jack could feel the sweat building on his own face and under his arms.

"Kong," Roxanne said urgently, as they all came to a halt. "What is it?"

Far above in the canopy a small mammal gave a panicky shrieking call, then others answered it in kind.

Hissing came from the trees. *Raptors!* Kong roared as two of the terrible creatures appeared in their path. As before, the creatures stepped with a gait that was almost mincing—until they blurred into acceleration. Kong roared again. Jack fired. The raptors were emerging from all directions. There were more of them this time. It seemed like an army. Some had wounds that must have come from bullets.

Goddamn, Jack thought, *those evil sons of bitches.* They were not just deadly killing machines, they were also smart. They'd fled the earlier battle, but now they'd come back with reinforcements.

"You ready to rock, Falcon?" Coffey said.

"Yeah, Donut," Falconie said with a grin of anticipation. "Let's takes 'er up."

Coffey called over his shoulder to the rest of the team in the back of the Super-Osprey. "Here we go, boys. It's showtime!" The VTOL craft's twin turboprops blasted the dry sand and it lifted slowly into the air.

Falconie had all his buddies with him but they'd left that little wimp, Valdez, at the base camp. He'd just have to get by for an hour or so, or however long it took, without the commando team to do his bullying for him. If he got into trouble they could pick up the pieces when they got back. By then, Denham would be dead and no one else would give any opposition. Valdez could play big-shot scientist however he wanted. What he didn't know about were Falconie's *special* orders from Charlton Hemming himself: arrange an accident for Denham before he left the island. There was no need to do that on the first day they were here, but fate had handed them an opportunity too good to pass up.

With Denham out there in a jungle more dangerous than he'd counted on, what better time to make sure that he died? If these dinosaurs, or whatever they were, didn't get him first, Falconie and his team would make sure the job got done.

Falconie adjusted the twin turboprops and the Super-Osprey moved forward over the ancient stone wall and across the green canopy of the tropical forest. The craft's maximum speed was over 400 miles per hour, but they didn't need that here, combing the island's forests and marshes. They'd take it slowly and find what they were hunting. Their cabin equipment picked up two sets of signals, which had to mean they were tracking both lost parties—Denham's group and Sanderson's. Both signals were crystal clear and in almost the same direction: roughly north east of the base camp. *Piece of cake,* Falconie thought. If only every job could be so easy.

Coffey pointed at an area of marshy ground not far from the cliffs on the island's eastern side. There was a thin veil of lingering wood smoke, while giant birds and flying reptiles gathered about, some circling, some rising or diving.

"Let's take a look," Falconie said.

They did a slow loop around the marshes. There was no mistaking the site where the expedition's chopper had gone down. The Jayhawk itself was a pile of crushed, twisted wreckage, with a huge mud-yellow dinosaur draped across it, obviously quite dead. Flattened, half-eaten human corpses lay in the dirt. Vultures, giant ravens, and huge, leathery flying reptiles were gathered there by the dozen, eating their fill, occasionally squabbling among themselves. The bigger scavengers gorged on the carcass of the giant reptile, leaving the human remains to condor-sized vultures. It seemed plain that nothing human had survived down there. Falconie saw the corpse of another giant dinosaur not far away with yet more of those goddamn scavengers enjoying the feast.

So that was the fate of Sanderson's team. Later on they could check it out more closely. Right now there was nothing they could do to save the explorers' lives, even if that had suited Falconie's plans, and there was still the radio signal from Denham's team for them to deal with. Denham and the rest seemed to be south of here, back in the tall forest. As they flew, Falconie got a fix on it from different angles. With that data, the Super-Osprey's inbuilt computer could triangulate a precise position.

If they could find a space big enough to land the VTOL craft, they'd soon find Denham's party.

"All right, Denham," Falconie said, more for his own benefit than Coffey's, "let's see if you're still alive." *And if you are, I'll damn sure do something about it.*

Once again, Kong threw himself at the raptors, but there were too many. He broke the back of one and threw it aside, but more attacked him with their sickle-like hind claws. He kicked one of the shark-toothed reptiles full force and it flew thirty feet through the air along the wide jungle path before slamming with a thud into a huge tree's ridged, buttressed trunk. Kong was taking wounds on his legs and arms but he was simply too big for the raptors to attack his vital organs. Unless they could cut his limbs out from under him, the raptors could not do him fatal damage.

Human beings lacked that size advantage. The raptors could seize the biggest man and tear him open in seconds. All around Jack, people were dying.

Quick sickle-slices dismembered Kowalski as he tried to fire. Roxanne slipped and fell to the ground—one reptile tripped over her as it raced a second too early for the kill. Jack fell back against the trunk of a giant emergent hardwood. Heart pounding in his chest, he wedged into position between two of the tree's twisting buttress roots. He saw no way to survive this latest ambush, but he wouldn't die without fighting to his last breath. As two of the raptors bent toward Roxanne where she lay on the ground, winded and helpless for the moment, Jack squeezed back the trigger of his dart rifle—and fired. He hit one raptor as Kong seized the other by its neck. The giant ape flung the thousand-pound killer dinosaur over his shoulder with no more effort than a child tossing an apple core. It crashed into a tree trunk and fell to the ground jerking in agony, its spine broken.

Kong roared with anger and pain from his wounds...and something even bigger roared back.

Only twenty yards away, that "something" pushed through the foliage, effortlessly bending palm trees as it went. It was huge and black-furred. If Kong had seemed like a living, moving mountain, he was now just a foothill. *This* was the real thing—an enormous male gorilla that made Kong seem puny. The full-grown male roared again. It stretched to its full height, its head up among the branches, and slapped its chest a dozen times. For the first time in his adult life, Jack felt like a helpless infant, overwhelmed by the thundering voice of an enraged father. He was nothing to this colossal creature. Nothing at all.

The giant slapped its chest another few times, then dropped to all fours. It rushed at a group of the raptors—half a dozen of them—scattering them like ten-pins. With its heavy left arm, it crushed a raptor against the ground. When it raised the arm a moment later, the pack-hunting dinosaur lay still. The other raptors turned their attention to this newest enemy, arching their necks and hissing angrily. Jack rushed from his position among the tree roots, kneeling at Roxanne's side to see if she was okay. She reached up to cling to him round the neck as both massive apes squared off against the raptors. The fighting was soon over. More raptors lay broken on the jungle path—the rest had fled into the forest.

It was clear that Jack and Roxanne were the only human survivors. Lying among the bodies of the raptors were the eviscerated corpses of all their colleagues. Jack dragged Roxanne back to the relatively shielded spot that he'd found among the buttress roots of the giant tree as the two victorious apes began to circle each other. "Uh-oh," Jack said. "They both want to be king of the jungle." Their circling became increasingly rapid. They snarled and exchanged angry glares, trying to stare each other down. Neither wanted to make the first attack, but neither was going to back off.

Suddenly both apes reared up. They roared at each other, baring their huge teeth and slapping their chests. The larger ape was at least five feet taller than Kong—more like Kong's "daddy" from 1933. *It must be twice Kong's weight,* Jack guessed, *or maybe even more.* Even Kong couldn't fight a monster like that! Compared to this full-grown wild ape, he was still just a kid.

Roxanne must have been thinking it, too. "No, Kong!" she screamed. Without warning, the beasts rushed at each other. Their tons of bone, muscle, and hide slammed together like two tourist buses colliding head-on out on the highway. In a blur of movement, they gripped and shook each other, tested their strength, tried to bite.

Kong got the worst of it. The wild ape tossed him like a strong man heaving a bag of cement. Kong fell against a thirty-foot palm tree, which splintered with the impact of his four tons. Then the larger beast was upon him, pounding on Kong's back with both of its huge fists. Kong twisted like a wrestler and snapped with his jaws, but the full-grown wild male was unfazed by it. Kong managed to squirm free and rolled onto all fours, snarling, the hair bristling all along his spine. He was ready to start again.

"He's going to get killed," Jack said, finally letting go of Roxanne. "Doesn't he know how to submit?"

"No one ever taught him," Roxanne said.

The apes bit and tore at each other. They pummeled each other with blows that would have flattened automobiles. The full-grown male slammed into Kong brutally and again sent him sprawling on the ground.

"Kong won't give up," Jack said.

"No, he's too stubborn."

"He's got to submit, Rox—or he's going to get *killed!*"

As the wild male bent over Kong, attacking with its teeth, Roxanne aimed her dart rifle and fired. She scored a clean hit but it only further enraged the giant. It turned away from Kong and looked angrily in Jack and Roxanne's direction. It snarled and roared and moved toward them with slow deliberation. This close up, its roars were painful to the ears. Again the giant gorilla snarled, revealing huge teeth that could crush a man's body. With their backs against the tree, there was nowhere for Jack or Roxanne to run... But then Kong leaped on the giant's back, dragging it to the ground under his weight. The two huge brutes landed almost on top of the dwarfed humans. They fought again—wrestling, biting, pounding, and tearing at each other.

For the first few seconds Kong seemed to give as good he was getting—but it couldn't last. The far larger and stronger ape soon threw him off and Kong landed heavily on his back with a loud expulsion of breath. It seemed that all the fight had been knocked out of him.

Desperately, Jack reloaded his own dart rifle. He fired quickly as the wild ape turned to consider him and Roxanne. Again it stood on its hind legs, lifting its head to roar at the forest canopy. It head and shoulders were up among the branches. Jack fumbled, got the rifle loaded, and aimed. You couldn't miss a target as big as that—it was like aiming at the sky. But striking it cleanly was another matter. As the ape flailed its arms, slapping its broad chest to display dominance, the dart struck a hairy forearm and spun away into the trees. At the same time Roxanne loaded her rifle. She fired! This time the dart hit the ape's chest and stuck there—a clean hit. The ape stared and snarled at the place where the dart had hit it, merely a pinprick for such a gigantic beast.

Jack looked wildly from one side to the other, trying to work out what to do next. His brain was going into overdrive, but reality gave it nothing to get a grip on.

For a moment the wild male ape merely glared at him and Roxanne, as if more bemused than angry at the efforts of its feeble human enemies. Then it raised its head once more and roared louder than ever.

There was an answering roar in the distance. Jack turned in that direction. *What the hell?*

Kong shook himself where he'd fallen. His body twisted in one powerful movement and suddenly he was on all fours again. He rushed his rival from behind, but it turned and batted him away much like a taller, stronger prizefighter could deal with a brave opponent. Both giant apes faced off once more, but as Kong circled him, the wild male finally started to look wobbly. The tranquilizer was having some effect. Perhaps sensing weakness, Kong attacked with renewed ferocity.

Yet again, there was a blur of muscle, fur, and the movements of powerful jaws. Both apes were now covered in blood. The larger beast used its weight and strength to push Kong to the ground, but didn't follow up with pounding or biting. It remained on all fours—roaring, shaking its head, then roaring again. Some of the power had gone out of its lungs. Kong bit, scratched, slapped, punched, and kicked his way free. He rolled to the palm tree whose trunk he'd almost broken when he'd landed on it a couple of rounds before. He stretched against the trunk on his hind legs, rising to two-thirds the height of the palm, and gripped it in a clumsy bear hug. He shook and pulled at the tree, breaking it off near the ground. Now he had a huge wooden weapon with one jagged, multi-splintered end.

The giant male lumbered toward him on its feet and foreknuckles, quite unsteady now from the massive dose of tranquilizer, but still conscious. Kong charged, using the tree trunk as a battering ram or a kind of monstrous lance. The splintered wood struck the wild gorilla in the middle of its body with all Kong's weight behind it. The giant went down in a heap. It quickly got to its feet but it looked confused and didn't move to attack.

Kong charged a second time with his makeshift lance, catching his rival at the shoulder. This time, the wild gorilla took several seconds getting up. As Kong brandished his weapon to attack yet again, the wild gorilla finally backed off. It snarled and roared one more time, still not wanting to submit, but then it hobbled clumsily back into the jungle, bending or snapping the unfortunate trees in its path. Kong threw down his tree-trunk weapon. He reared to full height, slapped his chest more times than Jack could possibly count, and roared in triumph—oblivious, it seemed, to all the wounds he'd suffered from killer vines, the carnosaur, raptors, and now the giant wild gorilla.

Once again, an answering roar came from somewhere in the reaches of the jungle. Kong's ears pricked up as he dropped the massive weight of his upper body back on his foreknuckles. The roar came one more time, perhaps a tiny bit closer—or was Jack just imagining that? Kong hesitated for a moment, looking first in that direction, then at Jack and Roxanne where they still huddled against their protective tree trunk. "What is it, Kong?" Roxanne asked. "What do you think it is?"

Suddenly, Kong ran in the direction of the sound, leaving his human friends alone.

TWENTY-SIX

It was no simple task finding a dry, clear space large enough for the Super-Osprey to land, but Falconie spotted a break in the trees just a mile from where he'd pinpointed Denham's position. He lowered the VTOL craft cautiously. *Gently, gently. Just kiss the ground.* As they landed, the wings brushed against some low shrubs but nothing big enough to damage them. They were in luck.

This was a fairly flat expanse of high, stony ground, with nothing but shrubs and grasses. Falconie hated leaving the Super-Osprey unguarded but there was safety in numbers—better not to leave anyone behind. The key was to act quickly then get back here. Give the island's megafauna as little chance as they could to take an interest in the aircraft. A compass reading told him the way to go. If the paths were not too tough they might locate Denham in an hour, maybe even less. Otherwise, they'd have to think of Plan B.

He had no intention of camping overnight, but one way or another they'd eventually find Denham and his party. With luck, Denham would already be dead, and they'd just have to identify the remains. That would be easy money. If not, Falconie would do what he was being paid for.

First, he radioed the base to report what had happened to Sanderson's party and to give his current position in the Super-Osprey. Valdez wasn't the sweetest guy in the world, but he wasn't in on Hemming's secret plans for Jack Denham. They'd have to keep him posted as if they planned to be Denham's saviors. That would be best for everyone.

Otani answered the radio; Falconie briefed her tersely, then demanded to speak with Valdez.

"Armando?" the scientist asked.

"They treating you right?"

"They know better than *not* to."

"Roger that, man. You heard what I told your little Jap friend?"

"All of it. That's a pity about Giles Sanderson—he was a fine scientist."

"I'm sure he must have been. We'll go and find Denham's group."

"Good hunting, Armando."

Yeah, dude—if only you knew.

Falconie signed off, and they all scrambled quickly from the Super-Osprey, checking in every direction for dangerous lifeforms. A huge, flat beetle scuttled over the stony ground, more insects droned from the forest all around them, and some birds flew overhead. But nothing here looked seriously dangerous. *Good.* Falconie went first, waving for the others to follow. He held his rifle, strapped across his chest, in both hands, ready to fire it at a moment's notice.

Walking single file, they headed into the trees, eyes peeled for any kind of path or trail that might take them in the right direction. Falconie's nerves were twitching, alert every second for ambush from the island's predators. As he went, he checked the ground below, the trees above, and in every other direction. Attack could come from anywhere.

He briefly considered splitting up his "rescue" party. All six of them were equipped with radio headsets to stay in touch with each other at short range. If they fanned out in their search for clues, they might find Denham's party sooner. But he dismissed the idea for the same reason that he'd not left a guard on the Super-Osprey. Safety in numbers—it was best not to take the risk. Despite Valdez's gloating back at the camp on the beach, Denham and the rest weren't fools or weaklings. If *they* were in trouble you had to start worrying.

Always thorough in his preparation, Falconie had researched their personal backgrounds. For their occupations and ages, those people were all quite fit. Denham and Blaine were experienced in the wild. They'd hiked plenty of jungles in their time. Denham himself was a serious mountain climber. People like that might make mistakes—anyone could—but not stupid beginners' errors. It must be goddamn *dangerous* out here in this jungle. What they'd seen of Sanderson's party was ample proof of that—that huge dinosaur, the crushed chopper, all those mean-looking scavengers. It was best to watch your every step and stick together.

All the same, the most dangerous species of all was Man. With the right training and equipment, a well-disciplined team of men could handle anything. That was where Denham and the rest really had made a mistake. This place was hostile; you had to treat it like an enemy force.

They found the path they needed—somewhat wider than Falconie had expected. It reminded him again of the size of the island's creatures, that they could clear such paths through the undergrowth. As he led the way between trees, creepers, and giant ferns, his confidence fell just slightly. A place like this could make you feel small. The largest trees soared far out sight, beyond the layers of greenery. Once you were among them, you were like an ant, passing by their enormous girths. You had to concentrate and keep your mind on what you were doing, or the goddamn jungle would swallow up your feelings.

They headed still deeper among the trees. Suddenly, there was a loud bird call—at least Falconie thought it might be a bird—from high overhead in the green canopy. It sounded almost like a rattlesnake, but much louder than *that*. Nothing appeared. They passed a fifteen-foot-thick tree trunk on their right and a dark brown beetle crawled downward on the trunk. It looked something like a cockroach, but over a foot long. *Goddamn ugly critter.* Falconie blasted it with a quick burst of fire from his M-16. Something bellowed in answer then crashed away through the bushes. He never saw what it was. Birds squawked in the bushes behind them. Insects droned all around.

Patiently, Falconie continued, one booted step at a time, occasionally checking his compass bearings as paths branched off each other, none going in exactly the right direction—they'd have to work their way by a zigzag route to Denham, Blaine, and the rest. Falconie decided to save his lungs and not to call just yet, though Denham's party could not be far away. Sound wouldn't travel all that well through the trees and scrub and over the noises of insects, birds, and God knew what else. They walked for five more minutes, then he tried calling for the first time: "Denham!" No answer came. They walked for *another* five minutes, enduring the heat and sweat, and the thickening clouds of flying insects. "Denham!" Falconie called again.

Coffey took up the theme. "Denham!" he called in his deep voice. "Denham, where are you, man?"

They continued forward, still zigzagging at times to test the paths. Falconie kept his rifle on "auto"—nothing was going to stop him now that he'd come this far. "Hey, Denham!" he shouted. Then he added, in a lower voice for the benefit of the others in his team, "Come on out, sucker. Come out here and get yourself killed."

Coffey laughed. "Yeah," he said. Then, in a sing-song voice, the huge man added: "Jack De-enn-ham. Come on out and plaa-ay."

That was when the hissing started. As they reached a wider section of the path, a strange reptile appeared in their way, standing on its hind legs. It was ten feet tall with beak-like jaws full of evil-looking teeth. Worse were the upward-then-downward recurved claws on its feet. Claws like sickles.

There was more hissing all around.

"Form a circle," Falconie said quietly. Then, louder—"Do it now!" He opened fire on full auto.

The ex-commandos stood back to back on the path, squeezing off three-round bursts as the nightmarish reptiles attacked from all sides. There was nothing else quite like this feeling, cutting loose with the M-16s on live targets. It was better than sex—like teaching poor old Mother Nature a lesson.

One of the nasties got past their hail of fire. With the swiftness of a striking snake, it caught Etting-hausen by the neck, lifted its leg...and struck. And struck again with its other clawed foot. The sickle claws tore at Ettinghausen's body armor—but the armor kept him alive for a few seconds. The reptile tossed him like a rag doll back to its ugly friends. Falconie kept on firing; there was nothing else for it. They took out the lizard that had attacked Ettinghausen, but others pounced on the man's body, quickly ripping through his armor and cutting him up like you'd slice a pear.

Shit! Falconie thought. *Oh man...just keep firing.*

The distant roar came again. "It's slightly different," Roxanne said. "I think that just might be a female."

"It seems like we've done our duty," Jack said, with a hollow laugh. "We came here to repatriate Kong." But was it as simple as that? Kong, he knew well, was covered in wounds from all his battles. If infection set in they might become serious. And how would he adapt to this place without human beings to care for him?

Roxanne must have been thinking the same way. "We've got to follow his trail," she said. "We need to know he's all right."

"Rox—"

"No time to *talk*, Jack!" She rushed onto the path where Kong and the wild male had fought, looked around to get oriented, then ran the way that Kong had gone.

"Roxanne, don't make things even worse!" Jack shouted after her. But she'd already vanished into the jungle. Jack tore off his backpack, which could only encumber him now. He kept his water canteen and swapped his dart rifle for Kowalski's Winchester Magnum, which lay on the ground beside its dead owner. Kowalski damn sure wouldn't be needing it.

Jack checked that he had plenty of ammunition, and as quickly as he could on his tiring legs, he headed after Roxanne. *Damn her, she should have waited.*

She'd gained a start and Jack had lost sight of her among the ferns, bushes, and trees. Roxanne was strong and athletic—not to mention a decade younger than he was—and she could cover ground quickly, even weighed down by her gear. But he figured he would catch up, as long as nothing killed him first. Her backpack was enough of a handicap to give him a fighting chance.

He had no trouble following Kong's path. The ape's weight had made deep tracks in the damp earth and he'd left a trail of freshly broken tree trunks and branches. Jack plunged along as fast as his tired legs would carry him, just hoping that Kong would clear aside any dangers before Roxanne reached them. He thought of that giant spiderweb that they'd seen on the first day just a few hundred yards from the beach. And that was the least of what she might encounter, running headlong in the jungle.

Fortunately, not much could stand in the way of a four-ton adolescent gorilla looking for a mate.

Burdened by his rifle and canteen, Jack was soon breathless with exertion. His lungs wanted to give out, but still he ran.

Kong and Roxanne were out of sight, but occasionally Kong roared from somewhere ahead. Jack stopped to catch his breath. *Goddammit, Roxanne!* he thought, as he bent over, panting. He took some last ragged, painful breaths, willed himself onward, started running again. After a hundred yards, he caught a glimpse of Roxanne as she ran around a bend in the trail. He called after her but she just kept running. She disappeared from view.

Keep going…keep going…

When he next he saw her, he'd gained a little. There was still no sign of Kong.

"Rox," he called, "let me catch up!"

She slowed down slightly, and he gained a few more yards. "Come on, Jack!" she called over her shoulder. "We don't want to lose him in the forest."

"Wait for me, please." He tried for a last burst of speed, but his legs seemed turned to jelly. He caught up at last but only because she let him. He grabbed her by the shoulder. "This would be a fine time to get yourself killed," he said.

That brought a spontaneous laugh. "When you put it like that, you've got a point." Not far away, Kong roared. "Well?" Roxanne said. "Coming?" She didn't try to run, but hiked briskly in Kong's direction.

Jack followed on her heels. "Roxanne—" They'd left the radio back with the dead bodies of their companions, but Jack figured they hadn't come all that far. If the rescue party homed in on the radio's signal they should see that he and Roxanne were not among the dead. As long as the two of them could stay alive long enough they would still be rescued, but they were adding to everyone's danger. Perhaps, he thought, they should just let Kong go, consider him repatriated. But Roxanne evidently had other ideas. She wanted to see it through, and he really couldn't blame her.

Well, they'd probably be safer if they stayed close to Kong. That was one justification for following him. If the big ape could keep his mind off sex for a moment, he might still give them some protection.

354

"Roxanne, *please* slow down. We'll find him together, but we've got to conserve some energy."

She turned and smiled wryly. "Come on, then. We'll get through this."

Jack wasn't so sure.

Ettinghausen was dead, but everyone else seemed okay. Falconie inserted a fresh magazine into his M-16. It looked like a case of humans 5, ugly monsters 1, he though grimly. Five of those walking death machines lay where they'd been gunned down by automatic fire. The rest had vanished into the trees—more proof that well-armed humans were the most dangerous beasts in the jungle.

He considered Ettinghausen's body, which had been dismembered by dozens of sickle-slashes from the reptiles' claws. There was no time to bury the corpse, or return it to the Super-Osprey. If they were going to get the job done, and get out of here still alive, they'd need to act quickly. If there was any time later, they might be able to do something about Ettinghausen. You didn't leave buddies behind, dead or alive. They ought to do something about the body. *Yeah*, he thought, *fat chance of that*. Ettinghausen's remains wouldn't last long in the jungle. Falconie had seen the island's scavengers in action and knew how they'd treat an unburied corpse.

"Come on," he said to the others. "We've got a job to do."

Dead buddy or not, the job came first—they had to make sure that Denham never returned from the island. If that meant shooting him outright, so be it, as long as it could be explained as an accident. One

RUSSELL BLACKFORD

thing that Falconie now realized plainly was that shooting accidents were all too possible. As long as there were no other witnesses, they could easily explain away the effect of a few "stray" bullets—but better yet would be making sure that Denham's body was never found. Let him die without leaving too much evidence. The fight with the reptiles had shaken Falconie a little, but he could also see advantages to the dangers of the island. Bodies might get scavenged. People might be eaten alive.

He headed on, hoping to pick up the tracks of hiking boots. There seemed to be more, and even broader, paths in this area, as if giant creatures had been wandering all round. The overlapping prints in the earth included some that could belong to huge primates, but there were still no signs of human prints. Then, some hundred of yards east of where they'd been landed, Coffey walked close to a huge tangle of thorny vines, which suddenly reached out tendrils to attack. One vine whipped around the big man's neck, while others gripped his arms and torso, trying to pull him apart and back into its vegetable mass.

Instinctively, Falconie fired his M-16. "Holy Jesus," he said.

"This really is a screw-up," Valdez said, standing at Laurel's shoulder as she struggled futilely to raise either exploring party on the radio. He actually seemed to be gloating about it.

Laurel ignored him, trying desperately to get through to Jack's group. It was bad enough to lose contact with Sanderson's team, but with Jack not answering now…"Is *someone* there?" she said into the radio mike. "Answer me, please."

"If any of them are alive, Falconie will find them," Valdez said. "It's just as well we arrived."

"Why don't you just shut up?" Mark said to him. "We could do without your help."

"But you couldn't," Valdez said.

It seemed that he had a point, but there was no need to rub it in so cruelly. Laurel decided to ignore him. "Is anyone there?" she said into the mike.

"You might as well give up for now," Valdez said. "Falconie will find them…or he won't. Either way, there's nothing you can do about it."

"You're way out of line," Mark said.

"Jack?" Laurel said. "*Anyone?*"

Valdez snatched the microphone from her hand. "You're wasting your energy."

"Listen, dude," Mark said, "our friends are dying out there in the jungle. If you don't think that matters, what kind of man are you?"

Valdez stared at him coldly, but his knuckles went white as he gripped the radio mike. "We're doing what we can. You should be thankful that Charlton sent us here."

"Why don't you take a one-way walk in the jungle?" Mark said.

Valdez handed back the mike with an ugly look that said, *I'll get you for this.*

Laurel took the microphone and gave Valdez a so-sweet smile, knowing she'd won a minor battle of wills. But Valdez was just a pawn in Charlton Hemming's plans. She imagined Hemming's expression when he heard the news—how he'd respond to their situation. He would probably be delighted if Jack were killed out there in the jungle.

Jack had always said that the toothy smile made Hemming look like a shark. Laurel thought of a hungry, grinning shark, gliding through the water.

A man-eater.

Jack and Roxanne marched purposefully, side by side, along the trail that Kong had made.

"If Kong's fine, at least we'll know we've done the right thing," Roxanne said. "We can go back with our consciences clear about that."

"That would all be great," Jack said with a strong note of irony, "if we hadn't seen so many people die and we weren't alone in a deadly jungle full of man-eating animals and plants. I think we must both be crazy."

"Listen!"

From up ahead came the sounds of two animals roaring. Roxanne stopped, concentrating on what she heard. She unscrewed the lid of her water canteen and raised it to her lips. She drank carefully, not wasting any precious water, then offered the open canteen to Jack. He took a few quick gulps and passed it back to her. The animals continued to roar.

"I'm not sure I like the sound of that," Roxanne said. "Let's check it out."

They walked with the lightest possible steps, though it was probably useless trying to sneak up on Kong and whatever he had found. Gorilla senses were far too sharp for that. They passed a tangle of killer vine, then a tree branch with some kind of buzzing, brightly colored wasp the size of a hawk. Three hundred yards on they came to the source of all the noise. Kong was with another gorilla at least as big as himself, but smaller than the giant male that he'd beaten off with their help.

"A female?" Jack asked in a whisper.

"I'd bet it's a fully grown female," Roxanne whispered back.

As they watched Kong tried to get around behind the female, as if he wanted to mate with her. She'd have none of it. She turned sideways and beat him across the face with her huge leathery paw. Kong tried again. She roared and cuffed him hard. They went through this routine several time before Kong roared back, expressing increasing frustration. Now they faced off, snarling and roaring, almost like rival males. Yet again, Kong tried to step around her. "Persistent, isn't he?" Jack said.

"Some men are worse," she said. Then she gave Jack a wide grin. "I think he's going to be all right."

"Aren't you worried about his wounds?"

"Yes, I am—they might be infected. I'd give him a course of antibiotics if I could, but what's in my first-aid kit wouldn't make any difference."

As they spoke the giant female struck Kong one more time. This blow, accompanied by an enraged roar was the most powerful one yet.

"Uh-oh," Roxanne said. "She's getting impatient with him. Better back off, junior."

The female shuffled away on her hind feet and foreknuckles, taking one of several trails that passed through here. Kong followed her warily.

"Seen enough yet?" Jack said.

"Let's find out what happens." Roxanne pointed at all the trails. "What do you make of those?"

Something clicked in Jack's mind. "Are you thinking what I'm thinking?"

"I'd say I am, Jack. But it depends on what you're thinking."

"I don't know…it's just a guess."

"Out with it! What are you *guessing*, then?"

He grinned. "Gorilla super-highway."

Falconie and the others fired their M-16s. Within seconds, they reduced part of the vine to matchwood, some of the rounds going close to Coffey's body.

Coffey dragged himself free and they all backed away from the plant. Falconie peered more closely at it from what he hoped was a safe distance. Then his eyes went wide with the possibilities. Tangled in there were all kinds of animal remains—bones, skin, rotting flesh. The vine infiltrated the branches of a group of trees and ferns maybe forty feet high. Its mass of thorny tendrils extended sixty feet back and forward along their path. It was big enough to entangle an elephant and use its carcass as fertilizer.

The mutant plant had almost made a meal out of Coffey. What else might it be able to do? Something like that could very useful. It could turn Denham into a tasty snack and no one need ever know how it had happened. This would all work out, Falconie realized. *No doubt about it.* It was a shame about Ettinghausen, but casualties happened in war, and they were most certainly in a war—against both Denham and the jungle.

Coffey was shaking and gasping, but he found an impact grenade in his webbing and loaded it into the launcher under the barrel of his M-16. "I'll show that son of a bitch," he said between gasps for air.

"*No!*" Falconie said. "We don't have time for that. If you're okay, let's move on."

"Goddamn son of a *bitch*."

"Are you okay or not, Donut?"

"Yeah, Falcon, I'm okay."

Falconie made sure that Coffey was telling the truth, that he'd be all right for the coming confrontation. His uniform was torn and there were still fragments of thorn lodged in the big guy's skin. Some might be hard to pull out of him or even carve out of his flesh.

But Coffey waved Falconie away. "I'm fine, man," he said. "Really, I'm fine."

"All right, then. "Let's move on. We'll fix you later."

They continued, watching even more carefully. An army of giant centipedes scuttled by, maybe forty or fifty of them. Then around a bend in the path they came to a huge animal like a rhino. It stood with its back to them on what was now a broad pathway through the forest with bent-over trees and broken branches. The beast must have heard or smelled them, for it turned, its small eyes looking baleful. It was a one-horned rhino, sure enough, but bigger than an African elephant. Rhinos were bad-tempered bastards, so Falconie didn't take a chance. Besides, this brute was in their way. "Hit 'em with the grenade, Donut! Now!"

Coffey fired.

As Falconie turned, raising one arm across his face, the force of the concussion struck him like a powerful hand. When he looked again, the giant mammal had been flung to the ground. It was a bloody, mangled wreck of a thing; most of its head had been blown off by the force of the blast.

Nature 1, humans 6.

They tiptoed past the carcass of the rhino as insects gathered on it—and then two giant vultures. Further on was another tangle of the thorny, meat-eating vine. They kept their distance on the other side but kept going. Then they found what they'd been looking for: marks on the ground from trudging boots among the tracks of various animals. Falconie pointed with a satisfied smile on his face. "All right, boys," he said. "Let's bag some human quarry."

TWENTY-SEVEN

Hemming had enjoyed his visit to Sri Lanka—he looked forward to coming back many more times to see his Skull Island venture prosper and grow. Island Properties Park was an excellent facility and he'd placed it capable hands. Likewise with his plans for dear old Jack. Valdez was nervous and overly eager to please, but he'd be efficient. Falconie was something else again. He was clearly *very* good at what he did, a man with no fumblings or excuses. Give him a job and he'd no doubt get it done.

Now that was the way to do business.

During the morning Hemming used his hotel phone to call four different government officials just to make sure that the local wheels were greased. Everything was running smoothly. Island Properties Park was good for Colombo's economy, which made it good news for these officials. By midday he was almost finished with them. "Thank you for this discussion, Minister," he said, rounding off his last and most important call. "I'd be delighted if you'd visit us next time I'm in Colombo. You'll find the facility very interesting."

"That would be my pleasure," the Minister said. He spoke with a perfect British accent, the fruit of an Oxford education.

"Goodbye then, sir. I'm sure we'll speak again soon."

"The best of luck to you, Mr. Hemming."

Half an hour later, Hemming checked out of the hotel and took a taxi to the airport. Soon he'd be back in San Francisco, shivering in the winter and dealing with everyday issues. But then there'd be calls from Falconie and Valdez. "Oh, poor Jack," he imagined himself saying at the sad news of his rival's death. The sooner that happened, the better.

He paid the smiling driver and stepped from the cab into the tropical sunshine. What a miracle life was! There was always more to look forward to.

Jack heard the sound of automatic weapons fire in the distance. Those were military rifles. Up ahead, Kong roared, as if in response.

"Yes," Jack said, "weapons. You know about that by now."

The giant female gorilla had outpaced them all, but Kong put on a burst of speed to catch up with her. "She's going somewhere," Roxanne said, striding out the distance.

"Everything that moves is going *somewhere*," Jack said. "What do you mean?"

"She's not stopping to eat or check anything out. What's the bet she's headed back to her nest?"

"What about those shots behind us?"

"Sounds like our rescue team, doesn't it?"

"It sounds like they're in trouble."

"Maybe not. It might be their idea of taking biological samples—machine-gun everything that moves."

"That figures," Jack said.

She gave him a quick glance. "Even if they *are* in trouble, we can't do anything about it. Let's follow Kong."

The distant firing continued, then died down. One way or other the rescue party's situation had resolved itself. Meanwhile, Jack had lost sight of Kong but not of the way he'd gone.

They were coming to what looked like the end of a tunnel, lit up with sunlight. They moved toward it, then into it—and gazed with wonder at what they saw. Here was a vast space, like a great, green cathedral a hundred yards across. Looking up, Jack could see that the jungle's high leafy canopy was almost unbroken, but muted emerald light streamed through to the damp earth nearly two hundred feet below. The lower layers of bushes and trees, the layers beneath the high canopy, were thinned out, leaving long grasses, scattered fruit trees, and some shallow streams and pools of water in the middle of the area.

None of that was so amazing.

But paddling in the water, like kids in a six-inch wading pool, were at least a dozen gorillas, each larger than Kong. On the other side of this space, several more of the giant apes played, slept, or merely walked about. One enormous male lay back on a nest of grasses, while females, younger males, and bear-sized gorilla kids moved warily around it.

"Jack?" Roxanne whispered.

"What?"

"Keep your voice down. Gorillas have sensitive ears—you don't want to upset them."

"All right," he whispered back.

"I feel like we're in the garden of the gods."

"It's awesome," he said as quietly as he could manage. "It really is. This is the most awesome sight yet."

The big female that Kong had been chasing headed for the water. She splashed across it, joining some of the other apes. Kong himself held back, watching from Jack's side of the water, as if unsure about joining the group.

"This is what we came to see," Jack said. He glanced over to where Kong was hesitating. "Do you think they'll take him in—the other gorillas, I mean? Will they accept him?"

"We'll find out." Roxanne sidled, partly crouched, closer to Kong's position. As Jack followed, Kong looked back at them.

"I hate to get anthropomorphic," Jack said when he'd caught up to Roxanne, "but it's almost like he's asking our permission to go."

"It's easy to project feelings onto animals."

"You don't think that's what he's thinking?"

Roxanne shrugged. "It might be something analogous," she said, still speaking very softly. "I wouldn't want to say more than that. I'm a scientist. When it's all said and done I don't like speculating about the untestable."

"Yeah, of course not."

"Kong is intelligent, but who can say what's happening in his brain? Maybe he's just getting used to all of this. Maybe he's wondering what *we're* thinking about it all—or something analogous to *that*." She gave a quiet laugh. "He's a gorilla, Jack...not human. He might understand more than we know, but if so, he can't explain it to us."

"Maybe if we'd taught him to sign—"

From the distance behind them came the sound of an explosion. Jack and Roxanne exchanged glances. "If you can't machine-gun it, just blow it up," Jack said.

"If they can blow things up, they're still alive," Roxanne said reasonably. "Let's see what Kong does. Whatever else he's feeling, he must be more confused than we are."

"Shit," Falconie said.

He'd fought in war, he'd killed men in cold blood and done worse things than that, but he'd never had to see anything like this. On the path, there were dead bodies everywhere, torn open like those goddamn reptiles had done to Ettinghausen. In a way, it was even worse. These people had not been wearing body armor and it looked like the sickle-clawed reptiles had simply split them—spilling their guts like you could split a coconut with a machete. Among the bodies were guns, packs, and pieces of abandoned equipment. Surely no one had survived this slaughterhouse.

And it was not just human bodies. Lying with them were those of many of sickle-clawed reptiles. Some had obviously been shot, but others looked like something enormously powerful had flung them against the trees or crushed them under its immense weight. They were scattered over a wide area, across and along the path.

That gorilla, maybe? Kong? But one thing was for sure: Kong wasn't here now, alive or dead.

Giant scavenging birds fed on the human and reptile corpses—dozens of vultures, and four of the huge black ravens. Beetles, centipedes, and a couple of huge scorpions crawled everywhere. Flies buzzed over the carrion. This was a scene of butchery as bad as in any war.

But there was more to it than that. One palm tree looked as though a giant had reached down and broken its trunk at the base—Falconie put two and two together as he saw the rest of the broken trunk lying on the path. Something huge really *had* twisted off the palm tree's trunk, then flung it about like a stick. There were broken branches everywhere, and even the ground looked churned up, like giants had fought here.

There were so many human corpses—but were any of them Jack Denham's? Some lay face down, some were horribly mutilated, and some were already half-eaten. But Falconie did a body count and it seemed that a couple were missing. They might have been carried off by predators, but then again maybe not. One or two people might have gotten out of this massacre alive.

"What now?" Coffey said.

"Keep your distance, boys," Falconie said. "Save your ammunition." He didn't want to fight all those scavengers at once. Some of them might fly off at the sound of rifle fire but some might turn on their attackers. They showed no fear of his party and the giant ravens just might be dangerous enemies. "Let's see what we can find out."

Signaling to the others to follow, he sidled carefully along the line of trees on one side of the path, keeping well away from the scavengers. The broken branches told of huge creatures that had burst onto this trail or off it. Maybe there would also be signs of human movements. Nothing attacked as Falconie led the way trying to interpret the marks on the ground and the damage to trees and bushes.

He found what he was after. There were the marks of human prints leading away from here. It looked like the bootmarks of two people running—maybe a woman followed by a man. Some of *his* booted prints overlay *hers*, so she was running ahead of him. Both sets of marks were fresher than the sole and knuckle prints of a giant simian creature. It all added up. "All right," Falconie said, "you've all seen—" He was going to say "worse," but that wouldn't have been true. "You've seen almost as bad."

"I think I'm going to be sick, man," Coffey said.

"No you're *not*." Falconie waited a few seconds to let that message sink in. "Listen up, all of you," he said. "None of the bodies look like Denham or like Roxanne Blaine. I think they're still alive—maybe the only survivors. They can't have gotten far." Those bootmarks were fresh, so Falconie's team was only a few minutes behind its quarry. "If we follow this trail we'll find them and then we can do what we have to do and get out of here."

It was tempting to forget about hunting Denham down. They could just let him and Blaine die in the jungle—tell Valdez and Hemming and that Otani woman that they hadn't been able to find them. But two people just *might* survive in the jungle for long enough to get back to the base camp. If luck was with them, if they hiked the distance without stopping for anything, a good walker like Denham or Blaine could easily do it in a day. After all they were still only a few miles from the beach, much as the terrain made the distances seem so much greater than normal. There was just that outside chance.

Back in 1933, two people had made it back to the beach, swimming in the river that flowed north/south from the island's volcanic mountain. The last thing Falconie needed was to have Denham and Blaine turn up still alive, but unwilling to return to the jungle. That would cause too many complications. *No, it's best to make absolutely sure.*

Falconie spoke grimly. "This job isn't over. Not yet, it isn't."

Hands firmly on his M-16 rifle, he turned from his troops to follow Denham's trail.

"All right," Coffey said to the others. "You heard the man."

After a few minutes Kong stepped closer to the center of the wild gorillas' space, walking on two legs over the muddy ground. Jack and Roxanne followed at a distance, crouching low in the grasses. With any luck they'd look inconspicuous, or at least harmless, to the other gorillas. Some of the gorillas glanced nervously in Kong's direction. None seemed to take any notice of the two much smaller primates that had followed him. With their sharp senses, the gorillas were surely well aware of Jack and Roxanne but they must have read them as posing no threat. *I hope it continues like that,* Jack thought. *If we just stay nice and quiet—*

There were distant shouts. "Jack Denham! Can you hear me? Dr. Blaine? If you're there, are you okay?"

Jack didn't recognize the voice. By the sound of it, it was someone who didn't get his way by charm and diplomacy.

Roxanne whispered, "Sounds like our rescue party."

"Yeah," Jack said. "I guess that's what it is."

"Don't make any noise until you have to," Roxanne said. "Let's hope they'll get closer."

"Okay, advice taken."

"And don't stare at the gorillas. They might take it as a challenge."

Thirty seconds later, the voices came more loudly. "Jack Denham? Roxanne Blaine?"

"All right," Roxanne said. "Let's hope Kong's new friends don't get too upset with us." She yelled back, "This way!"

Jack joined in. "Over here!"

"Stay right where you are!" Falconie shouted. He broke into a medium jog, following the direction of the voices.

Coffey and the others followed close behind him. They went down one path, then had to deviate as it turned at an unexpected angle. It took a few minutes, but they came to a kind of clearing. They burst into it, and saw—

Giant gorillas. Emerald sunlight.

And Denham and Blaine crouched there, near one of those goddamn gorillas. *That must be Kong*, Falconie thought, but the ape looked different from all the photos he'd seen of it. For one thing, it was so huge. It must have grown since he'd seen it on television back in the States—and besides, you could never get a proper idea of how big an animal like that really was until you saw it up close. The other change was that much of Kong's fur was matted with dried blood.

The setting was spectacular, but Falconie had a job to do. "Dr. Denham and Dr. Blaine?" he asked, showing them a touch of respect.

"That's right," Denham said, drawing himself up to speak with them. He spoke in a low voice as if afraid the gorillas were going to overhear. "And who are you?"

Falconie leveled his M-16 at Denham's head, knowing the others would do likewise, ready to cut down both of the scientists if it came to that. "Don't worry about my name."

"What's going on?" Blaine said.

"Just drop your weapons, both of you. Drop them right now!"

"Charlton—" Denham started to say.

"Shut-tup, man! Just do it! Now!"

Denham and Blaine lowered their weapons to the ground as Falconie and his people circled them.

"That's better," Falconie said. "Now, Dr. Blaine, just slide off the pack." She did so, and Falconie nodded approvingly. "Good girl, no sudden movements."

"I'm not a *girl*."

"Whatever. Now, you're both going to walk out of here calmly. We'll be watching your every step, so don't try anything cute."

"What's this all about?" Blaine said angrily.

"That's for me to know." *Some of that carnivorous vine would enjoy these two,* Falconie thought. They could just disappear into a mass of it and never be found again. Should he knock them unconscious, then feed them to the vine? Or was it better to give them to those sickle-clawed reptiles that hunted in packs? Either way, it was probably best to kill them first...then he'd decide how to dispose of the bodies. *Kill first, vine later*, seemed like his best option.

"Did Hemming send you?" Denham asked.

"No, smart guy," Coffey said, "we came from the goddamn moon."

TWENTY-EIGHT

Kong roared. All through the huge space and all around them, other apes roared back.

Kong doesn't like guns, Jack thought. *He knows that we're in danger!*

The giant ape ran, but not toward the five paramilitary thugs with the M-16s. He ran back into the jungle foliage, moving on all fours—and faster than Jack himself would have guessed was possible. Even after everything he'd seen Kong do, the big guy's speed was shocking. He certainly moved faster than the thugs could ever have guessed. They opened fire, but they must have misjudged the speed of what they were seeing and aiming at. Kong got away, crashing into the bushes.

Jack and Roxanne hit the wet ground as bullets whistled around them. Kong was so smart. If he'd charged straight at his enemies, they would surely have gotten him no matter how fast he was. Jack hunted around on the ground for his Magnum rifle, but the guy who seemed to lead this team of mercenaries was already upon him. "Get up!" he said.

"You're Falconie?" Jack said. *This* was supposed to be his rescuer?

The man was not that tall, but he looked immensely strong. He was built like a powerlifter, or a small gorilla. "If you say so," he said. "Now get up! *Do it!*"

When they stood, Falconie slammed the barrel of his M-16 into Jack's stomach. Jack screamed and doubled over in pain. Falconie threw a hard punch at Roxanne—Jack didn't see where it hit her, but she went down. Jack made a mental vow to kill the man, but then an iron-hard boot-toe took him in the ribs, seeming to crush them. Something might have broken. For a second, the pain was unbearable.

Roxanne was an athlete and Jack was himself fit and strong—for a man now into middle age. But they were helpless against this one guy, even leaving aside his goon squad. This Falconie was some kind of highly trained killer. What rock had Hemming found *him* under? Was he buying murderers now? Falconie's men gathered around Jack, pointing their military rifles at his head as he gasped desperately for breath. The strength had totally gone out of him from those two bone-crushing blows. He wanted to fight back but there was too much pain. For the moment, it seemed to have paralyzed him.

"Get up!" Falconie said. "Both of you."

"Why?" Jack asked through gritted teeth. "Just so you can knock us down?"

There was roaring and howling all through the "cathedral."

"We should shoot them now and get out of here," one of the thugs said nervously.

Strong hands dragged Jack back to his feet.

Falconie drew back his right arm. "We won't shoot them." Jack tried to duck the punch, but it came faster than he expected, crashing against the side of his jaw. He stayed on his feet, but stars blinked before his eyes. "I'll show you how to kill a man," Falconie said.

But then there was more roaring. As Jack tried to
pull himself together to fight for his life—and Roxanne's—an enormous male gorilla ran out of the forest
into the apes' clear area. Judging by its wounds, it
was the same full-grown male that Kong had fought.
Even a massive dose of tranquilizer hadn't stopped it
before, merely slowed it a little. Now it didn't even
look slowed down. It looked like it had recovered.

It looked pissed off.

Automatic rifles fired on the giant male, opening
up shallow wounds in its chest but not stopping it.
Jack ducked for cover, covering his head with his
hands. Other apes were charging from the far side of
the clearing, and Kong himself made a leap from the
foliage, falling on the thugs as they ran for their lives.
A giant gorilla foot squashed one. Kong crushed
another in one of his huge hands...

But what mattered most to Jack was that Roxanne
was okay. He looked about quickly and saw her
crawling over to him.

In a matter of seconds, the guns had stopped firing.
There were crushed or torn bodies everywhere. Kong
had moved like a tornado. Either he or the wild male
had thrown the thug-in-charge toward the center of
the green cathedral, as easily as flicking a match across
the room. Falconie's body lay thirty feet away. His
body moved slightly, so there was still some life left
in him.

Jack could feel where the cruel aches would soon
be in his own body. Another few seconds and Falconie would have killed him with his bare hands.
There was no way he could have stopped it. Hemming
had hired himself a monster. There were five human
monsters here, but against creatures as powerful and

fast as the giant apes all their merely human strength had been worth nothing.

Kong and the giant wild male faced off against each other for the second time. Both were wounded and angry, but if it came to a battle to the death there could only be one outcome. Kong was still not full-grown. Without a lot of help, he could never defeat a creature like that. If he didn't submit, the wild make would surely kill him. The gorillas circled each other on all fours. Each gave a sort of cough, as if to say: "Here I am, buddy. Now, just back off!"

For God's sake, Kong, you can't be the boss here yet, Jack thought. *You still need to grow a bit.*

The wild gorilla reared up, slapping its chest, then it roared and charged. Kong met the charge, biting and struggling. He rolled free as his bigger rival forced him down. Seconds later, he was back on his feet and foreknuckles as the wild male roared again and bared its teeth. But this time, Kong acted differently. He turned and moved away...toward Jack and Roxanne. He looked down at them with concern as if his rival wasn't there. The enormous male slapped its chest once more, then walked off on all fours toward the center of the cathedral. It seemed to have lost interest.

"Good gorilla," Roxanne said to Kong. "You had to learn that you can't beat everyone."

"He's smart, all right," Jack said. "Give him a few years and he'll be running this place."

"Spoken like a true silverback, my darling."

"Yeah," he said, though it hurt to talk, "I've got a bit of it in me."

Roxanne took his hand and squeezed it, as they got to their feet. Wincing with every breath from where he'd been hit in the stomach and kicked in the ribs, Jack walked over to the Falconie, who hadn't moved for some time.

"What was this all about?" Jack said, standing over him.

The man opened his eyes slightly. "Find out," he said.

"I will," Jack said.

The man winced. "Good luck in the jungle, Denham. I'll see you in hell."

When Jack crouched down to check, Falconie had stopped breathing. It looked as if his back was broken, and he must have had massive internal bleeding. Roxanne came over, dragging her pack from where she'd dropped it in the mud. She crouched and started to rummage through it.

"What are you doing?" Jack said.

She tried a smile, but her lips were puffy. One had been cut open—so that was where Falconie had hit her. "I'm going to take some DNA samples."

"What?"

She found some of her narrow test tubes and her cutting implements. "I said, I'm going to take some samples. Wasn't that quite clear, Dr. Denham? These guys might have interesting DNA. And let's search their clothing, too—you don't know what we'll find."

As she did her ghoulish work on their attackers, Kong approached one of the other gorillas. Both apes walked on all fours, their weight on their front knuckles. It looked like Kong had found another young male to deal with. Would it treat him as an ally or a rival? When they reached each other, they both stood upright, face to face, not touching at first, just staring. Then they touched, slapping hands—and embraced. They fell to the ground together, intertwined, rolling over and over. *They're not just animals*, Jack thought. *They're not quite human—but they're more like us than unlike.*

None of the giant apes treated Jack and Roxanne like a threat. With the fighting over, they forgot about the little naked-faced primates. Somehow they were smart enough to distinguish between the quiet ones who were Kong's friends and the five noisy killers who'd followed them into the green cathedral.

"Just remember not to *stare* at them, Jack," Roxanne said, without looking up from her work on the body of the leading thug.

Kong and the other young male continued to wrestle playfully. For a giant gorilla, Kong grunted fairly softly. Despite all his wounds, it seemed like he'd come home.

Roxanne glanced up, smiling crookedly. "I'll be sorry to say goodbye to Kong."

"I'll miss him, too," Jack said. "But he belongs here."

Another enormous male came over to inspect Kong. It sniffed him carefully, then wandered off without trying to dominate or attack. Then a female came to check him out. She climbed over Kong, sniffing at every part of his body, as if he might be hiding something under his fur or smuggled in his hollows and creases. Satisfied, she walked away. Kong wandered among the rest of the group. Some of them sniffed suspiciously, but others appeared to be bored. None challenged his right to be there. The newcomer had been accepted.

The green cathedral was getting darker. Somewhere above the canopy, Jack realized, the sun must be low in the sky. That gave them another problem. Traveling at night in this deadly jungle was out of the question.

They had no idea what predators hunted in the dark, and you could easily blunder into tangles of killer vine or God only knew what else. There was only one place to spend the night that just might be fairly safe.

"Rox?" he said.

"What, Jack?"

"This isn't a romantic proposition—"

"Damn, and I *so* thought it was going to be."

"—but I think we're going to have to spend the night together."

"Here?"

"I can't think of anywhere safer."

She looked around with exaggerated skepticism. "Uh-huh," she said. "That's typical, Dr. Denham."

"What have I done wrong now?"

"Any excuse to spend a few more hours near your overgrown child substitute."

"Come here, Rox," he said.

She finished what she was doing and packed away her gear in its rigid metal box. Jack embraced her gingerly. If both of them were going to die, at least he could spend one night Roxanne's arms—though he was too badly hurt for anything that could count as pleasure. Somehow, they'd have to get some sleep—then shoot their way back through the man-killing jungle.

But tomorrow's another day, he thought, as he held her as tight as he dared. *Things can only get worse.*

Jack woke in the gorillas' green cathedral. He felt dirty, aching, and bruised—but at least he was still alive. Roxanne snored gently beside him, curled on her side. The first morning sun slanted through the forest canopy, bathing the gorillas' home in soft, greenish light. A few of the huge apes went about their inscrutable business, while most still slept in nests around the cathedral's perimeter. Kong had made a nest during the night and now he was sleeping like a baby. He had a lot to recover from.

Painfully, Jack propped himself on an elbow for a better look around. *Ugh!* His ribs really hurt where Falconie had kicked him. His jaw felt like it had swollen to the size of a football. *Bastard.* Roxanne stirred and rolled over onto her back. She gave a soft groan and opened her eyes. "What's the time?" she said sleepily.

"Rox?" he whispered.

"*Jack?*" She sounded surprised to see him beside her. Then her eyes went wide with recognition of what had happened—first-thing-in-the-morning memory rebooting. He knew the feeling well. She gasped, sat up suddenly, and glanced around in near-panic.

"We're safe," Jack said.

"Tell me this is real."

"It's real, darling. All of it."

This magical place was a fortress that even scavengers knew better than to invade. The bodies of the five dead men had been left alone, except by the ever-present flies and crawling things. Jack and Roxanne beat away some of the insects and other critters to raid the corpses for equipment. Moving about quietly, they armed themselves with M-16s, spare magazines, and grenades. It was one thing to have respect for Mother Nature, another to get yourself killed. They'd treat this like a full-scale military operation. On that score, Falconie had had the right idea.

"Good luck, kid," Jack mouthed silently to Kong's sleeping form. "I'm glad you've come home at last."

Kong gave a single snort and wriggled in his sleep. "*Au revoir*," Roxanne whispered.

Cautiously, they began to retrace their steps. Yesterday's bootprints were still partly visible—their own prints and the heavy prints of Falconie's men. Easier to follow was the fresh trail of broken foliage where giant gorillas had crashed through the trees. They soon reached the scene of their second battle with the raptors—the place where Kong had fought the wild male gorilla. Little remained of their comrades' bodies. Most of the bones had already been picked clean. Jack felt sickened by the sight and Roxanne shook her head in disgust. "Let's try just one thing," she said.

Equipment was scattered all about and some of the backpacks had been ripped open by scavengers or by the raptors' claws, but some stuff looked undamaged.

Roxanne found their radio set. "I want to see if it still works," she said, brushing dirt from it with her hands.

Jack called the base. "Jack Denham here. Can you hear me?"

"Jack!" It was Laurel's familiar voice. "We've been up all night worrying."

"I'm safe," he said. "So's Roxanne, but we're both hurt. Everyone else is dead."

Another voice cut in. "Jack Denham? This is Ramon Valdez."

"Nice to talk with you, Ramon," Jack said with false good cheer.

"Yes, Jack, of course."

"On the other hand, Ramon…"

"What, Jack?"

"Your boys tried to kill us."

"Um, Jack, what are you talking about?" Valdez said. "The men I sent to rescue you?"

"I told you. I mean the thugs who just tried to kill us."

"That's crazy, Jack. Why would they want to do that?"

"You tell *me*. They're all dead now—and they didn't talk much before they died."

"We sent them to find you and bring you back. They were sent in as a rescue team."

"Whatever you say, Ramon."

Laurel must have taken the radio mike from Valdez's hands. "Jack?"

"Laurel?"

Roxanne cut in, grabbing the microphone from Jack. "About the Super-Osprey," she said.

"What about it, Roxanne?" Laurel replied.

"Whereabouts did it land?"

"Near you," Laurel said, sounding puzzled. "Only about a mile from your signal. I can give you the location Falconie gave us."

"Yes." Roxanne's lips formed a knowing smile. "Please do that."

As they scouted around the site, the pattern of boot-prints showed where Falconie and his men had tramped through after the gorillas had fought.

"Look," Roxanne said, following the prints back along the path where they'd come the previous day. "If we can follow those, it might get a lot easier."

They followed the bootprints to where they diverged from the earlier prints of Jack's exploring team. "Looks like they came from *that* way," Jack said, pointing.

"Right," Roxanne said. "Well, let's see where it leads."

They walked carefully, watching out for dangers. They passed evil-looking spiders, centipedes, and insects, a pair of vultures, and a tangle of killer vine. Not far down the path lay the remains of a large, one-horned animal—*huge* by any standards other than Skull Island's. Its bones had been picked almost clean. "Watch what you're doing," Jack said as Roxanne stepped over to inspect it.

"Look," she said, pointing to the way its bones had been shattered and then at some scorch marks on the ground. "That thing wasn't killed by any dinosaur."

"Yep, gotcha." The rhino had been killed by an explosion. More of Falconie's work, then. Jack looked around for prints or other signs of tramping boots. "This way, Rox."

Not far from the rhino's bones was another tangle of killer vine, this one with some bits of cloth hanging on its outermost tendrils. Expended cartridges lay on the ground nearby. Jack and Roxanne eased carefully past, still following Falconie's trail. At this stage there seemed to be no need to speak. Now and then one or the other of them would point out signs of where Falconie and the others had been. Other than that, nods and grunts sufficed. At one point it seemed like they'd lost the trail, but they soon picked it up again. A pair of giant gaurs crossed their path but Jack and Roxanne ignored them. *Live and let live* seemed like a good maxim. They waited until the big herbivores were well gone, then continued.

What they found next surprised them—another battleground. It included the remains of a human body and what was left of its uniform. Once again the bones had been picked almost clean, but insects still crawled on it, finding whatever scraps of meat they could. Several raptor carcasses lay about the area, most of the flesh gone from their bones. There were signs of fighting all around, with the distinctive prints of charging raptors and those of running boots—plus many expended cartridges. It hadn't occurred to Jack that Falconie had lost one of his own men even before the gorillas had massacred the rest in the green cathedral. So, Falconie and the others had been in their own life-and-death battle with the raptors—and they'd lost only one man. All their armor and weapons must have stood them in good stead.

Jack looked around nervously, the short hairs rising at the back of his neck. He had the feeling that something was watching them. Where raptors had struck once, they could strike again. Well-armed though he and Roxanne were, he didn't like their chances—just the two of them—against another raptor attack.

He saw nothing untoward. No sounds came from the jungle above the background insect drone.

"You know what I've got to do, don't you Jack?" Roxanne said.

He knew. She'd find what tissue she could on the man's remains, and take a sample of it for DNA testing. It seemed ghoulish, but it was going to be their best evidence of just who these men were who'd attacked them. With luck, some of them might have had criminal records. If Jack ever made it out of here, he swore there'd be hell to pay for somebody—that

somebody being Charlton Hemming. People had
died. Hemming had tried to have him killed. Not only
him, but Rox!

This whole mess was going to find its way back
into the law courts and if anyone was going down it
damn sure had to be Hemming. "Hurry, Rox," Jack
said. "This place gives me the creeps."

"I'm working as quickly as I can," she said. "All
right…finished."

"Let's move, then. Quickly! We must be getting
close."

They lost the trail again, where Falconie's team had
zigzagged along some narrower paths, but they knew
they were in the right vicinity. The ground rose and
became stonier; the vegetation began to thin out. A
minute later they saw open sky ahead. Rushing forward, Jack saw the dark metallic hull of the VTOL
craft through the trees, taking up most of a flat area
with just a few shrubs and patches of long, tussocky
grass. Roxanne followed close behind.

No!

The Super-Osprey appeared undamaged, but there
were two raptors sniffing around it. Wherever there
was one or two, there was likely to be a whole pack.
Best to sneak away before the raptors noticed them.
Jack signaled to Roxanne to move back, to retrace
their steps while they still had their lives. But it was
too late. The raptors must have heard them or maybe
smelled them on the air. They suddenly looked Jack's
way. "Run!" Jack shouted.

Roxanne turned to run for her life, but two more
raptors appeared to block her path. "Oh my God!"
She opened fire with her M-16 as one of the reptilian

killing machines that had been sniffing around the Super-Osprey suddenly sprinted in Jack's direction.

Jack had the general idea of firearms and had used many kinds of rifles—but never a military weapon like an M-16. He knew enough to switch the selector to "auto"; as the raptor closed on him, he leveled the weapon and fired. It shot off a three-round burst, but all the rounds went wildly astray. The rifle's recoil wasn't as bad as he'd expected, but he just had to get used to its heft. The raptor almost reached him as he fired again. The reptile spun and collided with a tree, as the rounds struck it in the body at point blank range. Its partner stepped away from the Super-Osprey's shadow and approached more slowly. It hissed and arched its neck as it drew closer. Its rigid tail flicked from side to side.

The creature's eyes were focused on Jack's gun, as if waiting for him to pull the trigger. Jack fired another burst, which the raptor seemed to anticipate. It dodged to one side, then ran at him at full speed—it almost reached him as his next three-round burst took it in the chest.

Behind Jack, Roxanne was firing burst after burst with her M-16. He joined her, firing at the raptors that came from her direction. Couldn't those evil carnivores just give up? Surely they must have learned by now that armed humans were dangerous prey. Roxanne took out one of the raptors but more began to appear.

The two humans backed toward the Super-Osprey, reaching the clearing as the hungry raptors strutted after them. The damned things had a cunning, knowing look. This close up, those jaws and rows of shark-like teeth seemed as big as a T. rex's. "Jack,"

Roxanne said urgently, "I'm running low on ammo." They had grenades and spare magazines, but if they took their fingers off the triggers for even a second the raptors were likely to charge. If one of them—just one—got past the wall of fire, it would be all over.

"I'll cover you," Jack said. "Don't argue with me. Run for it! Do what you have to do."

The Super-Osprey was now so close—just a ten-meter dash. Roxanne didn't hesitate. In one swift movement, she unstrapped her rifle from around her body and threw it toward the raptors. They recoiled from the dangerous object, which gave her the time she needed. As Jack fired bursts to cover her, she stripped off her backpack behind her as she sprinted in the direction of the VTOL craft. *I know you're a good pilot, Rox. I hope you can fly that thing.* Jack inched away from the raptors. When he reached the backpack, he scooped it up, getting its strap over his left shoulder. He didn't dare check behind him to see whether Roxanne had made it. *Hurry, Rox!*

The raptors attacked and Jack fired. He knew that this was the end. Only one had to get past the bullets. Then the trigger jammed. *I'm dead,* he thought.

But Roxanne just might survive.

There was a thunderous sound as the turboprop engines started up. One of the raptors reached Jack, clutching for him with its front claws. Jack stabbed the rifle barrel hard into its guts—another thing Falconie had taught him. When he pulled the trigger a fraction of a second later, one three-round burst went through the raptor, stopping it in its tracks. But that was the last of his ammunition. The gun wouldn't fire again.

The other raptors had scattered at the unexpected sound of the noisy engines. That gave Jack a few vital seconds. As Roxanne cut back the power to the fans, he dropped the rifle and ran for his life toward the Super-Osprey. His heart was beating like a drum. One of the raptors came after him—he could hear its hissing breath at his back—and he knew he could never outrun it. Pounding with all the last strength in his legs, he reached the aircraft—Rox had left a rear door open for him—and he tried to scramble in. But just as he got a firm grip on what felt like the metal underside of a chair, the raptor leaped on his back. Its front claws ripped through his shirt in an instant. They raked flesh from both sides of his spine, as the VTOL craft lurched crazily skyward.

"Hold on!" Roxanne screamed out from the front of the plane.

Jack dragged himself into the cabin as the Super-Osprey kept climbing jerkily. His lungs were burning from exertion and he hurt like hell from where the raptor's claws had raked his back, but the raptor had fallen away, its grip broken by the rough take-off. *The rougher the take-off the better,* Jack thought, *just this once.* Perhaps it was just as well that Roxanne had never flown anything quite like this before. Improvisation sometimes had its merits. As the rotors changed position and the VTOL craft moved forward over the jungle, Jack rolled onto his back, gasping for breath—and immediately tightened up with excruciating pain. He twisted onto his side and lay there, trying to breathe, and just wishing the pain would go away.

Goddammit, *every* part of him hurt like hell.

He must have passed out, for the next thing he experienced was a feeling of controlled falling. The Super-Osprey was already landing, its spinning rotors blasting down against the tug of gravity. Roxanne must be learning how to handle the damned thing.

After what seemed like an eternity, she made a soft landing. Another eternity passed, or so it seemed to Jack, before she cut off the power. Hunched over in the craft's confined interior, she stepped back into the rear cabin to see him. The thought struck him like a revelation—however mangled he was, he was still alive. Another thought hit home like bullet—better yet, so was *Roxanne*.

"We're home?" he asked, still lying in pain on the hard floor of the cabin.

"Back at the base camp," she said. "We'll be safer here." She glanced quickly at her backpack lying in the middle of the floor. He'd managed to get it into the plane during that last frantic scramble. Then she looked back at him, lying there at her feet. Her eyes narrowed with concern. "You're covered in blood, Jack!"

"Yeah."

"You're hurt."

"What's a bit of pain?" he said. "You know what they say—it's always either fatal or bearable. Either way, there's no use in complaining."

Roxanne knelt to look closer at his wounds. "Don't be brave. How bad *is* it?"

"I think it's the bearable kind. Can you give me some help here?"

"Sure."

She offered her hands to pull him up. Awkwardly, he took them. "Thanks, Rox." His ribs now hurt just from breathing. As for his jaw, it might be days before he'd eat anything solid. His back was *really* starting to throb and his shredded shirt felt glued by blood to his deeply raked skin. An examination of the wounds in his back might be rather nasty. Something not to look forward to. He stood unsteadily, reaching around to find one of the rear-cabin seats. He lowered himself slowly, wincing with the pain and trying his best not to groan.

From outside came the sounds of approaching voices. He recognized Laurel's and Mark's...and that other voice must have been Valdez in heated debate with them.

"We'd better see what's going down," Jack said.

Roxanne bent over him, looking distraught. "Can you move, Jack? Are you *okay*?"

"I'll live...but it's no thanks to your boss."

"He's not my boss anymore," she said, straightening up. "He'll soon be getting my resignation." She looked him over, deciding what to do. "Come on, let me help you out of here." Once again, she helped him to his feet and they staggered out onto the sand where the whole base-camp team had gathered round.

Valdez looked like a cornered animal. "Um, Jack," he said, "Roxanne..."

The rest of the group parted to let them through. Roxanne gave a sharp look to Valdez as they went past but she said nothing.

"Whatever happened out there in the jungle," Valdez called after them, "it had nothing to do with me."

Jack stopped and gently disengaged himself from Roxanne's arms. He was hurting, all right, but not so badly that he couldn't stand. He turned to Valdez

391

to look him in the eye. "Those thugs came with you, Ramon."

"They were supposed to rescue you, Jack. That's all I know. I sent them as a rescue team. Maybe Charlton had told them something else." Valdez's eyes were pleading. "It's nothing to do with me."

"Maybe so, maybe not," Roxanne said. "You've damn sure got some explaining ahead of you." She took Jack's arm to help him to the tents.

One of the island's giant, shiny black ravens landed on the ancient stone wall that divided the beach from the jungle. It peered down at the human camp as if looking for something important. Finding nothing that it wanted, it squawked once, then took to the air with a flurry of beating wings. It circled twice overhead. Then, as if disillusioned with the small primate intruders, it flew back over the wall and the jungle. Squawking noisily, it headed toward Skull Mountain.

There was a knock at the cabin door. "Dr. Blaine?" Another knock. "Roxanne? May we come in, please?" It was Captain McLeod.

"The door's not locked," Roxanne said, too tired to get up from her cane chair beside the bunk.

The captain entered, looking solemn and benevolent. Jack was close behind, dressed in his favorite shorts, deck shoes, and white T-shirt. He looked very serious—with his neat, graying beard, he didn't look much like a cowboy.

"I'm sorry for the interruption," the captain said. "We sent that DNA data to New York, to Ms. Atchison-Collander."

"Yes, I know."

Mark had used the ship's lab to analyze the DNA from all six bodies—all of Charlton's thugs. Using the satellite link, they'd transferred the data to Jack's precious Maudie and let her pass it to Stanley Levin and the New York police. *They* could figure out the right jurisdiction to take it further. As Roxanne had realized that afternoon in the green cathedral, killers like Falconie and the others had probably killed before—or committed other violent crimes. If they had criminal records or their DNA matched that at other crime scenes, the case against Charlton would be so much stronger. That bastard had *used* her, treated her like a fool. *Soon, Charlton,* she thought. *You're headed for a fall.*

But she couldn't be certain of that. The evidence of what exactly had happened was in the middle of Skull Island, a place too dangerous for proper police investigation. Witnesses were dead. Bodies would quickly rot—or be eaten. Rains would wash away the marks of struggles. There was another struggle ahead to bring Charlton Hemming to justice. Valdez had become ever so cooperative, but she was sure he was not a murderer. He knew nothing about any secret plans between Charlton and Falconie's team.

"Maudie got back to us," Jack said.

"Well?" Roxanne looked from one man to the other. "Don't keep me in suspense."

"It's good news, Rox. There are plenty of DNA matches. Falconie's DNA is all over more crime scenes than you'd like to imagine. All the others had records of violence. We're starting to look pretty credible."

"I see." She gave a heartfelt sigh of relief. At least that gave them a chance.

The captain excused himself with a slight bow. "Let's go up to the deck," Jack said, when he was gone.

He was such a decent man. Why had she ever thought otherwise? Her doubts about him seemed like ancient history. He still walked stiffly after what he'd been through on the island. One of his ribs had been broken, and there were sixty-eight stitches in his back—she'd counted them herself when she'd put them there. Every movement seemed to hurt him. Meanwhile, she'd gotten off rather lightly. For days after that encounter in the green cathedral she'd felt the blow where Falconie had struck her in the face, but now it was just a bad memory.

Up on deck the day was bright and hot, though a light breeze made it bearable. Halfway between the ship and the shore a monster gull fished for giant trevally.

"How are you feeling?" Roxanne asked. "Happier?"

Jack hesitated. "Too many people have died, Rox. Some of them were like my family. It's hard to be happy."

"Okay."

"I *am* happy that we're friends," he said tentatively.

"I'm happy about that, too," she said. "Happier than you know."

"Uh-huh."

"You and I make a great team, Jack."

When they'd gotten back to the base from the green cathedral, Jack had wanted to abandon the whole expedition. "No," she'd insisted, "we just have to take it slowly." She hoped he accepted that now, though he still seemed almost shell-shocked. Since that day, they'd circled each other kindly but nervously, more like old lovers with lingering hurts than like brand new friends.

So many people had died—he was right about that, of course—but you couldn't just give up, not even because of that. The island was too valuable, scientifically as well as commercially. It was one of the wonders of the world. If you just walked away and tried to quarantine Skull Island, then all the suffering and all the deaths would have been for nothing. *That* would betray everything she and Jack stood for.

And besides, you couldn't put a genie back in its bottle. Too many people knew the island's location. The place couldn't be hidden anymore.

She took his hand and squeezed it firmly. "I know that we can't just shrug off all those deaths."

"*No*," he said meaningfully. "No, we certainly can't."

"But we have to keep going, Jack—despite them. That's not the same as shrugging them off." What she hoped he would understand was what she was really trying to say, the difficult message beneath the surface of her words. The message that she wasn't cold or callous or ruthless, but sometimes you just had to grit your teeth and push down all your terror, your self-doubt, even your pity. Some things were that important, some things had to be done. That was what life was for.

She wanted him to understand that. More importantly, she wanted him to love her.

"I'm already missing Kong," Jack said, blatantly changing the subject. "He'd become part of my life."

Yes, she thought, *your child-substitute*. But why was that so terribly wrong? Everyone needed someone, or something, to nurture. If it came to that, she would miss Kong too. "We can check out how the big guy's getting along," she said. "Just now and then."

Jack's face brightened little. "I guess so."

"He'll still be there when we've grown old and died."

"You think so, Rox?"

"Yeah…if no one trashes the island."

At last, he gave her the faintest smile. "I wonder how long giant gorillas live. We've only ever guessed about that."

"We'll find out—or someone else will, after us. There's always more to find out."

Some time soon, they would try once more to explore the island. Someone had to take that responsibility. When the time came, they'd take things much more slowly, work on a smaller scale. The jungle was so rich in unknown forms of life that they shouldn't try to understand it all at once. They'd start with the area near the beach, for that by itself was a biological wonderland. There was plenty of time. They had years ahead.

Roxanne kissed Jack lightly on the cheek, then joined him leaning against the ship's rail, gazing at the ocean. They watched the huge bird skimming over the sea. "You made me a solemn promise on the island," Roxanne said. "Do you remember?"

"I guess I do," Jack said, trying on a feeble attempt at a laugh.

"Maybe you should keep it."

"I'm *keeping* it," he said, frowning at her. "I'll always love you, Rox."

Roxanne smiled mischievously. "Prove it, you fool."

"Hey," he said, laughing. "Hands off! I'm still an invalid, you know!"

"Awww, poor Jack," she said. She flashed a quick grin. *"That* excuse won't last forever."

Out over the water, the monster gull suddenly dived. It came up with a fish that seemed as big as itself, then flew toward the sheer cliffs of the island, the wriggling creature clasped in its orange beak.